"Greg Cox gives us a new dimension of Khan, he is a flawed, tragic leader who is seen as a hero in some aspects, a madman in others. That new dimension only contributes to the magnitude of Khan's personality, making him once again the premier *Trek* villain of them all."

—TrekWeb.com

Praise for
THE EUGENICS WARS,
Volumes One & Two

"Cox writes with great wit and an obvious love of *Trek* lore, though his greatest accomplishment lies in the way he links together seemingly unconnected twentieth-century events into a complex conspiracy that makes *The X-Files* seem unsophisticated."

—TrekNation.com

"An ingenious blend of actual history and *Trek* mythology. . . . Cox's electric, fun-loving style of storytelling is the perfect medium to take the reader into the twenty-first century and beyond."

—Wigglefish.com

"One of the more interesting additions to the expanded *Star Trek* saga."

—*Science Fiction Chronicle*

ALSO WRITTEN BY GREG COX

Star Trek®: The Original Series
The Eugenics Wars, Volume One
The Eugenics Wars, Volume Two
Assignment: Eternity

Star Trek: The Next Generation®
The Q Continuum: Q-Space (Book One)
The Q Continuum: Q-Zone (Book Two)
The Q Continuum: Q-Strike (Book Three)
(Also available in a single volume
Signature Edition)
Dragon's Honor (with Kij Johnson)

Star Trek: Deep Space Nine®
Devil in the Sky (with John Gregory Betancourt)

Star Trek: Voyager®
The Black Shore

STAR TREK®
TO REIGN IN HELL
The Exile of Khan Noonien Singh

Greg Cox

Based on *Star Trek*
created by Gene Roddenberry

POCKET BOOKS
New York London Toronto Sydney

POCKET BOOKS, a division of Simon & Schuster, Inc.
1230 Avenue of the Americas, New York, NY 10020

This book is a work of fiction. Names, characters, places and incidents are products of the author's imagination or are used fictitiously. Any resemblance to actual events or locales or persons, living or dead, is entirely coincidental.

Originally published in hardcover in 2005 by Pocket Books

STAR TREK is a Registered Trademark of Paramount Pictures.

This book is published by Pocket Books, a division of Simon & Schuster, Inc., under exclusive license from Paramount Pictures.

ISBN-13: 978-0-7434-5712-5
ISBN-10:   0-7434-5712-9

This Pocket Books paperback edition June 2006

10 9 8 7 6 5 4 3 2 1

POCKET and colophon are registered trademarks of Simon & Schuster, Inc.

Cover design by Zucca Design, cover art by Keith Birdsong

Manufactured in the United States of America

For information regarding special discounts for bulk purchases, please contact Simon & Schuster Special Sales at 1-800-456-6798 or business@simonandschuster.com.

To John Ordover,
thanks for ten years of expert editing!

Acknowledgments

Thanks to Ed Schlesinger, Paramount, and the whole gang at Pocket Books for letting me continue Khan's story beyond *The Eugenics Wars*. As before, I have to thank Gene L. Coon and Carey Wilber for creating Khan in the first place, and Jack B. Sowards, Harve Bennett, and Nicholas Meyer for resurrecting Khan so memorably fifteen years later. They gave me plenty of great material to work with as I strove to connect the dots between "Space Seed" and *The Wrath of Khan*. I also need to acknowledge Vonda N. McIntyre, whose novelization of *TWoK* I consulted frequently (even if I occasionally chose to go another way), as well as the *TWoK* photonovel by Richard J. Anobile.

And then, of course, there are Ricardo Montalban, Judson Scott, Mark Tobin, and the late Madlyn Rhue, whose performances as, respectively, Khan, Joachim,

Joaquin, and Marla McGivers brought those characters to life in my mind.

Thanks also to the Katzel family, whose generous donation to the Science Fiction and Fantasy Writers of America Emergency Medical Fund, at a charity auction two summers ago, earned them a place among the superhumans. And to Inge Heyer and her scientific colleagues for helping me try to figure out what really happened to Ceti Alpha VI (although any scientific inaccuracies are strictly my own). And to the avid posters at alt.startrek.books and trekbbs.com for refreshing my memory on arcane points of Trek lore.

Finally, as always, thanks to Karen, Alex, Churchill, Sophie, and Henry, just because.

Have you ever read Milton, Captain?

—Khan Noonien Singh

PART ONE

A.D. 2287

1

Personal log, James T. Kirk, Stardate 8415.9.

No longer an admiral, I am a captain once more, but a captain, as of yet, without a ship. The Enterprise-A remains in spacedock, while Chief Engineer Scott prepares our new starship for final testing and service.

With time on my hands, and my future on hold, it is the past that occupies my thoughts. Old decisions, and new regrets, haunt me, compelling me to embark on a solemn pilgrimage to the site of what may have been one of my greatest mistakes. . . .

"We're approaching Ceti Alpha V," Sulu announced from the helm. "Switching to impulse."

"Very good, Mr. Sulu," Kirk responded. "As always, your piloting is to be commended."

The *Yakima* was a compact, warp-capable cruiser,

only slightly larger than a shuttlecraft. Besides Kirk and Sulu, the chartered vessel held only two other passengers: Spock and McCoy.

"I still think there are better places to spend our vacation time," McCoy groused. The doctor sat opposite Kirk in the cruiser's cabin-sized passenger compartment, next to Spock. Like the captain and Sulu, McCoy had eschewed his Starfleet uniform in favor of civilian garb. A rumpled brown jacket hung over his bony shoulders. "Next time we're going to Yosemite or something."

"Nobody forced you to come along, Bones," Kirk said with a smile. A turtleneck sweater and trousers served as casual attire. He knew McCoy too well to take the doctor's grumbling too seriously. "This is a personal matter, not a Starfleet assignment."

McCoy's tone softened. "That's what friends are for, Jim." All kidding aside, the doctor's innate compassion was written upon his weathered features. "You shouldn't have to make this trip alone."

"Indeed," Spock concurred. "For once, Dr. McCoy and I find ourselves in agreement." Clad in an austere black robe, the Vulcan maintained a dignified posture upon his seat. His hands were clasped before him as though in prayer. "One does not have to be human to understand that this particular voyage is bound to trouble your emotions."

That's putting it lightly, Kirk thought. It had been less than a year since the deadly return of Khan Noonien Singh, who had blamed Kirk for his disastrous exile on Ceti Alpha V. Since then, Kirk had often pondered whether Khan had been justified in his quest for revenge. *Was I wrong to maroon Khan and his followers there so many years ago? Am I responsible for all those deaths?*

Kirk felt he owed it to the memory of those who had died on Ceti Alpha V to visit the planet himself, and perhaps learn more of what had transpired there after he'd left Khan behind all those years ago. "Thank you," he told his friends sincerely. "I'm grateful for the company."

He glanced out a porthole at the surrounding space. The stars, which had been streaking by the windows at warp speed, coalesced into discrete points of light as the *Yakima* dropped to impulse. Isolated chunks of solid matter bounced off the cruiser's deflectors, while the ship gracefully wove through an obstacle course composed of larger rocky fragments.

"Heading through an asteroid belt," Sulu warned them by way of explanation. "Things could get a little bumpy."

"Wonderful," McCoy drawled, buckling his seat belt. "I'd forgotten how delightful this system is." He rolled his eyes. "You know, I never did understand how the *Reliant* managed to mistake Ceti Alpha V for Ceti Alpha VI in the first place. Mind you, I'm a doctor, not an astronavigator, but how do you misplace an entire planet?"

"More easily than you might suppose, Doctor," Spock replied. "This remote sector has not yet been extensively charted, so Captain Terrell had to rely on the *Enterprise*'s original survey of the Ceti Alpha system, conducted many years before. According to that survey, there was a total of only six planets in the system, bordered by an extensive asteroid belt." He tilted his head at the porthole, where myriad granite boulders continued to zip past the window. "As *Reliant* approached the system from the outside, they naturally assumed that the outer planet was Ceti Alpha VI—and mistook the remains of the *real* Ceti Alpha VI for a portion of the asteroid belt mentioned in the survey."

Exactly, Kirk thought. Reliant *had no reason to suspect that the sixth planet had been completely destroyed.* He seized on Spock's argument to help ease his own pangs of conscience. *Just as I had no way of knowing that Ceti Alpha VI was going to explode.*

Or did I?

Should I have looked harder? Anticipated every possibility?

The nagging questions gnawed at Kirk's soul.

"All right," McCoy conceded. "But that just raises another question. How in blazes did Starfleet manage to forget where we put Khan? Didn't they realize that maniac was, at best, only one planet away?"

"Blame Starfleet secrecy," Kirk explained grimly. He'd asked himself many of the same questions in the weeks after their return engagement with Khan. "The details of the *Botany Bay* incident had been classified top-secret by Starfleet, which didn't want to advertise the existence of a colony of genetically engineered superhumans on Ceti Alpha V. As a result, Captain Terrell, immersed in the equally top-secret Genesis Project, was completely unaware of the system's history." Kirk's frown deepened as he remembered how that lack of information had ultimately cost Terrell his life. "Lord knows it wouldn't be the first time that Starfleet's right hand didn't know what the left one was hiding."

"Or, to be more precise," Spock observed, "had hidden eighteen years earlier."

McCoy shook his head, still not satisfied. "But Chekov was right there on the *Reliant*, not to mention John Kyle. They *must* have remembered about Khan and the others. Hell, Khan personally attacked Kyle that first time around. I treated his injuries."

Kirk had to admit that Khan Noonien Singh was hard to forget. "I spoke with Chekov about this, afterward," he divulged. "You have to remember that Ceti Alpha VI—or, rather, what *Reliant* believed to be Ceti Alpha VI—was just one of several planets that he and Terrell had checked out in hopes of finding an ideal site for Stage Three of the Genesis Project. They'd had every expectation of Ceti Alpha VI being rejected as a candidate just like all the others." Kirk smiled wryly. "Apparently, Carol was being extremely picky when it came to choosing just the right planet for her experiment."

"Dr. Marcus is known for her rigorous scientific methodology," Spock confirmed.

Kirk knew that was high praise coming from a Vulcan. *I wonder how Carol is doing?* he thought sadly; it had not been easy telling her about David's death on the Genesis Planet. *Bloodthirsty Klingon bastards!*

He pushed his vengeful thoughts aside—for now. "Chekov was caught in a bind," he continued. "Like the rest of our original crew, including Kyle, he had been sworn to secrecy regarding the *Botany Bay* affair, on a strictly need-to-know basis. And, at the point that he

and Terrell beamed down to what they thought was Ceti
Alpha VI, Terrell did not need to know . . . not when
Chekov had every reason to believe that Ceti Alpha VI
would be quickly rejected as a test site, and that *Reliant*
would be leaving the entire system shortly."

Kirk sighed, sympathizing with the Russian officer's
dilemma. "Naturally, had Ceti Alpha VI been selected for
the experiment, Chekov would have immediately informed
Terrell of the existence of a human colony one planet away.
But that hadn't happened yet and, as far as Chekov and
Kyle were concerned, Khan and his followers were safely
stranded on Ceti Alpha V, without the means of space-
flight. They seemed to pose no threat to *Reliant*—or so
Chekov believed."

A reasonable assumption, Kirk thought, *if tragically mistaken*. The ghastly consequences of Khan's escape from
exile were still fresh in his memory. Not only had Clark
Terrell perished; Khan had also ruthlessly slaughtered
nearly the entire science team at the Regula I Space Laboratory, and later launched a sneak attack on the *Enterprise* itself. Kirk winced at the thought of the many
fresh-faced cadets who had lost their lives in the battle
against Khan, including Scotty's own nephew. According to the eventual Starfleet investigation, more than
three dozen people had died as a result of Khan's return,
not counting Khan's own crew, whose exact names and
numbers remained unknown.

And those were just the direct fatalities, Kirk realized.
Khan's escape had set in motion a chain of events that
had led to Spock's brief but harrowing demise, the
creation of the Genesis Planet, the destruction of the orig-

inal *Enterprise*, and the murder of Kirk's son. *Who was really to blame for David's death?* Kirk asked himself. *The Klingons? Khan? Me?*

Where did it all begin—and where in God's name will it end?

"Probably just as well that Chekov is not along for this trip," McCoy observed. "Pavel suffered enough on that godforsaken planet."

"Agreed," Kirk said. The stalwart Russian had volunteered to join them, but, on his doctor's orders, he had stayed behind on Earth in order to fully recover from the injuries he'd sustained during their recent whale-rescuing excursion to the twentieth century. "I'm sure Scotty and Uhura will appreciate his help getting the new *Enterprise* shipshape."

Plus, Kirk knew, *Chekov has his own burden of guilt to deal with.*

The *Yakima* executed a last few elegant maneuvers; then its flight path leveled out once more. The floating debris outside the porthole gave way to open space. "We're through the asteroid belt," Sulu reported. "Ceti Alpha V dead ahead."

Here we are, Kirk thought. The prospect of setting foot on the planet that had driven Khan mad cast a melancholy pall over Kirk's spirits. *All the more reason to see it for myself*, he resolved. *After all, I was the one who banished him here.*

"I hear what you're saying, Jim," McCoy said thoughtfully. He peered through his own window, watching warily for the first glimpse of their forbidding destination. "But, me, I'm inclined to blame that whole mess with the *Reliant* on nothing more complicated than Murphy's Law."

It was, Kirk admitted, as good an explanation as any.

Ceti Alpha V loomed into view. It was an ugly planet, its surface hidden beneath clouds of yellowish brown vapor that swirled madly in the planet's turbulent atmosphere. How very different it looked from the lush, green world Kirk remembered.

We're coming, Khan, he thought. *Let's find out what made you hate me so much. . . .*

2

The planet was just as desolate as Chekov had described it. High-velocity winds ravaged the surface, creating a perpetual sandstorm that severely impaired visibility. Filtered through the sulfurous atmosphere, the daylight had a sickly yellow tinge. Sand dunes rose and fell in all directions, along with stony outcroppings and rock formations worn smooth by the constant wind-blown grit. The fierce winds shrieked like a phaser on overload.

Kirk found it hard to imagine that Ceti Alpha V had ever been a Class-M planet. Even safely encased within the protection of his environmental suit, he could feel the force of the mighty winds blowing against him. Only his heavy-duty gravity books kept him standing, however precariously, amid the never-ending gale. He peered through the tinted visor of his helmet and was impressed, despite himself, that Khan had managed to survive at all in this grossly inhospitable environment.

"Good Lord, Jim!" McCoy exclaimed, his shocked voice emanating from the headset in Kirk's helmet. A medkit was slung over the doctor's shoulder, in case of an accident. "How could anyone live in this hellhole, let alone for eighteen years!"

"Fifteen years, by Khan's reckoning," Spock observed calmly, "given Ceti Alpha V's altered orbit." The dire conditions failed to rattle his composure. "In any event, life-forms can be remarkably tenacious, Doctor. My own ancestors thrived in the scorched deserts of Vulcan for countless millennia."

"Maybe so," McCoy retorted, "but this place makes Vulcan's Forge look like a tropical resort!"

Kirk's friends stood only a few meters away, sheathed in their own protective suits. Thankfully, the suits came in different colors, which made it easier to distinguish between the two men in the middle of a sandstorm. The doctor's suit was orange-and-black, while, appropriately, Spock's suit was a more severe black-and-white. Kirk's own suit was orange as well, posing a bit of a challenge for Spock. *Let's hope his superior Vulcan senses are all they're cracked up to be,* the captain thought.

The abrasive sand fought a (hopefully) losing battle against the enamel coating of the men's environmental suits. Kirk heard his own breath echoing inside the confines of his bulky helmet, along with the (also hopefully) steady hum of the suit's breathing apparatus. In theory, the atmosphere retained enough oxygen to support life, but Kirk had no desire to inhale a raging sandstorm. He took a cautious step forward, wary of the shifting landscape beneath his boots.

Static crackled in his ears and he heard a scratchy, distorted voice that he barely recognized as Sulu's. "Everything okay down there, Captain?"

"We seem to have materialized with all our parts attached, Mr. Sulu," Kirk answered, raising his voice in order to hear himself over the ceaseless keening of the wind. "The scenery leaves something to be desired, though."

"What's that, Captain?" Another burst of static punctuated Sulu's query. "Please repeat."

The fierce sandstorms, along with electrical disturbances in the atmosphere, were wreaking havoc with transmissions to and from the *Yakima*. Kirk found himself yearning for Uhura's singular knack with communications technology.

"We're fine!" he shouted into his helmet's built-in mike. "I'll contact you again—shortly. Kirk out."

Landing the cruiser in this tempest had never been an option, so Sulu had remained in orbit with the *Yakima*. Kirk wished he could have given Sulu an exact time to beam them back up to the cruiser, but, to be honest, Kirk wasn't quite sure how long this somber expedition was going to last. *What exactly am I looking for?* he wondered. *Absolution?*

Kirk raised a tricorder and scanned the horizon. According to the coordinates Chekov had provided, Khan's former abode should be somewhere in this vicinity, although the ever-changing topography of the windswept desert made it difficult to get one's bearings.

He eyed the tricorder's display panel attentively, watching for some indication of anything besides sand, rock, and haze.

Chekov and Terrell, he could not help recalling, had been looking for a particle of preanimate matter, only to run into Khan and his genetically engineered acolytes instead. It was a chilling thought.

At first, the instrument yielded no hint as to which way to go, but Kirk had not come this far just to give up. He fiddled with the sensor controls while methodically surveying every centimeter of the surrounding wasteland. His persistence paid off as the tricorder picked up faint readings of artificial alloys somewhere beyond a rocky granite ridge southeast of where Kirk and his companions were now standing. Duritanium mostly, plus composites of cobalt and molybdenum.

"This way," he said, gesturing toward the ridge. Leading them on, he trudged through the treacherous sand, walking directly into the rampaging wind. The smooth slope of the escarpment made for an arduous climb, and Kirk was breathing hard by the time he reached the top. Sweat soaked through the lightweight garments he wore beneath the environmental suit. Ceti Alpha V was supposed to have Earth-standard gravity, but the heavy ceramic-polymer shell of the suit felt like it weighed a ton. *I could use a bit of Khan's genetically enhanced strength and stamina right about now,* he thought enviously.

He paused atop the ridge, taking a moment to catch his breath. Spock and McCoy joined him, the doctor lagging behind his hardier Vulcan colleague. "Well, I'll be damned," McCoy muttered as he peered past the hill they had just climbed.

The crest of the ridge looked out over a shallow depression, partially shielded from the storm by steep granite banks, like the eye of a tornado. Less blowing sand meant better visibility, so all three men were able to see, nestled at the base of the hollow, several half-buried large metal structures. The sharp right angles of the rectangular buildings stood in stark contrast to the sinuous curves of the wind-crafted dunes and rock formations.

Just as Chekov described, Kirk thought. Unlike the unlucky Russian, he knew right away what he was looking at: a crude shelter fashioned of recycled cargo carriers, Khan's dismal abode during his long years of exile on Ceti Alpha V. The ugly, boxlike shacks were a far cry from the sumptuous palaces Khan had enjoyed during his glory days back on Earth.

Anxious to get a closer look, Kirk set out down the leeward side of the ridge. Haste warred with caution as he carefully descended the pebbly concave slope, being careful not to lose his balance. Despite his impatience, he had no desire to tumble down the ridge head over heels.

Behind him, McCoy and Spock made their way down with equal care, but that wasn't enough to keep McCoy's feet from sliding out from beneath him as he awkwardly negotiated a particularly treacherous incline in his gravity boots. He toppled backward, waving his arms in a futile attempt to regain his balance.

Fortunately, Spock was there to grab the front of McCoy's environmental suit, steadying the wobbly physician. "Careful, Doctor," he admonished McCoy. "As I have often noted, your impetuousness will be your undoing."

"There was nothing impetuous about it!" the doctor protested, not about to let Spock get the last word. "I just had a little slip, you pointy-eared rapscallion."

Even with the somber nature of today's outing, Kirk could not help but smile at his friends' familiar bickering. It was good to hear Bones banter with Spock again, especially considering that, not so long ago, Kirk had thought they had lost Spock forever.

Thanks to Khan and his insane lust for revenge, Kirk recalled angrily. *Khan may not have succeeded in killing me, but, like the bad marksman I accused him of being, he damn well murdered enough people in the process!*

Kirk still found it hard to accept that Spock had actually died, albeit temporarily, in this very sector less than a year ago. He winced at the thought of the Vulcan's agonizing final minutes in the *Enterprise*'s radiation-flooded engine room. *One more death laid at Khan's doorstep,* he reflected, *and perhaps, indirectly, at my own.*

Reaching the bottom of the slope, he arrived within moments at Khan's literal doorstep. The pitted exterior of the cargo bays had been stripped of paint by the wind and sand, exposing the dull gray metal underneath. Signs of corrosion mottled the pressed steel walls. Rusted metal blinds covered a single small window, concealing what lay within the makeshift shelter.

Kirk had seen shantytowns on desolate mining asteroids that looked more livable than this.

He waited for Spock and McCoy to catch up with

him, then took hold of a closed steel door, roughly fashioned out of an old bulkhead. Decrepit hinges creaked loudly as he tugged open the door, which led to a cramped vestibule that must have served Khan and his followers as a sort of primitive airlock. A second door occupied the far end of the entry. Stuck in its frame, the inner door resisted Kirk's efforts, and he had to ram it with his shoulder before it finally swung open.

Taking a deep breath, Kirk stepped inside the abandoned lair of Khan Noonien Singh.

The ramshackle interior of the shelter resembled a cross between an army barracks and a junkyard. The sturdy cargo carriers had been laid end to end, like old-fashioned boxcars, creating a chain of rectangular compartments. A phaser had clearly been used to cut doorways in the interior walls, connecting the chambers; the charred edges of the open portals were rough and uneven. Dark red paint still clung to the riveted steel sheets composing the walls, floor, and ceiling. A stamped white notice listing a compartment's loading capacity betrayed its origins.

In silence, the three men toured the linked compartments. Evidence of habitation, if only of a marginal nature, could be seen all around them: benches, cots, a charcoal stove. Pots and pans hung on the walls, along with coils of recycled cable and wiring. Food and fuel canisters littered the floor, which was only infrequently carpeted with ragged pieces of canvas. A run-down protein resequencer, which looked as though it was being held together by baling wire and tape, rested on a dusty countertop.

Kirk spotted a makeshift chess set, the pieces composed of leftover nuts and bolts. Like most everything else in this improvised habitat, including the very walls, the game had been constructed from cannibalized pieces of scrap. Kirk wasn't sure whether to admire Khan's ingenuity or to be appalled at the desperate straits that had obviously driven Khan and his people to make use of every stray fragment of material they possessed.

The men's heavy bootsteps echoed in the silence of the deserted shelter. Kirk felt as though he were exploring a tomb. *No doubt*, he thought wryly, *Khan would appreciate being compared to an ancient pharaoh.*

McCoy finally broke the funereal hush. "According to my tricorder, the air is definitely breathable." He peered at the lighted display panel on his instrument. "Slight traces of craylon gas, but nothing our lungs can't handle."

Kirk took the doctor's word for it and unfastened the airtight seal of his helmet. Lifting the headgear from his shoulders, he took an experimental breath. To his relief, he did not fall over, gasping.

The air was hot and dry, but just as breathable as McCoy had promised. Although uninhabited since Khan's escape from Ceti Alpha V a year ago, the shelter still smelled of unwashed human bodies crammed into close quarters for far too long.

I left more than seventy colonists here nineteen years ago, Kirk recalled. *How many of them survived in this miserable hovel?* Chekov had reported seeing only a couple of dozen followers with Khan, all of them noticeably younger than their hate-crazed leader. The explosive demise of *Reliant*, however, had made a final body count impossible. *Besides*

McGivers, how many men and women perished in this godfor-saken place?

"Shades of *Robinson Crusoe*," McCoy murmured, having removed his own helmet. He ran a gloved finger over the casing of a jury-rigged air purifier mounted to one wall, leaving a trail in the yellow dust covering the inactive mechanism. He shook his head at the meager living conditions implied by the ill-equipped shelter.

"Perhaps," Spock agreed, "if Robinson Crusoe was a genetically engineered superman." He rested his matte-black helmet onto one of the empty cots. "One can only speculate whether ordinary humans could have survived so long under such adverse conditions."

McGivers didn't, Kirk thought. The face of the lovely redheaded historian rose from his memory like a restless spirit. He had not known her well, but she had been one of his crew, before he left her behind with Khan and the others. *She chose to stay with Khan,* he reminded himself, *but did I leave her any choice? It was that or a court-martial. . . .*

Remembering what Khan had told Chekov about McGivers' death, Kirk looked about cautiously for the sealed terrarium in which Khan had kept his deadly Ceti eels. To his surprise, the transparent container was nowhere to be seen, although a circular impression atop a dusty tabletop hinted at where the terrarium had once rested.

That's peculiar, he thought. Had Khan brought his vile "pets" with him when he escaped the planet? If so, the creatures must have died when *Reliant* exploded.

"Looks like they left in a hurry," McCoy said, toying

with a ceramic cup he found next to a pile of dirty plates and utensils. "They left everything behind."

Kirk nodded. He had noticed the same thing. "After eighteen Earth-years, I imagine they were sick of looking at them," he guessed. *Plus, Khan was doubtless in a rush to claim his revenge.* A shelf of antique books caught his eye, and he scanned the titles on the spines of the volumes. *King Lear. Moby-Dick. Paradise Lost.*

Kirk was surprised that Khan had abandoned his precious library, but only for a moment. *After all those years, his superior brain must have memorized every word.*

"Look at this," McCoy said. He had stumbled across an old Starfleet-issue medkit. Blowing the dust off its lid, he opened the kit, which turned out to be almost completely depleted of first-aid supplies. Only a few skinny rolls of bloodstained gauze remained, along with a broken hypospray and a handful of empty medication cartridges. "Dear Lord," the doctor whispered.

Kirk remembered how appalled McCoy had been, during their trip to twentieth-century San Francisco, at the barbaric medical technology of the time. He could well imagine the doctor's dismay at finding even worse conditions in their own era.

McCoy glanced around the forlorn shelter. "Genetically engineered or not, how on earth did Khan and his people survive being cooped up in these broken-down cargo bays for eighteen years?"

"As a matter of fact, that was not what occurred," Spock said.

"What?" McCoy reacted. He turned toward their Vulcan companion, who surveyed the habitat's interior with a cool, analytical gaze. "What do you mean by that?"

"Surely, Doctor, you did not believe that these refurbished cargo carriers comprised the entirety of the survivors' dwellings." Spock gestured toward the shelter's sparse decor. "Use your logic. Do you see the resources to sustain a working colony, no matter how rudimentary? Where are the foodstuffs produced?"

Good questions, Kirk thought, even though he suspected he already knew the answers.

"So what's the story?" McCoy asked. Despite his skeptical tone, Kirk thought he caught a trace of hope in the doctor's voice, as though he was relieved to hear that the castaways' lives might not have been as bleak as they first appeared. "Don't tell me Khan built a Shangri-La just over the next ridge. This entire planet is one big wasteland."

"Precisely," Spock agreed. "The surface of Ceti Alpha V is nearly incapable of supporting life, which is why, logically, we must look beneath the surface."

"That's right," Kirk confirmed. "Kyle and the rest of the *Reliant* survivors reported finding some sort of underground caverns after Khan stranded them on the planet. Unfortunately, they were in no shape to explore them at the time."

Kirk felt a renewed surge of anger at Khan as he recalled the madman's brutal treatment of *Reliant*'s crew. Keeping only the engine-room company, whom he forced into service via the mind-warping Ceti eels, Khan had banished the rest of the crew—some three hundred men and women—to the planet's surface, but not before venting eighteen years of pent-up fury on the innocent Starfleet personnel. Throats had been cut, and bones broken, in a vicious prelude to the massacre at Regula I. At least ten victims had not survived their injuries, and the rest had been too hungry and hurting to do much more than survive.

Khan's idea of poetic justice, no doubt, Kirk thought resentfully. *Never mind that not one of those people was responsible for his exile here!*

"I don't remember anything about caverns," McCoy protested. He hesitated, a look of uncertainty upon his face. "At least I don't think I do."

"You weren't exactly yourself after Spock's death," Kirk reminded him gently. "You had other things on your mind."

Spock's *katra*, among other things.

"In my mind, you mean," McCoy retorted, giving the Vulcan a dirty look. "But I guess I can be forgiven for blanking on a debriefing or two." He glanced down at the scuffed duritanium floor of the shelter. "Caves, you say?"

Kirk nodded. "Kyle mentioned something about an access panel in the floor. Let's look for that."

"Of course, Captain," Spock said.

Borrowing Kirk's tricorder, the science officer scanned the floor. Kirk watched intently, holding his breath. *Where the devil is that panel?*

An electronic beep announced that the tricorder had found something. His gaze fixed on the sensor display, Spock crossed the compartment until he came to a stretch of floor covered by a torn canvas tarp. He kneeled and yanked the tarp aside with his free hand, exposing a hinged metal grille embedded in the floor. Rising, he nodded at the grille knowingly. "As I surmised, the fresher air is rising from somewhere below, from an underground cavern, either natural or otherwise."

Kirk opened the grille. A dusty steel ladder led down into a murky, unlit shaft. *What are you hiding down there, Khan?* he asked silently, but the vengeful tyrant was beyond answering. *What answers are buried beneath these huts?*

The captain made an instant decision. "Let's go," he declared, donning his helmet once more. He activated the suit's built-in searchlight and stepped onto the top rung of the ladder. "I want to see what's down there."

"Are you sure that's wise, Jim?" McCoy asked. Nevertheless, he dutifully reached for his own helmet.

Kirk paused upon the ladder. "Mr. Spock, do you detect any structural instability below?"

"Not in the immediate vicinity, Captain." He aimed the tricorder directly at the yawning shaft. "The dense mineral contains trace amounts of kelbonite, making it difficult to scan beyond, say, one hundred thirty-two point six meters."

Kirk smiled at his friend's unerring precision. "We'll take our chances then." He gave both men a serious look. "Our suits should protect us from any lurking eels, but keep a watch out anyway." He tapped the type-2 phaser affixed to the belt of his environmental suit. "If you see one, shoot to kill."

"No kidding," McCoy muttered. The doctor had seen firsthand the injuries an immature eel had inflicted on Chekov's cerebral cortex. *Thank goodness the damage wasn't permanent*, Kirk thought.

He activated his helmet's searchlight and resumed his descent down the ladder. The metal rungs were scratched from constant use and wobbled unnervingly. Kirk breathed a sigh of relief when he reached the bottom of the shaft, roughly fifty meters below the compartment above.

Turning away from the ladder, which rattled beneath the weight of first Spock, then McCoy, Kirk swept the darkness with the beam of his searchlight. He found himself in a lifeless cavern, which appeared to be the nexus of several subterranean tunnels that radiated out from the central shaft like the spokes of a wheel.

The walls of the tunnels were rough and uneven, as was the stony floor beneath his feet. Jagged stalactites hung from the ceiling, even though the dripping moisture that had formed them appeared to have dried out long ago. The massive excavation reminded him of the underground mining complex on Janus VI; Kirk half-expected to see a Horta come burrowing through the walls at any minute.

Reaching the floor of the cavern, Spock and McCoy added their own searchlights to his. The added illumination exposed curtains of solid calcite adorning the walls.

"Good Lord," McCoy murmured, taking in the gloomy ambience of the sepulchral vault. Kirk wondered if McCoy was also remembering Janus VI, or perhaps the menacing corridors of Roger Korby's underground sanctuary on Exo III.

"Fascinating," Spock remarked. He aimed the tricorder down one of the narrow tunnels. "I'm detecting a rather extensive network of underground chambers, linked by branching corridors." An opened vent in his helmet allowed him to sniff the air, which smelled only slightly better than the sour atmosphere in the cargo bays. "The fresher air is being generated in some of the chambers ahead. Possibly gardens of some variety?"

Kirk was impressed. "How large is this network?"

"Impossible to say, Captain," Spock replied. "As I mentioned, the presence of kelbonite makes long-range scanning difficult. There may even be additional levels deeper below us."

Kirk ran the palm of his glove over a section of wall that showed evidence of being chiseled by hand. "Did Khan and his people carve out this entire installation?" Even with eighteen years of superhuman labor, it seemed an enormous task to complete.

Spock shook his head. "More likely, they adapted an existing network of caverns for their own use. Portions of these catacombs appear to have been formed by natural geological processes, while other regions have been expanded and excavated by artificial effort."

"Perhaps they were driven underground," McCoy speculated, "by the cataclysm that devastated the surface?"

"A highly probable supposition, Doctor," Spock said.

Kirk glanced upward at the thick limestone roof of the cavern. A thought occurred to him and he activated the communicator in his helmet. "Kirk to *Yakima*," he said. "Can you read me, Sulu?"

Static alone greeted his hails.

Just what I was afraid of, Kirk thought. Between the

storm, the duritanium crates, and some five hundred meters of solid rock, they were effectively cut off from their ship. *Just the way Chekov and Terrell were, when Khan ambushed them.*

"Looks like we're on our own," he said with a shrug, knowing that Spock and McCoy had heard his futile attempt to contact Sulu.

"Well, that's a comforting turn of events," McCoy drawled.

Now what? Kirk thought, contemplating the profusion of tunnels leading away from the cavern. If Spock was right, it could take hours—if not days—to fully explore this underground labyrinth. This was a job for full-fledged archeological survey, not a trio of vacationing Starfleet officers.

Once again, he asked himself just what he expected to find here. *A sworn affidavit from Khan, exempting me from all responsibility for the castaways' fate?*

That hardly seemed likely.

"Captain," Spock called out. "I believe you should come here."

The science officer had wandered partway down one of the murky corridors, his searchlight probing the darkness ahead. A hint of excitement in his voice, discernible only to those who knew him well, galvanized Kirk, sending him running as fast as his weighted gravity boots would allow.

The tunnel was a short one, leading to a dead end about fifty paces away. Kirk found Spock facing the calcite-encrusted wall at the end of the corridor, scanning the obstruction with his tricorder. "What is it?" he asked. As far as Kirk could tell, the wall ahead appeared indistinguishable from the crumbling limestone all around them.

"This barrier is not what it appears to be," Spock reported. "I was searching for a section of cavern that was low in kelbonite when I discovered that this particular wall is, in fact, composed of reconstituted thermoconcrete, fashioned to mimic the look and texture of natural limestone."

Kirk's eyes widened. Thermoconcrete was a silicon-based building material used by Starfleet to construct emergency shelters and, on at least one occasion, to patch the wounds of an injured Horta. Kirk remembered leaving Khan with a quantity of thermoconcrete when he dropped off the colonists on Ceti Alpha V years ago.

"Well, I'll be!" McCoy blurted, joining them before the ersatz cave wall. "Sure would have fooled me."

"Not always the most difficult of accomplishments," Spock observed dryly. "Nonetheless, it is a highly effective exercise in camouflage."

But to what purpose? Kirk wondered. *Why would Khan go to such effort to disguise an artificial wall?* He stared at the rugged-looking barrier with suspicion. *What was he hiding, and who was he hiding it from?*

"Can you tell what's beyond this wall?" Kirk asked Spock.

"Affirmative, Captain." The Vulcan scanned the wall with his tricorder. "Sensors indicate another chamber, approximately fifty-nine-point-eight-seven-two cubic meters in size." His right eyebrow arched. "I am also detecting traces of organic matter."

"Organic?" McCoy echoed in surprise. "You mean there's something alive in there?"

Spock shook his head. "Life signs are negative. More likely, these readings indicate the presence of something that was once alive."

Curiouser and curiouser, Kirk thought. He swiftly made up his mind. "We need to find out what Khan's hiding in there." He glanced at the ceiling. "Mr. Spock, would you say that this wall is essential to the structural integrity of this tunnel?"

"No, Captain," Spock replied. "I would estimate that the odds of a cave-in are less than one-point-zero-four percent."

"Good enough for me," Kirk said. Drawing his phaser, he set it for maximum power and aimed it at the camouflaged wall. "You gentlemen might want to step back."

Spock and McCoy duly obliged, and Kirk squeezed the trigger. A beam of crimson energy struck the disguised thermoconcrete, causing it to glow brightly at the far end of the tunnel. The solid wall shimmered briefly, then dissolved into empty space, revealing an open archway into the chamber beyond. McCoy cast a nervous look at the ceiling, despite Spock's reassuring prediction, but the narrow passage showed no sign of collapsing. Only a sprinkling of charred powder fell upon the floor around the newly exposed entrance.

Kirk released the trigger, then set his phaser back on Kill. Barely waiting for the edges of the archway to cool, he rushed into the second cavern, then stopped in his tracks. His jaw dropped.

The chapel-sized grotto had been transformed into a tomb of breathtaking beauty and elegance, dominated by a pair of massive stone sarcophagi. The right-hand sarcophagus was starkly unadorned, but the lid of the left-hand sarcophagus had been sculpted in the image of an attractive woman in an old-fashioned Starfleet uniform. The woman's ample hair cascaded down onto her shoulders, while her classical features bore a wistful expression, touched by a profound sadness.

The figure lay gazing up at the ceiling. Kirk read the inscription engraved at the foot of the sarcophagus:

Marla McGivers Singh
Beloved Wife
2242–2273 Anno Domini
"A Superior Woman"

McCoy entered the crypt after Kirk. He looked about the grotto with a look of wonder on his careworn features. "Jim, take a look at this," he said, pointing to a small niche above the entrance. A much smaller sculpture, of a knight in shining armor and a woman in a medieval gown, was embedded in the niche. "That's from McGivers' quarters back on the old *Enterprise*."

Kirk dimly remembered the sculpture. McGivers' own work, as he recalled. Her quarters had been a veritable gallery of paintings and sculptures, all paying tribute to the great heroes and champions of the past. *Small wonder she succumbed so quickly to Khan's charisma.*

His gaze was drawn back to the chiseled lid of the sarcophagus. Although he had not laid eyes on the real

McGivers for almost nineteen years, he could see that
the likeness was remarkable. The exquisite craftsman-
ship of the sculpture, as well as the graceful lines of the
sarcophagus below, testified to hours of painstaking
labor and commitment. He had no doubt that this was
Khan's own handiwork, and that the second sarcophagus had been intended for Khan himself.

"He must have loved her very much," McCoy murmured.

Kirk had to agree. In truth, he had long suspected
Khan of simply using McGivers, of taking advantage of
her hopeless infatuation in order to secure her cooperation in his failed attempt to capture the *Enterprise*. But
this remarkable memorial belied such a cynical interpre-
tation, as had the intensity of Khan's fervent desire for
revenge. Kirk could no longer deny that some sort of
deep and lasting love had blossomed between Khan and
the smitten young Starfleet officer.

Had McGivers made the right decision, going with
Khan? Was the love she found worth the price she ultimately paid? Kirk didn't know how to answer those
questions. He looked again at the inscription on her
bier, taking note of the dates engraved there. Marla
McGivers had been only thirty-one years old when she
died. . . .

Should I return her remains to Earth? Kirk wondered
momentarily. As he recalled, she had possessed no close
family ties back home, something which had made her
semi-mysterious disappearance a bit easier to pull off.
Officially, Lieutenant Marla McGivers was listed as
"Missing" in Starfleet's public records.

"Impressive," Spock observed, joining them within the tomb. "A burial site transformed into an artistic expression of love. Not unlike the Taj Mahal in Khan's native India."

"Why, Spock," McCoy said. "I never knew you were such a romantic!"

"I assure you, Doctor, my appreciation is purely aesthetic." Spock scanned the streaked marble coffins with his tricorder. "Curious," he remarked, raising a quizzical eyebrow. "Although Lieutenant McGivers' coffin contains merely her physical remains, I am detecting a variety of artifacts within the second sarcophagus, including a quantity of data-storage disks."

Data disks? Kirk's mind seized on the possibilities. McGivers was a historian, he remembered; she surely would have wanted to document the colonists' experiences on the planet. Had she kept a careful log of everything that happened to Khan and the others?

"I want those disks," he decided. Stepping forward, he gripped the massive stone lid of the right-hand sarcophagus. "Gentlemen, your assistance, please."

Spock responded promptly to Kirk's request, but McCoy hesitated. "I don't know, Jim," he said. "Doesn't this strike you as a bit, well, ghoulish?"

Kirk shook his head. "Khan's atoms were scattered all over the Mutara Sector," he reminded the doctor. "There's no body here to disturb." He glanced at the adjacent tomb. "Besides, I don't think McGivers would mind. As a historian, she knew that sometimes you have to unearth the past in order to learn more about it. If these are her records, she would have wanted them read."

He and Spock took up positions at opposite ends of the sarcophagus. He dug his fingers into the seam beneath the marble lid, securing his grip. The heavily insulated gloves of his environmental suit made holding onto the lid a bit tricky, but Kirk thought he could manage. "On my count," he instructed Spock. "One . . . two . . . *three!*"

The immense slab was difficult to lift. Kirk grunted inside his helmet, straining to budge the stubborn immovable object. Spock's Vulcan strength came to his rescue, and the lid came loose at last. Conscious of the intricate stonework, the two men carefully laid the marble slab on the floor, leaning it up against one side of the sarcophagus.

That was rough, Kirk thought. He suspected he'd be feeling the ache in his muscles for some time to come. *Let's hope it was worth the effort.*

He took a second to catch his breath, then peered into the shadowy recesses of the sarcophagus. As expected, no mummified remains greeted his gaze, only a packet of compact data-storage disks, of the sort used in old-style tricorders, plus one more thing: a large leather-bound book about the size of a computer display panel.

What's this? Kirk felt a tremor of excitement as he gingerly lifted the mysterious volume from its hiding place within Khan's coffin. While the other two men looked on, he flipped over the front cover of the book. He eagerly scanned the first page, on which was handwritten, in bold cursive letters, *"The Personal Journal of Khan Noonien Singh."*

Kirk could not believe his luck. Khan's own memoirs! Along with, most likely, Marla McGivers' account of the colony's history on Ceti Alpha V. *Perhaps*, he thought, *I should not be too surprised to find these waiting; given Khan's enormous ego, it's only natural that he would want to set down his life and times for posterity.*

"It seems Khan left us his journal," he told Spock and McCoy, showing them the inscription on the book.

"Indeed," Spock said. He sounded impressed, albeit in a cool Vulcan manner. "This could be a significant historical document, Captain."

McCoy, of course, had to question their good fortune. "I don't get it. Why would he leave this behind? Why not take it with him aboard the *Reliant*?"

Kirk thought he knew the answer. "Khan probably had a premonition that he might not survive his quest for revenge. He was basically taking on all of Starfleet, after all. I'm guessing he left his journal behind, along with McGivers' disks, because he wanted some record of his struggles to endure just in case he ended up going out in a blaze of glory." Kirk shook his head. "Khan had a weakness for grand suicidal gestures. Remember how he tried to blow up the *Enterprise*'s engines after his takeover failed? And how he activated the Genesis Device when *Reliant* was defeated?"

In truth, Kirk suspected, *I don't think Khan really cared what happened to him as long as he took me with him. The idea of dying in battle against his archfoe probably appealed to his warped sense of grandeur. Like Holmes and Moriarity, or Ahab and the whale. . . .*

"Sounds like Khan all right," McCoy agreed. "Hell,

as I recall, he almost destroyed Earth back in the 1990s, when it looked like he was losing the Eugenics Wars."

"Precisely," Spock stated. "With his Morning Star satellite weapon. Thankfully, he was convinced to choose exile in the *Botany Bay* instead."

Kirk contemplated the volume in his hands. Perhaps these records would tell them more about Khan's state of mind? He handed the data disks over to Spock. "Take a look at these," he instructed. "Let's see what we have here."

Spock loaded the first of the disks into his tricorder. The glow from the instrument's viewscreen highlighted the stark planes of Spock's face as his Vulcan mind swiftly absorbed the information scrolling across the screen. "As you surmised, Captain," he confirmed, "the disks appear to contain a record of the colony's experiences as chronicled by Lieutenant McGivers." He continued to scan the viewscreen with interest. "It is quite compelling."

For himself, Kirk could not resist the temptation to open the dusty journal and start reading immediately. As the words leaped out at him, perfectly preserved by the arid atmosphere of the underground tomb, Kirk could almost hear Khan's deep, resonant voice speaking to him. . . .

PART TWO

Paradise Lost

3

A.D. 2267

DAY ONE

The buzzing of the transporter beam faded away and Khan found himself standing for the first time on the soil of Ceti Alpha V. His eyes, accustomed to the unobtrusive lighting aboard the *Enterprise*, blinked against the harsh glare of the midday sun, which blazed brightly in the sapphire sky of this brave new world. He felt like Columbus or Armstrong, boldly setting foot on the brink of a vast and unexplored frontier.

Here I will build an empire, he vowed, *even greater than the one I left behind.*

A stark red jumpsuit clothed his muscular frame, and his chin was held high despite the blinding sunlight. His

sleek black hair was knotted at the back of his neck.
Dark brown eyes gazed out at the world with confidence and keen anticipation. He started to raise his
hands, to shield his eyes, then remembered the sturdy
steel bonds locking his wrists together.

Captain Kirk was taking no chances, not that Khan
blamed him. He had, after all, briefly captured the *Enterprise* and tortured Kirk nearly to death, so the captain's
precautions were only logical. *I would have done the same,*
Khan admitted.

A full contingent of Starfleet security officers were also
on hand to ensure Khan's cooperation. They stood,
phasers at the ready, all around the unrepentant superman, while more of their number kept watch over the
mass of Khan's followers, who waited silently for their
leader a few meters away.

At Kirk's insistence, Khan—and one other—were the
last of the exiles to be transported to the planet's surface,
the better to keep the ruthless Sikh dictator under wraps
until the very last minute. There would no replay of
Khan's previous escape from custody.

A gentle hand grasped his, and he glanced down at
the woman who had beamed down alongside him: Lieutenant Marla McGivers, late of Starfleet. His accomplice
in his short-lived takeover of the *Enterprise*, and his
eventual undoing as well.

A woman of the twenty-third century, born some
three hundred years after Khan and his fellow expatri-
ates, she was a willowy beauty whose graceful figure
was well displayed by her crimson Starfleet uniform. A
short skirt and polished black boots displayed a pair of

slender legs, while her auburn hair flowed freely over her shoulders, just the way he liked it.

"So this is our new home," she whispered, a trace of apprehension in her voice. Chestnut eyes, tastefully highlighted by pale blue eyeshadow, took in the untamed river valley before them. Thorny shrubs and scattered palm trees dotted the grassy savanna stretching beyond the shores of a mighty river. To the northeast, a range of snowcapped mountains rose in the distance, no doubt many days' journey north. Over the roar of the coursing river, the caws and squawks of the native wildlife could be heard. Avian life-forms, boasting impressive wingspans, circled slowly above the grassy plains, although whether they were predators or scavengers Khan could not tell.

He squeezed her hand reassuringly, taking care not to damage her fragile, merely human bones. Unlike Khan and his other followers, Marla was not a genetically engineered superhuman; small wonder she faced their new life with some trepidation. Khan was deeply aware of just how much she had sacrificed to be with him. *Like Eve with Adam,* he mused, *she has turned her back on the paradise of the twenty-third century to dwell with me in the wilderness.*

A young Russian ensign—Chekov, by name—stepped forward from the ring of security officers. Khan recalled that the youth had shown courage during his short-lived takeover of the *Enterprise*, leading a failed charge to retake engineering from the superhumans; that the Russian's charge had failed did not diminish his valor in Khan's eyes.

"Excuse me, Mr. Khan," he said, a trifle nervously, "but I'm to inform you that *Enterprise* will be departing shortly. As arranged by Captain Kirk, the provisions for your colony have already been delivered to the planet's surface." The youth gestured toward an assortment of bulky metal cargo containers, resting safely distant from the muddy banks of the river. "Besides your supplies from the *Botany Bay*, Captain Kirk has also provided you with some essential technology from our ship's stores."

"I see." Khan nodded in approval. "I am certain that all is in order, per your captain's instructions." Kirk himself had chosen to take his leave of Khan in the transporter room of the *Enterprise*; their farewells had been terse and unsmiling, as befitted two recent adversaries. "Just as I am certain that my people and I shall thrive and prosper far beyond James T. Kirk's expectations."

"Of course," Chekov agreed diplomatically. He glanced at Khan's wrist restraints and removed a small electronic device from his belt. "If you'll just raise your hands, sir, I'll remove your manacles now."

"Thank you, Mr. Chekov," Khan said, smiling slyly. "But that will not be necessary." Extending his arms in front of him, he clenched his fists tightly and exerted his strength. His eyes narrowed in concentration and a grimace twisted his lips as he pitted his more-than-human sinews against the impregnable steel cuffs. Twenty-third-century alloys surrendered with a metallic shriek as his bonds twisted and snapped apart, freeing his hands without assistance from Chekov or any other mortal.

That's better, Khan thought. He enjoyed the startled expressions of his captors. *Let them not forget my true superiority.*

The Russian gulped, even as the wary security officers shifted into a higher state of alertness. A half-dozen phasers pointed in Khan's direction, but their regal target showed no sign of alarm. Calmly, unhurriedly, he raised his empty palms to demonstrate that he meant Chekov no harm.

Flustered, the young ensign handed Khan the electronic key anyway, then turned toward Marla. Pity softened Chekov's expression as he addressed his soon-to-be-former crewmate. "Er . . . some of your friends aboard the *Enterprise* asked me to give this to you," he said, producing a small object wrapped in crinkly metallic foil. "To remember us by."

Khan looked on as Marla accepted the item, which turned out to be a silver medallion in the shape of the Starfleet emblem. Marla appeared touched by the gift, and her voice, when she spoke, was hoarse with emotion. "Thank you so much!" A sad smile lifted her lips. "It's comforting to know that not everyone on the ship hates me."

"Hate you? *Nyet!* No one hates you," Chekov insisted, perhaps a bit too quickly. Judging from scowls and stony glares of the red-shirted security guards, Khan suspected that the young Russian was not being entirely truthful. No doubt many of Marla's onetime comrades now regarded her as a traitor and a disgrace to her uniform. Khan only hoped that she did not see herself the same way.

I shall see to it, he pledged, *that she comes to know that she chose wisely. She shall have no regrets.*

"Are you sure about this, Lieutenant?" Chekov asked Marla, obviously reluctant to leave her behind with Khan and the others. "It's not too late to change your mind." He watched her face carefully for evidence of second thoughts. "Once the *Enterprise* leaves, you could be stranded here forever."

Khan bristled at the youth's presumption. *How dare this pup attempt to subvert Marla's allegiance, as if linking her destiny to my own is such a doleful fate?* He opened his mouth to rebuke the impertinent ensign, but Marla spoke first.

"I appreciate your concern, Pavel, but it's all right." She looked up at Khan without a trace of indecision. "I know what I'm doing."

Chekov nodded grimly. "Then there's only one thing left to do," he announced. He removed a phaser pistol from his belt and handed the powerful firearm over to Khan. "To defend yourself against hostile life-forms," he explained, "along with the antique guns and weapons stored aboard the *Botany Bay*."

"Excellent," Khan declared. Even outnumbered as he was, it felt good to have a weapon in his hand once more. "Tell Captain Kirk I am grateful for his foresight."

With no further business to conduct, Chekov and the other Starfleet personnel did not waste time returning to their ship. Khan watched in silence as the *Enterprise* reclaimed its own with a flourish of shimmering incandescent energy. In his mind's eye, he imagined Kirk upon the bridge, giving the command that would send

his magnificent starship hurtling away from Ceti Alpha
V, toward the distant reaches of the galaxy.

Khan allowed himself a fleeting moment of regret. If
only Kirk had not managed to regain control of *Enterprise* . . . ! It would have been good to be in command of
such a vessel, complete with its awe-inspiring phasers
and photon torpedoes. The *Botany Bay* had been state-of-
the-art when stolen from Area 51 back in 1996, but the
Enterprise made his primitive sleeper ship seem like a
rowboat in comparison. Who knew what sort of interstellar empire he might have carved with such a fearsome warship at his disposal?

But that was not to be.

Very well, he thought, turning his back on the past. Ceti
Alpha V was his future now, and he was determined to
make the best of it. Milton's immortal words came at once
to his mind: *"The world was all before them, where to choose
their place of rest, and Providence their guide."*

Taking a deep breath of the hot and arid air, Khan
surveyed his new domain. With an entire planet's worth
of landing sites to choose from, great care had been
taken in his selection of this particular location. Located
in the planet's southern hemisphere, this particular
geographic region was not unlike the fertile Indus River
valley that had served as the birthplace of Indian civilization. The nearby river was bounded on both sides by
endless kilometers of semitropical grasslands. In theory,
according to planetary modeling conducted back aboard
the *Enterprise*, their proximity to the river would lend
itself to agriculture, especially after the coming rainy
season, while the sprawling veldt no doubt abounded

with fresh game—as well as, he took care to remember, the attendant predators.

It appeared, in short, an altogether fitting place to found a dynasty, and to commence his inevitable reign over the entire planet.

Let us begin, he thought.

No longer separated from his people by the intrusive Starfleet myrmidons, Khan strode toward the waiting throng: his genetically enhanced brothers and sisters from the distant years of the twentieth century. The surviving crew of the *S.S. Botany Bay* had followed him from the dark days of the Eugenics Wars into an unknown future, in search of new worlds to conquer. Forty-one men, not counting himself, plus some thirty women besides Marla. Looking over the crowd, whose simple attire resembled his own, he spotted the faces of many of his most loyal lieutenants: Suzette Ling, Liam MacPherson, Vishwa Patil, and, of course, his faithful bodyguard from the old days, Joaquin Weiss.

The latter, a looming giant of man whose stolid expression was as blank and emotionless as a block of granite, stepped forward from the crowd, taking his place beside Khan as though the centuries they had spent in suspended animation had never transpired. Long ago, Khan had liber ated Joaquin from an Israeli prison, where the belligerent superman had been serving a life sentence for multiple assaults and homicide, and Khan knew that the brawny, brown-haired bodyguard would gladly die before letting any harm come to him.

"Greetings, my old friend," Khan said, grasping Joaquin's beefy arm. "Together again, just as before."

Joaquin grunted in agreement.

Letting go of the bodyguard's arm, Khan raised his voice to address his people. "Friends, comrades, fellow explorers, our time has come! Did I not promise you a new world, fresh and unspoiled and ripe for the taking? Across vast spans of time and space, we have at long last arrived at our glorious destination. Here, upon this virgin planet, we will plant our seed and build a civilization—a truly *superior* society—such as the universe has never seen before!"

Cheers rose from most, but not all, of the assembled castaways. Khan noted the discrepancy, but made no mention of it . . . yet.

"But first we must prove our worthiness to survive," he continued. "These early days will not be easy. We shall have to struggle to find food and shelter, and this alien world surely contains dangers that we can scarcely imagine. But I promise you, my brethren, follow me and I will lead you to greatness once more!"

"Like you did back on Earth?" a sarcastic voice called out. "Like you did aboard the *Enterprise*?"

Khan's eyes narrowed and his jaw tightened. "Who speaks?" he demanded coldly. "Show yourself."

A tall blond figure emerged from the crowd. Khan recognized Harulf Ericsson, a Scandinavian superman who had served as one of Khan's foreign operatives back on Earth. With a leonine mane of bright yellow hair, a fulsome beard, and a powerfully muscled physique, Ericsson was the very picture of his Viking ancestors. "I speak," he declared with distinct Norwegian accent. "And not just for myself."

Glowering murderously, Joaquin lurched toward Ericsson, but Khan held up his hand. "No," he said sternly. "Let him continue."

Ericsson needed no encouragement to voice his insolent slander. "Why should we follow you again, Khan, when you've led us to nothing but disaster! We fled Earth in defeat, driven off our own planet by our inferiors, and all because we mistakenly placed our faith in you. Then we spent centuries lost in space, trapped in cryogenic suspension, while our ship's life-support systems failed and many of our valiant comrades perished in their sleep! Then, finally, you revive us to capture the *Enterprise*, only to be defeated by Kirk and his minions—including her!"

He cast an accusing finger at Marla, who trembled but refused to shrink before Ericsson's vitriol. Khan smiled, proud of her for standing her ground.

In truth, he had been anticipating a challenge of this sort. Superior abilities ofttimes led to superior ambitions, and Khan had guessed that it would be only a matter of time before one of his followers sought to unseat him. Now, at least, he knew from which direction the threat came.

"I see," Khan responded, reining in his justifiable outrage. "Have you forgotten what became of the rest of the Children of Chrysalis?" he asked, referring to the top-secret project that had created Khan and the rest of his genetically engineered kin. "They are all long gone, exterminated centuries ago by fearful humans, who outnumbered them billions to one. We are all that survive of that noble breed, thanks to my bold decision to abandon Earth and strike out for a new homeworld somewhere in the stars. *You*, Harulf Ericsson, are alive only because I granted you a niche aboard the *Botany Bay*." Khan clasped his hands above his heart. "Your gratitude," he said sarcastically, "overwhelms me."

Ericsson scowled at Khan's gibe, unwilling to surrender just yet. "You may have been our leader back on Earth," he conceded, "but that was centuries and light-years ago." He glanced warily at the phaser lodged in Khan's belt, but kept on speaking, egged on by others of like sympathies, who clustered behind Ericsson like jackals hungering for a lion's kill. "A new world requires a new leader," he called out to Khan. "Why should that leader be you?"

"Because I am *Khan!*" Had there been a podium before him, Khan would have shattered it with his fist. Instead he looked away from Ericsson and his lurking band of jackals in order to speak directly to his people as a whole. "It has been said that to conquer without risk is to triumph without glory. We have suffered reverses, true, and grievous losses, but that is always the case when brave pioneers dare to open up a new frontier. It has cost us much to reach this shore, and yet more sacrifices may be demanded of us, but immortality lies within our grasp as well. Let us unite our efforts to forge a mighty empire!"

On Earth, back in the twentieth century, dissension and power struggles between the Children of Chrysalis had led invariably to the Eugenics Wars, with disastrous results for all. Khan had spent literally years caught up in a global struggle against his fellow superhumans. He did not intend to let history repeat itself.

He removed the phaser from his belt and openly handed it to Marla. *I need no weapon to squash this petty insurrection,* he thought scornfully. *Only the force of my own unyielding will.*

"Every one of you swore allegiance to me more than three hundred years ago," he reminded the assemblage. "But if anyone wishes to contest my rightful authority, let them step forward now . . . and wrest it from me with their bare hands!"

He locked eyes with Ericsson, silently daring the rebellious Norseman to make his move. Long seconds passed, as the entire planet itself seemed to hold its breath. Flanked by Joaquin on one side and Marla on the other, Khan faced his challenger unarmed. Part of him hoped that Ericsson would take the bait, so that he might nip this incipient mutiny in the bud. *"Now 'tis the spring, and weeds are shallow-rooted,"* he thought, recalling Shakespeare's immortal wisdom. *"Suffer them now and they'll overgrow the garden."*

But Ericsson was not so bold. He stayed where he stood, glaring at Khan in sullen silence, until the moment passed and it became clear that Khan had won the day.

"So be it," he said triumphantly, reclaiming the phaser from Marla. *Perhaps it is just as well,* he mused; his people's numbers were not so great that he could afford to sacrifice an able-bodied man so readily. *Our colony will need a diverse genetic pool to prosper, and every man and woman here possesses a unique combination of superior chromosomes that must be preserved for the benefit of generations to come.*

Choosing to be magnanimous in victory, Khan stretched

out his arms to symbolically encompass the fertile valley surrounding them, even as his memory harkened back to his vanished capital in northern India. "Welcome, my people, to New Chandigarh, birthplace of the glorious Khanate of Ceti Alpha V!"

Cheers rose from a majority of the gathered castaways, some, to be sure, more heartfelt and sincere than others. Ericsson and his treacherous coterie, foiled in their initial attempt at a coup d'état, dispersed back into the relative anonymity of the crowd, but Khan knew that he had almost certainly not heard the last of the bearded Norseman. *I shall have to keep a close watch on that one.*

For now, however, securing the basic essentials of survival took precedence. "Ling," he instructed the Asian superwoman, who had served on his personal security force back on Earth. "Take a dozen volunteers and begin collecting firewood. Patil, take a team down to the river to gather water. Remember, we shall have to boil the water before drinking it. MacPherson, let us discuss the matter of shelter. . . ."

There was much to do before nightfall.

4

Sunset found a rudimentary campsite in place just beyond the banks of the river, which Khan had already christened the River Kaur, after his martyred mother, the architect of the Chrysalis Project. At Khan's direction, a swatch of open ground had been hacked out from the chest-deep grass, creating a floor of reddish brown dirt about fifty meters in diameter. A wall of thornbush, uprooted by hand, surrounded the camp in hopes of deterring whatever hostile life-forms might prowl the veldt at night, while armed guards had been posted to watch out for any nocturnal predators. A dozen smoky campfires blazed within the enclosure, providing light and heat as well as an added degree of protection. Stars glittered like dilithium in the deep purple sky.

"I feel as though I have traveled backward in time," Marla dictated into her tricorder, completing her description of the settlement, "perhaps to the founding of the original Botany Bay colony in eighteenth-century Australia. . . ."

That settlement, she recalled, had been populated by convicts deported from England, the women all convicted thieves and prostitutes. *As a disgraced Starfleet officer, I would have fit right in.*

Guilt, fear, and an undeniable excitement warred within her soul. Although she would always regret betraying Captain Kirk and the others, she found herself thrilled by the prospect of building a new life with Khan. All her life she had felt out of place in her own time, dreaming of the great deeds—and great men—of the past. Now at last she would be *making* history, alongside one of the most dynamic and charismatic figures in human history: Khan Noonien Singh.

She was not naive. As a historian, she knew just how difficult and dangerous their new life would be. The first generation of colonists at Botany Bay had lived on the knife edge of starvation for nearly five years, while they struggled to eke a living from the foreign soil, and many of the original settlers had not survived at all, succumbing to disease, hunger, and even cannibalism.

But they did not have a Khan to lead them! Marla reminded herself fiercely. She had faith in him. Together they would prevail over everything Ceti Alpha V had to offer. *It will all be worth it, as long as we have each other.*

She peered at the lighted display panel of her tricorder as she strolled across the camp. She had promised Khan a complete inventory of their supplies and wanted to make sure that she had not forgotten anything.

The night was hot and dry, and swarms of flying insects buzzed about her annoyingly. In theory, according to the *Enterprise*'s environmental projections, they had arrived at this location during the height of the hot season, a few months before the monsoon. Marla glanced upward at the stars. *Let's hope we have a roof overhead before the rain starts,* she thought.

Among the unfamiliar constellations, one particular heavenly body stood out from the rest, a large orangish orb that resembled a small moon. *That must be Ceti Alpha VI,* she guessed; the lifeless world was Ceti Alpha V's nearest planetary neighbor. She recalled, from a briefing aboard the *Enterprise*, that the two planets were currently in synchronous orbits, which meant she could expect to see Ceti Alpha VI in the sky quite frequently over the next several months. Marla wondered if she and Khan's descendants would someday set foot on the planet above, when their newborn nation gained the resources to venture out into space. Given the colony's primitive beginnings, that could be many generations away. . . .

Scanning the campsite for Khan, she spotted him several meters away, conferring with Liam MacPherson. According to Khan, the lanky, redheaded Scotsman had been one of Khan's chief scientific advisors back during the Eugenics Wars, and Khan obviously valued MacPherson's opinion regarding the future of New Chandigarh. Marla paused in her tracks, reluctant to interrupt Khan while he was busy.

She was disappointed to see Joaquin standing guard only a few paces away from Khan, his arms crossed atop his massive chest. The thuggish bodyguard had not left Khan's side for a minute, and Marla was already finding his constant presence oppressive, especially when she remembered the brutal way Joaquin had struck Lieutenant Uhura back on the *Enterprise*. Thank goodness Khan had prevented Joaquin from hitting Uhura again. The man was obviously a brute.

As if he had heard her thoughts, Joaquin turned his head toward Marla. His perpetual scowl deepened as he spotted her standing by. He stared at her with undisguised animosity. *Guess the feeling is mutual,* she realized. Despite the stifling heat, a chill ran down her spine.

The bodyguard's baleful glare made her uncomfortable, so she turned away and headed toward the nearest campfire. She wasn't actually cold, but perhaps the smoke would discourage the cloud of gnat- and mosquito-like creatures enveloping her. She swatted uselessly at the airborne pests, while double-checking her computerized inventory lists one more time. *Let's see, the* Enterprise *left us about one dozen high-intensity plasma lights. Those should last at least twenty-five years or so. And we've got approximately 250 kilograms of silicon-based thermoconcrete. I wonder how many shelters you could build with that?*

Intent upon her tricorder, she accidentally bumped into another woman from behind. The woman, an Amazonian female with dark skin and braided black hair, spun around angrily. "Watch where you're going, you Starfleet slut!"

The sheer venom in the woman's voice caught Marla by surprise. "I'm sorry," she offered hastily. "I apologize."

"For what?" the woman demanded. "For your clumsiness, or for double-crossing us back on the *Enterprise*?" In the heat of the night, the irate woman had discarded her standard-issue jumpsuit in favor of the lightweight, golden-mesh garment she had worn while sleeping in suspended animation aboard the *Botany Bay*; the sparkling metallic fibers clung to the sculpted contours of a powerfully muscled body. "Don't think anyone has forgotten who released Kirk from the decompression chamber!"

Marla backed away, acutely aware that the other woman was a head taller than her and at least five times stronger. "I'm sorry!" she pleaded, not really expecting the woman to understand. "I had no choice. The captain was going to die!"

"So?" the Amazon said with a sneer. "He was just an insignificant human—like you." She advanced on Marla, while harsh laughter and encouragement spilled from the bystanders around the campfire.

"You tell her, Zuleika!"

"Teach Miss Twenty-third Century a lesson!"

"Smash her skull in!"

Does the entire camp want me dead? Marla wondered in dismay. It certainly seemed so.

The woman (Zuleika?) shoved her with superhuman strength, and Marla's boots lost contact with the ground. She flew backward as though strapped to a malfunctioning jetpack, then crashed to the earth several meters away. Her back and shoulders hit the ground with a jolt, and she skidded backward for several endless moments before finally coming to a halt. Dazed, she lifted her head in time to see Zuleika snatch a burning brand from the fire and stalk toward Marla with murder in her eyes.

"You're not one of us!" the woman spat, towering over the fallen lieutenant. She lifted the torch high above her head, while Marla struggled to remember her Starfleet self-defense training, which she hadn't had cause to think of since her Academy days. "You don't belong here!"

This isn't fair! Marla thought, raising a hand in a hopeless attempt to block the coming blow. *I'm a historian, not a fighter!*

The torch came swinging down, trailing sparks like a meteor. Marla flinched in anticipation of the fiery impact. She could already feel the scorching heat of the flames as they dived toward her face.

"What is this?!" a commanding voice exclaimed. A powerful hand grabbed Zuleika by the wrist, halting the downward trajectory of the torch. An imposing shadow fell between Marla and her foe. "Stop this at once!"

The blazing firebrand retreated from Marla's face, and she looked up past the flames to see Khan standing head-to-head with Zuleika, his fist wrapped around the Amazon's wrist. "Explain yourself!" he demanded. He squeezed her arm hard enough to make Zuleika yelp in pain.

The woman's arrogance evaporated in the face of Khan's fury. "Lord Khan!" she blurted, an anxious expression upon her flawless, genetically crafted features. "This woman betrayed you!"

"That is between her and I," he said sternly, releasing her arm. Zuleika stepped backward, the torch dropping to her side. Her panicked gaze darted from right to left, searching for support from her comrades, but none came forward to defend her, not even those who had been enthusiastically cheering her on mere moments before.

Turning away from Zuleika in disdain, Khan reached down and gently took hold of Marla's hand. His touch sent spasms of relief through Marla, bolstering her spirits, and she marveled once again at his uncanny strength as he effortlessly lifted her back onto her feet. He placed a possessive hand upon her shoulder.

"Are you well?" he asked her urgently. "Shall I summon the doctor?" Marla recalled that Khan's followers included at least one superhuman physician. Hawkings or Hawkins or something like that.

She shook her head. She was more rattled than injured. "That won't be necessary," she whispered. *With my luck, the doctor would try to finish me off!*

Satisfied, Khan turned his attention back to Zuleika and the others.

"Understand this, all of you," he said, raising his voice so that the entire camp could hear. "This woman is under my protection. Anyone who threatens her shall answer to me." His formidable gaze swept over the varied faces of the onlooking superhumans. "Have I made myself quite clear?"

A chorus of muttered assents answered Khan's query,

but Marla could not help noticing the grudging, half-hearted nature of the responses. She was still persona non grata as far as her fellow castaways were concerned, no matter what Khan dictated. *Congratulations, Marla,* she told herself ruefully. *You're an outcast even among exiles.*

She blinked back tears, overcome by both her brush with death *and* her timely rescue. Her legs felt like rubber and she sagged against Khan, drawing on his strength and presence.

He's all I have left, she realized. *Without Khan, I would be completely alone.*

Somewhere out on the veldt, beyond the flickering glow of the campfires, an alien beast roared like thunder, sending another shudder through Marla's quaking frame.

Dinner consisted of Starfleet field rations in self-warming packets. Although Khan intended for the colony to be self-sufficient as soon as possible, saving their provisions from the *Enterprise* and the *Botany Bay* for emergency use only, he had made an exception for this first night on Ceti Alpha V. Tomorrow, they could begin hunting for food and game.

Marla sat alone by a smoldering fire at the outer fringe of the camp, transferring her personal log entries onto a data disk; it was her hope that her daily record-ings would someday provide valuable insights into the early days of New Chandigarh. She watched from afar while Khan mingled with his people, making a point of dropping by each of the campfires for a few minutes or so, to share a laugh and some words of encouragement. Marla understood why he was doing this; it was important to maintain the group's morale. Still, she couldn't help feeling somewhat lost and abandoned, like an Academy plebe attending her first collegiate mixer. The obvious mirth and camaraderie emanating from the other fires only heightened her sense of isolation.

Outside the camp, the night-shrouded savanna seemed alive with mysterious rustlings and cries. Unknown animals barked and howled in the darkness, making Marla wish she knew more about xenobiology. The irksome insects, undeterred by the smoke, were growing more aggressive by the hour, buzzing about her face and nipping at every centimeter of her exposed flesh. The voracious pests made the vampire ants of Borgo III seem like vegetarians.

Marla caught herself yearning for the controlled climate of the *Enterprise*. "Stop that," she whispered to herself. "It's too late for second thoughts." She had made her own bed; now she would have to sleep in it.

She washed down the last of her stewed tomatoes and dehydrated eggs with a gulp from her canteen. The decontaminated river water was lukewarm and tasteless, but she finished off the whole canteen in seconds, then found herself wishing for more. Alas, strolling down to the Kaur for a refill was not an option; Ling and her party had already reported sightings of large carnivorous reptiles dwelling along the banks of the river.

Marla wondered what other predators roamed this alien wilderness. *Enterprise* had not had time to conduct a full biological survey. *At least we don't have to worry about hostile natives,* she reflected. Captain Kirk had taken care to ensure that Ceti Alpha V had no sentient inhabitants.

The night seemed almost supernaturally dark by the time Khan finally completed his rounds and joined Marla by the fire. He dropped cross-legged onto the ground beside her. The flickering orange light of the flames caught the sharp angles of his majestic countenance, which were familiar to Marla from centuries-old historical photos as well as her own firsthand observations. His burnished bronze skin seemed to glow from within, as though lit by some unquenchable inner flame. A ceremonial silver dagger, or kirpan, was tucked into his belt along with the phaser. Despite the exertions of the day, he looked as strong and vibrant as ever.

The first time Marla had seen Khan, in that coffinlike hibernation niche aboard the *Botany Bay,* he had taken her breath away.

He still did.

"My apologies for making you dine alone," he said graciously. "Sometimes the responsibilities of command take precedence over more personal concerns."

"That's all right," she replied. "I understand." She glanced up to see Joaquin standing only a few meters away, watching over Khan like a Baneriam hawk. He eyed Marla suspiciously, as though expecting her to knife Khan at the first opportunity. *Doesn't he realize,* she thought, unsettled by the bodyguard's relentless scrutiny, *that I would rather die than hurt Khan, despite what happened on the* Enterprise?

Her discomfort did not escape Khan's keen powers of observation. "That will be all, Joaquin," he instructed the attentive bodyguard. "You may leave us now."

"But Your Excellency . . . !" Joaquin protested, alarmed at the prospect of leaving Khan alone with Marla.

Khan smiled indulgently at his servant's distress. "Do not trouble yourself, my old friend." A deep, resonant chuckle escaped his chest. "I think I can defend myself against a lone woman." He shared an amused look with Marla. "Not that I expect I will have to."

Reluctantly, Joaquin exited the scene, but not before casting one last glare at Marla, who breathed a sigh of relief as the bodyguard's hulking figure receded into the distance.

"You must forgive Joaquin for his diligence," Khan said. "Back on Earth, I had many enemies, and Joaquin was my last line of defense against traitors and assassins." Khan's voice and face grew more somber as his memory stretched back across the centuries. "He owes me his life, and will do anything to protect me."

"I see," Marla said. *At least we have that much in common,* she thought, although she still couldn't shake the image of Joaquin striking Uhura. *I'm not sure I'll ever be able to forget that.*

A momentary hush fell over the campfire. Now that she finally had Khan to herself, Marla found herself strangely tongue-tied. It dawned on her that this was the first time they had been alone together since Khan's defeat aboard the *Enterprise*; afterward, Khan had been placed under maximum security in the ship's brig, while Marla herself had been confined to her quarters until the ship arrived at Ceti Alpha V. Although they had seen each other briefly at their judicial hearing, when Marla agreed to join Khan in exile, they had largely been kept apart—until now.

Where to begin? Marla thought. "Thank you," she murmured, "for saving me . . . before."

Khan dismissed the incident with a wave of his hand, as though Zuleika's attack on Marla was of little consequence. "In time, my people will come to accept you," he promised.

Marla had her doubts, but chose not to contradict him. There was something else on her mind. "Khan," she began, "we've never talked about what happened on the *Enterprise*, when I helped Captain Kirk retake the ship."

Khan nodded gravely. Marla held her breath, waiting for his response. She was terrified of what he might say, but, for better or for worse, she had to know whether he blamed her for stranding them all on this remote and uncivilized planet. Deep down inside, did he distrust her as much as his people did? *Please, no,* she prayed desperately. *I couldn't bear it if he hates me, too.*

"I was angry at first," Khan confessed. He spoke slowly, as though considering every word. "But I had time to think in that lonely cell aboard the *Enterprise*, and I soon realized that I had placed you in an impossible situation; I should not have forced you to choose between your loyalty to me and your duty to your captain." He shrugged his shoulders. "It was a miscalculation on my part. I take full responsibility."

Thank the gods! Marla thought, feeling a dreadful

weight lift from her. Her heart pounded in her chest and she found she could breathe once more. "I was afraid you'd never forgive me," she admitted, her voice hoarse with emotion.

Khan smiled and took her hand. "What's done is done," he told her. "You proved yourself to me when you chose willingly to accompany me into the wilderness." He looked forward into the future, putting the past behind them. "We need not speak of this again."

A piece of burning tinder snapped apart in the fire, the sharp report sounding like an old-fashioned gunshot. Outside the camp, a nameless animal howled for its mate. Khan rose from the fire. Nearby a pair of navy-blue Starfleet blankets were stretched out upon the ground, atop a layer of strewn, freshly cut grass. It wasn't the most comfortable bed Marla had ever seen, but at least the grassy mattress provided a degree of padding.

"Come," Khan said, helping Marla to her feet. "The night grows late, and we have many long days ahead of us." He guided her toward the waiting blankets. "Let us retire for the evening."

Marla thought she was going to die of happiness.

Later, after they'd made love as much as their limited privacy allowed, they lay in each other's arms beside the fire. Marla rested her head upon Khan's shoulder, while draping an arm across his bare chest. Ceti Alpha VI shone down upon them. *Not quite as romantic as a genuine moon*, Marla thought, *but close enough for me*.

"Tell me about yourself," Khan urged her. He stroked

her unbound red hair. "You know everything there is to know of my illustrious history, yet I know so little about your past."

"There's not much to tell," she said. "I've led a pretty boring life, up until recently."

Khan gave her a skeptical look. "No false modesty," he chided her. "You are a Starfleet officer, a space explorer. Do not expect me to believe that you have not known remarkable experiences."

"But it's true," she insisted, "more or less." She snuggled closer to Khan, encouraged by his interest, despite her protestations. "My parents were killed in a transporter accident when I was very young, so I was raised by an older aunt and her husband. They were decent people, but somewhat aloof and set in their ways. I always felt like an intrusion into their well-ordered lives, which revolved around advanced subspace theory." She smiled ruefully. "Not exactly the most exciting environment for a young and energetic child!"

Khan nodded. "I can sympathize. I was reared by distant relations myself, after my mother perished in the Great Thar Desert. A civil engineer and his wife. Admirable individuals in many ways, but hardly my intellectual equals. I spent much time reading, in search of stimulation."

"So did I!" Marla enthused. She was pleased to discover they had this much in common, even coming from two entirely different eras. "History, mostly. The past always seemed more colorful and interesting than modern-day Earth."

"I, too, was drawn to accounts of the heroic past," Khan revealed. "Alexander the Great, Ashoka, Napoleon—these were my inspirations as a youth."

I can believe it, Marla thought. Who else would Khan Noonien Singh seek to emulate than the legendary conquerors of the past? She readily placed him among their ranks, and knew that his greatest triumphs were yet to come. *Our descendants will remember Khan as the first great ruler of Ceti Alpha V.*

"So how did you come to join Starfleet?" he asked.

Marla turned her thoughts back to her own early years. "Well, no surprise, I studied history at first, but academia turned out to be too much like my guardians' cloistered scientific milieu, so I applied to Starfleet Academy instead. I guess I figured that if Earth had become too placid and predictible, I could always find the excitement I was looking for out on the final frontier."

"And did you?" he pressed her.

She shrugged within his embrace. "I suppose. To be honest, I don't think Captain Kirk had much use for me. I almost never accompanied him on away missions, not even when we went back in time to 1969." A sigh of regret escaped her. "All I got to do that time around was pick out the landing party's wardrobe so that they could blend in with the people of your time."

It gave her a start to realize that, at the same time that the *Enterprise* was orbiting Earth in 1969, thanks to the slingshot effect of a dangerous black star, Khan and his fellow superhumans were being conceived in a top-secret laboratory in Rajasthan. *Who would have guessed we'd both end up on Ceti Alpha V three hundred years later?*

"If Kirk did not take full advantage of your talents," Khan said, scowling, "that was his mistake." His expression darkened slightly as he spoke of Captain Kirk. "I saw at once that you were a woman of exceptional qualities."

As much as she appreciated the compliment, Khan's enmity toward Kirk made Marla uncomfortable, so she hurriedly changed the subject. "In retrospect, life on the *Enterprise* did have its heart-pounding moments. We rode out some fierce ion storms, not to mention pitched battles against the Klingons, the Romulans, the Gorns, and other hostile races. I caught an alien virus once, along with the rest of the crew, and spent several hours proclaiming myself the Crown Princess of the Universe. I even got to meet Richard the Lion-Hearted, sort of"— she blushed at the memory—"on this bizarre shore-leave planet."

Khan listened attentively to her words. A sense of profound intimacy came over Marla, compelling her to open up her heart completely. "Even still," she admitted, "I never felt entirely at home aboard the *Enterprise*. There were adventures, yes, but they weren't *my* adventures; I was just along for the ride. I wanted something extraordinary to happen to *me*—something like you."

"And you shall not be disappointed," Khan promised. He lifted himself above her, his head and shoulders blotting out the sky before his lips descended to claim hers. His ardent kiss was more thrilling than any ion storm.

This feels right, Marla thought deliriously, meeting his passion with her own. *More than the Academy, more than the* Enterprise, *this is what I've been searching for all these years.*

Whatever came next.

5

Strident shouts and cries awoke Khan in the middle of the night. Instantly alert, he sprang to his feet, phaser in hand. His eyes scanned the enclosure, discovering a scene of utter tumult and chaos. The sleeping camp was now a jumble of confused and agitated people, all speaking and shouting at once. Shots were fired by one or more of the *Botany Bay*'s precious twentieth-century rifles, but what exactly was being shot at Khan could not immediately determine.

"Khan, what is it?" Marla asked from their primitive bed, where only moments before she had lain nestled within Khan's arms. He heard alarm, but not panic, in her voice. "What's happening?"

"I do not know," he said grimly. He handed her a knife that he had providentially set beside their blankets. "Stay here."

The commotion appeared to be centered around a fading fire at the other end of the camp. Khan rushed barefoot across the enclosure, shouldering his way through the frantic crowd. "Make way!" he commanded, brusquely shoving aside any man or woman who blocked his path. "Let me through!"

Within seconds, he arrived at the campfire in question, where he found the unmistakable evidence of some ghastly tragedy. Fresh blood spattered the tangled blankets surrounding the fire, while the faces of the nearest colonists bore the ashen imprints of shock and grief. Dr. Gideon Hawkins, the camp's resident physician, was already on the scene, but the distinguished African-American had no patient to treat, only a smear of blood upon the sheets.

"Dmitri!" one man cried out hysterically. "It took Dmitri!"

Khan recognized the name of Dmitri Blasko, a chemist who had worked on Khan's biological-weapons program back on Earth. Blasko had survived the destruction of Khan's laboratories during the War, only to meet, so it seemed, an equally violent end on Ceti Alpha V.

"Who took him?" Khan asked urgently, his commanding tone cutting through the hubbub. "How? When?"

"A beast, Lord Khan!" a pale-faced guard exclaimed. She kept the muzzle of her American-made M-16 rifle aimed at the darkness beyond the thornscrub piled around the camp, as if expecting something to lunge from the shadows at any moment. "It struck without warning, leaping over the wall. It grabbed Dmitri and hauled him back over the thorns before anyone even knew what was happening!"

"Good God!" Hawkins exclaimed, clutching his useless medkit. Frustration showed on the angular features of the doctor, who had once been one of Earth's premier surgeons before being forced to abandon his practice in the wake of the Eugenics Wars. "The poor soul!"

Khan silently cursed the fates. Their first night on the planet . . . and he had lost one man already. He had hoped that, combined, the fires and brambles would keep the native wildlife at bay, but clearly he had underestimated their ferocity. "What kind of animal?" he asked.

"I'm not sure, Your Excellency," the distraught guard answered. Khan identified her as Parvati Rao, from his palace guard. "It was dark and it all happened so bloody quickly. . . ." She searched her memory, while keeping her eyes and rifle aimed at the encroaching blackness. "Something like a lion, I think, or a tiger . . . but bigger and heavier!"

Khan nodded. Rao's vague description had the ring of plausibility; the boundless veldt would be the ideal habitat for such a creature. He stepped closer to the ring of thorns that had failed to preserve Blasko's life. Droplets of blood glistened upon the top of the spiky brambles. More of the chemist's blood, or had the beast scratched itself as well?

"Be careful, Your Excellency!" a gruff voice called out from behind him. Khan was not surprised by Joaquin's rapid arrival upon the scene. "The beast might still be near!"

Khan raised his phaser. "Quite true, my friend," he agreed. "I shall be on my guard."

He peered past the wall into the primeval night, hoping to catch a glimpse of the monster. The starlight, along with the glow of Ceti Alpha VI, provided only meager illumination, however, and even Khan's superior vision could not completely penetrate the darkness, let alone the concealing grass and brush. There could have been dozens, even hundreds, of stealthy carnivores stalking the savanna and he would not have seen them.

"Tiger, Tiger, burning bright
"In the forests of the night . . ."

For an instant, he thought he glimpsed two glowing amber eyes staring back at him from the shadows beneath a cluster of palm trees. His finger tightened on the trigger of the phaser, but he was reluctant to waste the weapon's precious energy unless he was certain of his shot. "Joaquin!" he called out softly. "Come see this!"

But by the time the giant Israeli reached Khan's side, the luminous orbs had disappeared, dropping beneath a rise in the terrain. "What is it, Lord Khan?" his bodyguard asked.

"Never mind," Khan said, shaking his head. "Perhaps it was nothing." He stepped away from the fence, convinced that tracking the beast would have to wait until morning. In the meantime, stronger precautions had to be made against the possibility of another attack. "Build up the fires and double the watch," he instructed Rao. "Use up all our firewood if necessary. We can gather more tomorrow."

His eyes probed the camp, searching for safer territory within the enclosure. "Tell everyone to move their blankets closer to the center of the camp, away from the fence. We need to put more distance between—"

Terrified shrieks, coming from the other side of the camp, interrupted Khan in midsentence. *Marla!* he thought in alarm, before realizing that the screams came from a slightly different direction. Snatching up a burning branch from the fire, Khan raced toward the site of the new attack, leaping over the scattered campfires and dodging panicked colonists running in the opposite direction. Khan felt like a salmon fighting its way upstream, but he arrived at the northwest corner of the camp just in time to glimpse a huge, shaggy form partially illuminated by the reddish glow of a dying fire. A helpless human form thrashed wildly within the creature's immense jaws. The scent of freshly spilled blood polluted the air.

The monster sprang into the air, its powerful hind legs propelling it over the briar fence. *No!* Khan thought vengefully. *You'll not escape again!* With lightning-fast reflexes, he fired his phaser at the beast. An incandescent beam of crimson energy sliced through the darkness, striking the creature's right flank and causing it to emit a tremendous roar of pain and fury.

Momentum carried the wounded monster over the wall into the surrounding brush. For a second, Khan heard it thrash and hiss in the high grass, but the violent noises ceased almost immediately. *Is it dead,* Khan wondered, *or merely lying low?*

He was tempted to go out and search for the creature's body, but common sense dictated that he wait until dawn, especially since there might well be other predators lurking just beyond the briar barrier. Besides, he had other matters to attend to now, like identifying the dead.

"Who?" he asked a pair of bystanders, who had been drawn back to the site by the lethal brilliance of Khan's phaser beam. Daniel and Amy Katzel were siblings, their genetic profiles differing by only a single chromosome.

"Gorinksy," Daniel answered.

"And Lutjen," Amy added.

Two? Khan's heart dropped at the news. He had seen only one victim carried off. "Both?" he asked incredulously.

The Katzels nodded in unison. "There were two attacks," Amy said, "one after another." She shuddered at the memory.

"Gorinsky was standing guard," Daniel stated, "but the creature grabbed him before he could fire a single shot." A fallen rifle, lying atop the bloodstained earth, verified the man's story. "Then the second animal came over the fence and pounced on Lutjen. . . ."

So, Khan thought, *the animals hunt in groups.* A useful piece of data, although purchased at far too dear a cost. *Two men and one woman,* he counted, numbering the casualties. New Chandigarh's population was shrinking by the moment.

Khan clenched his fist. Rage and frustration gnawed at his soul. He had not brought his people across the galaxy, and three centuries into the future, just to satisfy the bloodthirsty appetites of some ravenous beasts. He snatched up the abandoned rifle and tossed it to Joaquin, who, along with Dr. Hawkins, had lost no time in being at Khan's side once more.

"Join the others in the center of the camp," he instructed the Katzels, who eyed Khan's phaser pistol as though it was their best and only hope. "Joaquin and I will stand watch."

Khan stood like a statue behind the bloodstained brambles, every one of his superhuman senses focused on the menacing shadows surrounding the camp. *When and where*, he wondered, *will the demons strike again?*

He would sleep no more tonight.

Neither, he suspected, would anyone else.

6

They found the remains of Eric Lutjen less than three meters away from the camp. All that remained of the ill-fated superman was grisly morsels of flesh and bones, including a skull from which every trace of skin had been stripped away. Dried blood splashed the long grass around the ghastly sight. Winged condor-like scavengers of prehistoric proportions had already descended on the creature's leavings, and the loud report of a rifle shot was required to disperse the enormous birds before Khan could take possession of the bones.

"Gather the remains," he commanded his party, which had emerged from the camp after sunrise. Noon was still hours away, but the suffocating heat was already reminiscent of Calcutta in March. The sunbaked dirt around the campsite had yielded no useful tracks, but it had been easy enough to follow Lutjen's blood through the brush to the site of his killer's feast. "No follower of mine shall be left as carrion, not while it is within my power to prevent."

He looked in vain for the carcass of the wounded beast itself. Had the creature fed on Lutjen despite its injury, or had another predator stumbled onto the colonist's defenseless body? Despite his words, he wondered if he would find the remains of Blasko and Gorinsky as well, or had they been dragged too far into the veldt to be recovered?

It was an inauspicious beginning to their first full day on Ceti Alpha V.

"Oh my God, Khan," Marla exclaimed, averting her eyes from their gruesome discovery. Her alabaster skin grew paler still, and Khan feared she might vomit. "It's horrible!"

No doubt such butchery was a rarity in the pristine world of the twenty-third century. Khan came from a different, more violent era, however, and he looked on the bloody spectacle without flinching. "You must learn to be stronger," he counseled her, not unkindly. "Ours is a raw and primeval world now, with nature red in tooth and claw."

"I know," she said a trifle queasily. With obvious effort, she regained her composure, fighting back the nausea through sheer strength of will. She forced herself to watch intently as Parvati Rao collected the scattered pieces. "I'll try," she promised Khan.

He smiled, proud of her recovery. He had originally questioned the wisdom of bringing her along on this expedition, but, given the incident with Zuleika Walker, he understood why she hadn't wanted to be left behind at the camp. *It is well*, he thought, *that she has not proven a liability*.

"Are you quite certain, Lord Khan, that you hit the beast?"

Harulf Ericsson craned his neck and made a show of searching fruitlessly for the wounded monster. A mocking undercurrent in his voice belied the innocuous wording of his query. "Perhaps, in the dark and confusion, your beam went astray?"

As with Marla, Khan had been reluctant to leave Ericsson back at the camp, but for completely different reasons. Better to have the smirking Norseman nearby than give him an opportunity to stir up trouble and sedition in Khan's absence. *Keep your friends close*, as the saying went, *but your enemies closer*.

"My aim was true," Khan asserted. There had been no further attacks after he'd shot the escaping beast in midspring, which implied that, if nothing else, the unleashed phaser beam had scared away the pack of predators for the night. Khan found it hard to believe that any mortal beast, however fearsome, could have traveled too far from the camp after being blasted by a phaser set on Kill.

"So where then, Your Excellency, is the animal's body?" Ericsson asked sardonically, earning him a murderous glare from Joaquin, who hefted his rifle ominously. Khan gestured for Joaquin to back down; for the moment, there were more pressing dangers than Ericsson's mocking tone.

Where was the body indeed?

"Khan, look!"

Marla pointed toward the west, where a flock of the giant condors was even now descending on some unseen piece of carrion, which appeared to be sheltered beneath a thicket of shrubs and palm saplings approximately one-point-five kilometers away. *Something* was clearly attracting the scavengers: possibly the beast, its two missing victims, or both.

"An excellent observation," Khan declared, turning to address the entire search party. "We shall investigate at once."

"As you command," Ericsson said with questionable sincerity.

Joaquin led the way, hacking his way through the heavy brush with a three-hundred-year-old machete. It was hard going, especially with the sun blazing high overhead, and Khan's red coverall was soon soaked with sweat. There was no question of stopping to rest, however, not while the fate of the wounded carnivore remained unclear. Khan held on tightly to the grip of his phaser, just in case the daylight held its own dangers.

A faint lowing noise caught his attention, and he glanced toward the horizon in time to see a herd of immense, bisonlike creatures grazing upon a rolling stretch of savanna. *The natural prey of last night's intruders?* Khan speculated. *And perhaps suitable game for my people as well.*

The party paused briefly to watch the distant herbivores. "It is curious," Khan remarked to Marla, who appeared grateful for a short respite. "For an alien world, the flora and fauna here seem strangely familiar. Condors, bison, palm trees, great cats of some variety . . .

I would have expected extraterrestrial life-forms to be more exotic."

"This sort of parallel evolution is surprisingly common throughout the known galaxy," Marla informed him. Perspiration bathed her lovely features. "You met Mr. Spock, for example. His people, the Vulcans, are remarkably human in appearance, despite having evolved on a different planet in a distant solar system."

Her chestnut eyes took in the wild landscape. "From the look of things, I'd guess that the biology of Ceti Alpha V is equivalent to Earth's own Pleistocene Epoch, complete with a tendency toward gigantism in the larger vertebrates." She glanced upward, where another enormous condor could be seen soaring through the sky. Khan estimated the bird's wingspan to be nearly six meters across. "Of course," Marla added, "it's too early to be certain of anything."

"Spoken like a historian," Khan said with a smile. Marla's theory appealed to him; better to conquer a world of giants than a planet of pygmies. Prehistoric man had survived and prospered during the Pleistocene. He and his people, supremely gifted as they were, were sure to do even better. "Come," he instructed the others, impatient to get back to the business of empire-building. "Let us complete our trek."

Arriving at last at the verdant thicket, they were rewarded with the sight of a large, tawny form stretched out beneath the meager shade of a few palms and sycamores. The hindquarters of the motionless beast were lost beneath the underbrush, but the creature's feline head and forelimbs were clearly visible. Khan's wide-eyed gaze was instantly drawn to a pair of huge ivory tusks jutting from the great cat's upper jaw.

"A sabertooth!" he gasped out loud.

"*Smilodon fatalis*," Marla confirmed, her hypothesis looking better and better. "Such as prowled the Earth over one million years ago. During the Pleistocene, to be exact."

The beast was at least three meters long, possibly more, while Khan guessed that the massive carcass had to weigh at least two hundred kilograms. Its huge, serrated canines were the size of daggers and its titanic front legs looked strong enough to bring down an ox, let alone a healthy human being. Brown and golden stripes streaked its shaggy pelt, the better to prowl unseen through the high summer grass.

A scorch mark on the creature's right side made it clear that this was indeed the very beast Khan had blasted with the phaser.

"Is it dead?" Joaquin asked. Machete in hand, he placed himself between Khan and the inert sabertooth, but Khan stepped out from behind his bodyguard in order to inspect the animal more closely.

It certainly looked lifeless enough. The still and silent smilodon lay flat against the earth, its eyes closed. The megacondors, disturbed by the human's arrival, had flapped away from the carcass, taking roost in the upper branches of some nearby palms, but Khan saw no evidence that the scavengers had begun feeding on it.

What were they waiting for?

Rao, who had borne the awful duty of carrying Lutjen's mutilated remains in a canvas bag, was less patient.

"Goddamned monster!" she cursed at the man-eater, charging forward to jab the carcass with the muzzle of her rifle. "You should be extinct, not Lutjen and Blasko and Gorinsky . . . !"

"Stop!" Khan called out in warning, but, hungry for revenge, the crazed soldier paid him no heed. An electronic hum filled the air and Khan turned to see Marla scanning the sabertooth with her tricorder.

"Watch out!" she cried. "It's still alive!"

As if on cue, the "dead" smilodon suddenly roared to life. Amber eyes flashed with savage fury, and its lips peeled back, exposing razor-sharp tusks and teeth. A ferocious snarl drowned out Marla's voice. A great feline claw swiped out, tearing through Rao's left thigh. Crying out in anguish, she collapsed onto the ground, even as the sabertooth lunged forward. . . .

A crimson beam struck the beast between the eyes. It reared backward in shock, clawing at the air, then fell like a rock back onto the grassy sward. Switching off his phaser, Khan glanced quickly at Marla.

"That did it," she reported, keeping her tricorder aimed at the smilodon. "It's dead."

Not soon enough, Khan thought bitterly. Lowering his phaser, he hurried to Rao's side. Hot blood gushed from angry gashes in the Indian guardswoman's thigh, while Rao clenched her teeth and tried to keep from whimpering. Khan instantly regretted not including Dr. Hawkins in the search party, just because he had been reluctant to risk the camp's only physician. "The medkit!" Khan shouted.

Marla quickly furnished him with one of the many

Starfleet medkits Captain Kirk had provided the colonists with. The futuristic drugs and equipment were foreign to him, and he swiftly moved aside to let Marla take charge. He prayed that her Starfleet training had included basic first aid and field medicine.

"Save her," Khan said tersely. "I will not lose another loyal soldier."

Marla gulped. "I'm a historian, not a doctor, but I'll do what I can," she promised, examining Rao's injuries with a small handheld scanner. "Broken bones, torn arteries . . . this looks bad." She drew a silver metallic instrument from the medkit and pressed it against Rao's shoulder. Khan heard a hiss of pressurized air. "That should help with the pain," Marla stated, and Khan noted a look of immediate relief on Rao's face, even as Marla reached for some manner of surgical laser. "Now I just need to stop the bleeding."

With admirable speed, Marla cauterized and bound Rao's wounds, then encased her upper leg in some sort of fast-setting plaster. "That should hold for now," Marla told Khan, "but we have to get her back to the camp and Dr. Hawkins. She needs rest to recover from the shock and blood loss."

"Of course," Khan agreed. At his command, Joaquin and Ericsson constructed a simple travois from the foliage at hand and placed Rao carefully atop a layer of matted grass and leaves. Despite the severity of the situation, Khan derived a degree of pleasure from assigning Ericsson the onerous task of dragging the travois and Rao all the way back to the camp.

"Go," he commanded the Norseman. "Watch over

your patient," he added to Marla. He looked over the bloodstained thicket with a calculating eye. "Joaquin and I will follow after you shortly. I am not quite done here."

Marla looked puzzled, but did not question him. *Faith and discretion*, he noted approvingly. *Two laudable qualities in a woman.*

He watched as Marla and Ericsson departed with Rao, then turned to inspect the dead smilodon and the adjacent scrub. Careful scrutiny failed to discern any trace of the two missing colonists, let alone any evidence of more sabertooths. Khan guessed that the injured smilodon had managed to drag itself to the relative sanctuary of the thicket, but that the creatures' true lair was elsewhere.

I will find their den, he vowed.

But not today.

He nodded at Joaquin and drew his dagger from his belt. He knelt beside the lifeless animal, grabbed its skull by the ears, and cleanly sliced its throat. "Let us claim our trophy," he said.

As Khan had expected, the sight of the man-eater's tawny pelt produced an incredible reaction upon his return to the camp, one more than worth the time it had taken to gut and skin the dead sabertooth. Heartfelt cheers and cries of relief greeted Khan as he strode across New Chandigarh bearing the striped hide across his shoulders like Hercules of old. Behind him, Joaquin dutifully carried the creature's tusks, plus several kilograms of bloody red tissue. "Fresh meat for all!" Khan announced extravagantly. "We shall not dine on Starfleet charity tonight!"

His words inspired another wave of jubilation, but Khan did not fool himself into thinking that a single dead cat ended the threat posed by the sabertooths. Ceti Alpha V had claimed first blood, and Khan had seen that blood partially avenged, but, in his heart, he knew the colony's battles had only just begun.

"*A hard beginning maketh a good ending*," as the proverb goes, he thought. *Let it be so here.*

In his absence, New Chandigarh's fortifications had been significantly improved. The briar fence was twice as high now, while a buffer zone of cleared land now extended two meters beyond the walls in all directions. Huge steel cargo carriers had been dragged into place to serve as watchtowers facing the four corners of the compass. Searchlights, powered by a portable generator, were mounted atop each of the improvised watchtowers.

Excellent, Khan thought. The prowling sabertooths would not so easily take them unawares tonight. He prayed that the camp's strengthened defenses would spare them further depredations, at least until they had time and material enough to build a proper stockade.

The bulky cargo bays looked particularly substantial. Khan made a mental note to convert them into sheds or confinement cells at some point, after they'd been fully emptied of provisions. In the meantime, heavy canvas tents, rescued from the three-hundred-year-old stores of the *Botany Bay*, had been raised within the encampment, providing further shelter from the coming night.

After checking on Parvati Rao, who had thankfully survived being dragged back to camp, Khan conducted a thorough inspection of the settlement. He was gratified to see that, as per his commands, every colonist went about his or her business armed, with a rifle, pistol, blade, or axe. *A good start,* he concluded, *but we still need more weapons. Spears, bows, arrows. . . .*

New Chandigarh's sole phaser rested securely against his hip, but Khan knew he could not rely on its awesome power forever. Eventually, its energy would run low, as would their limited supplies of ammunition and gunpowder. The sooner the colony began manufacturing its own armaments, the better.

But first Khan had a more somber duty to perform.

"The deaths of our beloved comrades—Eric Lutjen, Dmitri Blasko, and Nadia Gorinsky—are a sobering reminder of the challenges we will face in conquering this primeval world. But do not lose heart," Khan instructed his people. "I remind you that each of us has already cheated death, awaking to new life hundreds of years in the future, long after our ancient enemies have faded into history."

The memorial service was held shortly before sunset, before another night of terror could begin. Lutjen's sundered remains were cremated atop a blazing pyre, rendering them immune to further desecration. That the bodies of the other two victims had not yet been recovered galled Khan's soul, although he took care to keep the bitterness from his voice as he presided over the ceremony.

"Mourn our departed friends we must, but we will honor them best by meeting the hardships ahead with courage and determination. Only by carving an empire out of this forbidding wilderness can we ensure that our comrades' names will be remembered forever!"

His people nodded, their dismal faces lit by the fiery glow of the burning pyre, whose crackling flames matched the anger blazing deep inside Khan's heart.

Someday soon, he promised himself, *I will hunt the rest of the sabertooths to their lair.*

7

THREE MONTHS AFTER DAY ONE

"Toxic. Toxic. Edible."

A variety of alien roots, nuts, berries, and grubs were laid on a blanket at the edge of a newly cleared field. Marla knelt in the dry red dirt beside the blanket while she scanned the samples with her tricorder. *Just our luck*, she thought wryly. *Only those squirmy yellow worms are safe to eat.*

"Dammit," Parvati Rao swore, obviously sharing Marla's reaction to the revolting-looking grubs. She leaned against her walking stick as she looked over the blanket's contents. "I had high hopes for those juicy orange berries."

Marla shook her head. "You'd be dead before you finished off a handful of them." She rose and brushed the dust from her skirt. A wide-brimmed hat, made of woven grass, protected her head from the blazing sun overhead, but offered no relief from the sweltering humidity, which indicated that a rainy season was approaching, just as the *Enterprise*'s planetary modeling had predicted. "Spread the word to the others to leave those berries alone, no matter how succulent they look." She shrugged off her own disappointment, even though her mouth watered at the sight of the tempting fruit. Khan had them all on strict rations, and Marla was hungrier than any modern, twenty-third-century human should ever expect to be.

Beneath her fraying Starfleet uniform, her body felt bonier than a Vulcan matriarch's. Marla guessed that she'd lost at least ten kilograms since setting foot on Ceti Alpha V, with no end in sight. They weren't exactly starving—hunting and gathering turned up enough food and game to live on, augmented by carefully regimented nutritional supplements from their provisions—but at times Marla thought she would kill for a working food slot. Her historian's imagination was haunted by visions of the Donner party and the famine on Tarsus IV. . . .

"Maybe we'll have better luck tomorrow," she sighed.

Testing the local flora and fauna for toxicity had become a regular part of Marla's routine. With the colonists clearing fields in anticipation of the coming monsoon, new samples were turning up almost daily. So far she'd identified about a half-dozen native life-forms as suitable for human consumption, along with a number of nasty poisons to avoid.

"Anything else?" she asked Daniel Katzel, who was standing guard over the field. The former computer hacker stood a few paces away, dividing his attention between Marla's survey and the ongoing effort to clear the field of leftover roots and rocks.

"You bet," he answered brusquely. Daniel's face was shaded by the brim of his hat. He put down his rifle and picked up a Starfleet-issue specimen jar. "Take a look at this little bug-eyed monster."

Something gray and scaly skittered inside the transparent aluminum canister. "Goddamn!" Parvati exclaimed as Daniel brought the jar closer for the inspection. "What the bloody hell is that?"

Parvati's casual profanity betrayed her twentieth-century roots, but Marla knew what she meant. The creature inside the jar was truly hideous, like some mutant hybrid of a wood louse and a scorpion. Roughly thirty centimeters in length, from its pincers to its tail, the life-form appeared to be a mollusk of some sort, possibly a gastropod or chiton, whose dorsal shell consisted of overlapping plates of horny armor. Slitted red eyes peered malignantly from the creature's skull, while a pair of vicious-looking pincers protruded from its open maw. An angry noise, somewhere between a squeal and a snarl, escaped the trapped specimen as its pincers scratched furiously at the transparent walls of the jar.

As a Starfleet officer, Marla had been trained not to judge alien life-forms by their appearance. Even still, something about the caged mollusk sent a shiver down her spine, as though someone had walked upon her grave. . . .

"Found it burrowing underneath a rock," Daniel explained, "like a Plutonian sand-spider on *Captain Proton*." Three centuries in hibernation had not diminished Katzel's enthusiasm for the classic science fiction of his own era. "Damn near took off Rodriguez's toe with those pincers."

Parvati shuddered in sympathy, no doubt recalling her own close encounter with the local wildlife. "Well," she asked hesitantly. "Can we eat the bugger?" Judging from her dubious tone, Marla suspected that, despite the food shortage, the other woman was praying the answer was negative.

"Let's see," Marla said, scanning the creature through the walls of the canister. "Hmm. Not exactly toxic per se, but I'm detecting some sort of odd neurochemical in the specimen's offspring, which seem to be present in larval form beneath the creature's outer shell." She adjusted the tricorder's controls, trying to get a more precise reading, only to be interrupted by an electronic beep from the instrument. The readout on the display screen wavered, then dissolved into visual static.

"Hell!" Marla cursed. Clearly, Rao's penchant for profanity was rubbing off on her.

"What is it?" the other woman asked.

Marla smacked the side of the tricorder with her hand, but the display did not right itself. "I was afraid of this," she admitted. "It's exhausted its energy supply." She looked up from the unresponsive device. "I need to get a fresh power cell back at the camp." Strapping the tricorder over her shoulder, she glanced over at the walls of New Chandigarh, about thirty meters away. "I'll be right back."

"Want me to join you?" Parvati asked.

Marla shook her head. While she appreciated the offer, the other woman's leg had never fully recovered from the sabertooth's attack; indeed, Rao had only recently graduated from a crutch to a walking stick. Marla would make better time on her own, plus why subject Parvati to an extra hike if it could be avoided? "Don't worry about it," she said. "Why don't you keep an eye on our ugly friend there? I'm sure Khan will want to see it when he gets back from the hunt."

Khan remained obsessed with tracking the sabertooths to their lair. Although they had not lost another colonist to the man-eaters since improving the camp's defenses, there had been any number of close calls; just yesterday a trio of smilodons had attacked a party of would-be ranchers trying to corral some of the local bison. One man's back had been severely mauled before the predators were driven off, and the entire ranching expedition had been forced to retreat in disarray. Every night Marla could hear the deadly cats prowling the veldt, to the fury of Khan, who had never forgiven the smilodons for slaying three of his people on that ghastly first night. Marla knew he would not rest until he'd repaid that debt in the sabertooths' blood.

Sometimes his passion for revenge frightened her. *It's probably just as well*, she thought, *that Captain Kirk and the others are all light-years away by now.* She never wanted to come between Khan and his wrath.

"Sounds good," Parvati said, assenting to Marla's

wishes, so Marla set off through the fields toward camp. It was at least forty-five degrees Celsius, and the combined heat and humidity sapped her strength, leaving her drenched in perspiration. As far as she was concerned, the monsoon couldn't come too soon, and not just because they needed the rain for their crops. She was tired of being hot and dirty and dusty all the time. What she wouldn't give for a decent sonic shower . . . !

No more of that, she scolded herself. Self-pity was a luxury she was doing her best to overcome, along with the gnawing ache in her stomach. *Maybe I should have grabbed a few of those grubs to munch on.* To her slight dismay, the squiggly worms were sounding better and better.

The gates of New Chandigarh soon came into view, and she took a moment to admire the progress the colony had made since their arrival on the planet. Barbed wire and a high metal fence, cannibalized from construction materials found in the cargo bays, had replaced the wall of thorns, although four of the now-empty cargo carriers still served as watchtowers. Crude doorways, carved out by a red-hot phaser beam, provided entrance to the converted metal shells.

A crimson banner, bearing the image of a crescent moon superimposed upon a sun, fluttered from a flagpole rising from the center of the camp. The flag had been designed by Khan himself, Marla knew, during his reign on Earth three hundred years ago. Together, the sun and the moon symbolized totality—everything in the world, all that Khan had once intended to rule.

Just as he now intended to rule Ceti Alpha V.

Meanwhile, the original tents had given way to roughly fifteen one-story huts, of a primitive "wattle-and-daub" variety. *Not unlike the early structures at the first Botany Bay colony in Australia,* she reflected. Horizontal lengths of saplings, harvested from a grove of palm trees they'd discovered farther down the river, had been stretched between four sturdy timber posts, creating walls that resembled antique washboards. Thatched roofs covered the tops of the newly built huts, while canvas from the discarded tents provided an additional level of insulation for the ceilings.

Back in the eighteenth century, Marla knew, such crude structures had been plastered on the outside with mud, but Khan had shrewdly realized that sunbaked mud would be unlikely to survive the coming monsoon. As a result, the walls of the huts had been lightly daubed with fast-setting thermoconcrete, of the sort used to construct emergency shelters by Starfleet landing parties. Marla took pride in having suggested the idea to Khan in the first place; ironically, despite a lifetime devoted to the study of the past, she now found herself the colony's resident expert on "future" technology and materials.

Not that my fellow colonists appreciate my efforts, Marla thought, the buried resentment surfacing against her will. *At least not most of them.*

She pushed the painful knowledge aside with effort, returning her attention to the growing settlement. Someday, she hoped, there would be time to manufacture actual bricks from the clay by the river, and stone tiles to replace the thatched roofs. She envisioned graceful brick buildings rising from the camp's humble beginnings, adorned perhaps with polished marble, or rare woods imported from the great deciduous forests to the south, to make New Chandigarh a city worthy of Khan's ambitious dreams of empire.

But for now, of course, hunting and farming took priority.

Thunder rumbled in the distance, somewhere to the southwest. Marla sniffed the breeze. Was it just her imagination or was there a wisp of ozone in the air? *Another electrical storm on the way,* she surmised. Another sign, along with the mounting humidity, that the rainy season should be arriving any day now.

Bring it on, she thought eagerly. *Anything to cool things off a bit!*

Trudging wearily through the feverish heat and dust, she walked through the front gate of the colony. No friendly faces or salutations greeted her return to the camp—only a few sullen and/or disinterested glances from men and women who quickly went back to their respective chores, turning their backs on Marla.

She was used to the cold-shoulder treatment by now, but it still hurt. Her standing in the colony remained a work-in-progress that, unlike New Chandigarh itself, was going nowhere fast. At Khan's insistence, the others tolerated her presence, some more grudgingly than others, but Marla knew that she was still regarded as an outsider and an inferior. For a moment, she regretted leaving Parvati Rao behind in the fields; thanks to Marla's lifesaving medical assistance during that first sabertooth-hunting expedition, the Indian guardswoman was about the only human on the planet, aside from Khan himself, who actually treated Marla like a friend.

Marla crossed the campsite in lonely silence. Her Starfleet medallion dangled from a chain around her throat, and she guiltily tucked it into the neck of her sweat-stained blouse, safely out of sight. She wasn't ashamed of her past—on the contrary, she remained proud to have served, however briefly, in Starfleet— but, for Khan's sake, she thought it wise not to flaunt her divided loyalties in the face of the other colonists. Why mark herself with a scarlet letter, as if she wasn't already enough of a pariah?

"Well, well," a mocking voice called out, "if it isn't Khan's pretty little pet!"

Marla recognized the voice and her heart sank. *Great,* she thought. *Just what I* didn't *need right now.*

She turned to see Zuleika Walker tending a large pot of boiling water, not unlike a witch brewing her cauldron—if your typical witch looked like a towering dark-skinned Amazon, that is. Weeks of strict rations had stripped every ounce of excess body fat from the woman's body, making her formidable musculature all the more imposing. As usual, she wore only a revealing shroud of golden mesh, as a concession either to the heat, her vanity, or both.

"What do you want, Zuleika?" Marla asked apprehensively. Although the hostile superwoman had not threatened Marla physically since their first night on the planet, she seldom missed an opportunity to give Marla a bad time, if only when Khan was not around. After the incident with the torch, Marla couldn't help feeling uneasy at the sight of Zuleika in close proximity to another fire.

"Want?" the other woman replied. Her dark eyes flashed indignantly. "I want to be somewhere civilized, with indoor plumbing and air-conditioning, not playing *Gilligan's Island* on Ceti Alpha V, wherever the hell that is, but I guess that's just not going to happen, is it, Mary-Ann?" She spat at the dusty ground between them. "I was a supermodel-slash-assassin back on Earth. Now look at me!"

Marla didn't quite get all of the woman's archaic references, but the message—and the attitude—was clear enough. *Fine,* Marla thought angrily. She was tired of taking the blame for all the rigors of frontier life. What did Zuleika expect when she signed aboard the *Botany Bay,* a pleasure cruise to Risa? "I don't have time for this," she responded.

She made sure Zuleika got a good look at the Colt automatic pistol (which would have been the envy of Lieutenant Sulu back on the *Enterprise*) tucked into the wide black belt around her waist. There had been some controversy, mostly generated by Ericsson and his lackeys, about Marla receiving the pistol, while many of the other colonists had to make do with axes and spears, but Marla found herself glad that Khan had remained adamant on this point; amid all these genetically enhanced physical specimens, her gun served as a much-needed equalizer.

Just call me Annie Oakley, she thought.

She turned her back on Zuleika, but could not resist glancing backward over her shoulder as she marched away from the other woman. Thankfully, Zuleika appeared content, for now, simply to shoot daggers at Marla with her eyes. "Go ahead, walk away," she called out. "I'm not going anywhere—and neither is anybody else!"

Marla made a mental note to ask Khan what a "supermodel" was. Some sort of genetically engineered prototype?

The bulk of her Starfleet gear was stored in a half-finished shed not far from Khan and Marla's own private hut. The basic wooden construction had been completed, but only the bottom third of the shack had been daubed with thermoconcrete, to provide a secure foundation. They were starting to run low on thermoconcrete, Marla knew; she wondered if there would be enough to finish the shed before the rains hit. If not, they might have to move the supplies back into one of the original cargo carriers.

Thunder rumbled again, and Marla caught a glimpse of lightning to the south. *That could be dangerous,* she fretted, worrying about the colonists still out in the fields. They'd already had to stamp out a few scary brushfires, although so far there had been no casualties.

As she wound through rows of huts, on her way to the storage shed, she spotted Paul Austin, one of Ericsson's cronies, loitering nearby. A sunburnt American, with ruddy skin and tattoos, he was leaning against a typical hut, smoking a cigarette made from a local plant that bore some slight familial resemblance to Terran tobacco. Marla shook her head; of all the barbaric habits that Khan's people had brought with them from the twentieth century, smoking was one of the most baffling. Why inhale noxious fumes, when even the humans of their own era knew it was bad for them?

Intertwining snakes, spiders, and scorpions covered the tattooed American's bare arms and chest. The revolting creature Daniel Katzel had just discovered would have fit right in.

Conscious of Marla's scrutiny, Austin crushed his cigarette beneath his heel and strode away, perhaps concerned that Marla might report him to Khan for shirking. He needn't have worried; Marla figured she was unpopular enough without becoming the camp snitch, which was one of the reasons she tried not to complain to Khan about the harsh treatment she got from Zuleika and the others.

It worried her, though, that Austin had been lurking so near Khan's quarters—and the supply shed. What if he wasn't just taking a smoking break?

Quickening her step, she arrived at the shed, where she was relieved to see Vishwa Patil, a security officer who had once been stationed at Khan's fortress in northern India, standing guard over the precious supplies. Meticulous about his appearance, despite the rough conditions, he sported a trim military haircut along with an impressive handlebar mustache, whose oiled tips curved upward below his cheeks.

A padlock and chains provided additional security for the shed, of a sort; the chains could not stop Austin or any other colonist from breaking in, of course—Marla still remembered Khan snapping his manacles in half in front of poor Chekov—but a broken lock would alert her if someone had been at her carefully hoarded Starfleet gear.

"Good afternoon," she greeted Patil. "I need to retrieve a new fuel cell."

The stern-faced Indian nodded and stepped away from the door. Although clearly uninterested in small talk, the guard knew that Khan had granted Marla full access to the shed. *Thank heaven for small favors,* she thought; after Zuleika, she wasn't up for another argument.

Marla unfastened the lock and pulled the door open. She stepped inside, leaving the door open to let in the daylight. More light filtered in through the cracks between the unplastered saplings. After her exhausting hike in the sun, the relative shade of the thatch-covered hut came as a welcome change.

Her eyes adjusting to the shadows, she quickly inventoried the contents of the shed, which included spare medkits, life-support gear, hazard vests, tritanium-mesh blankets, snow gear, a universal translator, antigrav cargo pallets, electronic clipboards, transtator components, protein resequencers, plasma lights, generators, rechargers, and other Starfleet-issue equipment. No communicators, though; Captain Kirk hadn't wanted to give Khan the capacity to lure unsuspecting starships into a trap.

To her chagrin, she found only two fully charged power cells left for the tricorder. *I'll have to remember to recharge my old one,* she realized; a somewhat time-consuming procedure. Recycling and cannibalizing their existing equipment was a way of life on Ceti Alpha V.

After all, we can hardly requisition Starfleet for fresh supplies.

It occurred to her that there were probably a few more cells stored in one of the old cargo bays that now served as watchtowers. Not wanting to place all their eggs in one basket, Khan had made sure that reserves of their most essential supplies were safely tucked away inside the impregnable steel carriers. *I should probably check on those supplies as well,* she thought.

Without warning, the door slammed shut, leaving her in the dark. A heavy weight hit the ground outside. She heard footsteps and called out, "Patil?"

No answer.

Marla hurried to the door, only to find it locked from the outside. Thunder boomed overhead. She shoved on the door with both hands, but it refused to budge. Something large and massive was wedged against the other side. Marla was trapped. "Patil?" she yelled again, more anxiously this time. Had something happened to the guard? "Let me out of here!"

She smelled smoke. A sudden fear gripped her heart.

Oh no!

But it was already too late. The dry timbers surrounding her caught fire immediately, the flames quickly blocking every avenue of escape. Choking black smoke filled the shed, and Marla dropped to the floor in search of purer air, even as the acrid fumes invaded her nose and lungs.

For a second, she considered trying to dig her way out of the burning hut, but the thermoconcrete foundation rendered that scheme unworkable; there was no way she could tunnel deep enough to escape the hut before the flames consumed her. She could feel the heat of the roaring blaze all around her, scorching her skin.

In desperation, she fired her pistol into the air, praying that someone in the camp would hear the shot and come to her rescue. "Help!" she cried hoarsely, choking on the smoke. "Patil! Somebody! Help me!"

But no one answered.

8

The hunt was on, and Khan did not intend to return empty-handed. He, Joaquin, Ericsson, and one more colonist, Karyn Bradley, pushed their way through the tall grass in search of the elusive sabertooths. *Fortune will be with us today,* Khan thought confidently. *I can feel it in my bones.*

A hot wind blew across the savanna, causing the yellow grass to rustle and stir like waves atop the sea. Khan took care to march directly into the wind, so that his scent would not precede him.

"Your Excellency, look." Joaquin pointed to a clump of impervious "axebreaker" trees not far away. Such thickets, they had learned, offered shade and the occasional waterhole, which often attracted the beasts they sought. Khan was encouraged to see birds nesting in the upper branches of the trees, confirming the locale's appeal to the indigenous wildlife.

He nodded in agreement, and the hunting party stealthily made their way toward the dense green grove. Khan was armed with his phaser, which never left his person, while Joaquin and Bradley both carried American-made rifles, from the *Botany Bay*'s original stores. Ericsson sullenly carried the rest of their gear through the intense humidity. The Norseman's once-fair skin had long since been browned by the merciless sun. His only weapon was a handmade stone axe.

As they approached the thicket's outer fringe, their efforts were rewarded by the unmistakable rumble of a purring smilodon. Signaling the others to silence, Khan cautiously drew back the fronds of a leafy bush in order to peer deeper into the sylvan bower. His blood surged in anticipation of the kill. *The beast's tusks and hide shall serve as testaments to my revenge.*

His eyes beheld a massive sabertooth, stretched out on the undergrowth between two thick tree trunks. The stripped bones of an unfortunate bison were scattered upon the floor, and it required little imagination on Khan's part to imagine the mangled skeleton of one of his people in place of the dead ruminant's bones. Sated and content, the smilodon dozed placidly in the shade, seemingly oblivious to the arrival of the four superhumans. Its eyes were closed in slumber, and its steady purr sounded like the murmur of a well-tuned motor.

Perfect, Khan thought with pleasure. The specters of his martyred followers rose up in his memory, demanding vengeance. Khan slowly raised his phaser, taking careful aim at the sabertooth's colossal skull. The weapon was set to Kill, not disintegrate; Khan had no desire to forgo his trophy. *I will teach this planet that there is a new and greater predator on Ceti Alpha V.*

Then, at the worst possible moment, the wind shifted, carrying Khan's scent into the thicket. Amber eyes snapped open and the recumbent sabertooth sprang into action, every sense alert to danger. In haste, Khan fired at it, but the animal had already bolted for safety, taking cover behind the broad tree trunks. The deadly crimson beam blackened the bark of a guiltless axebreaker, even as the fleeing smilodon suddenly veered toward Khan, lunging at him with its powerful foreclaws extended. Tusks like daggers sliced through the air between them.

Khan swung his phaser around, desperately trying to meet the creature's charge with another blast of energy. Gunshots rang out behind him, however, and the beast was sent hurtling backward, turning a somersault in the air. Patches of bright red blood burst from the sabertooth's tawny hide. An anguished roar joined the echo of the two, almost simultaneous rifle blasts.

Khan risked a glance behind him, where he saw both Joaquin and Bradley standing with their rifles still poised against their shoulders. The scent of gunpowder assaulted his nostrils. A look of vast relief flooded Bradley's freckled countenance, although Joaquin's face remained as stoic as ever. Ericsson, if anything, looked distinctly disappointed by Khan's survival.

The smilodon crashed to earth, then instantly broke for the relative cover of the deep grass. Khan's gaze snapped back to his prey in time to see the wounded sabertooth disappear into the rustling waves of yellow and brown.

"Hurry!" he shouted to the others, eager to claim the beast that had attacked him only seconds before. "We must not let it get away!"

There would be time enough to thank his defenders later. For now, the hunt continued. Phaser in hand, Khan charged into the brush. His boots pounded loudly against the earth as he ran after the vanished smilodon. He heard Joaquin and the others running behind him, Ericsson cursing in Norwegian beneath his breath.

Despite its injuries, the sabertooth made good time through the grassland, easily outdistancing its determined pursuers. But although Khan could not catch even a glimpse of the departing animal, a trail of smeary bloodstains made tracking the big cat mere child's play. *There are advantages*, Khan noted, *to old-fashioned ammunition;* a phaser blast left no bleeding wounds.

Joaquin caught up with Khan, jogging only a few paces behind his leader. "Beware, Your Excellency," he huffed. "A wounded animal can be more dangerous than ever."

True enough, Khan acknowledged, without slowing his pace. "You know, my friend, I might have slain the beast myself, back there by the thicket."

"Of course, Lord Khan," Joaquin agreed readily. "But I did not wish to take that chance." He gripped his rifle with both hands as he ran. "Forgive me for my presumption."

Khan smiled, amused by the bodyguard's apology. He was not so proud that he begrudged a legitimate attempt to protect his life. "It is of no matter," he assured the other man.

The trail of blood led uphill, toward a stony ridge overlooking the savanna. The sabertooth was seeking higher ground, Khan surmised. He was undaunted by the climb ahead; the upward chase would leave any ordinary man winded, but Khan and his people all had fifty-percent superior lung capacity. If anything, he increased his pace as he reached the base of the ridge.

A puddle of warm blood, filling a shallow depression in the rock, verified that they were still on the right track. Bradley winced at the sight of the crimson pool. "It's bleeding badly, poor thing." A note of sympathy, and regret, entered her voice. "It's a shame we have to kill it." Her eyes entreated Khan. "Are you certain we can't somehow coexist with these animals?"

Khan recalled that the tall brunette had been an academic back on Earth, sheltered somewhat from the crueler realities of life. "Homer said it best," he informed her. "'There are no compacts between lions and men, and wolves and lambs have no concord.'" He shook his head solemnly. "On Ceti Alpha V, the only endangered species is us."

"Yes, Lord Khan," she said, tightening her grip upon her rifle. "I understand."

Splashes of red led them up the side of the ridge until they came to the entrance of a cave, tucked into the gap between two flanking boulders. A scraggly bush partially concealed the open cavity, which appeared to lead deep into the craggy bluff. Crimson smudges stained the thornscrub.

Khan's face lit up. Could it be that, after months of searching, he had found the man-eaters' den at last? He eagerly chopped away the prickly shrub, clearing the entrance. His eyes probed the darkness beyond, but saw nothing but shadows. He unclasped a palm-sized flashlight from his belt and stepped toward the gaping maw.

"Your Excellency!" Joaquin exclaimed. "You cannot mean to enter the cave."

"That is precisely what I mean to do," Khan declared. He had not hunted the sabertooth all this way just to turn back now. He raised his hand to forestall further debate. "Do not attempt to dissuade me. The beast dies today."

An unexpected voice spoke up. "Then let me go first, Lord Khan," Ericsson volunteered, without his usual sarcasm. "Your safety is paramount."

Khan's eyes narrowed as he examined the Norseman, surprised by the man's offer. Was Ericsson simply trying to get back into Khan's good graces, or had he some darker motive? Khan saw no obvious flaw in the other man's proposal; indeed, it would be safer to have the possibly duplicitous Norseman in front of him than behind him. *And I hardly wish to leave him standing guard outside the cave, where one convenient "avalanche" could bury the rest of us alive.*

"Very well," Khan stated, stepping aside to permit Ericsson full access to the cavern's entrance. "Bravery is a trait I seek always to encourage." He quickly assigned the others their duties. "Bradley, you will stand watch outside the cave. In case of a collapse, it is imperative that you get assistance from New Chandigarh to dig us out." He turned to Joaquin, whom looked perturbed by these recent turn of events. "You, my friend, will follow after me into the cave, and we shall not emerge until the creature's lifeless body is in my possession."

The unhappy bodyguard nodded. "As you command."

Khan handed Ericsson the palm light, half-expecting the bearded man to ask for a rifle as well. Instead Ericsson simply drew his stone axe with his right hand while accepting the flashlight with his left. He shined an incandescent beam into the mouth of the cave, but the light provoked no response from whatever dwelt within. "Into the *mistenkelig* breach," he muttered, ducking his head as he entered the darkness, with Khan and Joaquin close behind him.

A sloping path led them down a narrow tunnel defined by smooth limestone walls. Khan peered past Ericsson's shoulder, watching for the telltale gleam of angry feline eyes, while listening carefully for any signs of life. He heard Joaquin gulp nervously, and glanced behind him to see his loyal servant eyeing the jagged ceiling with obvious mistrust.

No doubt, Khan realized, the stalwart bodyguard was recalling that perilous incident in 1993, when an earthquake, triggered by a rival superman, had trapped him and Joaquin beneath the ruins of an ancient Hindu temple. Both men had nearly died that day, so Khan could not fault his old friend for experiencing a touch of claustrophobia, no matter that the sacred caves of Ajorra were now many light-years and centuries away.

Perhaps, Khan thought, *I should have left Joaquin outside and brought Bradley instead.*

The temperature grew notably cooler, causing the perspiration on Khan's clothes and body to grow cold and clammy. As they rounded a corner, venturing ever deeper in the subterranean recesses of the cavern, they disturbed a multitude of batlike creatures sleeping amid the stalactites overhead. The sound of countless leather wings flapping wildly briefly filled the underground chamber, before the agitated nightflyers fled toward the lower depths. Khan listened to the flapping recede into the abyss, leading him to wonder just how extensive this cave system was. *Something worth exploring at some future date,* he resolved. *Today I have bloodier business to conclude.*

The pungent smell of bat guano permeated the air, mixing with a musky animal odor that grew stronger the further they explored. Leaving the bat chamber behind, they came to a smaller grotto with two branching exits. No obvious bloodstains betrayed the route taken by the wounded smilodon.

"Which way now, Lord Khan?" Ericsson asked. Khan thought he detected a tinge of impudence in the man's voice, but could not have sworn to it.

Khan sniffed the air. The animal scent was heavy here, but offered little clue as to which way to proceed. He stepped away from Ericsson, toward the right-hand corridor, only to stumble over something that clattered against the flowstone floor.

What is this? Khan wondered, a terrible suspicion already dawning in his soul.

Ericsson's search beam, turned in Khan's direction, confirmed his fears: a grotesque assortment of well-gnawed bones were scattered about the grotto, along with scraps of fabric and pieces of jewelry. Khan realized that he had finally found the dismal resting place of the two missing colonists. Shattered skulls and jawbones made readily apparent the once-human nature of the debris.

"Gorinsky. Blasko," he pronounced solemnly. Looking up and down the tunnels to make sure his flanks were covered, Khan tucked his phaser into his belt, then knelt to gather up the disordered bones. He had promised these victims honorable cremations and he would not suffer their remains to lie in this abhorrent state one moment longer. "A bag," he instructed Joaquin. "At once."

A feral growl intruded on the moment, seizing Khan's attention. Luminous yellow eyes, growing larger by the instant, glowed in the darkness as an enraged smilodon came charging at Joaquin, who fired his rifle with commendable speed. The bloodthirsty sabertooth took multiple shots, but kept on coming, driven by a relentless primeval fury. An earsplitting roar echoed within the enclosed confines of the creature's lair.

Khan jumped to his feet and reached for his phaser, brandishing a fractured jawbone in his free hand. Before he could fire, however, Ericsson's voice shouted urgently: "Watch out! Behind you!"

The search beam swung around to reveal *another*

smilodon, crouching atop a limestone shelf overlooking the boneyard. Intent on rescuing the dead colonists' remains, Khan had not even noticed the shelf was there.

Until now.

The second sabertooth sprang at Khan, who cursed himself for thinking only in two dimensions, even as Joaquin continued to fire at the original predator. Dueling snarls competed with the sharp report of the rifle. Khan dropped to the floor, ducking beneath the claws of the pouncing smilodon, which nonetheless sliced through the back of his jumpsuit, tearing deep gouges in his flesh. The animal landed heavily on the ground, sending bones flying in every direction. Crazed by the scent of fresh blood, it instantly went for Khan again.

Ericsson hurled his axe at Khan's attacker. The crude weapon spun through the air, coming to rest deep in the sabertooth's back. The beast let out a roar of anguish, and angrily turned on Ericsson. Khan took immediate advantage of the smilodon's distraction by taking aim with his phaser and blasting the enraged creature with a beam of concentrated energy. Taking no chances, he upped the setting on the phaser, disintegrating the beast entirely. Within seconds, all that remained of the second smilodon was a faint afterglow, which swiftly faded from sight.

Khan took a second to process the sabertooth's demise, then hurriedly checked on Joaquin. To his relief, he saw that the first smilodon was finally dead, lying flat upon the bone-strewn floor less than ten paces away from Joaquin. Smoke issued from the muzzle of the bodyguard's weapon, which remained raised and ready. "Your Excellency," he said in alarm. "Your back!"

Blood streamed from five deep cuts in his jumpsuit; a few centimeters deeper and the sabertooth's claws might have severed Khan's spine. "It is nothing," Khan insisted, dismissing the sharp-edged pain with a wave of his hand. "The animal drew first blood, but mine was the killing blow."

Joaquin did not question Khan's assessment of his injuries. "We should leave," the bodyguard stated bluntly. "There might be more animals."

Rising to his feet, Khan nodded in agreement. The tigers of his native India tended to hunt alone, but who knew how alien sabertooths behaved? Bandaging his wounds could wait until they were safely clear of the predators' lair. In any event, Khan was satisfied with the outcome of the hunt. He had achieved two kills, one for both Blasko and Gorinsky. That was enough for today.

He turned toward Ericsson. "My thanks," he said, "for your timely warning and intervention." The man's axe had been disintegrated along with the second smilodon, so Khan presented Ericsson with his own knife. *Perhaps,* he thought, *I have misjudged the man.*

Or perhaps not. It occurred to Khan that Ericsson might have saved him simply because the Norseman doubted his ability to escape both sabertooths on his own. Still, Ericsson had performed bravely in battle, and that, too, was all that Khan required today. *His courage has bought him a chance to regain my favor,* Khan decided. *We shall see whether he wastes that opportunity or not.*

They exited the caves with no further incident, dragging the carcass of the original smilodon behind them. From its multiple gunshot wounds, many more than Joaquin could have inflicted during the attack in the grotto, Khan deduced that this was the very beast whose bloody trail had led them to the cavern's entrance. They brought Gorinsky's and Blasko's bones as well, mixed together in a single canvas bag. Perhaps, back at the camp, they could take the time to separate the two victims' remains.

Emerging from the chilly gloom of the cave into the searing heat of the sun, they rejoined Bradley upon the exterior of the rocky bluff. Her eyes widened at the size of the dead smilodon and she started to ask about the kill . . . when an unexpected noise suddenly rang out across the savanna, coming from the direction of New Chandigarh.

Gunshots.

Alarmed, Khan peered toward the distant camp, raising a hand to shield his eyes from the glare. Despite the height of the ridge, and his own superior vision, he could not quite make out the origin of the gunfire. "Binoculars!" he demanded tersely, and Bradley thrust a pair of field glasses into his hand.

He pressed the binoculars against his eyes, quickly locating the outer walls of the colony, as well as the crimson flag above them. To his dismay, he saw large quantities of black smoke rising from somewhere within the settlement.

A fire? Gunshots? Obviously, there was trouble back at the camp, but he could only guess how serious the crisis was. *Marla*, he thought anxiously. Was she safe, or had the unknown calamity already claimed her life, along with the lives of perhaps many others? *I must know what has transpired, as fast as humanly possible.*

All thought of skinning and gutting the dead saber-tooth, not to mention tending to the bleeding claw marks on his back, vanished from his mind. "Hurry!" he told the others, lowering the binoculars. "We must return to camp at once!"

Let Marla be safe, he commanded the fates, all too aware that an uncaring universe did not always bend to his decrees. *Let her still live. . . .*

9

The mysterious gunshots had long since fallen silent by the time the hunting party reached the gates of New Chandigarh. Coal-black plumes of smoke continued to rise toward the sky, but Khan was relieved to see that the entire colony had not apparently burned to the ground. He raced through the open gate, ignoring the hails of the guards, and headed straight for the source of the smoke, which, he noted with alarm, appeared to be very near the location of his own hut. His concern for Marla's safety grew at a geometric rate as he rushed across the camp.

He broke through a crowd of onlookers to discover a smoldering pile of cinders and burning timbers where once a storage shed had stood, only a few meters away from the hut he shared with Marla. The fire itself was dying now, reduced to a smoking remnant of its former self. Khan's anxiety began to lessen, until he failed to spot Marla's face among the colonists circling the ruins.

He spotted Vishwa Patil standing nearby and immediately stepped in front of him. "Report," he demanded. "What happened here? Were there any injuries?"

Where is Marla? he added silently. His flesh still screamed where the sabertooth had slashed him, and the back of his jumpsuit was soaked with blood, but Khan was barely aware of his own injuries. An ominous feeling cast its pall over his soul.

"There was a fire," Patil explained, his face blackened with soot. "It's . . . unclear . . . how it began. I was standing guard by the door, when something struck me from behind." He reached back to massage the back of his skull, wincing as he did so. "When I came to, the shed was already on fire. Arson . . . lightning . . . I don't know." He glanced upward at the sky, where inky clouds drifted toward the camp from the south, adding to the foreboding atmosphere. "We used CO_2 and water to put the blaze out."

Khan nodded impatiently. "What of casualties? Was anyone harmed?"

Patil hesitated before answering. "Lieutenant McGivers," he said finally, "entered the shed right before the fire broke out. I was watching her from the doorway, in fact, when I was knocked cold." He shook his head ruefully. "I believe she . . . did not escape."

The security officer flinched in anticipation of Khan's wrath, but Khan's first reaction was one of profound grief—and guilt. *My beautiful Marla,* he mourned, *the fairest flower of this brave new era. You might have been hap-*

pier, and lived far longer, had I never awoken in your time. Only his iron self-control kept even a single tear from welling in the corner of his eye. *I would have wished for you a more joyous fate.*

The depth of his sorrow caught him by surprise. Back on Earth, when he had ruled as prince over millions, there had been paramours aplenty—"A bevy of fair women," in Milton's phrase—but none that stood out from the others. War and conquest had been his priorities then; he had always assumed that there would be time enough later, after he achieved dominion over the Earth, to select a queen, sire a dynasty. In the meantime, he had amused himself with the world's most beautiful courtesans and superwomen.

So how was it, he pondered, *that I lost my heart to a hero-worshipping historian from another century? Was it because, unlike those who came to me at the height of my power, Marla stayed by my side even as I faced eternal exile from the world she knew?*

He stared at the fiery wreckage, where Marla's charred remains were doubtless buried beneath the embers. His mother, Khan recalled, had also died in flames, consumed by a nuclear explosion beneath the sands of the Great Thar Desert in northwestern India, nearly three hundred years ago. *What cruel fate,* he lamented, *decrees that the women closest to me be immolated upon the flames of destiny?*

He stepped closer to the dying fire, drawn by an irresistible compulsion to come nearer to Marla's buried ashes, and his gaze fell upon a scorched metal padlock, connected to an unbroken length of chain. The padlock, he noted at once, was still closed, confirming his worst suspicions. A large metal storage locker was sunk into the earth right where the shed's doorway had once stood. If Marla had indeed been within the shed when the fire began, why would the door be locked from the outside, plus blocked by the heavy locker? And why else would Patil have been rendered unconscious first?

Only one answer presented itself, and a fearsome rage stirred inside Khan. Vengeful eyes scanned the faces of the crowd, seeing there apprehension and concern, but no trace of sorrow for the woman whose bones were now baking beneath the ashes. "Who?" he whispered hoarsely, softly first, but then in a booming voice that hushed all others. *"Who is responsible for this?"*

A chorus of denials and protestations of innocence greeted his implied accusation:

"Lightning?"

"A stray spark?"

"An accident!"

Khan did not believe a word of it. He was fully aware of just how unpopular Marla had been among the citizens of New Chandigarh. He knew that many still blamed her for their banishment to this primitive world. He had hoped that, in time, his people would come to value Marla as he did, but clearly he had underestimated the murderous enmity directed against her, and this fatal misjudgment had cost Marla her life.

But if he was too late to save her, he could still avenge her death. *Murder, though it hath no tongue, will speak with most miraculous organ. . . .*

"Hear my words!" he warned his people, speaking

loudly enough to be heard by all. "I will uncover the truth, and those who are responsible for this heinous crime will pay with their unworthy lives. This I swear upon the pyre before us, and—"

A miracle, of sorts, cut short his oath. Gasps arose from the chastened onlookers as, without warning, something stirred beneath the wreckage. Carbonized saplings shifted and crumbled, falling away as though something—or someone—was struggling to rise up through the charred debris.

Khan's heart skipped a beat. He rushed forward and began tossing the smoking timbers aside, heedless of the dwindling flames. "Marla?" he shouted over the crackle of burning wood. "Marla!"

A hoarse cough answered his frantic call. A convulsive motion disturbed the pyre and a blackened, shrouded figure suddenly erupted from the cinders, like an unearthly revenant haunting the site of its own cremation.

But this was no ghost. Marla stood before him, wrapped from head to toe in an apparently flameproof blanket. A translucent mouthpiece, which Khan recognized as part of a Starfleet breathing apparatus, masked the lower portion of her face. Soot and ash obscured what he could glimpse of her face; only her unmistakable chestnut eyes made her identity crystal clear.

Khan recalled that the torched shed had housed much of their limited supply of Starfleet paraphernalia. Clearly, Marla had used the futuristic equipment to protect herself from the enveloping smoke and flames. *Ingenious!* he marveled. Marla had once more proven herself worthy of his love.

"Khan," she whispered through the face mask.

Visibly exhausted by her ordeal, she teetered upon unsteady legs. Khan scooped her up in his arms, blanket and all, and carried her safely clear of the baking ruins. Her weight was a welcome burden, easily borne.

"The doctor," he demanded. "Without delay!"

Gideon Hawkins hurried to Khan's side, clutching a Starfleet medkit. As his medical expertise was now some centuries out-of-date, Marla had wisely taken the time to familiarize the doctor with the contents of the medkit.

Khan reluctantly set Marla down so that Hawkins could examine her. As the soot-covered blanket came away, Khan saw that the breathing mask was connected by a length of tubing to a rectangular silver box belted to Marla's waist. To his relief, he discerned no serious burns on her person, a diagnosis that the doctor soon verified. "She seems all right," Hawkins said. The angular planes of his gaunt face had grown even more pronounced on the colonists' thin rations. He fingered the flame-resistant blanket that had saved Marla's life. "A remarkable material."

He helped Marla remove the mask from her face. She coughed loudly a few times, expelling some leftover smoke from her lungs, but then began to breathe more easily. Khan's worries faded as it became clear that Marla would recover.

Fate has been kind, he realized.

Relief gave way to renewed anger that anyone would dare to endanger Marla's life in the first place. "Who did this?" he interrogated Marla, his eyes blazing in fury. Hawkins began to protest, but Khan silenced him with a curt gesture. His justice would be neither denied nor delayed. "Tell me," he entreated Marla. "Who is to blame?"

Marla shook her head. "I don't know," she croaked hoarsely. Where the breathing mask had covered her face, her flesh was unmarked by soot, giving her partially blackened face the look of a carnival disguise. "I'm not sure."

Her answer did not satisfy his need for vengeance. Scowling, his dark eyes searched the faces of the onlooking crowd, hunting for a likely suspect. His gaze lit on the striking features of Zuleika Walker.

"You!" he accused, pointing at the former assassin. Khan had not forgotten Zuleika's unprovoked attack on Marla on their very first night on the planet. "What have you to do with this?"

The startled woman blanched at Khan's irate tone. "Nothing, Your Excellency!" she protested fearfully. "I swear it!"

Vishwa Patil spoke up. "She may be lying, Your Excellency. I am told that she quarreled with Lieutenant McGivers right before the fire." He glared scornfully at Zuleika and fingered the bump at the back of his skull. "She spit at McGivers and called her names."

"Who says this?" Khan demanded.

Patil pointed at Paul Austin, whom Khan recognized as one of Ericsson's cohorts. "Is this true?" Khan asked.

Austin muttered something under his breath, too low to be heard. He gave Marla a dirty look, as though blaming *her* for this tense encounter.

"Speak up!" Khan insisted. "Did you see Zuleika Walker accost Marla?"

"Maybe," the tattooed man conceded grudgingly.

Zuleika tried to back away into the crowd, but Patil and his fellow security officers blocked her exit. Khan turned his forbidding gaze upon the nervous ex-supermodel. "Do you deny these reports?" he asked her harshly.

"N-no, Your Excellency," Zuleika stammered. "I mean, it's true we had words—but I never tried to kill her!" She gulped out loud. "Not tonight, that is. Not this time!"

Khan had heard enough. "Seize her," he ordered.

"Wait," Marla started to object, but a sudden coughing jag rendered her incapable of speech. Her fragile body was racked by the ragged coughs.

"This is too much for her," Hawkins insisted. "She needs rest."

Khan saw Marla struggle to regain her breath. Perhaps the doctor had a point after all. He turned back to Zuleika, who was now flanked by Patil and a full security team. "Imprison her," he instructed, confident that the assassin was safely in custody. "I will administer my justice in due course."

He watched with satisfaction as Zuleika was dragged away, still frantically proclaiming her innocence. Her failure to take responsibility for her actions further condemned her in his eyes.

She could expect no mercy.

10

"Khan, you can't! It's inhuman!"

Marla had regained her voice, no thanks to Zuleika Walker's perfidious efforts, but Khan was surprised to hear that voice raised against his intention to banish Zuleika from New Chandigarh upon the morrow.

"It is no more than she deserves," he told Marla in the privacy of their hut. Outside, the sun had fallen, bringing an end to a day of both triumph and treachery. Thunder boomed overhead and a sprinkling of rain fell upon the thatched roof, giving them just a taste of the coming monsoon. "Indeed, she should be thankful that I chose banishment rather than a public execution."

The latter had been tempting, but Khan had feared its effect on the camp's morale. Besides, he did not wish to sully the belated cremations of Gorinsky and Blasko by holding them in conjunction with a far less heroic death. Better that Zuleika simply disappear into the wilderness, where her eventual demise would go unwitnessed and unmourned. *Let the beasts of the field devour her ignoble bones,* he thought coldly.

"But it's still a death sentence!" Marla protested. She rose from the humble bed upon which she had been kneeling. A pair of rectangular storage lockers—one from the *Botany Bay*, one from the *Enterprise*—completed the hut's spartan furnishings, aside from a few of Marla's paintings and smaller sculptures, salvaged from her quarters aboard the *Enterprise*. A portrait of Khan, regal in an elegant white turban, occupied a position of honor upon the western wall. A library of data disks rested upon a roughhewn shelf. "She won't stand a chance on her own."

"What of it?" Khan shrugged his shoulders as he removed his shirt, preparing for bed. Fresh bandages covered the claw marks on his back, which had required multiple stitches. "I find it puzzling that this disturbs you so. The woman tried to burn you alive."

"We don't know that for sure," Marla insisted. "There's no proof." She crossed the hut to join Khan by the door. A carpet of woven grass protected her feet from the crude dirt floor. "I told you, I didn't see who locked me in the shed."

Khan tried to remember that Marla came from a rather overcivilized culture, where war and capital punishment had been all but abolished. "I am confident of her guilt," he said firmly. "Do you doubt that this woman means you ill?"

"She's hardly the only one," Marla replied. "In case you haven't noticed, I'm about as popular as Typhoid Mary."

Her sarcasm irked Khan, who was beginning to find this entire discussion tiresome. He had dealt with saber-tooths and a murderous arsonist today; the last thing he needed was an overwrought woman, who lacked the understanding to see what needed to be done.

"I am aware of everything that transpires in this camp," he informed her brusquely. His palms, which had received a few minor burns when he tried to dig Marla free from the smoldering ruins, stung like the devil, while his back felt as though it had been flayed alive. The various pains added to his worsening mood. "You must trust my judgment in this."

Marla refused to let the matter rest. "But she hasn't even had a fair trial! I don't want an innocent woman to die just because you suspect she tried to hurt me."

"Due process is a luxury we cannot afford," Khan said bluntly. He spoke to her as he would to a naive child. "This is not one of your pampered Federation outposts, enjoying the security of Starfleet's protection. We are on our own here, and I cannot risk harboring a viper within our midst."

If Marla caught the warning tone in his voice, she paid it no heed. "But what if the viper is someone else? I told you, I saw Paul Austin not far from the shed, smoking a cigarette no less!" She shook her finger at the air, like a defense attorney playing to the jury. "Maybe he did it. He's one of Ericsson's cronies, and they're always trying to stir up trouble."

Khan's patience was nearing its end. "Do you think that I have not already considered every possibility?" he asked, grabbing on to her wrist ungently. "Ericsson and his followers have no reason to eliminate you; frankly, you are more of a political liability to me alive."

A hurt expression came over Marla's face, and Khan regretted the harshness of his words. "I'm sorry," she said in an acid tone, as he released his grip on her wrist. She tried and failed to keep the tears from streaking down her face. "I didn't realize I was such an impediment to your plans." She retreated to their bed, where she collapsed onto a grass-stuffed mattress. "Maybe Zuleika—if she really did set that fire—was just trying to do you a favor."

Khan briefly considered apologizing. Marla had endured much today, after all. But then she might feel encouraged to reopen the debate regarding Zuleika's fate, and that would not do. *She must learn not to question my authority*, he resolved. The future of New Chandigarh depended on his superior will and judgment, and no one, not even Marla, could be allowed to challenge that.

Doing his best to ignore the muffled sobs coming from the bed, he lay down beside her. Rain dripped from the ceiling, despite the protective tarp underlying the outer thatchwork. Khan made a mental note to have the roof reinforced before the heavy rains arrived. Marla kept her back to him, her face turned to the wall, but he could sense her unhappiness, and he blamed Marla's would-be assassin for causing this rift between them. The sooner he concluded this wretched business, the better. *In time*, he felt certain, *Marla will see the wisdom of my decision.*

Perhaps in the morning.

The prisoner stood before him, bound in the very chains that had trapped Marla within the burning shed. Khan appreciated the poetic irony of the situation.

He gazed down at Zuleika from atop a temporary dais constructed of the camp's last surviving antigrav lift, which had thankfully been employed elsewhere when the shed was torched. Aside from the guards manning the watchtowers, practically the entire colony had gathered to witness Khan pronounce judgment on the accused arsonist. Marla, the intended victim of Zuleika's crime, waited off to one side, her face downcast. Khan suppressed a frown; Marla had clearly not moved beyond last night's quarrel.

No matter, he thought. Zuleika needed to be dealt with, even if Marla lacked the strength to see this. "*One man with courage makes a majority*," *as the American president Andrew Jackson once said, and a true leader, such as myself, must always be prepared to rule on matters of life and death.*

Ominous gray clouds hung over the camp, adding to the somber atmosphere. "Zuleika Walker," he began, "you have endangered the safety of New Chandigarh, and defied my own incontrovertible edict, by attempting to take the life of one of your fellow colonists. For this unforgivable offense, I hereby sentence you to eternal banishment from this settlement and the surrounding lands."

Zuleika's eyes widened in horror. "No, Lord Khan! Not that!" The chains about her wrists rattled as she lifted her arms in a desperate appeal for mercy. "I have always served you well. Remember the Indian cabinet member? The UN ambassador?"

Khan was unmoved by the woman's pleas. True, Zuleika had been a useful assassin back on Earth, but that was before she turned her homicidal talent against one whom he had declared under his protection.

"My decision is final," he stated.

All the strength seemed to evaporate from Zuleika's athletic frame, and she sagged against the stone-faced guards flanking her. Khan carefully scanned the faces of the other colonists, looking to see how Zuleika's well-deserved punishment was playing with the rest of his followers. Did the disgraced assassin retain any sympathy among her fellow castaways? He was not about to change his decree, but it was best to know whether Zuleika's dire fate would provoke division and controversy within the camp.

But the expressions of the onlookers, which ranged from grim to carefully neutral, offered little clue as to what subversive undercurrents might be roiling beneath the surface. *There is no art to find the mind's construction in the face*, Khan reflected, after *Macbeth*. Yet at least no one seemed inclined to voice any objections to his decision.

Until Marla spoke up.

"No, Khan," she said decisively, stepping forward to stand between him and the prisoner. "I can't let you do this. I'm the supposed victim here. I should have some say in the matter."

Khan's jaw dropped, caught off guard by Marla's unexpected rebellion. *She dares to challenge me here, in front of the entire colony?* Dismay warred with anger, with the latter quickly claiming victory. Questioning him in the privacy of their hut was bad enough, but to undermine his authority in public?

No. This cannot be allowed.

"Silence," he rebuked her. "You forget yourself."

Marla refused to back down. "I mean it, Khan." She took a deep breath, as though readying herself for a plunge. "If you banish Zuleika, you banish me as well."

"Huh?" the prisoner reacted in surprise. She stared at Marla in disbelief. "What the hell?"

Under less grave circumstances, Zuleika's nonplussed reaction might have bordered on comical, but Khan saw nothing humorous in the situation, which was rapidly escalating beyond his control. He wished he could erase Marla's rash ultimatum from existence, turn back the clock just a few precious moments, but, no. Her fatal promise hung before them all, demanding a response.

"You are overwrought," he suggested, giving her a chance to take back her words, "no doubt traumatized by your terrible ordeal." He looked down at her with a show of pity and understanding. "Perhaps you should return to your hut."

"I'm not going anywhere," she said decisively, "except maybe into exile." She squeezed between the stupefied guards to stand beside Zuleika. It was impossible to say who looked more dumbfounded, the guards or the prisoner. "You heard what I said. If Zuleika goes, I go."

The stunned crowd held its breath, waiting for Khan's reaction. Joaquin glared murderously at Marla, a look of spiteful vindication upon his face. Out of the corner of his eye, Khan thought he spied Ericsson smirking at his predicament. The sight added to his mounting ire.

Very well, Khan decided, hardening his heart. As much as he cherished her, Marla had given him no choice. *I cannot tolerate such flagrant insubordination, not even from her.*

"So be it," he announced. "You will each be given water and a weapon and escorted from boundaries of the colony. You have until nightfall to leave this territory. If either of you is seen in New Chandigarh again, your lives are forfeit."

He stepped down from the dais, knowing that he had lost Marla for the second time in as many days, this time forever. He took one last look at her lovely face, saddened by the grief and disappointment he saw there. Alas, he also discerned no weakening in her resolve.

"Good-bye, Khan," she said, unable to entirely quell the tremor in her voice. Her large chestnut eyes shimmered wetly.

"Take them away," he commanded.

11

"I don't know what you think you're proving," Zuleika snarled as she hacked her way through the damp grass. Her machete decapitated the tall, yellowish brown blades as though they were prisoners of war enduring a mass execution. "You're just going to end up dead anyway."

Marla hiked behind Zuleika, using a stone-tipped spear as a walking stick. Trying to keep up with the powerful superwoman had her breathing hard, and her legs were aching already from the fast-paced trek through the savanna. Clearly, Zuleika was taking Khan's sunset deadline very seriously.

What am *I trying to prove?* Marla wasn't sure she could explain it to herself, let alone the other woman. *Am I crazy, abandoning Khan and the safety of the camp to brave the wilderness with a woman who probably tried to kill me?* When you put it that way, it sounded positively insane.

But this isn't really about Zuleika, she realized. *It's about what kind of a woman I can live with being.* She loved Khan, but she had to stand up to him, too, for the sake of what was left of her self-respect. She had let her passion for Khan overcome her conscience aboard the *Enterprise*, and, as a result, Captain Kirk had been tortured nearly to death. *Never again,* she vowed. *I have to stand by my principles, even if it costs me my life.*

"I'm doing this because I'm a Starfleet officer," she told Zuleika, not expecting the other woman to understand. "And a civilized human being."

Zuleika snorted in derision. "Not much to brag about, if you ask me." For once, she had clothed herself in one of the *Botany Bay*'s standard-issue red coveralls, practicality apparently winning out over exhibitionism. "Ordinary humanity has been obsolete since the seventies, and I mean the nineteen seventies."

We've done all right over the past few centuries, Marla thought. *Warp travel. World peace. The Federation. And all without starting down the slippery slope of human genetic engineering.*

She didn't have the inclination, or the energy, to debate the matter, however. Besides her spear, she was also carrying a full canteen, a pistol on her hip, and a torch she had snatched from a campfire on her way out of New Chandigarh. She didn't need the latter to see by—twilight was still hours away—but she hoped that the torch would help scare away any lurking predators, and make it easier to light a fire of their own come nightfall.

The grass was still wet from last night's showers, so Marla didn't have to worry about accidentally starting a brushfire. Pendulous gray clouds blotted out the sky, promising more rain to come. Marla prayed that the bleak, overcast day would discourage any remaining sabertooths from venturing out into the veldt.

The women were heading north, toward the equator. If they lived long enough, they might actually reach the vast, uncharted rain forests beyond the savanna, where they figured food and game would be more abundant. For now, however, Marla just aimed to find a convenient stand of trees around sunset, where they could take shelter for the night. Sleeping in the branches, high above the prowling wildlife, sounded marginally safer than camping out on the ground.

Or so she hoped.

Marla fought the temptation to glance behind her. Chances were, she would still be able to see smoke from the colony's many campfires rising up to meet the clouds. Part of her hoped that Khan would come to his senses, look past his immense pride, and start searching for her, but she knew that this was only a foolish dream; for better or for worse, Khan was not the kind of man who changed his course once he made a decision.

I will never see him again.

Her throat ached, not just from thirst, and she took a gulp of purified water from her canteen. "We should stick close to the river," she suggested to Zuleika. They would need to refill their canteens soon enough.

"No kidding," the other woman replied sarcastically. She didn't bother turning her head to look back at Marla. "But not too close. You seen some of the scaly monsters they've got swimming down there?"

"Just a glimpse or two," Marla admitted, but she knew what Zuleika was referring to. Although she had never been invited to help fetch fresh water from the Kaur, she had heard stories from the colonists who had ventured down to the riverbanks, always in the company of an armed security team. Apparently Ceti Alpha V's tendency toward gigantism where its fauna was concerned was not confined to dry land; there had been many sightings—and narrow escapes—regarding crocodiles and turtles of prehistoric proportions. Marla herself had once spied from the watchtower, via Khan's binoculars, the head of an enormous crocodile rising from beneath the flowing surface of the Kaur. Although much of the creature's armored body had remained submerged, the supercroc's jaws alone appeared to be as long as Marla was tall, which would make them nearly two meters in length.

Not unlike Earth's own primitive Sarchosuchas, she reflected, which was believed to have weighed almost eighty kilograms and been about the length of a small shuttlecraft. Marla shuddered at the thought; a monster like that could drag down a bison or sabertooth with just one snap of its jaws. She didn't want to think about what it could do to mere homo sapiens, genetically engineered or otherwise.

"Trust me," Zuleika insisted. "Down by the river is one place you don't want to spend too much time, not unless you're properly armed." She cast an envious glance at the Colt tucked into Marla's belt.

Forget it, Marla thought. *I'm not that idealistic.* For all she knew, the pistol was the only thing keeping Zuleika from killing her once and for all—that and the fact that they were going to need each other to survive on their own. *For the time being, this gun is staying right where it is.*

They came to the brim of a shallow valley, which stretched across their path for what looked like kilometers. A narrow stream, perhaps no more than ankle-deep, trickled down the valley's center, heading for the Kaur farther to the east. A stand of sycamores and papyrus had grown up along the sides of the brook.

Marla peered nervously at the darkening sky, where the clouds were growing heavier and more ominous by the minute. She was uneasy about descending into the gully just as a storm threatened, but there didn't seem to be any alternative; to go around the valley might take hours and there was no guarantee that higher ground could be found. And they *did* need fresh water. . . .

Zuleika didn't hesitate before starting down the slope. Perhaps she was even thirstier than Marla, if such a thing was possible, or maybe she was just determined to put as many kilometers as possible between them and the camp. With a shrug of resignation, Marla followed closely behind her.

The angle of descent was not too steep, and Marla had to admit that the gradual decline came as a relief after long hours of hiking across the grassy plains. Thorny acacia bushes gave way to mingled willows and papyrus reeds. She tried not to think about the uphill climb awaiting them on the other side of the valley.

They had just reached the bottom of the slope when the first heavy raindrops pelted Marla's face. *Uh-oh . . .* but it was already too late. Within seconds, the sky turned black as midnight. A howling wind came whipping up the valley, tossing Marla's hair about wildly. Sheet lightning strobed the darkness. Water fell from the sky like an ion cascade.

After weeks of teasing, the monsoon had finally arrived.

Almost before they realized what was happening, both women were soaked to the skin. Marla's torch was doused instantly, and the ground beneath their feet dissolved into sludge. The tiny stream, which had barely merited the name moments before, quickly swelled into a rushing cataract, topped by frothing white water.

An icy dread gripped Marla's heart.

"We have to get out of here!" she shouted over the rampaging wind and rain. Zuleika nodded in agreement, her worried features devoid of her customary attitude and hauteur. Marla envied the other woman's short, tightly beaded hair; at least she didn't have windblown tresses flying in her face.

Frantically, they tried climbing back the way they had come, but their boots slipped repeatedly upon the muddy incline, trapping them at the bottom. Marla discarded her worthless torch and grabbed on to some reeds, but the stalks came free from the soaked hillside, roots and all, sending her tumbling back toward the overflowing stream. Marla held on tightly to the shaft of her spear, determined not to let go of the weapon. More water gushed over the lip of the valley, pouring down the slope to join the swiftly growing floodwaters.

Marla felt like she was drowning. The water was everywhere . . . in her eyes, in her mouth, beneath her hands and knees. Somewhere nearby, Zuleika let loose with an impressive barrage of late-twentieth-century profanity. From the sound of it, the volatile superwoman was just as overwhelmed by the deluge as Marla was, the sheer power and enormity of the storm rendering the genetic disparity between them insignificant.

Not even Khan could stand against this, Marla guessed. A diabolical irony stabbed at her soul. *I've been waiting so avidly for the monsoon! Now it may be the death of me. . . .*

A tremendous roar, coming from upstream, drowned out Zuleika's volcanic curses. Wiping the rain and hair from her eyes, Marla looked up in time to see a colossal wall of water barreling toward her like a tidal wave. The onrushing torrent stretched from one side of the valley to the other, offering no hope of refuge.

Beam me out of here! she thought fervently, even though she knew that wasn't going to happen. . . .

The flash flood struck with the unbelievable force, snatching up both women and carrying them along in its unstoppable rush toward the River Kaur. Marla held on to her spear with both hands as she was tossed about wildly by the turbulent waters. She tried holding her breath, only to end up gasping for air whenever her face bobbed above the spuming whitecaps. Uprooted bushes and branches smashed against her, the jagged twigs tearing at her flesh. The brutal current spun her about randomly, so that she barely knew which way was up. Once she collided with what felt like another human body, but the flood whisked her away from the other woman before she could even determine if Zuleika was still alive.

Khan! she screamed silently. *Help me—please!*

A wave splashed against her face, invading her mouth and nose. She gasped and sputtered, spitting out a mouthful of muddy water before the flood pulled her under again. . . .

Khan looked on grimly, accompanied by Joaquin and Vishwa Patil, as a team of colonists sifted through the charred remains of the storage shed. Alas, there appeared to be little to salvage; the advanced twenty-third-century equipment had all been destroyed, leaving them only whatever Starfleet equipment remained in the original cargo bays. Of this shed's contents, it seemed only Marla and her protective blankets had survived.

Marla.

A pang pierced his heart. Despite his stony exterior, doubts and second thoughts plagued him. Had he rushed to judgment regarding Zuleika Walker? What if Marla had been right and Zuleika had indeed been innocent? If so, he had condemned both women to certain death on the basis of an overhasty decision. *"Impatience will be your fatal flaw,"* an old acquaintance had once warned him, back during the Eugenics Wars. Could it be that this flaw had cost Marla her life?

His eyes probed the crime scene before him, searching for proof of Zuleika's guilt or innocence. Between the fire, the rain, and the frantic efforts of the firefighters, however, the site was far from pristine. The sodden ground had been trampled over by multiple feet since the initial attack on Vishwa Patil, meaning that any revelatory evidence had been hopelessly lost.

Not that there was likely to have been many clues to begin with; setting a dry wooden shed on fire with a piece of tinder was not exactly a crime that required extensive effort or preparation. As Marla had rightly pointed out, most anyone could have snapped shut the padlock and lighted the blaze, all in a matter of minutes.

He turned toward Patil, who was also contemplating the burnt wreckage. An ugly scab covered the bump at the base of his skull. "You saw or heard nothing?" Khan asked the Indian security officer.

Patil shook his head. His imposing mustache vibrated as he spoke. "Nothing, Your Excellency."

Khan clenched his fists in frustration. There had to be some way to uncover the truth. "You did not smell smoke?"

"The camp always smells of smoke," Patil said with a shrug, "what with the cooking fires, campfires, and such. The Walker woman was boiling a big pot of fresh water maybe twelve meters away." He rubbed the sore spot at the rear of his head. "Raised quite a bump, she did. I suppose I should be thankful that she dragged me away from the shed before putting the torch to it." A mournful sigh escaped his lips. "By the time I came to, only a few moments later, the entire structure was ablaze. I tried to get to the door, to set Lieutenant

McGivers free, but the smoke and flames . . . they were too much for me."

He showed Khan his palms, which were still reddened where the fires had lightly scorched him. They matched the burns on Khan's own hands.

Khan frowned. Now that he heard it again, something about Patil's story did not ring true. Why would Zuleika be so crude as to hit Patil with a rock, especially if her true target was Marla, not Patil? Zuleika was an assassin par excellence; she could swiftly and efficiently render a man unconscious with her bare hands, simply by clamping on to the appropriate pressure point. And why, having spared his life, would she take the chance of him recovering in time to rescue Marla? Again, she had the talent and skill to safely incapacitate him for hours.

Suspicion flared in Khan's mind. "Tell me," he asked sharply, invading the other man's personal space. "How did you know that Zuleika was busy boiling water if you were standing by your post?"

"Um, I'm not sure," Patil answered. He stepped backward, retreating fearfully from Khan's scrutiny. "I must have heard as much from someone else . . . after the fact, that is."

Khan was not convinced. To the contrary, the guard's uncertainty, and sudden nervousness, reinforced Khan's sense that Patil was hiding a particularly heinous secret. He cast a meaningful look at Joaquin, who instantly seized Patil from behind. "Lord Khan!" the guard cried out in alarm. "I don't understand!"

"The truth!" Khan demanded. There was no time for

further games or evasions, not with Marla and Zuleika facing unknown perils at this very moment; for all he knew, both women were already dead.

He took hold of Patil's throat and squeezed.

Patil gasped out loud. "Please, Your Excellency!" he squeaked. His face turned red, then blue. Bulging veins throbbed upon his brow. "I can't breathe!"

Khan squeezed more tightly.

Patil's eyes protruded from their sockets, the bloodshot orbs seeing neither mercy nor hesitation in Khan's own eyes. "Yes! All right!" Patil choked out. "I confess, it was me!"

I knew it, Khan thought. He released his grip enough to let Patil speak more easily.

"Forgive me, Your Excellency!" Patil gasped as he spoke, hungrily sucking air into his lungs. His agonized face pleaded for mercy. "I did it for you, Lord Khan! The Starfleet woman was a wedge between you and your true followers, giving your enemies an issue to use against you." The words came pouring out of him now, in a desperate effort to justify his actions. "You were blind to the threat she posed, and I could not stand by and let you be brought down by a woman again, like on the *Enterprise*, and back on Earth. . . ."

Khan knew to whom the latter remark referred: the Lady Ament, once one of his most trusted advisors during the glory days of his reign on Earth. An exotic beauty of great intelligence and charm, she had ultimately proven to be a double agent employed by his enemies. Along with the meddlesome Gary Seven, she had played a key role in his eventual downfall.

Even after three hundred years, Ament's betrayal still rankled, but Khan had never made the mistake of equating that feline traitoress, long dead by Joaquin's hand, with Marla. They were two very different women. Indeed, they could be truly said to be not even of the same species.

"So, you see, Your Excellency," Patil insisted, "I sought only to rid you of an inferior specimen who stood between you and your greatness." Only Joaquin's unbreakable grip kept the confessed arsonist from dropping onto his knees to beg for his life. "Perhaps I erred, but, I beg of you, do not condemn me for an excess of loyalty to your cause!"

But Khan had already stopped listening to the security officer's excuses. Marla, and the possibility that she might still be alive, was all that concerned him now. Intent on finding her, he casually withdrew the silver dagger from his belt and thrust it directly into Patil's heart.

The man convulsed once, then expelled his last breath. Joaquin checked the pulse at Patil's throat, confirming that he was dead, then dropped the corpse onto the muddy ground beside the blackened ruins of the shed. The rest of the salvage team watched the execution in stunned silence.

Khan did not bother to address the crowd. His mind was kilometers away, where Marla and Zuleika faced every manner of peril Ceti Alpha V had to offer. "Hurry!" he called out to Joaquin. "Gather a search party. Get every man or woman the camp can spare. We must set out at once."

"But, Your Excellency!" Joaquin protested. "The Starfleet woman defied your will!"

"With good reason, it appears," Khan stated. "I am not so proud that I do not know when I have made a mistake. Do as I instruct."

The bodyguard appeared less than enthusiastic at the prospect of Marla's return, but not enough to defy a direct order from his master. "As you command," he assented, and hurried to round up the search party.

Thunder rumbled overhead. The sky darkened dramatically, and a heavy rain began to fall. A hot, humid wind blew against his face, and Khan recognized the long-awaited onset of the monsoon.

No matter, he resolved, even though the sudden downpour left his dark hair plastered to his skull. The camp was well prepared for the rain, being safely distant from the riverbank, but he knew the surrounding countryside was awash with dry riverbeds that would rapidly fill with water. Storm or no storm, he would not rest until he found Marla again.

Perhaps it was not too late to save her.

Swept along by the flood, Marla fought to gain some control over her watery tumbling even as the surging torrent punched its way through the grass and scrub, rushing downhill toward the River Kaur. Eventually, after what felt like an eternity being tossed about like flotsam, she sensed the current begin to slacken as the natural gully widened and leveled off, causing the cataract to spread itself thinner. A stand of palms swayed before the force of the flood, and Marla managed to halt her progress by wedging the shaft of her spear between two unyielding saplings.

The besieged trees bent but did not break. Marla gripped the horizontal spear with white knuckles, letting the worst of the torrent pass over her until at last the fleeting water left her behind, lying facefirst upon the muddy underbrush, gasping for breath. *I did it!* she thought, amazed at her own survival. *I'm still here.*

But what about Zuleika?

The sudden cloudburst had faded to a drizzle, giving Marla a chance to catch her breath. Drenched and exhausted, she climbed slowly onto her knees, then leaned on her spear as she dragged herself up to a standing position. Gallons of water seemed to stream from her soaked hair and shredded uniform, joining the muck beneath her feet. The faded red fabric of her Starfleet uniform hung in tatters upon her shaking frame. Amazingly, her pistol was still secured to her belt, which struck her as nothing short of miraculous.

She turned toward the Kaur, looking for Zuleika. At first all she saw was uprooted bushes and branches, but then she spotted a sludge-covered figure at the very edge of the Kaur, which seemed to have swollen beyond its usual boundaries, flooding the surrounding banks. *Great for agriculture,* Marla noted, *but maybe not all that safe for the two of us.*

Never mind keeping a safe distance from the river. The Kaur had come to them.

"Zuleika!" Marla called to the prone figure. *You can't be dead,* she thought anxiously. *You're a superwoman, remember?* Marla couldn't believe that she was running to the rescue of her worst enemy. She doubted Khan would approve. "Can you hear me?"

The downed Amazon lifted her head in response to Marla's cry. She started to lift herself from the mire, then collapsed, wincing in pain. "I think I broke a rib," she gasped. Her spear lay by her side, proof that Zuleika had also managed to hang on to a weapon during their tumultuous ride down the flooded valley. Her machete, on the other hand, was nowhere to be seen.

Marla tried to imagine what kind of impact could have fractured one of Zuleika's superdense bones. *Must have been hit dead-on by a floating tree trunk,* she guessed, *or maybe she bounced off a boulder on her way down. Probably would have killed me. . . .*

"Hold on!" she called to the other woman. Using her spear as a cane, she descended toward the river, trying hard not to lose her balance upon the muddy ground, which oozed disconcertingly beneath her boots. "I'll be right there!"

She hoped Zuleika wasn't too badly injured. The odds against their continued survival were bad enough already. She could only pray that the superwoman's recuperative abilities were as enhanced as the rest of her.

But as she hurried to reach Zuleika, something else got there first.

Marla's eyes widened in alarm as a huge, muck-encrusted mass rose out of the turbid water at Zuleika's feet: a monstrous river turtle the size and shape of an inverted bathtub. A curved beak gaped open, revealing rows of pointed yellow teeth. The prehistoric chelonian was quite obviously a carnivore—and very hungry.

"Behind you!" Marla shrieked, alerting Zuleika barely in time.

Snatching up her spear, Zuleika rolled onto her back and thrust the point of the lance into the monster's beak. The turtle hissed angrily, and a musky odor filled the air. The beak snapped shut, breaking the spear in two. The creature shook its head wildly, trying to dislodge the business end of the spear from its gullet. Zuleika dragged herself backward through the mud, desperate to distance herself from the mammoth alien.

Marla took advantage of the animal's distraction to draw her gun. Was the antique firearm powerful enough to penetrate the turtle's bony shell? Marla wasn't sure, so she aimed for the turtle's exposed head.

She pulled the trigger—and nothing happened.

What? Her heart plummeted as she realized that the flood had somehow rendered the ancient pistol inoperative, and at the worst possible moment.

By now, the monster turtle had disgorged the offending speartip, and was once more advancing on Zuleika. Four massive claws propelled it through the mud and its head extended out from its shell, like a cobra striking out from beneath a concealing boulder. Zuleika screamed and jabbed at the head with the bottom of her broken wooden shaft, as the fanged beak snapped viciously at the air.

Marla ran toward the unequal battle, splashing through the mud. She lunged between the giant turtle and Zuleika, and began thrusting her own spear at the fleshy opening beneath the monster's carapace. The turtle's head whipped around savagely at the end of its snakelike neck, attempting to take a bite out of its new attacker. Cold reptilian blood spilled onto the mucky ground, adding a bright crimson tint to the reddish brown quagmire. Marla felt like a cavewoman locked in some primeval struggle for survival.

She jabbed her spear at the turtle again, but her thrust missed its target, sliding off the mud-slick dorsal plates instead. Momentum almost carried her forward onto her face, but she threw herself backward at the last minute, only to land on her back less than a meter away from Zuleika. Like the other woman, she hastily positioned her spear between herself and the hissing turtle. Gasping fearfully, Marla had no reason to expect that her weapon would fare any better against the enraged reptile.

The turtle hesitated, uncertain which tasty morsel to go for first. Its head swung back and forth between Marla and Zuleika, who each expected to be devoured at any moment. Despite the blood leaking from the monster's throat, Marla knew their time was running out. *This is it*, she thought. *We're history.*

Abruptly, something else surfaced from the flooded riverbank. A gigantic upper jaw lined with knife-sized fangs opened up behind the monster turtle, then came crashing down on the unsuspecting chelonian, chopping it in two. A huge scaly snout tossed the bisected turtle into the air, swallowing first one half, then the other. Slitted yellow eyes, with vertical pupils, gleamed with cold-blooded satisfaction, then turned their implacable gaze on the two vulnerable women.

Marla instantly recognized the head and forequarters

of a full-grown supercrocodile. Its cruel saurian features resembled a Gorn's, only six or seven times larger. Despite the croc's timely intervention, Marla knew that they had merely exchanged one predator for another even deadlier. Her paltry spear was nothing but a toothpick compared with the sheer immensity of the tremendous reptile.

The crocodile finished off the last of the turtle, then slid toward Marla. Silty water streamed from the dorsal crests running along its back. Marla took aim at the creature's right eye, determined not to surrender her life without a fight. She drew back the spear for one last desperate thrust.

Then, without warning, a coruscating beam of scarlet energy lit up the murky scene. The beam struck the crocodile squarely in the side, incinerating it instantly.

Marla looked to see Khan standing on a grassy rise overlooking the river. His raised phaser was still aimed at the now-empty place the supercroc had occupied only a heartbeat ago. There were other colonists accompanying him, but Marla only had eyes for Khan, who looked even more magnificent than she remembered, like Perseus rescuing Andromeda from the sea monster.

I don't believe it, she thought, tears of joy streaming down her face. *He didn't abandon me after all.*

Moments later, she felt his strong hands lifting her from the muck. She gratefully relinquished her spear to Parvati Rao, as Khan helped her back up the hill. Not far away, Dr. Hawkins and the Katzel twins tended to the injured Zuleika.

"Forgive me," Khan entreated her. A blanket was thrown over her tattered uniform. "I should have listened to you more attentively, and heeded your counsel." She heard regret in his voice. "I should have never forced you to take such risks."

It was worth it, Marla thought. She had proven something to Khan—and to herself. She could stand up to Khan without necessarily losing him. They could clash and still come back together again. Now, at long last, she knew for certain that their love was strong enough to overcome the vast differences in their histories and temperaments. *I can be his conscience*, she resolved, *and he can be my strength.*

Together, there's nothing we can't endure.

12

SIX MONTHS AFTER DAY ONE

"I now pronounce you partners for life."

Nearly the entire colony had gathered outside the camp for a mass wedding presided over by Khan himself, who stood beside Marla atop a sturdy wooden dais erected for the occasion. Garlands of brightly colored flowers festooned the platform, adding a suitably festive touch, while a trio of musicians played a lively raga on handcrafted wooden instruments.

Khan smiled, looking out over rows and rows of paired colonists. Two by two, they stood in a cleared field awaiting his blessing. It was a cool, clear day in New Chandigarh, typical of the mild weather that had graced the colony since the end of the rainy season. Sunlight radiated through a majestic blue sky, and a gentle breeze rustled through the veils and flowers adorning the various brides.

All is well, he thought. "Be fruitful and multiply," he exhorted his people.

His injunction was hardly necessary; many of the women assembled before him were already pregnant, the couples having paired off quickly over the last six months. New Chandigarh's population now consisted of thirty-nine men and thirty women, resulting in a total of thirty-two couples, counting two male-male pairings. That left five men still unattached, Khan noted; a potential source of tension, unless a few of the women ended up widowed—which, given the hazards of life on Ceti Alpha V, was a very real possibility.

For the moment, however, he preferred to focus on the celebration at hand. Among the newly wedded couples, he glimpsed the ever-faithful Joaquin, now united with none other than Suzette Ling, whom Khan believed to be already with child. *Excellent*, Khan thought, looking forward to the birth of a brand new generation of superhuman beings, the first to be conceived on Ceti Alpha V.

Harulf Ericsson had found a bride as well—Karyn Bradley, whom he had bonded with over the course of various hunting expeditions. Khan judged this a good thing; perhaps domestic bliss would curb the Norseman's dissident tendencies. Certainly, Khan had not wanted Ericsson fomenting rebellion among the remaining single males, whom were likely to be discontented enough as was. *I must take pains to reward those men with other privileges*, he thought. *Perhaps extra rations or opportunities for advancement?*

Sitar and shenai music played in the background as Khan basked in the jubilation of his people. He had donned his finest attire for the occasion, a golden Nehru jacket sporting an embroidered honeycomb pattern; it was, he recalled, the same outfit he had worn to his state dinner aboard the *Enterprise.* Now, as then, his hair was tied neatly in the back, exposing his regal brow.

From his elevated vantage point, he could view acres of crops rustling in the fields outside the walled encampment. Wheat, oats, barley, corn, and rice, all growing from Earthborn seeds stored aboard the *Botany Bay.* Later, perhaps, there would be time to experiment with the native flora, in search of viable foodstuffs, but for now he chose to rely on proven staples from Earth. *We must plant soybeans next,* he reminded himself, *to replenish the soil.*

Planted in the immediate wake of the monsoon, the terrestrial crops appeared to be growing successfully, despite a never-ending battle against indigenous pests and weeds. Thornbush fences served to protect the fields from the larger herbivores, even if it was still not safe to dwell outside the camp after dark. Thankfully, the sabertooths had little interest in corn or rice.

Khan estimated a good harvest in another three months or so. Perhaps then, he reflected, he would be able to increase his people's daily rations, which still remained barely above subsistence levels. *A hard life, but a good one,* he mused, pleased with the colony's progress. For where he stood, New Chandigarh looked to be, if not yet thriving, then on the verge of doing so. *We are carving out an empire here, precisely as I envisioned.*

A gentle hand reached over and squeezed his own. "Forgetting something?" Marla teased.

"Never," he assured her, turning his gaze from the ripening fields to his own beauteous bride. As was only fitting, Khan intended his own nuptials to serve as the grand finale of the day's festivities.

Marla looked suitably ravishing in a metallic-silver sari stitched together from the fire blanket that had saved her life. A touch of gold piping around the hem was all that remained of her storm-ravaged Starfleet uniform. Borrowed golden mesh, salvaged from the *Botany Bay*'s hibernation suits, served as a veil. Fresh-cut flowers were braided into her auburn hair, no doubt with the expert assistance of her two eager bridesmaids, Parvati Rao and Zuleika Walker. The latter, ironically enough, was now one of Marla's closest friends, despite having tried to kill her many months before. Their joint banishment, as unjust as it had proven to be, had yielded that benefit at least.

Neither woman occupied the dais, as both were currently accompanying their own grooms in the field below, but Khan spotted them beaming encouragement to Marla from the first row of married couples. Their respective spouses, Rodriguez and Talbot, looked more than pleased with their catches.

As well they should be, Khan thought.

Still, as lovely as the two grinning superwomen were, in their own individual fashions, Khan knew that Marla easily surpassed them both. *A superior woman,* he judged once more, despite her humble genetic origins. *Sometimes, it seems, the random shuffling of ordinary chromo-*

somes can produce a masterpiece. His own mother, after all, had been conceived in the traditional manner, but her formidable intellect and vision had given birth to the Chrysalis Project.

Marla herself was not yet with child, but Khan was in no hurry. In truth, he hoped to see the first few harvests brought safely to fruition before exposing an heir to the uncertain fortunes of this alien world. Better to tame the vast wilderness before siring a dynasty. . . .

"Friends, comrades!" he addressed the crowd, without letting go of Marla's hand. "My heart shares your joy on this happiest of days. Now bear witness as I gladly join my destiny to the woman standing beside me."

The jubilant cheers that greeted his declaration had the ring of sincerity; Marla's standing in New Chandi-garh had risen significantly since she'd made her heroic stand in defense of Zuleika. Even Joaquin seemed some-what less suspicious of Marla, although Khan had largely given up hope of Joaquin and Marla ever becom-ing friends.

In addition, her historical knowledge of frontier colonies, both on Earth and beyond, had proven invalu-able to the struggling colony. It was Marla, for example, who had first suggested that the fledgling farmers fertil-ize their fields with potash, derived from the ashes of burnt timber. She had also recommended that they turn over the sod, just as the original Botany Bay colonists had, so that the wild grass and weeds could compost into the soil before the sowing of the precious Terran seeds.

The truth of the matter was that, despite their enhanced

intelligence and educations, very few of Khan's people had much hands-on experience with primitive agriculture; they were all warriors and scientists and technocrats. *We have been fortunate to have Marla among us*, Khan acknowledged.

He turned toward his bride, who clutched a bouquet of alien blossoms to her chest. Her radiant face, bronzed by months of arduous labor beneath the sun, managed to blush endearingly. She smiled back at him.

"Marla Madlyn McGivers," he began. Although raised as a Sikh, albeit a fairly secular one, Khan was inclined to create his own traditions, and, as there was no one on Ceti Alpha V whose authority exceeded his own, he found it altogether proper that he officiate over his own wedding. "Do you take I, Khan Noonien Singh, as your lawfully wedded husband, to share the bounty and adversities of this brave new world as my one and only queen?"

Marla's brown eyes glistened wetly. Her hand trembled in his. "I do," she answered without hesitation.

"I accept your pledge," he said solemnly, "and make one of my own, that I will honor, cherish, and protect you all the days of my life." He reached into his pocket and retrieved an ivory ring, painstakingly carved from the tusk of a sabertooth. Their intertwined names were engraved on the ring's polished interior. "I give you this ring as a pledge of my eternal love."

A pang of regret stung him. Back on Earth, he could have lavished precious jewels and fine silks upon Marla; here on Ceti Alpha V, he had to make do with far cruder materials.

Not that Marla seemed to care. She choked back an ecstatic sob as he deftly slipped the handmade ring onto her finger. It fit perfectly, just as Khan knew it would.

Hands linked, they turned to face the assembly. "Brothers, sisters," Khan proclaimed proudly, "I present you with Marla McGivers Singh!"

Applause and celebratory shouts rang out across the field, even as Khan lifted Marla's golden veil and bent to impart a loving kiss.

Before their lips could touch, however, a frantic cry of alarm cut through the cheers and clapping. Khan looked up in anger. *Who dares disrupt this sacred moment?*

His searching eyes quickly located the source of the disturbance. A gigantic bison had invaded the ceremony, sending the rows of couples running madly for safety. An adult bull, whose curved horns looked to be a full three meters long from tip to tip, stampeded wildly into the empty field. Its shaggy head and humped shoulders bore a carpet of matted black fur. Bloodshot eyes blazed with bestial fury. Foam dripped from its frothing snout.

"What in the world?" Marla whispered.

Khan stepped protectively in front of her. "Stay back," he warned, raising his phaser, which never left his person, not even on the day of his wedding. He tried to take aim at the charging bison, which was zigzagging erratically across the field, making it difficult to target. *Wretched animal!* he thought, furious at the beast for spoiling the moment. *I'll blast you out of existence!*

Marla laid a restraining hand upon his arm. "Khan, wait. There's something wrong with it."

Khan hesitated. There was something to what Marla

was saying. The bison behaved as though it were deranged, chasing frenziedly after seemingly invisible tormentors. It tossed its titanic skull from side to side, impaling the empty air upon its horns, and clawed at the ground with its hooves. Clearly, something had driven it completely insane.

"Yes," he agreed, nodding at Marla. If the beast was infected with some unknown pathogen, he wanted a specimen left for analysis. He ratcheted down the phaser's setting, so as to kill but not disintegrate.

It came charging directly at the dais, giving Khan the perfect opportunity. He calmly pulled the trigger and watched as the crimson beam struck the bull directly between its rolling, red eyes. The creature fell heavily onto the soil, joining the trampled bouquets and veils littering the field. Scattered colonists, seeing the bison fall, halted their headlong flight, and began inching back toward the wedding grounds.

Khan moved faster than any of them. Leaping from his platform, he rushed to the carcass. He kept his phaser ready, just in case the beast was playing possum, but, on closer inspection, the bison appeared to be well and truly dead. He knelt by the animal's head, then jumped backward in surprise.

Something gray and slimy was emerging from one of the dead bull's tufted ears.

"What?" he exclaimed.

The escaping parasite was only a few centimeters long and coated with blood and mucus. Chitinous gray scales covered its body and a tiny red tongue flicked out from between a pair of evil-looking pincers. Segmented legs propelled the tiny creature onto the dirt at Khan's feet.

He instantly recognized the revolting parasite for what it was: a miniature version of the so-called Ceti "eel." In fact, the dangerous life-form was closer to a mollusk, but someone early on had described one of the creature's larvae as an eel and the name had stuck. By any name, the colonists had quickly learned to watch out for the "eels" and their vicious pincers.

But what was this immature mollusk doing inside the dead bull's skull? Could it be the reason for the bison's apparent madness?

The slimy creature wriggled toward Khan. He was tempted to crush it beneath his heel, but he drew his dagger and speared it on the knife's point instead. The twitching eel was pinned to the ground like a captured butterfly.

A crowd of onlookers had gathered to witness Khan's inspection of the dead bull. "A container!" he demanded, and Keith Talbot, Zuleika's groom, came forward with a carved wooden goblet, no doubt intended for the postwedding refreshments. The athletic, dark-skinned Canadian had once analyzed spy photos as part of Khan's intelligence force. Khan accepted the cup gratefully and transferred the trapped eel to the container, being careful to keep the parasite safely stuck upon his blade.

"Should I get my tricorder?" Marla asked, appearing at his side. Unlike Khan and his weapons, she had not thought to bring scientific equipment to her wedding.

Khan shook his head. "Perhaps later."

Raising his gaze from the wooden goblet, he swiftly located Dr. Gideon Hawkins among the spectators. "I want you to perform an immediate autopsy on this bull," he told the doctor, gesturing toward the immense carcass. "And take a look at this eel as well."

Marla had once told Khan of the various bovine and other animal-based diseases that had contaminated Earth's food chain not long after the Eugenics Wars. He had no intention of letting a similar epidemic endanger the colony's food supply, especially since he had long-range plans to domesticate the native megabison. "I want to know what was wrong with this animal—and as soon as possible."

Hawkins sighed, no doubt seeing his wedding night plans evaporating before his eyes. The doctor's new partner was a onetime professional cricket player named Panjabi. "Yes, Your Excellency," he acceded without argument. "I'll get right on it, although I admit veterinary medicine is a bit out of my field."

Khan had no doubt the expert surgeon would do his best. "Thank you, Doctor," he said graciously. "My apologies for calling you away from your worthy spouse."

Rising from his kneeling position, he turned toward Marla. "My apologies to you as well. This cannot be the wedding day you envisioned."

Marla shrugged and smiled ruefully. "That's Ceti Alpha V for you. Always full of surprises." Her gaze fell upon the cup in Khan's hand—and the bloody eel trapped therein. Her smile faded and she shuddered involuntarily.

"Damn, I don't like those things," she admitted.

Khan could hardly blame her.

". . . despite the disruption caused by the insane bison, today's weddings marked a historic turning point in the development of New Chandigarh, symbolizing the entire colony's mutual commitment to building a new future on Ceti Alpha V. A more superstitious perspective might see the bull's intrusion as a bad omen, but I prefer to take a more positive outlook. The joint ceremony bonded us as a community, just as Khan intended."

Khan.

Marla clicked off her tricorder. She cast a yearning look at the door of the hut, but Khan was nowhere to be seen. The sun had fallen outside, leaving Marla to dictate her notes by the light of a single tallow candle. She sat alone on the modest bed she shared with Khan, waiting for her brand-new husband to return from his conference with Dr. Hawkins.

Not exactly the wedding night I envisioned, Marla thought, sighing. She wasn't bitter or resentful, though; she knew that Khan was only seeing to his responsibilities as leader. *It would be the same if I were married to a Starfleet admiral.*

None of which made her feel any less lonely—and impatient for Khan's return.

A cool breeze rustled the curtains over the door and Marla shivered upon the bed. Her wedding dress had been neatly folded and tucked away at the bottom of a storage locker, so she waited for Khan wearing only her veil and a clingy negligee made of the same shimmering golden mesh. A floral perfume, extracted with effort from the native blooms, scented her skin, which she had scrubbed clean with a sponge and a bowl of hot water. Her ivory ring gleamed in the candlelight, and Marla took a moment to admire the elegant wedding band. That Khan had crafted the ring himself only made her cherish it more.

All over the camp, she knew, happy couples were busy celebrating their nuptials in the privacy of their own huts. *And here I am, all dressed up and nowhere to go.*

She heard a familiar tread outside. Her heart pounded in excitement as a gloved hand reached into the hut and drew back the curtain. Khan stepped inside, still wearing the golden honeycombed outfit he had donned for their wedding. He appeared lost in thought, a concerned expression upon his face. Specks of dried blood dotted his jacket. *From the bull's autopsy,* Marla guessed; no doubt Khan had assisted Hawkins with the procedure.

Her heart went out to him. She couldn't imagine a worse way to celebrate one's wedding. Dictating log entries by candlelight sounded positively romantic in comparison.

"Khan?" she asked him gently. "Is everything all right?"

His expression lifted somewhat as he laid eyes on Marla and the slender golden filaments draped over her body. "Ah, my beauteous bride!" he exclaimed, beaming proudly at his wife. "Forgive me for leaving you alone on our wedding night."

"That's all right," she assured him. Rising from the

bed, she laid her tricorder on top of her locker before joining Khan by the door. "I understand. I have to share you with your people."

Khan drew the curtains shut behind them, cutting them off from the world outside. "My attention, perhaps," he admitted, "but never my heart." He wrapped his strong arms around her. "That belongs to you alone."

His words thrilled Marla beyond all measure. *It was worth waiting all these hours just to hear him say that,* she thought happily. His body still felt tense, however, and she sensed that he had not yet shed the cares of the day. "Was it bad?" she asked him. "The autopsy."

He shrugged. "Disturbing," he conceded. "Dr. Hawkins dissected the beast's brain and found severe damage to the cerebral cortex. He theorizes that larval versions of the eel nest within the brains of the bison, emerging only when they are fully developed or when their hosts expire. An insidious arrangement that results in brain damage to the hosts, causing the sort of erratic behavior we observed today." His hand dropped instinctively to the phaser on his hip. "Hawkins suspects that the bull would have died eventually even if I hadn't killed it."

Marla shuddered in his grasp. "How horrible!"

"Perhaps," Khan said, "but nature is often cruel and savage. In any event, there is no indication that this parasitic relationship poses any threat to the colony, provided we take care not to consume the brains of any infected beasts."

He shook his head. "But this is not a fit topic for so auspicious an evening." He gazed down at Marla with loving eyes and stroked her hair possessively. "We will speak no more of this tonight."

Marla was just as eager to change the subject. Wordlessly, she helped Khan undress, feasting her eyes on his superhuman physique. But as her fingers traced the claw marks upon his back, Khan scowled and pulled away; to his mind, Marla knew, the scars were a gross betrayal of the physical and mental perfection upon which he prided himself.

She saw it differently. "In the past," she whispered, gazing on the wounds without revulsion, "Earth's greatest carpetmakers would take care to include a deliberate imperfection in even their most exquisite designs, which only made their rugs all the more authentic and valuable." She circled around him and softly kissed the claw marks, one by one. To her, the marks proved that he was flesh and blood, just like her. They reminded her of their common mortality, not to mention of the sacrifices he had made for them all. "These scars only make me love you more."

Khan permitted the kisses, then turned to face her. His scowl dissolved into a look of pride. "You are as wise as you are lovely," he declared, lifting her veil in order to gaze into her adoring eyes. "Truly, a woman worth traveling across the galaxy to find."

He scooped her up into his arms and carried her to the bed, where his hungry fingers peeled away the golden negligee, which suddenly felt constricting and cumbersome. "In naked beauty more adorned, more lovely than Pandora," he recited above her.

As she gasped out loud, unconcerned whether the

entire camp heard her, she couldn't help remembering the first time she and Khan had made love, back in her cluttered quarters aboard the *Enterprise*. That had been a rough, almost violent encounter in which Khan had driven her to ecstasy in order to secure her allegience. Tonight, by contrast, she truly felt that Khan cared about her just as much as she worshipped him.

"You have no regrets?" he asked as they came together in the candlelight. The rich orange glow of Ceti Alpha VI filtered through the curtains over the door, throwing an almost supernatural radiance over their passion.

"I wouldn't change a thing," Marla answered.

13

A FEW NIGHTS LATER

"Tell me more of these Klingons," Khan said.

He and Marla rested side by side upon the pitched roof of their hut, enjoying the starry night sky. Above them, Ceti Alpha VI glowed brightly in the glittering firmament, outshining its celestial neighbors with its constant orange brilliance.

"As you wish," his wife agreed readily. Khan knew she enjoyed entertaining him with tales of mankind's exploration of space—an entire era of human achievement that he had quite literally slept through. "To be honest, I've always been secretly fascinated by the Klingons, even though that wasn't something I ever wanted to admit, given the current political situation." Her brown eyes gleamed with enthusiasm as she warmed to her subject. "They're magnificent warriors, with a rich and glorious culture. Ruthless, yes, but with their own distinctive code of honor." She smiled warmly at Khan. "Not unlike a certain Sikh I know."

Khan placed his arm around her shoulders, savoring a rare peaceful moment. *I would have liked to have met a Klingon,* he mused. He could not help wondering what might have happened had a Klingon vessel discovered the *Botany Bay* instead of Kirk's ship. *I suspect I would have fared well among such a people....*

His eyes searched the heavens, where, according to Marla, a vast assortment of alien species and civilizations populated the quadrant: Vulcans, Romulans, Andorians, Gorns, Thasians, and many others. He contemplated the myriad stars overhead. Who knew what exotic worlds orbited those distant suns?

An unexpected flicker caught his eye, and he stared in amazement as Ceti Alpha VI exploded in the night sky.

The familiar orange orb flared more brilliantly than ever before, so that, for a moment, the night seemed transformed into day. Before Khan's startled eyes, the planet's crust came apart, exposing its volcanic mantle and white-hot core. Seconds later, the core itself ignited into a starburst of glowing fragments spreading outward in all directions.

Khan's heart stood still. He heard Marla gasp beside him and knew that she had also witnessed the shocking spectacle. She grabbed for her tricorder, rushing to record the event for posterity. His mind raced frantically, searching for an explanation, even as he struggled to grasp the possible consequences. *This bodes ill*, he realized at once. *But to what degree? And how soon?*

"Khan," Marla whispered anxiously. "What does this mean?"

Ceti Alpha VI, he recalled, was only twenty-one million kilometers away. Was it even possible that Ceti Alpha V might remain untouched by its neighbor's destruction?

The planet's wildlife gave him his first answer.

From the grasslands beyond the camp's gates, a cacophony of howls and roars and squeals disturbed the night, as though every living thing within earshot was crying out in alarm. The clamor awoke the entire colony, causing startled men and women to come pouring out of their huts. Khan spotted Parvati Rao and her husband, Armando Rodriguez, among others.

The earthquake struck next. A thunderous rumbling, like the churning of mighty turbines, drowned out the squawks of the agitated animals, and the building beneath Khan and Marla began to shake violently. Khan's memory instantly flashed back to the great quake that had struck central India in 1993; he and Joaquin had been literally buried alive during that disaster, and thousands of their fellow countrymen had perished. An agonizing sense of déjà vu filled his heart with dread.

No, he thought. *Not again. Not here.*

He and Marla were in a precarious situation, he realized, as the thatched roof trembled beneath their feet. Reacting swiftly, he sprang to the ground, landing unevenly upon the quivering soil. "Jump!" he called out to Marla, holding out his arms to catch her. "Hurry!"

She obeyed without hesitation. Khan breathed a sigh of relief as she landed safely within his grasp. He supported her weight easily, thanks to his incomparable strength. Hesitant to place her down upon the unstable ground, he cradled her against his muscular chest as he looked about in dismay.

Pandemonium engulfed the camp. Men and women stumbled about randomly, shouting in confusion. Unable to maintain their balance, many colonists fell to the ground, where they tried without success to climb back onto their feet. Distraught husbands held on tightly to their pregnant mates, desperate to protect their nascent families. Khan saw Harulf Ericsson grab on to his wife, Karyn, only seconds before she tumbled backward into a blazing campfire.

The tremors kept on coming, increasing in intensity, and New Chandigarh started to come apart. Watchtowers swayed like reeds in the wind, and the tall wire fence came crashing to the ground, trapping unlucky colonists beneath the metal mesh and cruel barbed wire. "Over there!" Khan shouted to the nearest people still standing. Reluctantly putting Marla down, he pointed urgently at the pinned victims. "Help them!"

Even the thermoconcrete plaster supporting the wooden huts proved unable to withstand the colossal jolts. Cracks spread like forked lightning through the rough, gray walls. Thatched roofs tumbled inward, only moments before the huts themselves collapsed into rubble. Khan prayed that all his people had fled the huts before they caved in, but feared that some poor souls were now buried beneath the heavy debris.

"Oh my God!" Marla gasped, clinging to Khan for support. Her tricorder was strapped to her shoulder.

"Your Excellency!" Joaquin appeared at his side, Suzette Ling following closely behind him. The Israeli bodyguard was shirtless and barefoot, while his brand-new wife wore only a fraying cotton nightshirt. Khan was impressed to see that, despite the uproar, Ling had retained the presence of mind to grab a flashlight, while Joaquin himself clutched an M-16 rifle. "What are your commands?" he asked.

Khan scanned the scene, even as the relentless tremors threatened to topple him. If only the shaking would stop long enough for him to get his bearings! His eyes searched for sanctuary and quickly zeroed in on the solid-steel cargo carriers, which appeared to be enduring the quake better than the flimsy huts.

"The watchtowers!" he ordered. "Start herding the people into the towers." It would be a tight squeeze, but they might all fit, provided all the stores inside the converted carriers were tossed out. "Follow me!" he shouted to the nearest colonists, and began leading them toward the northwest tower. "Into the cargo bays!"

He had only taken a few steps, however, when the ground split apart before his eyes. An enormous fissure opened in the earth, cutting them off from the relative safety of the tower. Campfires and debris tumbled into the yawning chasm, which was rapidly joined by yet more gaps in the earth. Bottomless cracks snaked across the well-trod floor of the camp. Khan watched helplessly as Ali Rahman, a former member of his secret police, disappeared into a newborn cleft, his horrified screams swallowed along with his life.

Khan froze, staggered by the extent of the unfolding catastrophe. He kept waiting for the tremors to subside, but the situation seemed to be getting worse by the second, as though he had somehow invited the wrath of a vengeful god.

Then the volcanoes erupted.

A tremendous noise, like a thousand cannons going off at once, struck like a tidal wave, all but deafening Khan and the others. Aghast, he spun around to face the north, where the distant mountain range loomed above the horizon. His eyes widened in horror, and his jaw dropped open, as he saw great plumes of ash and lava spewing from the shattered caps of the formerly snow-capped peaks. Streaks of purple lightning added to the satanic glow of the pyroclastic clouds. From where Khan stood, his arms wrapped protectively around Marla, the entire range appeared to be erupting. Ash blackened the sky, blotting out the stars.

Seconds later, the first lava bomb hit the camp. "Watch out!" Parvati Rao shouted out, a heartbeat before a blob of semimolten rock came plunging out of the sky. The bomb smashed into both Parvati and Rodriguez, killing them instantly.

"No!" Marla shrieked, as her closest friend was obliterated right before her eyes. "This can't be happening!"

But it is, Khan thought. *Whatever destroyed Ceti Alpha VI is lashing out at us as well.* For all he knew, the planet's very orbit was shifting. . . .

More bombs rained down on the camp, like the

American missiles that had destroyed his fortress in Chandigarh three hundred years ago. Blocks of ruptured granite, some as large as cornerstones, slammed into the ground all around Khan, forming craters in the trembling soil. Red-hot globules set fallen thatchwork and timbers aflame. Thick black smoke added to the chaos, making it difficult to see or even to breathe.

He heard a thudding impact nearby, and an anguished voice cry out. "Liam!" Peering through the smoke, he dimly glimpsed the scorched body of MacPherson, half-buried beneath a splatter of molten rock. The smell of burning flesh assaulted his nostrils, and he heard Marla gag at the acrid stench. A viscous stream of lava flowed off the corpse, igniting the strewn remains of a thatched roof, and a wall of fire rose between Khan and MacPherson, obscuring his view of the dead scientist—another survivor of the Eugenics Wars who would not live to see the Khanate reborn.

Damn you, Kirk, he thought angrily. *Why didn't you warn me this planet was unstable?*

Khan realized that there was no safety here, not even within the metal cargo carriers. The smoke and flames were spreading too fast. *We must flee,* he thought, *but to where?*

"The caves," he blurted out loud, remembering the murky underground lair of the sabertooths. Khan had heard of individuals who had survived deadly volcanic eruptions by hiding in caves or dungeons. Perhaps deep beneath the earth he and his people could find temporary refuge from the convulsions wracking Ceti Alpha V.

It was their only hope.

"The caves!" he yelled to Joaquin, his voice hoarse from the combined smoke and ash. He cupped a hand over his mouth to protect his lungs. "The den of the sabertooths! We must get the people there!"

Joaquin nodded in understanding, and began herding their party toward the front gate of the compound, now collapsed onto the ground along with the rest of the wire fence. He snatched up a torch from one of the burning huts, to add to the light provided by his wife's flashlight. The other colonists followed his example before braving the ash-shrouded darkness beyond New Chandigarh.

Khan grabbed on to one fleeing colonist, Daniel Katzel, and ordered him to stay behind and round up any other survivors. "Tell everyone to meet at the cavern on the ridge." He gestured emphatically toward the east. "We shall be waiting."

Assuming we make it there alive.

Khan held on to Marla's hand as they raced out of the disintegrating compound, their boots trampling over the fallen gate. A wave of despair washed over Khan as he saw fields of ripening crops ablaze, the neatly plowed rows thrown into disarray by the violent contortions of the earth. Before his anguished gaze, lava bombs set fire to acres of wheat, destroying in moments the work of months.

He shook his head once before looking away. They would mourn the crops later, if they survived. *Famine is the least of my concerns,* he thought morosely.

The tremors finally began to subside, at least until the inevitable aftershocks, but gaping chasms and spreading brushfires forced Khan and the others to zigzag through the devastated fields before they reached the open veldt, which was also being ravaged by the earthquake and volcanoes. Khan gripped his phaser in one hand while holding on to Marla with the other, but, for once, there appeared to be no danger from the sabertooths and other beasts; the planet's predators were too busy fleeing the ongoing cataclysm to bother with a few, equally panicked humans.

Their torchlit trek through the carnage was like some ghastly fever dream, punctuated by booming explosions and fragmentary glimpses of utter havoc and desolation. Bison, rodents, and other creatures lay dead throughout the sundered plains, their fresh carcasses going ignored by scavengers. A megacondor crashed to the ground, its mighty wings weighed down by a coating of heavy ash. Lush groves of trees were now a collection of jagged stumps and broken timbers; Khan skirted the wrecked copses as much as possible, for fear of falling tree trunks.

He spotted a live sabertooth pinned beneath the weight of a toppled palm tree. The great cat thrashed frantically, clawing at the earth with its forepaws and roaring like a demon, but was unable to free itself. In a rare moment of mercy, Khan used his phaser to put the crazed beast out of its misery.

Marla staggered and fell, her merely human endurance unable to keep up with the breakneck pace of Khan and the other colonists. "Go on!" she urged him. Her chest heaved as she gasped for breath, exhausted. "Don't let me slow you down!"

"Never!" Khan stated emphatically. Her courage and willingness to sacrifice herself provided him with a surge of pride in the midst of the holocaust. "Not while I breathe!"

He scooped her up into his arms and hurried after Joaquin and the others. He kept his eyes fixed on the refugees' torches, for fear of losing sight of the party. There might still be safety in numbers, despite the overwhelming scale of the disaster.

Finally, after a harrowing journey through the flaming veldt, they arrived at the base of the stony ridge holding the entrance to the smilodons' onetime lair. Khan was relieved to see that the rugged granite outcropping appeared to be intact, despite the earthshaking tremors. "This way!" Joaquin shouted gruffly at the party, leading the way. Suzette Ling searched the upward path with the beam of her flashlight.

Khan placed Marla back upon the ground, but kept one hand on her shoulder as he helped her climb the steep incline. "No one enter the cave until I give the order!" he called out to the rest of the party, squeezing his way toward the front of the procession. He suspected that any remaining sabertooths would have already fled the vicinity, but he wished to take no chances. He had already lost several followers to this unthinkable cataclysm; he was not about to lose another colonist to the tusks of a fear-maddened smilodon. "Beware of eels!" he added, as another possible hazard occurred to him.

It is no doubt too much to hope, Khan cursed silently, *that the fires and tremors might at least kill off those noxious parasites!*

A sudden aftershock rattled the cliff face, causing the climbers to drop to their knees and grab on to the ridge to keep from tumbling back down to the rock-strewn plain below. An avalanche of gravel, dirt, and ash cascaded down onto the refugees' heads and shoulders. Khan heard the sound of cracking stone, followed by an urgent cry from Marla. "Khan, watch out!"

Khan glanced up in time to see a large boulder plummeting straight toward him. He threw himself to one side, narrowly evading the boulder—only to hear a panicked shriek cut off abruptly. A hundred kilograms of falling granite collided with mortal flesh and bone, then smashed to earth seconds later.

No! Khan thought in rage and frustration. He peered down over his shoulder at a lifeless human form half-buried beneath the shattered remains of the boulder. "Who?" he whispered hollowly, dreading the answer.

"Kamala Devi," Amy Katzel answered, biting back tears.

Khan recalled a brilliant microbiologist who had also enjoyed a brief career as a Bollywood movie idol. His broad shoulders drooped limply, crushed beneath the weight of this latest tragedy. *So much talent and potential,* he grieved, *snuffed out in an instant.*

Like Parvati and MacPherson and Rodriguez. . . .

Despair beckoned, but Khan refused to surrender to hopelessness. Too many people, including Marla, still depended on him. Lifting his head, he waited for the deadly aftershock to subside completely, then completed his ascent to the cave entrance. Pitch-black shadows filled the gaping mouth of the cavern.

As a precaution, he fired a beam of killing energy into the tunnel, in the unlikely event that a smilodon, or perhaps a nest of Ceti eels, waited within. When no bestial cry greeted the phaser blast, he nodded at Joaquin to proceed.

The bodyguard stepped past Khan, his rifle ready. His wife aimed her flashlight ahead of him. Ducking his head beneath the lip of the cave entrance, Joaquin led the other colonists into the sheltering depths while Khan lingered outside, making sure no straggler was left behind.

From his perch upon the ridge, Khan could see clusters of other torches making their way across the midnight landscape below. Many of the scattered groups moved slowly and intermittently, as though possibly burdened by injured comrades among the survivors. He shuddered to imagine how many casualties the colony had suffered.

How many of my people are grievously wounded? How many dead?

"It's not your fault," Marla whispered, as if reading his mind. The sensitive historian had not yet followed the rest of the party into the caves. "This was like Pompeii or Krakatoa . . . there was nothing you could have done."

Khan drew little comfort from her words, no matter what truth they might hold. He was the colony's supreme commander; he should have been prepared for any catastrophe. "Go," he told her softly. "Stay close to Joaquin and Ling. They will keep you safe." He guided her firmly but gently toward the mouth of the cave. "I will join you shortly."

Perhaps sensing his need for solitude, Marla did not contest his decision. "All right," she said. "Take care of our people. I'll be waiting when this terrible night is over."

She disappeared into the cliff face, leaving Khan alone upon the ridge. In the distance, he spied flames and smoke rising from what had once been New Chandigarh. *All our work, all these months of struggle and survival,* he lamented, *swept away in a matter of minutes.*

It was too cruel.

INTERLUDE

A.D. 2287

The planet came apart?

Kirk paused in his reading. According to Chekov, Khan claimed that Ceti Alpha VI exploded six months after he and his followers arrived on this very planet, resulting in a global cataclysm that all but destroyed the world's ability to support life. But what had caused the disaster in the first place?

"I've never understood this," he said, lifting his gaze from Khan's journal. He glanced upward, as though peering through the roof of the cavern at the desolate wasteland above. "How could Ceti Alpha VI have exploded? This system seemed perfectly stable when we left Khan here, nineteen years ago." He shook his head in confusion. "Planets don't just explode."

"This is true," Spock agreed. Despite the weight of his environmental suit, he appeared completely at ease; Kirk

187

envied his Vulcan strength and endurance. "Unlike, say, the Genesis Planet, whose matrix was composed of unstable protomatter, conventional planets are not capable of spontaneous detonation. Other cosmological factors must have been at work."

"Such as?" Kirk prompted.

Spock gave the matter some thought. "It is impossible to determine for certain, at least not without a comprehensive gravimetric analysis, but it is possible that a miniature black hole, perhaps ejected from a binary system elsewhere, passed through the Ceti Alpha system. Its tremendous gravitational pull could have literally torn Ceti Alpha VI apart while simultaneously affecting the orbit of Ceti Alpha V." Spock arched a speculative eyebrow. "Such a disaster is theoretically possible, and fits the description provided by Khan."

Kirk nodded. Trapped as Khan was on a primitive world, without any advanced astronomical sensors, he would have had no way to know for certain what had caused the cataclysm, but he surely would have been able to observe the disappearance of Ceti Alpha VI . . . and feel the effects of its passing.

Makes sense, Kirk thought regarding Spock's theory. *More or less.* "Shouldn't we have noticed a black hole approaching the system when we were here before?"

"Not necessarily, captain. A black hole with mass sufficient to destroy Ceti Alpha VI might still have had an extremely small Schwarzchild radius." Spock was referring to the hole's outer boundary, the point of no return beyond which neither matter or energy could escape. "If the hole was traveling through empty space, as it would have been en route to the Ceti Alpha system, there might have been very little evidence of its passage."

I suppose, Kirk thought. Spock's explanation, plausible as it was, did not entirely assuage his sense of guilt for having missed the approach of the black hole so many years ago, if that was indeed what had set off the catastrophe. *It's possible we may never know for sure what really happened here.*

"What about some sort of artificial planet-killer?" McCoy suggested. The doctor leaned against the wall of the grotto, letting the crumbling limestone support his weight. "Like that doomsday machine we ran into way back when?"

Spock considered the notion. "Possible," he concluded, "but improbable. That particular mechanism was singularly methodical in its operation; it is unlikely that a similar device would have destroyed Ceti Alpha VI but spared the rest of the solar system."

"It was just a suggestion," McCoy muttered.

Kirk glanced at the chronometer on his environmental suit. They had been out of touch with Sulu for more than an hour now. *We ought to return to the surface soon*, he realized. Fortunately, many of the journal entries were brief or repetitive, containing only a terse listing of rations consumed, crops yielded, minor disciplinary infractions, and so on. He skipped over these entries in search of the overall history of the colony. *I can always examine the book more closely later on*, he reasoned.

The murky illumination made deciphering Khan's intricate handwriting difficult, and Kirk found himself pining for his reading glasses, which remained back aboard the *Yakima*. He had gotten about two-thirds of the way through the journal when a faint noise from outside the grotto caused him to look up from the book in surprise. "Did you hear that?" he asked aloud.

Neither Spock nor McCoy had time to respond before a pair of fists burst through the wall behind the doctor. A muscular arm locked itself around McCoy's throat, causing him to gasp for breath. Kirk and Spock reached for their phasers even as an unexpected figure appeared in the entrance to the grotto. "Drop your weapons," the newcomer barked, "or my friend will break your companion's neck!"

The speaker was a striking blond woman, who looked several decades younger than Kirk. Human in appearance, she aimed a wooden crossbow at Kirk while glaring at him and Spock with icy blue eyes. Her baleful expression made it clear she was deadly serious. "Your weapons," she repeated harshly. "Now."

A strangled croak from McCoy added emphasis to her threat.

"All right," Kirk said. Nodding at Spock, he placed his phaser down on top of Marla's sarcophagus. Spock did likewise, his stoic Vulcan features betraying not a flicker of trepidation. "Let him go," Kirk told the woman, gesturing toward McCoy. "We don't mean you any harm."

"Quiet!" the woman snapped. Keeping her weapon squarely pointed at Kirk's head, she stepped farther into the murky tomb, allowing more intruders to scramble through the open doorway. "Take their weapons," she instructed her cohorts. Kirk winced as their phasers were snatched up by eager hands. Almost as an after-thought, the woman shouted to her accomplice outside the grotto. "Let the hostage breathe . . . for now."

The arm around McCoy's throat relaxed slightly, and Kirk heard the doctor suck in the sere, stagnant air of the cavern. "Are you all right, Bones?" he asked, risking another outburst from the mystery woman.

"Well enough," McCoy croaked, the color slowly returning to his face. "I told you we should have gone to Yosemite, though."

"That's enough," the woman ordered. She took a moment to inspect her surroundings, scowling as her gaze lighted on the sarcophagus and its sentimental inscription. From her expression, and from the curious glances of her associates, Kirk guessed that their captors had never entered the crypt before. In fact, he would have been willing to bet good money that none of these strangers had even known the hidden grotto was here.

Were these people the reason Khan had disguised the entrance in the first place?

Like the woman, the other invaders were young, blond, and distinctly feral in appearance. Their golden tresses were wild and unshorn, while their sunbaked faces were smudged with dirt and soot. Their ragged clothing, such as it was, seemed to have been cobbled together from a motley assortment of scraps and debris, including old rags, blankets, upholstery, and broken lengths of electrical cable. Cannibalized circuit boards and transtators served as jewelry of a sort, along with various rings and bangles carved out of bone and ivory.

They looked, in other words, much the way Khan

and his followers had looked, right after their escape from Ceti Alpha V. *I don't understand*, Kirk thought. *I thought all of Khan's people died aboard the* Reliant, *during that final battle in the Mutara Nebula?*

He did not recognize any of the strangers from Khan's short stay aboard the *Enterprise*. Judging from their ages, he guessed that these were all second-generation superhumans, conceived during Khan's exile on this planet. But why hadn't they left Ceti Alpha V with the others?

The woman seemed equally puzzled by the presence of the three Starfleet officers. "Who are you?" she demanded. Her voice had a faintly Scandinavian accent. The tusk of a long-dead sabertooth dangled on a cord around her neck. "What are you doing here?"

Kirk welcomed the chance to explain. "My name is James T. Kirk." Habit almost caused him to add, "Captain of the *Starship Enterprise*," until he remembered that his starship was still in spacedock, many light-years away. Still, there was no reason to advertise that fact just yet. "We're here on a peaceful miss—"

But his name alone provoked an immediate reaction, interrupting his attempt to put his captors' minds at ease. "Kirk!" one of the young savages blurted, casting a shocked look at the woman with the crossbow. "Did you hear, Astrid? It's he, the Abandoner!"

Kirk kicked himself mentally. *I should have realized that I'd be pretty infamous among this crew. After all, I'm the one who exiled their parents here.* As inconspicuously as possible, he tucked Khan's journal beneath his arm. *The Abandoner? Is that how these people remember me?*

"I heard, Cesare," the woman, whose name was apparently Astrid, replied. She eyed Kirk dubiously, as though he had just claimed to be Kahless or Zefram Cochrane. "I'm simply not sure I believe it." She cast a worried glance at the doorway, perhaps aware that it was the only way in or out of the grotto. "There may be others. We should leave, as soon as I take care of one more thing."

She extended an open hand toward one of her followers, who immediately surrendered his captured phaser to Astrid, who briskly examined the weapon. "Exquisite," she pronounced, before taking aim at the marble sarcophagus. "A phaser, correct? I wonder if this weapon is half as powerful as we've been told?"

Realizing her intention, McCoy reacted in horror. "Wait! That's a woman's tomb!" Kirk placed a restraining hand upon the doctor's arm, to keep McCoy from lunging forward and provoking the guards. "You can't just vandalize it!"

Astrid sneered at the doctor's protests. "Not just any woman," she replied. "Khan's human whore." She gestured contemptuously at the magnificent sarcophagus. "She deserves no such tribute."

Kirk, too, was sickened by what he realized was about to happen, but there was nothing he could do. *I can't risk our lives for a relic, no matter how beautifully crafted.*

The woman fired the phaser. The crimson beam struck Marla's marble portrait, turning Khan's flawless re-creation of his wife's beauty into a charred ruin. Polished stone cracked and crumbled to ash before Kirk's eyes. He couldn't help feeling as though McGivers were dying a second time.

I'm sorry, Marla, he thought.

The phaser was not set to disintegrate the sarcophagus, but it made a wreck of the memorial regardless. Hours of loving effort were undone in seconds, rendering the sculpture completely unrecognizable. For good riddance, Astrid turned the beam on the engraved inscription as well, eradicating the last vestige of Marla's identity as thoroughly as that of a disgraced Egyptian queen.

"Dammit, Jim," McCoy muttered in disgust. "This is obscene." He glared at the mysterious woman. "She didn't have to do this!"

"Wanton destruction is seldom logical," Spock commented. A tinge of regret colored his voice. "More's the pity."

Astrid apparently disagreed. "That's better," she said finally, releasing the trigger. She eyed the disfigured sarcophagus with obvious satisfaction before turning her attention back to Kirk and the others. "Time to go," she declared.

At her direction, the barbaric youths escorted Kirk and his comrades out of the desecrated tomb. Additional castaways, all armed with spears and bows, waited outside the grotto, including a muscular youth who withdrew his arms from the punctured cavern wall. Kirk counted half a dozen young superhumans in all. Flickering torches, fueled by moss and dried dung, cast ominous shadows on the walls of the catacombs. Kirk watched with concern as a pair of castaways toyed with the captured phasers; he couldn't help remembering that the weapons were set on Kill.

A powerful hand shoved Kirk from behind, propelling him down a winding tunnel, which proved to be the first of many as their mysterious captors led the three friends through a bewildering maze of caverns and corridors, transporting them ever deeper into the hidden sanctuary beneath the planet's surface. Kirk tried to keep track of the various twists and turns, but soon doubted his ability to retrace their steps back to the abandoned cargo carriers. He could only hope that Spock's computerlike mind was coping better with the devious labyrinth.

The temperature dropped several degrees as they descended into the lower depths of the cave system, and Kirk was grateful for the multiple layers of insulation provided by his environmental suit. His eyes and ears kept busy as he marched, searching for possible avenues of escape, as well as for hints of the castaways' lives down here. At one point he thought he smelled some sort of organic fertilizer, and caught a glimpse of an underground garden in one of the adjacent chambers. Polished obsidian mirrors reflected and focused the light provided by a pair of old-fashioned high-intensity plasma lights that Kirk vaguely remembered including in the colonists' supplies many years ago. He heard a portable generator sputtering somewhere nearby, and was impressed that Khan and his people had managed to keep the aging mechanism running for more than eighteen Earth-years.

Looks like Spock was right about the survivors growing

their food underground, Kirk thought. *With a working pro-tein resequencer, they might even be able to convert the raw organic crops into a viable diet.*

Other chambers appeared to have been converted into barracks, storerooms, and even an armory stocked with primitive weapons: swords, spears, and crossbow bolts. *For defense against wild animals,* he speculated, *or some other threat?* In theory, all of the planet's larger predators were now extinct.

Finally, after a long and exhausting hike, they arrived at some sort of meeting hall. Stone benches, carved from preexisting limestone formations, surrounded a firepit stacked with lumpy fragments of coal. Kirk guessed that, since the cataclysm, timber had become too pre-cious to use for fuel. A wispy gray tendril of smoke rose from the burning embers, disappearing into a jagged shaft in the ceiling. Overlapping sheets of flowstone cur-tained the walls.

"Up against the wall," Astrid ordered, and her cohorts lined the three men up against a hardened tapestry of rock, as though preparing them to face a firing squad. "Remove your armor."

Damn, Kirk thought, as he reluctantly began to shed his environmental suit. Without the protective outfits, there was no way they could escape back to the planet's surface. He wondered if Sulu was already searching for them. If so, his efforts were doubtless in vain; they were clearly too far underground to be detected by the *Yakima's* sensors.

Summoned by the excited shouts of their captors, more men and women came running into the torchlit

hall. The new arrivals were obviously of the same breed
and generation as Astrid and the others; in their patch-
work attire, they reminded Kirk of J. M. Barrie's Lost
Boys, not to mention the feral "onlies" of Miri's planet.
He estimated that there were at least twenty adults,
along with a smattering of children and toddlers.

Kirk had to set down Khan's journal in order to
remove the outer layer of his environmental suit.
Beneath the protective shells, each man wore a tight-fit-
ting black bodysuit equipped with microprocessors to
monitor his life signs. Kirk could not help noticing how
much cooler the cavern felt now that he had lost a layer
of insulation.

To his dismay, the exiles confiscated Khan's journal,
along with Spock's tricorder and data disks. He was
tempted to protest, but thought better of it. Uncovering
Khan's past was no longer his top priority. *If I'm not careful,* he realized, *we could end up history ourselves.*

Astrid waited until her people snatched away the discarded segments of the environmental suits, then strode
up to confront Kirk and his fellow prisoners. "My name is
Astrid Ericsson," she identified herself proudly. One of the
captured phasers now resided in her hand. "I am in command here."

"Ericsson?" Kirk's eyes widened in comprehension.
"Daughter of Harulf?"

Azure eyes narrowed suspiciously. "How do you know
my father?"

Kirk hesitated. He didn't want to call further attention to Khan's journal, which currently rested at the feet
of one of Astrid's lieutenants; so far, the youthful cast-

aways had been more interested in their captives' high-tech artifacts—the suits, tricorders, and phasers—than in a musty old book. "I'm James T. Kirk, remember? I met all of the original colonists years ago."

In truth, Kirk barely remembered Ericsson. Khan had commanded more than seventy superhumans, all of whom had spent most of their time in the *Enterprise*'s brig before arriving at Ceti Alpha V. Only Khan had made any sort of an impression on Kirk.

Astrid appeared to accept his explanation, though. "Perhaps you are he," she said cautiously. Turning her attention to Spock, she scrutinized the Vulcan's exotic features. "The stories say that the Abandoner had an alien henchman, a humanoid with pointed ears, who looked like Satan."

Without warning, she grabbed Spock's arm and savagely bit down on his hand, tearing the skin. Green blood welled up, filling the indentations left behind by her teeth. She spit more emerald droplets onto the ground.

"Good God!" McCoy exclaimed, as shocked as Kirk at the young woman's savagery. "Are you out of your mind?"

Spock, however, took the incident in stride. "There are less invasive ways to confirm my ancestry," he observed coolly. "The tricorder, for instance."

Regardless, the sight of the inhuman green blood appeared to satisfy Astrid. Turning back toward Kirk, she got straight to the point. "Where is Khan?" she demanded.

Kirk was taken aback by the question. "You don't know?"

"All we know," she said heatedly, "is that the Tyrant, along with all his minions, vanished sometime in the last year." She gestured toward the surrounding caverns. "This was his stronghold . . . at least until our scouts reported it abandoned many weeks ago."

The Tyrant? Khan?

Kirk struggled to keep up with these unexpected twists. "I'm confused," he admitted. "If you're not with Khan, who are you?"

"We are the Exiles," she declared, raising her chin imperiously. "Sworn foes of the despot, Khan Noonien Singh, and all who serve him. For over a decade, we have lived only to bring his diabolical reign to an end."

The last of the dissidents, Kirk realized, *led by the daughter of Khan's old nemesis.* Kirk recalled from Khan's journal how divisions within the colony had headed toward a breaking point in the years after the cataclysm. *I guess Khan chose to leave these rebels behind when he made his escape from the planet.*

"Fascinating," Spock remarked. "It appears that the Eugenics Wars repeated themselves three hundred years later, pitting superhuman against superhuman once more."

That explains that armory I glimpsed earlier, Kirk thought. *Khan and the Exiles were fighting a civil war here, right up to the point that Khan hijacked the* Reliant. *Khan probably sealed up Marla's crypt right before he left the planet, in order to keep the Exiles from desecrating his loving memorial—just as Astrid did, the first chance she got.*

Furthermore, he reasoned, Astrid and the rest of the Exiles must not have realized that Khan was missing until well after *Reliant*'s crew was rescued from the planet. Not too surprising, given the hostile relations between the two tribes; the Exiles probably kept pretty clear of Khan's territory until just recently.

"Enough!" Astrid snapped. "You cannot deceive us with such transparent playacting." She fondled the phaser in her grip and glared venomously at Kirk. "As leader of our tribe, I have sworn a blood oath to bring down the Tyrant. Do not attempt to shield him from our vengeance!"

"But Khan is dead!" McCoy blurted out. "He was blown to atoms nearly a year ago!"

Astrid reeled backward, looking as though she had just been struck by lightning. But she quickly regained her composure—and hostile attitude. "That's impossible! Do you take me for a fool?"

"He's telling the truth," Kirk insisted. "Khan and his people escaped Ceti Alpha V in a stolen starship, but the ship was soon destroyed in battle." He omitted mentioning the Genesis Device, which would only raise more questions in the woman's mind. "There were no survivors."

"Lies!" Astrid accused them, her Valkyrie-like features contorted in fury. "The Tyrant cannot be dead, not at the hands of mere ordinary humans. And a stolen spaceship . . . do you expect me to believe such nonsense?" She regarded Kirk with open suspicion. "If Khan died so long ago, what were you doing here now, in the tomb of his inferior wife, no less? Don't tell me that your return to this world is a mere coincidence."

Kirk was startled by the vehemence of Astrid's reaction. *But perhaps it's not so surprising*, he reflected. Khan's departure several months ago must have thrown these so-called Exiles into a state of crisis. If their entire community had always been dedicated to overthrowing the "Tyrant," his sudden disappearance had no doubt left them adrift. *No wonder she's so resistant to the idea; without a Khan to oppose, Astrid has no purpose in life.*

"We came . . . to pay our respects to the dead." Even as he spoke, Kirk was conscious of just how flimsy that pretext sounded, even if it happened to be true. "And to learn more about what transpired here after the disaster."

A scornful laugh escaped Astrid's lips. "You never cared what happened here before, so why now?" She clearly wasn't buying Kirk's explanation. "Let me get this straight. You came all this way, after all these years, just to mourn an old enemy." She sneered contemptuously. "Do not insult my intelligence!"

The woman's accusations stabbed Kirk in the heart. *Why didn't I ever check on Khan and the other colonists?* he asked himself, for maybe the millionth time since Khan's return. There were reasons, of course: his responsibilities to Starfleet, the ongoing cold war with the Klingons and the Romulans, dozens of other Federation colonies to look out for, a galaxy of new worlds and civilizations to discover. *I always just assumed that Khan and his people were capable of fending for themselves. Plus, given Khan's ambitions, and the danger posed by the superhumans, it had seemed wiser to leave Ceti Alpha V alone.*

Good reasons all, but were they enough to excuse him of responsibility for the tragedy that resulted?

"You're right," he confessed to Astrid. "I should have paid more attention to what happened here." It *had* been his decision, after all. "But that doesn't change the fact that your war is over. Khan is dead."

"So you say now," she responded. Kirk could tell from her voice and belligerent expression that she still refused to believe him. "But perhaps you and your companions will tell a different story after I've introduced you to a few of Khan's favorite pets." She turned to one of her nameless subordinates. "Get the eels."

Kirk remembered the missing terrarium. Apparently, Khan hadn't taken the loathsome, brain-warping parasites aboard the *Reliant* after all. "Wait!" he urged Astrid and the others. "You don't have to do that. We're telling you the truth!"

Before he could say more, another castaway came running up to the Exile leader. "Astrid! You must hurry! Tamsin is going into labor . . . and she doesn't look good! I think there's something wrong with the baby."

That was all McCoy needed to hear. "I'm a doctor. Let me help!" He nodded toward a nearby Exile, who was currently fiddling with the contents of McCoy's medkit. "That's my equipment there. Just give me a chance to see the patient!"

Astrid glanced at the medical hardware, as if confirming McCoy's description of the instruments. The hyposprays and trilasers, along with McCoy's passionate entreaties, seemed to convince her. "Very well," she finally agreed. "Get your things and come with me." She gave McCoy a warning look. "If this is a trick, I'll kill you myself—slowly."

"I've heard that before," McCoy muttered under his breath as he quickly gathered up his supplies under the watchful gaze of the scowling Exiles.

Astrid headed for an exit, then paused to look back at Kirk. "This is only a reprieve," she coldly informed him. "Use it to think better of your deceptions. We shall speak again, later."

Armed castaways escorted McCoy after Astrid, who issued a parting command to the Exiles standing guard over Kirk and Spock.

"Take them to the Pit."

Kirk barely had time to glance back at Khan's journal before the guards took them away.

PART THREE

Khan Agonistes

14

They spent nearly a week underground, hiding from the cataclysm. Violent aftershocks rocked the caverns, resulting in frequent rockfalls and tunnel collapses. The shell-shocked survivors were forced to constantly relocate in order to keep one step ahead of the cave-ins, while their escape route back to the surface was soon sealed off by tons of collapsed granite and limestone.

Khan barely slept, relying on his superhuman stamina to sustain him while he tended to what remained of his followers. He moved restlessly from chamber to torchlit chamber, checking on the wounded and offering whatever encouragement he could to the beleaguered refugees. "Take heart!" he urged a cluster of huddled

207

colonists, including Harulf Ericsson and his pregnant wife, Karyn. "We shall come through this trial, this I promise."

Ericsson stared back at Khan with malice in his icy blue eyes. He held his tongue, however, so Khan left the Norseman behind to comfort Karyn as best he could in these dismal circumstances.

Conditions were brutal, not to mention claustrophobic. The forced evacuation of New Chandigarh had been rushed and disorganized, with no time available for planning or provisions. The fleeing colonists had brought only whatever weapons, implements, and articles of clothing they had managed to grab on to while running madly from the tremors and falling lava. Blankets were in short supply, a serious problem given the coolness of the lower caverns, where the temperature seldom climbed above twelve degrees Celsius. Even with their genetically enhanced immune systems, many of the survivors found themselves succumbing to disease; fevers and hacking coughs were soon common.

Food and water had become an issue, too. With their rations left behind, doubtless lost in the blaze that had consumed the camp, the starving colonists were forced to scour the crumbling catacombs in search of cave-dwelling beetles, millipedes, spiders, salamanders, and even the occasional Ceti eel. Khan watched in dismay as a handful of bedraggled men and women dug through piles of accumulated bat guano looking for the pale, colorless worms and insects living in the dung. (The bats themselves were long gone, having presumably fled the cavern the night Ceti Alpha VI exploded.)

How the mighty have fallen, he thought, *where once we lived like princes of the earth*. He found himself pining for a raw bison steak, dripping with blood, or the barbecued haunch of a freshly bagged sabertooth. Even the processed blandness of Starfleet rations sounded like caviar compared to the squirming vermin they were forced to subsist on.

Their water supply was limited to the paltry moisture that trickled down the cavern walls or dripped from stalactites, which was not nearly enough to slake the thirst of so many trapped men and women. Khan's own mouth felt as dry as the Great Thar Desert where he was conceived. His skin felt like sandpaper.

We cannot stay down here much longer, he realized. Soon enough they would have to brave whatever awaited them on the surface of the planet. *I can only pray that the worst of the disaster has passed.*

A flashlight beam lit up the former bat cave, heralding the approach of Gideon Hawkins. The haggard physician had been entrusted with one of the refugees' few flashlights, owing to the paramount importance of his duties. Khan was thankful that Hawkins, at least, had survived the catastrophe . . . so far.

"Greetings, Doctor," Khan addressed him. Both men's coveralls were torn and caked with grunge. "How fare your patients?" Inwardly, he braced himself for Hawkins' answer. Every time he saw the doctor, Khan half-expected to hear of yet another fatality among his people.

So far, the death count stood at nine. Five men and four women, not counting the unborn children extinguished along with their unfortunate mothers, or lost to miscarriages in the aftermath of the disaster. The total human population of Ceti Alpha V had been reduced to a mere sixty men and women, many of them ill and/or wounded. Counting those superhumans who had perished in hibernation aboard the *Botany Bay*, Khan calculated that he had already lost nearly thirty percent of his original entourage.

It was a sobering, and deeply disheartening, figure.

"No new fatalities," Hawkins assured him quickly. The doctor's knuckles were wrapped around the handle of a medkit, which he had been shrewd enough to hang on to when he fled New Chandigarh. "But Hans Steiber's leg has gone gangrenous. I'm afraid I'm going to have to amputate . . . with your permission, of course."

Khan nodded grimly. "I trust your judgment, Doctor. Can I be of assistance?"

"Actually, I could use a hand," Hawkins admitted. "Saraj and your wife are swamped tending to the other patients."

Bidding farewell to the worm-hunters, Khan followed the doctor back to the shadowy grotto that now served as their makeshift infirmary. Roughly a dozen colonists, suffering from everything from broken limbs to third-degree burns, were stretched out on the dank floor of the cavern, atop whatever blankets or padding the nurses had managed to scrounge up. Khan spotted Marla, along with Saraj Panjabi, circulating among the patients. Marla was wringing a damp rag above the parched lips of Paul Austin, trying to squeeze a few more drops of water out of the wet cloth. Khan's mouth watered at the sight of the precious moisture.

He made eye contact with his wife, who smiled wanly at him in return. It pained him to see how thin and debilitated she looked. Dark shadows gathered beneath her sunken brown eyes, while her once-lustrous red hair now looked dry and lifeless. Her durable red jumpsuit was streaked with dirt and coming apart at the seams. The tricorder hanging from her shoulder looked in better shape than she was. *And yet she keeps on working,* he noted proudly, *as befits the wife of a Khan.*

Reluctantly, he returned his attention to the matter at hand. "Over here," Hawkins said, guiding Khan toward a dimly lit side chamber just off the main cavern. He tied a soiled rag over his mouth and nostrils and gestured for Khan to do the same. "I moved Steiber in here to isolate him from the other patients."

The entrance to the crypt was narrow enough that Khan and the doctor had to squeeze through one at a time. Inside they found the former financier and money launderer trembling beneath the flickering light of a single torch, which was jammed securely into a crack in the cave wall. Steiber's face was ashen and his entire body trembled uncontrollably. Beads of sweat, which he could ill afford to shed, dotted his febrile brow.

"H-h-herr Khan," he greeted Khan through cracked and bleeding lips. He tried to sit up, but could barely lift his head from the cold stone floor. "F-forgive my weakness."

"Do not trouble yourself," Khan told the man, gesturing for Steiber to lie back down. "Save your strength for your recovery."

Hawkins drew back a sheet, exposing Steiber's left leg, which had been severely burned when a lava bomb set fire to the high grass through which he had been running. Gangrene had set in, despite the doctor's best efforts, turning the limb black and spongy. Khan could smell the rotting flesh even through the handkerchief covering the bottom half of his face.

"I tried to halt the infection," Hawkins insisted, "but it resisted even the strongest Starfleet antibiotics." He placed the flashlight onto a rocky ledge, positioning it so that the incandescent beam added to the illumination provided by the sputtering torch. "Some damn local bug, I guess, that nobody's ever run into before."

Another unanticipated blessing of Ceti Alpha V, Khan thought mordantly. Not for the first time, he cursed the day Kirk first told him of this planet. *It's been six months since we were left here. Surely, the* Enterprise *will be back to check on the colony soon, especially after Kirk learns what happened to this solar system. . . .*

Opening his medkit, Hawkins took out a hypospray and surgical laser. Steiber's bloodshot eyes widened in fear at the sight of the latter instrument, but Khan placed a steadying hand upon the German's shoulder. "Courage," he said softly. "Your sacrifice will not be forgotten."

Hawkins pressed the hypospray against Steiber's neck, and the patient's eyelids drooped mercifully. "That's the last of the anesthetic," the doctor announced with a scowl. "Should be enough to take care of the worst of the pain, but I'm going to need you to hold him still, just in case."

Khan took hold of Steiber, being careful to keep his bare hands away from the gangrenous flesh. "Proceed," he instructed the doctor.

He did not avert his eyes as the doctor's trilaser neatly severed the rotting limb from the rest of Steiber's body, cauterizing the wound as it did so. A shudder went through the German as the scalpel did its work, but Steiber remained unconscious. When he was finished, Hawkins tugged on the sheet beneath the amputated limb, pulling the leg away from his patient. "That needs to be disposed off," the doctor said. He cast a meaningful glance at the phaser on Khan's belt. "If that is agreeable to you."

"Of course." Khan did not wish to waste the phaser's energy frivolously, but recognized the importance of eliminating every last trace of the infectious mass. A quick burst from the phaser disintegrated the foul-smelling leg before it could spread its contamination elsewhere. The stomach-turning odor lingered in the musty air of the cramped isolation chamber.

Khan looked down at the unfortunate Steiber, who was now minus a limb, but looking even more pallid than before. "Will he recover?" Khan asked the doctor.

"Perhaps," Hawkins answered. "If shock, starvation, and dehydration don't kill him first." He looked Khan in the eyes, an intense expression on his face. "I'm not just talking about Steiber. My patients need fresh air and sunlight, not to mention decent amounts of food and water, if they're going to survive. They need to get out of these godforsaken caves," he said forcefully. "We all do."

Khan remembered Marla's sunken eyes, and the pathetic sight of superior men and women digging in the muck for beetles and grubs. Thirst and hunger ate away at his own iron will and endurance. He glanced upward at the uncounted meters of solid rock cutting them off from the surface.

"Your point is well taken, Doctor."

Despite Hawkins' concerns, Khan waited until another forty-eight hours passed without any aftershocks before deciding that the time had come to lead his people back into the light. Leaving the doctor and his partner to care for those who remained too weak for the climb, Khan told Marla and the others to gather up their things and follow him.

Let us hope, he thought solemnly, *that the disaster has left us something to rebuild upon.*

With Khan in the lead, the threadbare procession wended its way toward the surface. Collapsed tunnels and piled rubble forced frequent detours, so that the route seemed much longer than Khan remembered. Hours passed, many of them spent digging through great heaps of limestone with their bare hands, an exhausting task at the best of times, let alone after several days of hardship and privation. By the time they reached the former lair of the smilodons, Joaquin and Ericsson and Zuleika and the other workers were practically dead on their feet.

"Soon," Khan promised his weary followers. He felt

like Orpheus ascending from the underworld; he was half afraid to look back at Marla for fear that she would disappear back into the depths if he did so. "Our long confinement is almost over."

So near the surface, however, they discovered that an enormous cave-in had placed several tons of broken granite between them and the sunlight. Despairing groans erupted from the marchers behind Khan as the beam of his flashlight exposed the monumental boulders blocking their path.

"What now, glorious Khan?" Ericsson mocked, fatigue and disappointment overcoming his better judgment. He sneered at Khan through his yellow beard. "Thanks to you, we're all buried alive!"

Khan's own temper was at its limits. Handing the flashlight over to Ling, he angrily drew his phaser, then reconsidered at the sight of the Norseman's pregnant bride, now leaning on Ericsson for support after the long and arduous climb. Karyn Bradley's swollen abdomen carried the hope of the colony, Khan realized.

He lowered the phaser. "I will pardon your insubordination one last time," he informed Ericsson, "for the sake of your wife and unborn child, who will need your strength in the days to come. But do not tempt me further."

He turned to contemplate the collapsed exit. There was no way Joaquin and the others could be expected to tunnel through so much packed rock, not depleted as they were, but perhaps there was another use to which he could put his phaser?

"Stay back," he instructed, raising the weapon once

more. He set the phaser at its highest setting, then unleashed a coruscating beam of crimson energy against the stubborn obstruction. He smiled tightly as, millimeter by millimeter, the phaser beam slowly ate away at the heaps of granite. *We have not come this far to turn back now,* he vowed.

A warning light on the phaser flashed, indicating that the weapon was not intended to run at maximum power for such a continuous length of time. But Khan was determined to free his people. Ignoring the warning, he switched off the safety override. A high-pitched squeal soon emerged from the phaser, the shrill noise jabbing through Khan's skull like a drill.

"Khan, stop!" Marla cried out in alarm. "It's overloading!"

He felt the phaser heating up within his grip, but he refused to let go of the weapon. Instead he kept blasting away at the cursed rockfall, squeezing every last erg of blazing energy out of the overtaxed weapon. He peered intently past the glowing aura of the phaser beam. Was it just his imagination, or could he see a sliver of open air beyond the closed-off exit of the tunnel?

"Back!" he warned the wide-eyed throng behind him. "Keep your distance!"

The phaser's wail grew louder and shriller. Its metal grip grew hot to the touch, burning his naked palm. Khan gritted his teeth and kept on squeezing the trigger, as another snatch of Milton raced through his brain: *"Long is the way and hard, that out of hell leads up to light."*

"Khan!" Marla called urgently. He heard her struggling against some restraint and guessed that Joaquin or one of the others was holding her back. "It's going to explode!"

That is precisely what I intend, he thought, ignoring the searing heat against his hand. Wisps of white smoke rose from his clenched fist. The sickening aroma of burning flesh filled his nostrils, just as it had the night of the cataclysm. Destructive energy flowed like lava from the phaser's emitter, even as the whine of the weapon climbed toward an ear-piercing crescendo. Solid stone melted and crumbled before the incalescent beam.

Just a few more moments, Khan resolved, enduring unimaginable pain. He waited until what he judged the absolute last second, then hurled the smoking phaser at the rubble with all his strength, while simultaneously throwing himself in the opposite direction. "Take cover!" he shouted to Marla and the others.

A blinding flash ignited behind him, and he squeezed his eyelids shut as he flew through the air, feeling a blast of intense heat at his heels. He expected to crash onto the floor of the tunnel, but Joaquin appeared to break his fall and he slammed into the bodyguard's meaty chest instead. Joaquin grabbed on to Khan, holding him upright. "I am here, Your Excellency," he assured Khan. His stolid face was as red as a boiled lobster, his once-brown eyebrows singed into near nonexistence. "You shall not fall."

Planting his feet firmly on the ground, Khan stared past Joaquin. The rest of the survivors were all prone upon the rocky floor, where they had dived to avoid the scorching blast. Marla was pinned beneath the heavier form of Zuleika Walker, whom Khan suspected had prevented Marla from running to his side. *For which I shall be forever grateful*, he thought.

Marla stared up at him in horror. "Khan . . . your hand!"

A quick glance confirmed what his screaming nerve endings were telling him with every passing second: his right hand was a blackened ruin, charred and oozing. Khan winced at the sight. He had seen enough of combat in his day to know that the hand would be forever scarred no matter what treatment he received. *I shall have to wear a glove*, he thought without emotion.

The pain was almost unbearable; his hand felt as though it were trapped in the heart of a nuclear reactor, or perhaps the flames of perdition itself. A lesser man would have already succumbed to shock and agony, but Khan gave his injury only a moment's regard. A more important matter commanded his attention: Had he succeeded, or had it all been for naught?

Were they still trapped beneath the earth?

Clutching his still-smoking hand against his chest, he spun around toward the sealed-off cave entrance. His heart pounded as he saw with relief that the wretched dead end was no more; the explosive detonation of the phaser had blasted through the last of the barrier to the open air outside. A frigid wind blew into the tunnel, bringing some small fraction of relief to his throbbing hand.

Yes! Khan exulted. *I have set my people free!*

One thing concerned him, though. By his calculations, it should be daylight upon the surface, but the open archway revealed only darkness and shadows. The beam of a flashlight, wielded by Suzette Ling, probed beyond the cavern, revealing a strangely nocturnal sky.

An ominous feeling penetrated the waves of pain crashing against Khan's tortured consciousness. He did not like the look of this.

Why was it so dark outside?

15

"Nuclear winter," Marla said. "That's what they used to call it."

Khan stared upward at the dim, sunless sky. Although it should have been high noon, it was as black as midnight all around them, thanks to an oppressive cloud of ash and dust hanging over the land, blotting out the sun. No doubt hurled into the atmosphere during the vast volcanic eruptions, the airborne debris seemed to wrap Ceti Alpha V like a shroud, even though at least a week had passed since the cataclysm. "I recall the theory," he said dourly.

"It's more than a theory," Marla insisted, ever the historian. Her somber tone matched his own. "Back on Earth, the Third World War produced dense black clouds that blocked out ninety percent of Earth's sunlight for over a month. Temperatures dropped dramatically, and the entire food chain almost broke down. Millions of people died from starvation and exposure."

Her graphic description made the Eugenics Wars suffer by comparison. Khan felt grateful to have missed such a catastrophe—at least until now.

Along with the rest of the colonists, save those left behind in the underground infirmary, Khan and Marla huddled behind a pile of fallen tree trunks, seeking a momentary respite from the fierce winds that now seemed to afflict the surface. Much as Marla recounted, it seemed to be much colder outdoors than it had been in the caves, so the survivors crowded together against the splintered timbers in a pathetic effort to stay warm. Khan guessed that it was below two degrees Celsius at least.

Now swaddled in bandages torn from the sleeve of Marla's coverall, his hand still throbbed but somewhat less than before, perhaps because the nerve endings had been permanently damaged. Khan briefly regretted leaving Dr. Hawkins back in the caverns, before returning his attention to the ash-clotted sky.

"Could volcanoes alone produce a cloud of such magnitude?" he asked aloud. "Perhaps a meteor strike as well?" He had seen Ceti Alpha VI explode with his own eyes; was it possible that fragments of the demolished planet had struck its sister planet elsewhere, perhaps even on the far side of the world? Such an impact might easily produce a global winter such as that which had killed the dinosaurs millions of years ago back on Earth.

"I hope not," Marla said, easily following the train of

his thoughts. He felt her shiver in his arms. "The last thing we need is a full-scale mass extinction."

Khan agreed wholeheartedly. His heart ached for his poor, beleaguered people should such a dire calamity befall them, on top of all the other grievous reverses they had already endured. He gazed past Marla at the rest of the party, now crouching in the dirt behind what used to be a thriving grove of axebreaker trees. One of the men, a battle-scarred soldier named Huang, lifted his head from the clump of shivering bodies, a perplexed look upon his face. He probed his ear with one finger, as though trying to dislodge something.

Khan opened his mouth to ask Huang what the matter was, only to be interrupted by a sudden clap of thunder overhead. Mud began to rain from the sky, pelting the colonists with heavy, reddish brown droplets. Khan decided that it was time to get the procession moving again. He was anxious to discover what remained of their old encampment. "We have rested enough," he announced, rising to his feet despite the deluge. He raised his voice to be heard over the wind and rain. "The sooner we reach New Chandigarh, the sooner we may find shelter from the storm."

Better to raise slim hopes, he reasoned, *than no hope at all.*

Groaning audibly, the party rose and shambled after him, all except for Huang, who remained sitting on the ground, staring blankly ahead of him. *What the devil is wrong with the man?* Khan wondered irritably. *Has the strain proven too much for him?* If so, Khan was surprised; Huang had served with distinction in his forces back on

Earth. "You heard me, Huang," he barked. "Get up and join the rest of us!"

"Yes, Your Excellency," the soldier said, somewhat mechanically. Khan's impatience faded as Huang obediently caught up with the other colonists.

Stepping out from behind their improvised windbreak, the survivors were immediately buffeted by a near-cyclonic wind that sent their unbound hair and tattered garments flapping wildly. Crude bandannas, composed of whatever stray fabric presented itself, covered their noses and mouths, providing a degree of protection against the windblown dust and gravel. Swirls of ash spun like dervishes in the ever-shifting gale. Marla kept directly behind Khan, her thin arms wrapped around his waist, while he strove to shield her from the full force of the wind.

An M-16, strapped to Khan's back, served as a replacement for the destroyed phaser, in the unlikely event that they encountered any dangerous wildlife. Only a handful of firearms had escaped New Chandigarh with the surviving colonists, and Khan had been careful to assign them only to his most trusted lieutenants—Joaquin had another rifle and Ling had a handgun.

Khan hoped to find more guns and ammunition back at the camp. With the phaser gone, the twentieth-century firearms had become the state-of-the-art on Ceti Alpha V.

The party staggered forward, advancing slowly across the murky, blighted landscape. By the light of Ling's busy flashlight, they caught glimpses of the devastation wrought by the earthquakes, volcanoes, and ensuing darkness. . . .

Where the high grass had not been burned to the ground by brushfires, the grass and scrub were shriveled and dying, literally starving for sunlight. Blackened stumps marked the site of once-green thickets, while the surviving trees were skeletal, stripped of their leaves by the wind and cold. Burns and gouges scarred their bark, reminding Khan of his raw, red, right hand. Frost-covered animal carcasses littered the broken plains, many already reduced to naked bone. An entire family of sabertooths lay rotting amid the cremated stubble, their mighty tusks proving no defense against the merciless cataclysm that had ravaged their world.

Khan had witnessed many disasters in his time, including the 1984 chemical accident at Bhopal, but the scale of the destruction he now saw left him speechless. It was as though the entire planet had been laid waste.

A plaintive lowing caught Khan's ear, and he spied a paltry herd of bison, consisting of less than a dozen members, rooting in the mud for a few last blades of dry brown grass. The hungry beasts were already noticeably emaciated, their ribs showing through their withered hides. Khan made a mental note to return and slaughter the bison later, before the scant meat on their bones was wasted.

Nuclear winter indeed, Khan thought. He shuddered to imagine what was left of their crops. *Starvation might be our lot as well.*

The falling mud turned the barren earth beneath them into a sucking quagmire that only impeded their progress further. They trudged through the ankle-deep sludge, fighting both the wind and the muck for what felt like hours, before they finally arrived at the outer perimeter of their former home. A disconsolate moan emerged en masse from the throats of the exhausted colonists.

Even though Khan had prepared himself for the sight, the awful reality was almost more than he could bear:

The fields outside the camp, which only weeks ago had burgeoned with ripening wheat, corn, and rice, had been completely destroyed, burned by the fires and later buried beneath centimeters of ash and mud. *And even if they had somehow miraculously survived the disaster,* he realized, *this unnatural winter would have murdered the surviving crops as surely as any deadly lightning bolts or lava bombardment.*

"Oh, Khan," Marla murmured, sharing his grief and horror at the sight before him. "All that work, all our hopes . . ."

She did not need to complete the sentence. Khan knew they were all thinking the same thing. Glancing backward to check on his people, he saw strong men and women sobbing openly. Ericsson let loose a stream of Norwegian obscenity. Ling kept repeating, "No, no, no," over and over again. Huang stared vaguely. Even the stoic Joaquin allowed his brawny shoulders to droop in despair.

Let them grieve, Khan thought grimly. He lacked the heart to fault them for any show of weakness. Not even superhumans could be expected to endure defeat after defeat without complaint. *No chromosome*, he mused, *no matter how cleverly engineered, can fully prepare a soul for purgatory.*

But the worst was yet to come.

Looking past the decimated fields, he allowed himself to gaze upon what once had been their home.

New Chandigarh was a memory. Its fences and huts were no more, buried beneath the sodden residue of the disaster. Shards of shattered thermoconcrete jutted from the sludge. Only a handful of durable cargo bays had survived, and even they had been tossed about like a handful of dice, landing at odd angles and locations throughout the ruins of the colony. Khan's weary muscles ached at the prospect of turning the massive cargo carriers upright once more. He could only hope that some of the supplies inside the steel crates remained intact.

"At least some small shelter remains," he observed to Marla, wanting sorely to offer her some small morsel of consolation. "We may be able to escape the deluge within the cargo bays."

"Of course," she responded. She seemed as eager as he to cast a positive light on matters, and Khan was grateful for her support. More and more, they seemed to be of one mind, complementing each other perfectly. *I chose well*, he thought.

Perversely, the rain chose that moment to let up, although the clouds above remained as black and impenetrable as ever. Khan shook the mud from his long black mane, and turned to address his people. It was vital, he knew, to present a brave face to all assembled, despite his own crushing heartache.

"My friends," he said gravely, "I know how discouraged you must feel for, in truth, I share your sadness at what has become of our former home. It is as though a vengeful Fate has singled us out for torment and persecution." He shook his head mournfully before raising his chin proudly and thrusting his unscarred left fist at the lightless sky. "But I defy whatever power conspires against us. We shall come through this trial, just as we have triumphed over all that has tested us before, both on Earth and beyond."

His dark eyes searched the faces of the crowd, looking for some sign that his words were taking root in their hearts. Ericsson scowled through his beard, but wisely held his tongue. Zuleika wiped a tear from her eye and stiffened her spine accordingly. Marla held out her tricorder, recording Khan's speech. Huang stumbled forward to the front of the crowd, seemingly drawn by Khan's stirring oratory. He nodded solemnly, hanging on his commander's every word. "Yes, Your Excellency," he murmured. "As you command."

Suzette Ling, on the other hand, appeared bereft of hope, despite Khan's rhetoric. "But how can we begin again?" she asked him despairingly. "We've lost our homes, our food, our friends!"

Joaquin moved to silence his distraught wife, but Khan gestured for him to let her be. Unlike Ericsson's persistent challenges, there was no malice or insubordination in Ling's desperate queries. She spoke from pain, and no doubt fear for her unborn child. She deserved an answer.

"We have no other choice," he told her gently. "We

must rebuild, rise up from these ashes, or all that we have accomplished so far will have been in vain." He raised his voice, knowing Ling's doubts surely lurked within the hearts and minds of the others. "What would you have us do?" he asked the crowd dramatically. "Lie down and die?"

"Yes, Your Excellency," Huang answered unexpectedly. Before Khan's startled eyes, the veteran soldier lay down in the muddy field and closed his eyes. He crossed his arms atop his chest and sank limply into the mucky ash and silt. His jaw dropped open and his breathing slowed, presenting an eerily effective impersonation of a corpse.

Khan was seldom at a loss for words, but found himself momentarily dumbfounded by Huang's bizarre behavior. *What is the meaning of this?* he thought in bewilderment. *Has the man gone completely mad?*

"Enough!" he shouted finally. Frustration won out over confusion in his voice. "Stand up at once."

"Yes, Your Excellency." Calmly, without apparent embarrassment, Huang lifted himself from the ground and stood before Khan. The back of his scalp and jumpsuit were completely caked with mud. Slurries of discolored water streamed down his clothes. "As you command."

"Do you mock me?" Khan asked savagely. He advanced on Huang until his angry face was only centimeters away from the soldier's. "Do you dare?"

Huang flinched in the face of Khan's obvious displeasure. "No, Lord Khan," he insisted. "I only did as you instructed." He raised a hand to his temple and winced in pain. His right cheek began to twitch uncontrollably. "Forgive me, Your Excellency."

Khan's anger was not yet appeased. "Explain yourself!"

"I'm trying, Lord Khan!" Huang said anxiously. "I obeyed all your commands!" He seemed to have trouble speaking. "P-P-Please tell me what you want!"

Khan seized the man's throat, determined to choke a coherent answer from the babbling soldier, but Marla ran forward to intervene. "Khan, wait!" she cried out. "There's something wrong with him. I think he may be sick. Remember that bull at our wedding!"

Khan froze. He suddenly remembered seeing Huang dig his finger into his ear back by the downed axebreakers. The soldier started acting peculiarly right after that, Khan realized.

Another, older memory flashed through his brain: a slime-covered eel wriggling out of the ear of the insane bison. The bull's autopsy, revealing the parasitic nature of its relationship with the eel larva, had been distasteful, but Khan had never suspected that an eel could infest a human's brain as well!

He let go of Huang, who dropped slackly onto his knees. Glassy eyes stared at a muddy puddle in front of him. His jaw sagged open and a trickle of saliva dripped from the corner of his mouth. Khan found it hard to believe that this same man had once single-handedly repelled a team of Russian commandos. Had an alien larva succeeded where the Russians had failed?

It seemed that another danger, besides starvation, now lurked in the ruins of Ceti Alpha V.

16

Khan stood upon the riverbank, contemplating his domain.

The omnipresent clouds of ash had thinned at last, although it was difficult to tell given the sheer amount of dust and grit blown about by the constant winds. As they had discovered in the long months since the cataclysm, Ceti Alpha V's very orbit and rotation had shifted, bringing both shorter days and perpetual gales. The latter scoured the devastated landscape day and night, hastening the rapid deterioration of the ecosystem.

Is the entire planet dying, Khan could not help wondering, *or just this particular region?*

The once-mighty Kaur was now a dying stream,

which seemed to grow smaller and shallower each time Khan and his people came in search of water. Sparse vegetation grew along the edges of the stream, sprouting up through the crumbling skeleton of a dead super-crocodile. Khan could see the formerly fertile valley turning into a desert before his very eyes. *"Regions of sorrow, doleful shades,"* he mused, after Milton, *"where peace and rest can never dwell. . . ."*

Such was Ceti Alpha V becoming.

Beneath him, in the deepening gorge, a party of colonists secured fresh supplies of water. Empty turtle shells, left behind by their possibly extinct former owners, served as convenient containers. Like Khan himself, the water-bearers were swathed in overlapping layers of heavy fabric, so that they resembled desert bedouins. Every square centimeter of their skin was carefully covered, and the ends of his headcloth, or kaffiyeh, were wrapped tightly around his face and neck. Makeshift visors, composed of volcanic obsidian, painstakingly polished by hand, hid their eyes.

How cruelly ironic, Khan reflected. Back on Earth, in the final days of his reign, he had attempted to destroy the planet's ozone layer in a pyrrhic act of revenge against a world that had spitefully rejected his benevolent rule. In the end, he had ultimately opted to spare Earth, choosing exile in the *Botany Bay* instead, but it seemed that his intended sins had come back to haunt him nonetheless. Since Ceti Alpha VI exploded, it had become evident that the disaster had shredded its sister planet's ozone layer, exposing at least this portion of the planet to fierce ultraviolet rays that further ravaged what life remained. Khan and the other castaways had been forced to shield themselves from the sun in order to avoid the cancer and blindness that had already afflicted some of their companions.

Was there merely a hole in the ozone layer above them, such as once formed above Antarctica, or was the whole world similarly undefended? If the latter, Khan feared what the ultraviolet barrage could be doing to the entirety of Ceti Alpha V's native fauna and flora. Suppose the UV rays killed off the tiny phytoplankton at the base of the marine food chain? The planet's teeming oceans could soon become a vast aquatic graveyard, just as its land-based plants and animals appeared to be going the way of Earth's dinosaurs.

Khan was well familiar with doomsday scenarios, having devised more than a few of them himself. But how far beyond the distant horizon did the devastation truly extend?

Soon, he resolved, *I must seek answers to these questions.*

A cloaked figure trudged up the sandy slope. Khan recognized Joaquin from his stature and lumbering gait, as well by the rifle strapped to his shoulder. The weapon was wrapped in plastic sheeting, in a possibly vain attempt to keep the sand from getting into the precious firearm. "The water canisters are filled, Lord Khan," he announced.

"Excellent," Khan stated approvingly. "Let us not linger then. I have seen enough of this wasteland today."

The trek back to their new home was a long and wearisome one. The original site of New Chandigarh, now cruelly exposed to the elements, had long since been abandoned in favor of the primeval caverns, which provided better protection from the unrelenting wind and radiation. All that survived of their old settlement was the surprisingly durable cargo carriers, which now rested at the bottom of a rocky hollow above a newly carved cave entrance. The bulky metal compartments had been transported, via backbreaking labor, to this new site, which provided (relatively) easy access to the vast warren of tunnels and grottoes beneath the surface.

The colonists called their new home Fatalis, after the sabertooths who had once made it their lair. The name had an appropriately foreboding ring to it.

Khan opened the door to the nearest cargo bay, letting the heavily laden water-bearers enter first, before stepping inside and sealing the door behind him. Along with the others, he shed his protective outerwear, revealing a faded red coverall patched with bits of animal hide, electrical cable, and insulation; as their original clothing slowly disintegrated, the castaways' attire was increasingly becoming a hodgepodge affair held together by whatever scraps could be salvaged from the ruins of the original colony. With every day, he and his people were looking less like pioneers and more like barbarians.

He kept his right glove on.

Descending a ladder into the caverns below, Khan was greeted by a guardsman bearing grim news. "Welcome back, Your Excellency," the sentinel said. Cataracts had invaded his left eye, leaving him half blind. "Dr. Hawkins requests your presence at the infirmary." He shook his head gloomily. "Dumas is in a bad way, I'm afraid."

No doubt, Khan thought sourly. He expected woeful tidings; it was positive news that came as a surprise these days. Despair and self-pity threatened to unman him. *Must I be confronted with fresh tragedy within seconds of my return? Can I not savor a moment's surcease from sorrow?* Responsibility overcame exhaustion, however, and he nodded in acknowledgment. "Very well. I shall seek out the doctor at once."

He would have preferred to reunite with Marla first, but apparently that was not to be. Accompanied by Joaquin, he headed straight for the subterranean infirmary, where he found Hawkins kneeling at the side of Marcel Dumas, the latest victim of the dreaded Ceti eel.

Khan saw at once that Dumas was in the final stages of dementia. The former speechwriter and propagandist thrashed wildly upon the floor of the cavern, his arms and limbs tightly bound by leather straps skinned from the hide of a dead bison. Insanity contorted the Frenchman's once-handsome features into a grotesque mask. Foam spewed from the man's twisted lips. Bloody veins inflamed maniacal eyes. Inarticulate grunts and moans echoed off the cavern walls.

Sadly, Khan had seen such symptoms many times before. As the bison had vanished into extinction, the eels had swiftly sought out new hosts for their young— namely the hard-pressed colonists. Somewhere deep inside Dumas's brain, Khan knew, a growing eel was coiled around the man's cerebral cortex, exerting an ever-increasing pressure. "I take it, Doctor, your treatments have proven unsuccessful once again."

Hawkins wiped his forehead with the back of his

hand while he inserted a protective rubber tile between Dumas's teeth. "I've tried herbs, spinal massage, even acupuncture," he lamented, "but nothing has expelled the parasite or alleviated the symptoms. If I was back on Earth, I could attempt radiation or brain surgery, but under these conditions?" He threw up his hands. "Nothing awaits Dumas but a slow and agonizing death."

"I understand," Khan said. Without further discussion, he reached down and placed the palm of his gloved hand over Dumas's mouth and nostrils. He clamped down firmly, cutting off the flow of air to the man's lungs. Dumas's bound body jerked briefly, then fell still.

Khan removed his hand. He rose from the dead man's side, then waited patiently for Dumas's killer to flee his cooling corpse. Within minutes, a slime-covered eel emerged from the victim's ear canal and wriggled onto the floor of the cavern. Khan allowed himself a thin smile as he crushed the vile mollusk beneath the heel of his boot.

There was no need to preserve the creature. Hawkins already had plenty of specimens to study. Counting Huang, the first victim, Khan had lost seven followers to the eels since the disaster a year ago. Another three colonists had succumbed to disease and skin cancer, leaving behind only fifty remaining adults, plus a handful of underfed infants. Khan wondered morbidly where the eels would plant their insidious offspring should the rest of the colony join the bison in oblivion.

The castaways had taken to sleeping with wads of material stuffed in their ears, but still the eels managed to claim a new victim every few months. Dissection of captured eels revealed that they appeared to be subsisting on minute traces of organic matter left behind by the mass extinction, as well as raw nitrates and other substances. Khan suspected that the widespread ash and dirt still contained a few microscopic extremophiles, such as Earth's near-indestructible tardigrades, that perhaps served as food for the deadly eels, while the colonists themselves provided hosts for the next generation of parasites.

Khan gazed down at the latest fatality. It was Dumas, he recalled, who had drafted the official denials whenever Khan's political enemies accused him of plotting to conquer mankind. That these denials were utter fabrications did not diminish his service to Khan's cause.

"Remove his brain for your research," Khan instructed Hawkins coldly. "Have the rest of him taken to the fertilizer pits."

Alas, he couldn't even offer Dumas a decent burial or cremation. Like the rest of their dead, his remains would be composted to provide nutrients for Fatalis's struggling underground gardens. "I will extend my condolences to his widow."

As always, his mind added darkly. Paying his respects to grieving spouses was another duty he had become far too familiar with. His memory summoned a picture of Dumas's wife: a military strategist named Savine. *I shall visit her shortly*, he vowed, *but not right away*.

First, he would find Marla. He needed to see his own wife again, if only as a relief from the never-ending death and decay. "If that will be all, Doctor," he informed Hawkins, "I will take my leave."

Knowing there was nothing more he could do here, Khan left the doctor with his lifeless patient. Joaquin followed him dutifully as he traversed the winding tunnels, which were lit by flickering torches and the occasional patch of phosphorescent mold. Although a few generators and power cell rechargers had survived within the impervious cargo bays, electricity was too precious to waste on mere illumination, except here and there.

As they traveled, Khan heard stone axes and picks chipping away at the surrounding limestone, as a team of workers sweated to expand and improve upon their underground habitat. The smell of unwashed bodies permeated the closely packed catacombs. At times the corridors were so narrow that only a single individual could pass through them at a time. Deferential colonists stepped aside, or backed up entirely, to allow Khan and his bodyguard to proceed unhindered. Joaquin ducked his head to avoid scraping his skull on a low-hanging ceiling.

They passed the armory, where the colony's dwindling supply of guns and ammunition was kept under twenty-four-hour guard. Although most of their ammo had been destroyed when New Chandigarh burned to the ground, roughly half a dozen guns and rifles had survived. Khan hoped someday to manufacture fresh ammunition for the weapons, but, for the time being, food and water took priority over munitions.

A pang of hunger struck Khan, and he searched his pockets for what remained of his day's rations. He found only a gnawed-upon piece of dry sabertooth jerky and a small ball of rice. His stomach groaned as he considered his meager fare. Saving the rice for later, he chewed on the jerky to dull his hunger.

It didn't work.

A year after the destruction of their crops, the colony was barely getting by. The cyclonic winds and UV radiation made farming on the surface impossible, even if all the arable soil hadn't already dried up and blown away. Furthermore, in a fiendish irony, the most successful survivors of the disaster—the Ceti eels—were too indigestible to eat. The castaways' only hope for sustenance came from growing limited quantities of hand-pollinated Terran crops underground, using Starfleet-provided "plasma lights" in lieu of sunlight. A battered portable generator provided just enough electricity to keep the subterranean gardens viable, while the colony's few surviving protein resequencers allowed them to satisfy their most basic nutritional requirements.

Thank the Fates, he thought, *that we managed to find enough seeds beneath the burned-out fields to keep going.* He and many others had dug beneath the charred crops and volcanic ash with their bare hands in search of scorched kernels of corn and seedlings of rice, while every available man and woman had carted armloads of dead wildlife and flora back to the caves for composting. *It is a miracle that we have managed to cultivate any fresh food at all*, Khan reflected. He doubted that mere ordinary humans could have done the same.

Except for Marla, of course.

He found her, as he expected, at Fatalis's nursery, in a relatively cozy grotto whose vaulted ceiling had been meticulously pruned of any threatening stalactites. Empty storage bins had been converted into cradles for roughly a dozen precocious infants, who were already developing at an accelerated rate. Wire mesh, recycled from the fence that had once surrounded New Chandigarh, was stretched over the tops of the cradles in hopes of protecting the babies from lurking eels, although Khan placed rather more faith in the constant vigilance of Marla and her staff. He marveled that so many children had managed to survive so far. *Only their superior genetics*, he theorized, *have allowed them to endure such harsh conditions.*

Marla looked up as he and Joaquin entered the grotto. A drowsy infant was nestled in her arms, while the tattered remains of Khan's golden Nehru jacket was draped over her shoulders. Her eyes lighted up at the sight of her husband. "Khan! You're back."

"Indeed," he assured her. "Know that I will always return to you."

Marla strolled past a row of improvised cradles to join them. "Good afternoon, Joaquin." She handed the baby in her arms over to the towering bodyguard. "Say hello to your son."

"Hello, Joachim," Joaquin said gruffly. A rare smile appeared upon his stolid features as the baby gripped his thumb with a tiny fist. "You feel strong today. Good."

The blond, blue-eyed infant bore little resemblance to either Joaquin or Suzette Ling. Curiously, as an unforeseen side effect of the genetic tinkering that had performed on their parents, all of the colony's children had been born blond and Caucasian, regardless of their parents' ancestry. "Shades of *The Midwich Cuckoos*," Daniel Katzel had commented upon the birth of the first batch of babies, referring to one of his favorite science fiction novels. Khan could not help wondering what his own mother, the Sikh scientist responsible for the Chrysalis Project, would have had to say about this peculiar development; no doubt she never intended the second generation of superhumans to resemble the results of a Nazi breeding program. . . .

"Shirin delivered a fresh supply of water earlier," Marla informed Khan. Her Starfleet medallion dangled on a chain around her neck. "I'm glad the expedition to the river went well. We needed the water badly, for the nursing mothers as well as the babies."

The nursery was Marla's domain, where she and a small, rotating staff watched over the Grandchildren of Chrysalis while their overworked parents strained to eke out a living beneath the ground. Marla ran the nursery with energy and enthusiasm, even though (or perhaps because) she had not yet borne a child of her own, nor even succeeded in becoming pregnant.

Reluctantly, Khan had begun to suspect that Marla's unrefined DNA was incompatible with his own. *A pity*, he thought, although his regret was tinged with relief. In a colony with better prospects, Marla's inability to produce an heir would have posed a significant problem; under the circumstances, however, Khan thought it almost better not to bring another innocent child into the abysmal purgatory Ceti Alpha V had become.

His gaze drifted to rows and rows of populated

cradles. Here was the future of his people, if any such thing existed. A high-pitched wail rose from a steel bin and a tired-looking colonist hurried to check on the cradle's small occupant.

What sort of world would these children inherit? Khan somberly looked ahead, searching for a way to provide the next generation with a less precarious existence.

It was clear that Kaur River Valley held little promise for his people; desertification was proceeding apace and he could all too easily foresee a day when the former grasslands would become as dry and inhospitable as the Sahara. *We must seek out greener pastures,* he realized, *but where?*

He smiled sadly at Marla, knowing he would soon have to leave her again. Her flowing hair and chestnut eyes called out to him, as did the gentleness of her touch. He was not eager to tear himself away from her, for who knew how long, but his mind was made up.

There can be no more delay, he vowed. *I must leave this place—and learn what has become of the rest of the world.*

For better or for worse.

17

"Sandstorm!"

The small expedition, which consisted of Khan, Joaquin, Ericsson, Keith Talbot, and an experienced cartographer named Debra VonLinden, had been following the dwindling Kaur toward the sea, where Khan hoped to find a safe harbor for his people, in more ways than one. So far, however, all they had discovered was kilometer after kilometer of dried-up grasslands, whose once-loamy soil was now barely held in place by the dying foliage. The savanna was evolving into a desert, with all its attendant dangers. . . .

Ericsson's cry jolted the party, which had already been battling wind and sand for days now; Khan found it difficult to envision what constituted a storm in this hellish environment. Were they not already trapped in a tempest without end?

Still, his visored eyes saw what Ericsson saw: an opaque black cloud rolling across the floor of the desert at an incredible speed. Heat lightning flashed in its wake.

"Link arms!" he called out, with only moments to spare before the storm was upon them. Throwing his wooden staff to the ground, he hastily hooked his elbows around those of Joaquin and Talbot, while Ericsson and VonLinden formed a chain connected to Joaquin. "Hold on! Do not let yourself be separated from the group!"

The sandstorm struck with the force of a monsoon, almost knocking Khan off his feet. In an instant, visibility was reduced to less than a meter. Despite his protective burnoose and headcloth, the abrasive wind and sand pummeled him mercilessly. Every minute tear or aperture in his desert garb was invaded by jets of flying grit that scoured his skin raw. More sand made it past his visor, forcing him to squeeze his eyes tightly shut. Ducking his head as much as he could, he breathed shallowly through his nose while keeping his jaws clenched together to keep from choking to death.

The roar of the storm was deafening, making speech impossible even if he dared to open his mouth. Khan fought to maintain his footing, and to hold on to the rest of the expedition, who were, quite literally, being sandblasted where they stood.

We must make for higher ground, he decided. The individual sand grains propelled themselves by bouncing off the desert floor; perhaps it was possible to get above the densest portion of the storm. *Even the slight-*

est degree of relief might make the difference between life and death!

He remembered seeing a steep rise in the riverbank perhaps five meters to the left. Trusting his memory, he tugged on his companions and began marching in what he prayed was the right direction. The wind and sand hit them crossways, making progress difficult and navigation all but impossible. Khan believed he was trudging toward the eastern bank of the riverbed, but could not be certain that the relentless pressure of the storm had not already driven them off course.

To his relief, the parched ground beneath his feet began to slope upward . . . an encouraging sign. Half-guiding, half-dragging his companions, Khan made it a couple of steps up the sharply angled grade before disaster struck.

Talbot slipped, nearly pulling Khan down with him. Khan tried to yank the other man back onto his feet, only to feel Talbot's arm begin to slip away from him. Khan almost lost hold of him entirely, but, at the last minute, the stumbling man grabbed on to Khan's wrist. *Hold on!* Khan commanded silently; he had no desire to inform Zuleika Walker that he had lost her husband. *Hold on for your life!*

In the commotion, however, Talbot's kaffiyeh came loose, giving the homicidal storm the opportunity it needed. The wind stripped the protective headcloth from Talbot's face, and he let out a horrendous scream as the razor-sharp sand abraded his exposed flesh. Instinctively, he let go of Khan's wrist in order to throw his hands in front of his face.

"No!" Khan shouted, receiving a mouthful of grit. He reached frantically for the endangered colonist, but the storm drove them apart in a matter of heartbeats. At once, Talbot was completely lost to sight.

Grief, and an excruciating sense of failure, jabbed Khan's heart. He knew better than to chase after Talbot. There could be no hope of finding him in the middle of a sandstorm; Khan would only be risking the rest of the expedition by doing so. Reluctantly, he returned to climbing the slope before him, using his now-free hand to help assist his ascent. He could feel Joaquin's weight pulling on his other arm, and he hoped with all his heart that Ericsson and VonLinden were still linked to Joaquin and each other in turn.

Slowly, fighting the storm with every step, they reached the top of the bluff, which, if not entirely free of the battering wind and sand, at least seemed to be above the worst of the tumult. The wind was still just as ferocious, but the churning sand was a few degrees thinner, making it a little easier to breathe. The surviving explorers huddled together atop the rise, turning their backs to the storm as they leaned on each other to anchor themselves against the gale.

We may survive this yet, Khan realized. *And all it cost was the life of a loyal follower.*

In the end, the storm vanished as swiftly as it had arrived. Squinting through his visor, Khan watched the deadly black cloud roll northward, shrinking in the distance as it left them behind. With luck, the storm would dissipate long before it reached the vicinity of Marla and the others, who, in any event, were hopefully safe beneath the earth in their underground sanctuary.

Such sandstorms, he suspected, would soon become a way of life upon these dying plains. *All the more reason to seek out a less inhospitable environment elsewhere.*

A dusty haze still swirled in the air, but Khan judged it safe to move on. After all, this was about as clear as the weather ever got these days. Gesturing for the others to follow him, he cautiously descended back toward what remained of the River Kaur. The heels of his boots caused avalanches of freshly deposited sand to flow in rivulets toward the floor of the riverbed. Reddish brown dust coated everything in sight, from jutting stones to patches of scraggly brush. Even the silty stream seemed muddier than before.

Khan felt the effects of the storm as well. Beneath his robes, his skin felt sandpapered. Irritating granules of grit infiltrated every crack and wrinkle in his body. His mouth tasted of dirt, and he would have killed for a glass of clear, cool water.

They found Talbot about seven meters from the bottom of the incline. His body lay sprawled upon the ground, half-buried in fresh sand. His face was raw and bleeding and caked with dust. More sand poured from the dead man's mouth and nostrils; Khan did not need to perform an autopsy to deduce that Talbot's windpipe, and perhaps even his lungs, were clogged with sand.

Forgive me, Zuleika. Your husband shall not be returning to you.

I wonder if any of us shall.

Only days away from Fatalis, and they were already one man down. The expedition was off to a bad start. . . .

"Perhaps we should turn back?" Ericsson suggested. His Scandinavian accent was muffled by the folds of his kaffiyeh. The blackened lens of his visor concealed his scheming blue eyes.

Khan bristled at the suggestion, but resisted the temptation to lash out at the other man. He had, as was his custom, brought Ericsson along to keep him from stirring up trouble in Khan's absence. He was willing to squash Ericsson once and for all, if necessary, but so far the Norseman had managed to steer clear of any outright insubordination. Perhaps because only Khan and Joaquin were equipped with rifles.

"Go back to what?" VonLinden answered harshly. The mapmaker had lost both her spouse and her child to the Ceti eels. "I have nothing to return to."

Khan made the decision for them all. "No," he said firmly. To return to the caverns now, without discovering a new home for their people, was to condemn the entire colony to a hopeless existence beneath an expanding wasteland. "We will continue onward as planned."

His hope was that his people could build a new life upon the shore of the unnamed sea to the south, where they might be able to survive by fishing or whaling. Certainly, the history of their homeworld was full of peoples and cultures who had thrived in proximity to the sea. Even if the surface of Ceti Alpha V had been laid waste, Khan dared to dream that the planet's oceans still held enough life to sustain a growing colony.

Not New Chandigarh, he mused, *but perhaps New Mumbai or Goa.*

"But—" Ericsson began to protest. He looked to Von-Linden for support, but the shrouded widow shrugged fatalistically. Joaquin remained mute, his obedience to Khan's will beyond question. Realizing he was outnumbered, Ericsson wisely curtailed his objections. "Very well, Your Excellency," he surrendered, with only a hint of rancor in his voice.

That left only Talbot to be dealt with.

"Strip him," Khan ordered, nodding toward the corpse. They could not afford to sacrifice a single item of food, equipment, or clothing, even if that meant that Talbot must go to his eternal reward as naked as a newborn babe. Still, Khan resolved to see the man's body decently cremated before they moved on.

It was the least he could do for one who died under his command. *Rest in peace, my servant. Your part in our long ordeal is over.*

Ericsson knelt to claim Talbot's possessions and supplies. A gloved hand touched the dead man's sand-flayed countenance and a drop of blood attached itself to his fingertip. He lifted the finger before him and paused, contemplating the glistening crimson bead for several long seconds. "Lord Khan," he said at last, "I hesitate to even suggest this, but, with food and drink in such dangerously short supply, I feel compelled to point out that, just perhaps, our departed comrade can provide one last, life-sustaining service for us all."

Khan realized at once what Ericsson was suggesting. Anger flared within him and he savagely kicked the kneeling man in the ribs. "Never speak of such things again!" Khan snarled. Beneath his visor and kaffiyeh, Khan's face recoiled in disgust. "Castaways we may be, desperate and forlorn, but cannibals? Never!"

In truth, the awful possibility Ericsson alluded to had haunted Khan's mind for months, ever since the cataclysm first threatened them all with famine. But he had resolved, firmly and irrevocably, that some things were worse than starvation. He and his people were a superior breed, the next stage in human evolution, and they would not debase themselves by sinking to such primitive depravity.

I have been called ruthless, Khan reflected, *and with good reason. But there are some lines I will not cross!*

Clutching his side, Ericsson scrambled away from Khan's wrath. "Forgive me," he pleaded. "I didn't mean to offend. The sand . . . the wind . . . I wasn't myself, believe me!"

Khan stared at the backpedaling Norseman with contempt. It was one thing to entertain such a hideous notion in the dark night of one's own soul, but to actually suggest such a thing . . .

If only Ericsson had died in the storm instead!

"I can't believe you're trying to steal vital resources from sick people!"

Gideon Hawkins' indignant voice rang out across the nursery, threatening naptime for any number of infants. Marla winced at the noise.

"Dying people, you mean!" Suzette Ling retorted. "My security teams are too thirsty and hungry to do their jobs properly, yet we're still wasting precious food and water on invalids who already have one foot in the grave!"

High-pitched squeals erupted from the nearby cradles, much to Marla's annoyance. "That's enough!" she told the quarreling colonists. She clicked off her tricorder. "Let's take this elsewhere before you wake up the entire nursery."

Leaving the crying babies in the charge of her staff, Marla led the doctor and the security chief into an adjacent grotto, about the size of a turbolift. With any luck, the thick limestone walls would keep the argument from spreading out into the rest of Fatalis. "All right," she said, reactivating the tricorder in order to record the debate; Khan would want to know what took place in his absence. *Good thing I just recharged the power cell*, she thought. "What's all this about dying people?"

This wasn't the first dispute she'd had to arbitrate since Khan left her in charge of the colony weeks ago. Marla was starting to feel like a substitute teacher, constantly being tested by a classroom of unruly students. *Ah, for the good old days, when nobody ever wanted to speak to me . . . !*

She never thought she'd miss being persona non grata.

"Not all my patients are terminal," Hawkins insisted. "Most are merely suffering from infection or malnutrition, but they certainly won't recover without adequate rations of food and water." He glared at Ling, who had started this fracas by asking Marla to divert extra rations to her security patrol instead. "This is just like you mili-

tary types, always placing 'security' above health care."
He laughed derisively. "Security! Who the hell are we at
war with on this godforsaken planet?"

"The eels!" Ling shot back. "As you should know
better than anyone else." The severed pincers of over a
dozen dead eels adorned Ling's ragtag garments, like
medals won in combat. "I have teams of searchers
combing the tunnels for eels night and day, but they
need to be sharp, alert—not groggy from hunger and
dehydration."

The Asian security chief looked to Marla for support,
a smugly confident look upon her face. Marla sometimes suspected that Ling had married Joaquin primar-
ily because of the bodyguard's close ties to Khan. She
probably expected that connection to give her an edge.

Forget it, Marla thought. Khan had entrusted her with
leadership of Fatalis in his absence and she intended to
be scrupulously fair and evenhanded, much as Captain
Kirk had been back on the *Enterprise.* "Perhaps we can
work out a compromise here."

"A compromise?" Ling echoed incredulously. Both
she and Hawkins looked extremely dubious.

No surprise there. Marla had already discovered that
the hardest part of governing a colony of genetically
engineered supermen and superwomen was managing
their conflicting egos; these were not people accustomed
to accommodating the opinions of others. *Small wonder
the Eugenics Wars broke out so quickly back in the 1990s,* she
reflected; it took a personality as large as Khan's to get
any amount of superior humans to work together without conflict.

Despite her supposed "inferiority," Marla suspected that she had better people skills than most of the imperious Children of Chrysalis. *I wonder if that's why Khan left me in charge.*

"I refuse to compromise where my patients' care is concerned," Hawkins blustered, crossing his arms atop his chest. His bloodstained labcoat was stitched together from pieces of a mutilated sleeping bag. A rusty stethoscope dangled around his neck like a tribal talisman.

"You may have to, Doctor," Marla said thoughtfully. Khan's silver dagger, his kirpan, was thrust into Marla's belt as a symbol of Khan's authority; at times like this Marla would have preferred a working phaser pistol. "Every unit in Fatalis is strapped for resources, not just Medical and Security. Farming, childcare, construction, water-gathering . . . these are all essential functions, too." She shook her head sadly. "We have to make hard choices every day."

"On Khan's orders, I'm already euthanizing the eel victims as soon as they're diagnosed," Hawkins pointed out unhappily. "Don't ask me to starve my other patients, too."

Marla felt a pang of sympathy for the besieged doctor, who reminded her somewhat of Dr. McCoy. Ceti Alpha V would be hell for any conscientious healer. So many patients lost, so little that could be done to help them.

Still, Ling, despite her irritating sense of entitlement, had a point. It was important to keep the most productive members of the colony safe, and every eel Ling and her people caught might mean one less hopeless case in the infirmary.

"Here's what I suggest," Marla declared, looking the doctor in the eye. "I'm sorry, but you're going to have to perform triage even more strictly. Cut the rations of the patients least likely to recover by thirty percent."

"Thirty percent!" Hawkins exclaimed. "That's barbaric."

We're living in caves, haven't you noticed? A humorless smile lifted the corners of Marla's lips. *Barbaric is standard operating procedure. . . .*

She held up her hand to forestall further discussion, then turned her gaze on Ling. "But you have to give up something, too," Marla told the other woman. "In exchange for the extra rations, you're going to give the infirmary increased priority. I want the main grotto and all side chambers swept for eels every forty-eight hours."

"Forty-eight hours?" Ling stared at Marla as though she had lost her mind. "You've got to be joking!"

"Take it or leave it," Marla said bluntly. She knew that if she didn't extract some sort of concessions from Ling, she'd have every team leader in Fatalis demanding extra rations before nightfall. "Or, if you prefer, you can take this matter up with Khan when he returns."

"If he returns," Ling muttered.

"When he returns," Marla insisted. She rested her sweaty palm on the hilt of Khan's dagger. At the back of her mind was the unsettling awareness that the other woman could break her in two if she wanted. "If that's all for now, I still have work to do in the nursery— including looking after Joachim," she added pointedly.

Neither Ling nor the doctor appeared entirely happy with the compromise, but, to Marla's relief, neither seemed inclined to push their luck further. She waited until both parties exited the small grotto, then slumped limply against the cold stone wall. Pent-up tension leaked away, leaving her feeling completely drained.

Where are you, Khan? she wondered anxiously. She switched off the tricorder, just in case it was running out of juice, too. *I can't keep doing this without you.* Ling's implication, that they might never see Khan again, had shaken Marla more than she had let on. She drew the kirpan from her belt and stared at it with melancholy yearning. The metal dagger felt very heavy in her hand.

Come back to me, Khan. Please.

18

Khan rose before dawn, then roused the others. His bones and muscles ached from a long night spent sleeping upon the rough earth, with only his desert robes to cushion him. "It is time," he croaked tersely, his mouth too dry to say more. Thirst and hunger consumed his thoughts.

Groaning, Ericsson and the rest climbed to their feet. They shook their burnooses thoroughly, just in case a Ceti eel had slithered into their cloaks sometime during the night. Thick wads of recycled insulation were extracted from their ears and carefully inspected for signs of larvae. Khan did the same, before staggering down into the empty riverbed; he had insisted that they always sleep above the former banks of the Kaur, so as to be prepared in the (highly) unlikely event that a flash flood came rushing down the bone-dry arroyo.

The Kaur itself was no more. Rather than stretching all the way to the sea, the once-mighty river had gradually dwindled away to nothingness, finally disappearing entirely into the rocky floor of a desiccated gully. Khan and the rest of the expedition had left the last pathetic trickle behind days ago, but Khan knew that there might still be some moisture lurking beneath the arroyo—if he and the others moved quickly enough.

His gloved fingers dug into the parched earth, taking hold of a large stone and turning it over. As expected, a thin layer of moisture clung to the underside of the rock. Khan pulled open his headcloth beneath his visor and gratefully licked the pre-morning dew from the stone.

It was an old Bedouin trick, one that had kept him alive since the Kaur expired and their canteens went dry. Khan savored every drop, knowing that it might well be the only water he drank all day. He licked the stone dry, then looked around for another rock.

Nearby, the other explorers emulated Khan. They dug in the dirt silently, needing neither conversation nor instruction. At this point, they all knew the routine by heart. Khan watched as Debra VonLinden sucked the dew off the scraggly branches of a leafless bush. Joaquin let out a grunt of satisfaction, and Khan saw that the bodyguard had managed to capture a small lizard by the tail. *Excellent*, Khan thought approvingly. The lizard's meat and blood were worth its weight in gold; upon such scavenging did the expedition depend for their very existence. Khan shuddered, imagining their situation years hence, when and if the rats and lizards died out completely.

They had been traveling for weeks, and their original provisions had long since been consumed. Insects, reptiles, and small rodents provided their only meals, while dew, blood, and the occasional small waterhole served to slake their thirst—at least enough to survive. Khan was glad, however, that he had left Marla behind; no ordinary mortal could have endured such extreme deprivation.

What is Kirk eating now? he wondered enviously. *The* Enterprise's *convenient food slots had offered all manner of tempting dishes and libations, from fine wine and cuisine to cups of ice-cold chai. . . .*

Joaquin snapped the lizard's neck, then dutifully offered it to his commander. Khan's mouth watered at the sight of the uncooked reptile, but he waved it aside. There was meat enough for only one person upon the lizard's frame, and Joaquin deserved it as much as he. "It is yours, my friend," Khan insisted. "Enjoy it. I can find my own meals."

Easier said than done, he added privately. His stomach felt as empty as that of a Calcutta beggar. *But perhaps luck will be with me today.* Through the visor, his dark eyes searched the arid gully for any hint of wildlife. Patches of scrub sprouted from the floor of the arroyo, while bright yellow streaks hinted at sulfur deposits, yet Khan detected not a flicker of movement, not even the furtive stirring of an (inedible) eel. Fresh meat, it seemed, was not on the menu this morning.

"Khan!" Ericsson called out abruptly. Khan was startled by the obvious excitement in the man's voice. Ericsson was practically hopping where he stood, pointing eagerly to the west. "Look . . . rain!"

Rain? Khan could not believe his ears; he had almost forgotten such a phenomenon existed. Rising to his feet, he looked intently to the west, expecting to see nothing more than an obvious mirage. He felt another surge of anger toward the Norseman. *How dare he raise our hopes in this manner!*

But Ericsson was not mistaken. On the horizon, roughly two kilometers away, a pendulous gray cloud hovered over the withered landscape. Khan could see dark sheets of rain pouring down beneath the cloud. Compared to the scant moisture provided by the dew-coated rocks, the distant deluge looked like salvation itself.

Khan was not willing to wait to see if the rain would come their way. Instead he ran up the western bank of the arroyo, clutching his empty canteen as he did so. "After me!" he exhorted the others, who required little prodding to race toward the beckoning rain. Four pairs of dusty boots smacked against the crumbling earth as the party sprinted frantically across the desert as fast as their depleted bodies would allow. Khan could not tear his gaze away from the miraculous rainfall, terrified that the downpour would cease before they got there. His heart pounded, his lungs burned, and his legs ached from the punishing pace, but he never once thought about slowing down. The skeleton of a gigantic saber-tooth appeared in his path, but Khan leaped over the sun-bleached bones in a single bound. Reaching the rain was all that mattered.

At last, after an exhausting run through the wind and the dust, the weeping cloud filled the sky only a few meters away. Summoning up one last burst of speed, he dashed beneath the cloud, then skidded to a stop. He turned his face and open hands upward to greet the falling rain. He licked his chapped lips in anticipation of the cool, refreshing water striking his face.

But not a drop did he feel.

He blinked in confusion. *What cruel joke is this?* Peering upward through the obsidian lenses of his visor, he could see the rain issuing from the bottom of the billowing cloud, but the ground and air around him remained as dry as the barren plains they had crossed to get here. Khan glanced about him at his equally confounded followers. Although the upper halves of their faces were concealed by their visors, Khan could see confused frustration twist their mouths into grotesque expressions. "I don't understand!" VonLinden cried out, with an edge of hysteria. "What's happening? Why can't I feel the rain?"

Khan grasped the truth. "Phantom rain," he said bleakly, familiar with the concept even if he had never witnessed the phenomenon in person. "The rain is falling, yes, but it is evaporating before it hits the ground."

He could not think of a more sadistic twist of fate.

"*Helvete!*" Ericsson swore vehemently. Bent over, gasping for breath, he still managed to spew an impressive stream of obscenities in his native tongue. He angrily hurled his canteen at the uncaring cloud, but his throw fell far short of its target and the hollow canteen clattered to earth several meters away.

A few paces away, Joaquin said nothing, but his meaty fists were clenched tightly at his side.

They stood for several minutes in the shadow of the cloud, watching the phantom rain streak the sky many kilometers above them, maddeningly out of reach. Khan raged silently at whatever malignant gods or spirits governed Ceti Alpha V. *Better to see no rain at all,* he brooded, *than to be tormented so!*

He forced himself to look away from the tantalizing cloudburst overhead, turning to look back the way they had come. Exhausted by their headlong, and ultimately fruitless, stampede across the desert, he dreaded hiking back to the faraway arroyo.

They had no other choice, though. Although the Kaur no longer stretched all the way to the sea, Khan still intended to follow its former path to the end, no matter how long it took and how many rocks he had to lick to stay alive.

"Come," he informed the others. Retying the loose ends of his kaffiyeh beneath his visor, he set out for the dried-out riverbed—and whatever lay at the end of its meandering path. "We have a long way to go."

"We should have stayed on Earth," VonLinden said gloomily. She trudged like a zombie through a narrow defile at the bottom of a deep canyon. Towering granite cliffs hemmed her in on two sides as the expedition trekked single-file through the gorge, still following the path of the extinct river. "We don't belong here."

"Such defeatism is beneath you," Khan reprimanded her. He paused to look back over his shoulder at the three explorers behind him. In their all-concealing robes, the party resembled a procession of hooded specters.

His stern voice echoed off the canyon walls. "It is beneath us all."

His words appeared to strike home. "My apologies, Lord Khan," VonLinden replied. "It is just that I am so hot . . . and tired . . . and hungry."

Khan sympathized with her distress. The temperature had been steadily rising over the last several days, making a hard journey even more torturous. Despite the shade provided by the canyon walls, Khan felt as though he were marching through an oven. Sweat soaked through his dusty garments, wasting moisture he could ill afford to lose. His skin felt dry as parchment, while his sunken eyes were dry and scratchy. A throbbing headache, no doubt induced by fatigue and dehydration, pounded beneath his brow.

"I understand," Khan told the despairing cartographer. Knowing how much she had already lost, he was reluctant to upbraid her further. "But we cannot allow our iron resolve to falter. This planet is our home now, and we must bend it to our will."

Or die trying, he thought to himself.

The uneven ground beneath his boots was studded with jagged boulders; Khan guessed that not long ago, back when the Kaur still flowed freely, foaming rapids had carpeted the floor of the canyon. Now, alas, those turbulent whitecaps were gone, leaving only a rocky obstacle course behind, sloping gradually downward toward the far end of the gorge. A hot wind blew up the canyon, and it required all Khan's discipline not to shrink before the torrid blast. The rustle of the explorers' robes joined the vicious pulsebeat in his ears.

The heat was oppressive enough that Khan had seriously considered traveling by night and sleeping by day. But with the stars still obscured by airborne dust, nights on Ceti Alpha V were perilously dark. It was safer, if infernally more uncomfortable, to cross the blighted land while the sun still shone through the constant haze.

Even in daylight, the rough terrain made hiking difficult. It was necessary to watch one's step carefully, lest one slip and sprain an ankle or worse. Even still, loose rocks often shifted beneath Khan's feet, threatening his balance.

His eyes carefully scanned the canyon floor. A vein of exposed coal reminded Khan of Kirk's encounter with the Gorn on Cestus III. Marla had told Khan of the incident, which had taken place not long before the *Enterprise* discovered the *Botany Bay* floating derelict in space. Khan had to admit that Kirk had shown considerable ingenuity in manufacturing a weapon to defeat the Gorn from the raw materials he found upon the planetoid.

Impressive—for a mere human.

The thought of Kirk brought a scowl to Khan's lips. More and more these days, he found himself blaming the captain for the tragedies that had befallen the colonists. Surely Starfleet's vaunted technology should have warned Kirk that this star system was unstable! Had Kirk merely been criminally negligent, or had he deliberately stranded Khan and the others on a planet faced with imminent disaster? And why had he not returned to rescue the imperiled colony?

Ordinary humans have always feared their superiors, Khan thought darkly. *Perhaps Ceti Alpha V was simply*

Kirk's way of eliminating me and mine without getting his hands dirty?

His dire suspicions were interrupted by the unmistakable sound of waves crashing against breakers. His heart leaped upward. They had reached the sea at last!

"Listen!" he shouted to his fellow explorers. "Can you hear that? Our destination calls to us!"

The joyous news galvanized Joaquin and the others. Forgetting their fatigue, they came running down the gorge faster than Khan would have imagined possible. Their breakneck descent through the rugged pass defied caution, but Khan could not condemn them for their impatience. He shared their eagerness to look upon the fabled shore after so many days of weary journeying. Khan's only regret was that poor Talbot was not there to join in the celebration. *Perhaps I shall name the harbor after him*, Khan thought, *so that his sacrifice will not be forgotten.*

A short run brought Khan to the end of the canyon. He emerged from the defile to find himself at the foot of a monumental cliff, facing a craggy beach upon which pounding green waves crested and ebbed. Beyond the shore, the unnamed ocean stretched for as far as the eye could see, perhaps all the way to the other side of the world.

We made it! Khan exulted. He felt the way Lewis and Clark must have felt when they first viewed the Pacific Ocean. Or perhaps Moses, gazing upon the Promised Land to which he would lead his suffering people.

Behind him, Joaquin, Ericsson, and VonLinden came racing out of the gorge, only to come to a sudden halt at the sight of the ever-rolling waves. "I can't believe it!"

VonLinden exclaimed tearfully. "Look at all that water! It goes on forever!"

"*Milde Makter!*" Ericsson exclaimed. For once, his words seemed to hold no subversive undercurrent. "I thought I'd never see waves again."

Joaquin joined Khan upon the beach. "Your will has triumphed once more," the giant bodyguard said. He dipped his head in respect. "I never doubted you."

Would that I always possessed such confidence, Khan thought. Even now, having reached the end of their long journey, Khan knew that he would not be completely at ease until he had verified that the emerald sea held enough life to sustain his famished people.

His gaze scoured the marine landscape, looking for signs of a thriving, or at least recovering, ecosystem. It concerned him that no avian life-forms populated the dusty sky above the harbor. Where were the gulls or albatrosses diving for fish among the waves? The lack of winged predators did not necessarily mean that the sea was devoid of ready food, but it gave him pause. *Is it possible,* he worried, *that we have come all this way for nothing?*

His worries mounted as he stepped nearer to where the tide beat against the shore. To his dismay, the spray-soaked rocks were free of clinging algae or barnacles. Indeed, the slick, black breakers looked as though they had been assiduously cleansed of every last trace of life. Khan's expression darkened beneath his wrappings. *I do not like the looks of this.*

The sound of racing footsteps seized his attention. He looked up to see Debra VonLinden running recklessly toward the sea. Her eager fingers tore the visor from her

face, then tugged at the folds of her dust-covered kaffiyeh and burnoose as she headed straight for the beckoning waves—and the soothing relief they seemed to
promise.

An overwhelming sense of alarm came over Khan.
"Wait!" he called out urgently, but the heat-crazed colonist
was apparently beyond heeding his strident warning.
"Stop! Halt at once, I command you!"

VonLinden didn't even slow down. Leaving a trail of
ragged fabric behind her, until all she wore was a grimy
cotton shift, she dived headlong into the bright green
waters, immersing herself completely. Khan held his
breath in horrified anticipation. *Perhaps my caution is
unfounded,* he thought anxiously. *Perhaps there is nothing to
fear?*

A moment later, VonLinden rose like Aphrodite from
the surf . . . only screaming in agony.

Khan and the others watched in horror as the
woman's flesh began to bubble and dissolve before their
eyes. Smoky fumes rose from her reddened skin. Her
brunette hair came away from her skull in clumps. She
clutched at her eyes with clawlike fingers and started to
stagger toward the shore, away from the caustic waves
that were eating her alive.

Instinctively, Khan rushed forward to assist her, but
Joaquin held him back. "No, Your Excellency!" he insisted,
determined to keep Khan from sharing VonLinden's fate.
"It is too late for her!"

He spoke the truth. Khan abandoned his effort to
break free of the bodyguard's grip. He knew he could do
nothing but watch another loyal follower die.

VonLinden managed only a step or two before collapsing facefirst into the water, which roiled feverishly around her prone form. Emerald water frothed crimson as the mapmaker's body twitched convulsively, then fell still. Burnt flesh continued to bubble and melt upon her frame, until gleaming shards of bone began to show through.

Khan heard Ericsson vomit onto the beach behind him. As much as he disliked the man, he allowed Ericsson this moment of weakness. Even for one accustomed to violent death, as Khan most assuredly was, he had to concede that VonLinden's final moments had been hideous beyond belief.

Even Joaquin sounded shaken by what he had just witnessed. "I don't understand," he confessed. His usual gruff monotone contained an almost imperceptible tremor. "What happened to her? What is wrong with the sea?"

Khan had already identified VonLinden's killer. "Acid," he intoned. Underwater eruptions, no doubt triggered by the cataclysm, had obviously released enormous quantities of volcanic gases into the ocean, rendering it highly acidic. "The very sea has turned to acid."

He dropped to his knees as the full implications of this revelation sunk in. Debra VonLinden's death, ghastly as it was, was almost inconsequential compared with the true horror of what they had discovered.

This lethal shore held no future for him or his people. The nameless sea was a dead one, murdered by the disaster as surely as the Kaur River Valley had been. *There is no escape*, Khan realized numbly, *from the infernal wasteland Ceti Alpha V is becoming.*

We are trapped in Hell.

"That's it," a sour voice pronounced. Khan turned his head to see Ericsson rising from the rocky beach. A puddle of his own vomit congealed at his feet. "We've reached the end of our rope. We're done for."

"No!" Khan roared. He lunged to his feet and grabbed the collar of Ericsson's burnoose. "This is not the end!" he railed passionately, as much to himself as to the faithless Norseman. "Khan Noonien Singh will never surrender, not to this accursed planet and not to the treacherous vagaries of fate." *Not to mention the shameful neglect of James T. Kirk.*

"Hear me now, Ericsson, you doubting turncoat. I shall show you that the superior man never bends before the cruelties of fate, no matter how hopeless the odds. Let this entire planet die a slow and miserable death. Let Kirk and Starfleet forget us entirely. I will keep you and the rest of my people alive—this I swear upon my sacred honor."

He shook his fist at the dust-shrouded sky.

"Do you hear me, Kirk? *I will survive!*"

19

FOUR PLANETARY YEARS LATER

The enormous salt pan stretched for kilometers in every direction, its crystalline crust crackling beneath Khan's boots as he climbed out of the glittering white depression. A procession of salt-bearers marched behind him, each heavily laden with weighty blocks of salt. Muddy brown sunlight filtered through the perpetual clouds of dust. Fierce winds whipped the ends of the travelers' robes.

Khan reached the southern lip of the pan and shook his head at the dispiriting view that greeted him. A fitting verse resounded in his brain:

"*And yonder before us lie,*

"*Deserts of vast eternity. . . .*"

Five years had passed since the cataclysm, as years

passed on Ceti Alpha V. The once-lush surface of the planet now resembled Earth's Sahara Desert. The River Kaur had dried up completely, leaving behind an arid landscape constantly scoured by gusts of windblown sand and gravel. Swirling dust devils prowled the sandscape, lurking in ambush behind evolving granite formations sculpted by time and erosion. Heat waves shimmered above the barren ground, while shifting dunes were driven hither and yon by the unceasing wind. Far to the north, snowless black peaks jutted above the badlands.

Khan pined for the relative comfort of Fatalis, still three days away by foot. Not for the first time, he longed for camels or horses to ease the difficulty of expeditions such as this one. Alas, as far as he knew, the deadly eels were the only indigenous animals still alive on Ceti Alpha V, aside from whatever microscopic organisms the eels themselves might be feeding upon. *Of all creatures to survive the cataclysm,* he thought ruefully, *why those vile parasites?*

Despite the best efforts of the entire colony, they had lost four children, and at least one adult, to the eels over the last few years. Factoring in additional deaths by disease and accident, Fatalis's total population had been reduced to no more than forty-six adults and perhaps half as many infants and toddlers.

Beneath his kaffiyeh, Khan's scowl deepened. The empire he had hoped to build was shrinking with each passing year.

Just as Kirk had always intended?

His grip tightened around his axebreaker walking

stick, as he imagined the Starfleet captain's throat within his grasp. By now, Khan had abandoned all hope of the *Enterprise* returning to rescue them. Kirk had clearly forgotten the benighted colony, either deliberately or otherwise. At times, Kirk haunted his thoughts; in his bleakest hours, Khan could almost hear Kirk whispering at the back of his mind, mocking him. . . .

A heavy thud interrupted Khan's dour ruminations. He turned to see one of the marchers crouching upon the desert floor. Canvas bags, heavy with life-giving salt, rested upon the rock and sand beside him. "Please," a voice gasped from beneath the wrappings of his head-cloth. "I can't go on. I need to take a break, just for a minute or two."

Khan recognized the voice, and distinctive trappings, of Paul Austin. *Ericsson's crony,* he thought disdainfully. *I might have known.* It seemed that the Norseman and his allies were constantly undercutting his authority, one way or another. *I will have no more of it.*

Angrily, Khan stalked back to where Austin knelt. He resented every step he was forced to backtrack. "Get up!" he commanded the American. A working pistol was hidden beneath the folds of Khan's burnoose, but he had no intention of exposing it to the blowing sand just to threaten one insignificant shirker. "On your feet at once!"

Austin shook his head. "Please, Your Excellency! Just let me rest for a second." His breath came in pants, punctuating his sniveling pleas. "I'm wiped out!"

Khan had no patience for such whining. Every moment's delay kept him away from Fatalis and Marla, and put the caravan at greater risk of being caught in a sandstorm. Austin could not be allowed to get away with his malingering, especially not in front of the other colonists, who were gathering in a circle around Khan and Austin, waiting to see what happened next. Some of them, Khan noted, were already shifting the salt bags from their shoulders, in preparation for sitting down as well.

A few more minutes, and he might have a full-scale mutiny on his hands. . . .

"Get up, I command you!" Khan repeated warningly. Joaquin positioned himself at Khan's right side, adding his own considerable presence to his leader's. "Do not disgrace yourself by behaving as pitifully as a mere human!"

Austin made a pretense of trying to rise, only to drop back onto the ground. "I'm sorry . . . I can't!" He pointed a gloved finger at the canteen dangling from Khan's waist. "Perhaps if I could just have a few drops of water?"

"What? You dare!" Khan could not believe the man's audacity. The caravan's water rations had been carefully calculated to get them to a hot spring several kilometers away, which would provide their next and only chance to refill their canteens before setting off on the final leg of their journey home. "You will drink when I tell you and not before!"

He lashed out with his staff, striking Austin sharply across his back. The indolent American yelped in pain and toppled forward, throwing out his hands to break his fall. Showing no mercy, Khan jabbed the wooden pole into the man's side, just below his ribs. The flame-hardened staff met only slight resistance from Austin's desert robes.

Khan smiled cruelly as Austin cried out again. Usually, he regretted having to resort to such draconian measures, as was required more and more frequently these days, but right now it felt good to expend his anger and frustration on a deserving target. Khan only regretted that he was not beating Kirk or Ericsson instead.

Gasps, and muttered protests, rose from the rest of the caravan. A few of the braver souls stepped forward as if to intervene, but Joaquin silenced the dissidents by drawing a handmade basalt dagger from his belt. Back on Earth, the bodyguard had always preferred blades to guns, and had dispatched many an enemy with nothing more than a well-aimed throwing knife, as his fellow colonists clearly remembered.

"Stop . . . no more!" In an impressive burst of energy, Austin clambered to his feet before Khan could administer another blow. He grabbed frantically for his discarded salt bags and slung them over his shoulders, wincing as he did so. The heavy bundles flopped against his bruised flesh. "I will carry on, as you command!"

"So," Khan said sarcastically, "it seems some strength remains in you after all. At least when you are properly motivated." He swept his gaze over the other bearers as he rested the foot of his staff against the ground. His scrutiny lingered on Ericsson, whom he spotted lurking at the rear of the crowd. He imagined he could see the Norseman's spiteful blue eyes through the tinted visors shielding the other man's face. *Send your jackals against me as many times as you dare,* Khan thought defiantly. *This dismal world is mine to rule, such as it is.*

"We have wasted enough time here," he said sternly. "I will tolerate no further delays—from any of you!" He turned his back on Austin and returned to the front of the procession, trusting Joaquin to watch his back. "Onward," he declared, striding forward across the sands. "And heaven help the next grumbler who incurs my wrath!"

Deserts of vast eternity swallowed the sound of his marching footsteps.

Azar Gorge had been named after Shirin Azar, the Persian geologist who had discovered it while foraging for coal many months ago. Unlike the gullies dug out over centuries by the now-extinct Kaur, this deep ravine dated back no further than the cataclysm, when the very land itself had been torn apart by violent seismic forces. A gaping wound in the planet's hide, the gorge was over thirty meters deep and ten meters across.

The entire caravan seemed to breath a collective sigh of relief as Khan and the other thirsty colonists entered the northern end of the gorge. Gravity, along with impatience, quickened the travelers' weary stride as they descended a well-worn path toward the canyon floor, which was pockmarked by bubbling geysers and hot springs. Steam moistened the air, while the towering walls of the ravine provided protection from the abrasive winds blowing across the desert above. Thick black lines streaked the canyon walls, marking exposed layers of bituminous coal. Alien cacti and other succulents sprouted from the flinty soil.

Khan magnanimously stepped aside to permit his followers access to the springs ahead. "Rest and refresh yourselves," he instructed the exhausted bearers, and this time no one disputed his commands. Bags of salt hit the ground in a hurry as the colonists hastened to refill their canteens and water gourds at one of the seething hot springs. As a bonus, the boiling water was already purified, which meant that the impatient bearers could drink their fill as soon as the water cooled.

Although too geologically unstable to settle upon, the Azar Gorge had become one of the colony's primary water sources, supplemented by a network of solar stills installed in the desert above Fatalis. *What a shame*, Khan reflected, *that the gorge is located over a day away from the colony itself. Life would be slightly less challenging were the precious springs closer at hand.*

Content to let his people drink before him, Khan sat down upon a flat-topped boulder safely clear of the nearest geyser. His tired legs were grateful for the break, yet Khan resisted the temptation to sigh audibly, lest it be taken for a sign of weakness. As the canyon walls provided shelter from the fierce winds and UV rays, he loosened the folds of his kaffiyeh and breathed deeply of the comparatively dust-free air. He saw that many of his followers were shedding the outer layers of their desert garb as well.

Joaquin stepped forward and extended an open hand. "Your canteen, Your Excellency. Let me refill it for you."

"Thank you, my old friend," Khan replied, handing Joaquin the canteen as requested. At least he could always count on Joaquin's loyalty, despite the discontent brewing in other quarters. "Your thoughtfulness is much appreciated." He was surprised at how hoarse his voice was. "My mouth feels as dry as the Kalahari."

Joaquin nodded gravely. "I shall return shortly."

The bodyguard's heavy tread receded as Khan closed his eyes, permitting himself a rare moment of repose. The steamy, humid atmosphere reminded him of the imperial sauna back at his old palace in Chandigarh. It saddened him to recall that the magnificent fortress no longer existed, having been bombed out of existence centuries ago, in the closing days of the Eugenics Wars. According to Marla, a thermoconcrete landing pad now occupied the site; no plaque or monument commemorated his reign.

"*I don't know if you're going to like living in our time,*" she had cautioned him years ago, in his temporary quarters aboard the *Enterprise*. How tragically prophetic those words had proven!

He turned his thoughts toward Marla in an effort to rescue his spirits from the melancholy overtaking them. Her steadfast love had been the only bright spot over all these long years of exile and suffering. Without her, even for all his superior will and intellect, he might well have gone mad. She was Eve to his Adam, exiled from Paradise together:

"*I feel the link of nature draw me: flesh of my flesh,*

"*Bone of my bone, thou art, and from thy state*

"*Mine shall never be parted, bliss or woe . . .*"

Joaquin's returning footsteps disturbed his reverie. Khan kept his eyes closed, prolonging for a few more moments his escape from this hellish world, only to hear Joaquin freeze in his tracks. The bodyguard gasped out loud.

What the devil? Khan's eyes snapped open in irritation. "Lord Khan!" Joaquin exclaimed, over a sudden rumbling noise overhead. Sand and gravel rained down on Khan's head and shoulders. The rumbling grew louder, all but drowning out Joaquin's frantic shout: "Beware!"

Avalanche! Khan realized at once. He leaped to his feet, but Joaquin was faster still. The bodyguard charged forward, knocking Khan to one side, then throwing his massive frame over Khan to shield him from danger. Khan's face smacked against the floor of the canyon. He tasted blood and dirt upon his lips.

Boulders crashed to earth less than a meter away. The deafening roar of the landslide filled Khan's ears and the ground beneath him shook as though the cataclysm itself had returned. Sprawled upon the rocky floor, beneath Joaquin's protective weight, Khan braced himself for the crushing impact of some colossal fragment of stone. It seemed he was destined to be buried alive, no matter how many times he narrowly escaped that particular doom. . . .

Farewell, Marla, my love. May you keep my memory alive.

But, to his surprise, the thunderous roar gradually diminished in volume, until all that remained was the faint skittering of a few last rivulets of dirt. Joaquin stirred above him, and Khan felt the bodyguard rise to his feet, apparently unharmed. A cloud of dust, stirred up by the avalanche, enveloped the air around the two men. Khan coughed on the dust, spitting out blood from a torn lip.

"Your Excellency!" Joaquin called out in alarm. "Are you well?"

Khan took a quick inventory of his vital organs and bones. "Do not distress yourself," he assured the body-guard. "It seems I have come through this trial more or less unscathed, thanks to your timely intervention."

Joaquin offered his hand, but Khan chose to rise under his own power. He stood up slowly, brushing the powdery debris from his robes. The other colonists, attracted by the clamor, came running to investigate. Khan raised his hand to indicate that he was quite unharmed, to the disappointment, perhaps, of Ericsson and his fellow malcontents. *You shall not be rid of me quite so easily,* Khan gloated.

The thought sparked an immediate suspicion in his mind. What had triggered the landslide in the first place? He peered upward at the rugged cliff face. A tell-tale trickle of loose scree marked the path of the avalanche. Khan instantly spotted a narrow ledge not far from where the rockfall appeared to have originated. A skilled rock climber could have easily attained the ledge and set off the landslide from there, retreating back to the bed of the gorge amid the confusion and clouds of dust. Khan imagined Ericsson or one of the others using a walking stick as a lever to start an avalanche directly above Khan's head.

Traitor! Assassin!

Suspicion turned to certainty within Khan's mind; it could be no coincidence that the rockface chose that particular moment to rain down upon him. "Who?" he demanded furiously. "Who among you is responsible?"

"Lord Khan?" Ericsson blurted, feigning ignorance. Khan was not surprised to see the rebellious Norseman in the forefront of the crowd. He had removed his kaffiyeh and visor, revealing a golden beard now streaked with gray. His blue eyes mocked Khan with their ill-disguised malice. "I don't understand."

"Do not dissemble!" Khan raged, his temper pushed to its limit by this brazen attempt on his life. The dusty haze began to settle at last, clearing the air between him and other colonists. He searched their faces, determined to find the guilty party. "I know an assassination attempt when I survive one." He grabbed on to Ericsson's collar and all but yanked him off his feet. "Where were you mere minutes ago? Up there on the cliff above me?"

Ericsson refused to flinch before Khan's fury. "Of course not, Lord Khan," he insisted. "I was refilling my canteen with the others." He tipped his head toward his fellow colonists. "Ask anyone."

Khan turned his volcanic gaze upon the assembled bearers. "Is this true?" he barked, still holding on to the collar of Ericsson's dusty burnoose. "Answer me at once!"

Murmured assents and nodding heads replied, but Khan's anger was not assuaged. "Then who was it?" His suspicious gaze alighted on Paul Austin; he could well see the impertinent American serving as Ericsson's cat's-paw once again. "One of you *must* have seen something!" Khan accused the others. "Tell me the name of the assassin now, or I will hold you all responsible!"

Silence, and sullen looks, were all that the members of the caravan offered up in response. Their mute complicity further infuriated Khan, who felt betrayed beyond measure by their galling ingratitude. *For five and a half years, I have devoted my every waking hour to keeping my people alive—and this is how they repay me!* "Vipers!" he cursed them. "Conspirators, all!"

"Your Excellency!" Ericsson protested, his voice all wounded innocence. He smoothly extricated his collar from Khan's grasp and stepped back from Khan. "It was a freak accident, no more. You know how unstable this gorge is!"

"No one is such a liar as the indignant man," Khan thought; so said Nietzsche, who knew well the ambitious heart of the Superman. Khan's lips curled in disdain. "Very well," he snarled. "If none among you will come forward with the truth, then you will all pay the price for your reticence." He paused for emphasis. "There shall be no more food rations until we return to Fatalis!"

A collective wail erupted from the throng. "You can't!" Amy Katzel cried out, a look of utter disbelief upon her face. Other voices took up her anguished cry. "It's not fair!"

Khan braced himself for whatever was to come. If the caravan was going to rise up in open mutiny, now would likely be the moment. His hand dropped to the knife upon his belt. He heard Joaquin take up an aggressive stance behind him. *Let us see,* he mused, *how deep this insurrection runs.*

"You have brought this on yourself by refusing to name the would-be assassin among you," he decreed. His stony face betrayed not a flicker of trepidation. "My decision is final."

He saw anger and resentment in the faces and postures of the people before him. Fists were clenched and several eyes looked to Ericsson for a signal. Several meters away, an awakening geyser bubbled ominously, threatening to spill over at any minute—like the tensions simmering between Khan and the other colonists. Khan waited to see if either geyser would erupt.

But Ericsson merely shrugged. "Too bad we no longer have a phaser," he remarked as though to remind the others of how Khan had inadvertently destroyed the weapon years ago. "It would have made cleaning up this debris so much easier."

Turning his back on Khan, he headed back toward the hot springs with his canteen in his hand. The moment passed, and the crowd began to disperse, muttering darkly among themselves. Khan and Joaquin soon found themselves alone amid the newly fallen rubble. The confrontation appeared to be over . . . for now.

Intriguing, Khan thought. He could only assume that if Ericsson was not yet ready to force the issue then the Norseman must not have been certain that he enjoyed the support of the entire caravan, not to mention a majority of the colonists back at Fatalis. *Not every heart has turned against me, it seems.*

Still, today's brush with death had been a close one. *I can take no chances*, Khan realized. *I must be on my guard at all times.*

Joaquin retrieved Khan's walking stick from the scree and brought it over to his leader. The axebreaker staff would be a formidable weapon, if need be. "You must be careful, Your Excellency," the bodyguard grunted. "Your enemies plot against you."

"I know, my friend. I know." *Thank the heavens*, Khan thought, *that I can always depend on Joaquin.*

And Marla, of course.

20

"Have you got it?" Ericsson asked.

He held a rag over his mouth and nostrils as he spoke, due to the nauseating stench coming from the compost pit a few meters away. The rotting waste matter turned his stomach, but that was exactly why he had chosen this spot for the meeting; with luck, the fetid atmosphere would guarantee their privacy. Ericsson couldn't imagine anyone visiting the pit unless they absolutely had to.

"Well?" he repeated impatiently. "Do you have it or not?"

Saraj Panjabi looked about furtively before answering. Beads of sweat dotted his brow. Fear showed in his darting eyes. "Are you sure it's safe?" he whispered.

"No one is listening," Ericsson assured him. "Austin is standing lookout in the corridor, just in case."

Panjabi nodded, looking only slightly less nervous. He swallowed hard and took a deep breath. Reaching under the edge of a ragged vest, he drew out a transparent plastic vial and handed it to Ericsson. Inside the vial, a slimy black eel larva wriggled against the sides of the container, searching for a way out of the vial—and into the nearest convenient ear canal.

Ericsson could not repress a shudder at the sight of the dreaded creature. He double-checked the seal on the container, making sure it was intact. Only then did he smile in anticipation of what was to come. "Perfect," he declared. He eyed Panjabi cautiously. "The doctor won't miss this specimen?"

Panjabi shook his head, revealing a mutilated profile. Khan had sliced the man's left ear off after Panjabi had been caught stealing from one of the colony's underground gardens. *Bloody tyrant!* Ericsson thought angrily. Khan's punishments were growing increasingly severe as the embattled dictator struggled to maintain control of Fatalis.

"The larvae are hidden beneath the dorsal ridges of the adult eels," Panjabi reminded Ericsson. As the doctor's husband and number one orderly, the Indian superman had easy access to Hawkins' medical laboratory. "No one will ever notice that one small larva is missing."

Ericsson chuckled. "Just so long as no one blows the whistle in the next few hours." He tucked the vial into the pocket of his tattered jacket. "If all goes as planned, we won't have to worry about Khan's so-called justice much longer."

"But what if something goes wrong?" Panjabi fretted. He wrung his hands together apprehensively. "Perhaps this isn't such a good idea. . . ."

"It's the only way," Ericsson said sharply. He couldn't allow the other man to back out now. It was too late for second thoughts. "Khan is guarded night and day. If we want to get rid of him for good, this is our best shot."

Just be ready to head for the hills, he added silently, *if the plan goes awry.* They were playing a dangerous game here, and the consequences of failure were almost too ghastly to contemplate. *But we're not going to fail,* Ericsson thought. *This time tomorrow we'll be running Fatalis.*

"Trust me," he promised Panjabi. He patted the pocket containing the stolen larva. He visualized the obscene parasite squirming within the vial, eager to find an unwilling host. "Khan will never see this one coming!"

"Lady Marla?"

Marla was heading back to her quarters, after a long day looking after the colony's children, when a voice called out to her from behind. She turned to see Karyn Ericsson hurrying down the torchlit corridor toward her.

She paused to let the other woman catch up with her. "Yes?" she asked patiently, despite her fatigue. Her ubiquitous tricorder was slung over her shoulder, ready to disgorge another day's worth of recordings onto her dwindling supply of data disks. "Can I help you?"

"I'm sorry to bother you," Karyn said. The former college professor, whose dark hair was cut just below her ears, had an anxious expression. "But I was wondering if you could spare a few moments to come see Astrid?"

"Is something wrong?" Marla asked. She had noticed that Karyn's daughter had not shown up for class today. Along with Joachim, five-year-old Astrid Ericsson was one of Marla's prize pupils. Even among a brood of genetically enhanced prodigies, all of whom were maturing at an accelerated rate, Astrid was smart and capable beyond her years. Marla had already pegged the little girl as a rising star and likely future leader of Fatalis. "Should we go find Dr. Hawkins?"

Please, Marla prayed, as a sickening notion occurred to her, *don't tell me the eels have gotten to another child. . . .*

Karyn shook her head. "I don't think she's sick. Something's bothering her, though, and she won't tell me what it is." Worry deepened the furrows on the woman's face. "She won't eat, she won't do her homework, she's barely speaking. I was wondering, perhaps you can talk to her?"

That's odd, Marla thought. She couldn't think of anything that might be troubling Astrid. The little girl had gotten a perfect score on yesterday's quantum mechanics exam and was well liked by her peers. *What on earth could be bothering her?*

"Of course," she volunteered, sympathizing with the obviously worried mother. "I'll be happy to talk to her, if you think it would do any good."

Karyn beamed in relief. "Thank you so much," she said, taking Marla's hand. "I'm sure you can find out what the problem is. Astrid thinks very highly of you."

Then how can I say no? Marla thought, shrugging her

shoulders in resignation. She cast a wistful glance in the direction of her own quarters as Karyn guided her in the opposite direction. She had been looking forward to spending the evening with Khan, in the privacy of their own chambers, but apparently that was going to have to wait a bit. *A teacher's work is never done, I suppose.*

Karyn and Harulf Ericsson lived in a block of rough-hewn apartments carved out of one of the lower levels of the underground complex. Marla felt a familiar pang as she and Karyn passed various other families retiring for the night; after five years of marriage, she and Khan still had no children of their own and by now Marla had pretty much given up on the prospect. For years she had nursed a secret fear that Khan would seek out another woman to bear him an heir, yet Khan had never even spoken of looking elsewhere, choosing instead to groom young Joachim as his future successor.

Then again, Marla mused, *Astrid Ericsson may have something to say about that further on down the road.*

A hanging metal curtain marked the entrance to the Ericssons' quarters. Karyn pulled the curtain aside and gestured for Marla to step inside. "Go on," she urged pleasantly. "Astrid is waiting."

But instead of the precocious child, Marla found Harulf Ericsson and Paul Austin instead. The two men grinned wolfishly as she entered the cave. Marla suddenly sensed that she had made a frightful mistake. "What—?" she began, backing away, only to feel Karyn's hand clamp tightly over her mouth. The other woman shoved Marla toward the waiting men, who pounced forward to seize her. An old piece of rubber, cut from the sole of a discarded boot, was thrust between her jaws and tied in place with a gag. Austin yanked on her arms, trapping them behind her back. Marla struggled to free herself, but the superman's grasp was too strong.

She was caught.

I don't understand, she thought. *Why are they doing this?*

Harulf Ericsson smiled at her predicament. "Why, *Lady* Marla," he said sarcastically, making a joke of her title. "How nice of you to grace us with your *exalted* presence. I'm sure our humble abode hardly compares to the one you share with our glorious leader, but we're hoping to improve our situation soon—with your generous assistance."

What does he mean by that? Marla wondered fearfully. Her heart pounded in her chest as she tried to anticipate Ericsson's plans for her. Her eyes searched the cramped, sparsely furnished cave, but saw nothing that offered any hope of escape. Astrid, she could not help noticing, was nowhere to be seen. *Probably off with a babysitter*, Marla guessed. She realized now that this had nothing to do with Ericsson's daughter—and everything to do with his ruthless ambition.

She cursed herself for her naïveté. *I should never have trusted Karyn, no matter how talented her daughter is.* She felt a surge of anger at the duplicitous mother. *But how dare she take advantage of my concern for the children!*

Not a trace of remorse showed on Karyn Ericsson's face as she joined her husband in front of their captive. Marla wanted to shout at them both, tell them how despicable they were, but, gagged as she was, she couldn't even threaten them with Khan's wrath. A chilling thought occurred to her: *They wouldn't risk provoking Khan like this—unless they never expected me to see him again.*

"I'm sorry our daughter isn't here to welcome you," Ericsson continued, "but there's someone else I'd like to introduce you to." Karyn fetched a sealed clay jar from a limestone shelf and offered her husband a pair of metal tongs. Ericsson carefully opened the container and reached in with the tongs. "And here he is."

Marla's eyes widened in horror as she spotted the greasy larva squirming in the tong's grip. *No!* she thought, literally frozen in shock. *Not that! Anything but that!*

Panicked, she fought to break free of Austin's grasp, but the tattooed superman held her fast as Ericsson approached her, bearing the quivering eel in his tongs. He lifted her hair with his free hand, exposing the area around her right ear. *Please, no!* she pleaded with her eyes. *Don't do this!* But Ericsson ignored her petrified expression, lifting the tongs toward her ear. Marla flinched in terror as she felt the slimy larva come into contact with her skin.

The next few seconds felt like an eternity. The eel slid upward, leaving a trail of mucus behind it. She felt the larva navigate her lobes, then slide implacably into her ear canal. A searing pain erupted inside her head as the larva burrowed through her eardrum on its way toward her brain. Relief, of a purely physical nature, came a few moments later, as the eel sprayed some sort of anesthetic goo inside her ear, sealing the gap in the perforated eardrum; apparently, the parasite had no intention of rendering its host crazed with pain—at least not yet.

It doesn't matter, Marla thought numbly. She knew there was no possible hope for her now.

She was a dead woman.

But what did Ericsson hope to gain from killing her? Revenge?

She could feel the eel moving through her inner ear. She felt a growing pressure within her skull, like a tumor at work, and a sort of fog descended on her thoughts, along with a peculiar sense of detachment. . . .

It was like one of those dreams where one is acting and watching oneself act at the same time. One knows what's going to happen, but goes through the motions anyway, like an actor following a script laid out by one's unconscious mind. Marla felt like an outside observer in her own body, listening to her heart calmly settle down as though nothing horrible was happening to her.

As though she hadn't already been murdered.

In a grotesque parody of compassion, Karyn Ericsson wiped the blood and mucus from the outside of Marla's ear, concealing any evidence of the larva's passage. Harulf watched Marla's face carefully while he waited for the larva to complete its trek to her cerebral cortex. He stared into her eyes as if he expected to see the deadly eel staring back at him.

He snapped his fingers in front of her face. "Are you still there, Lady Marla?" he asked. A pitiless smirk showed through his beard. "Nod if you can hear me."

Never! Marla thought defiantly, determined not to

cooperate with her killer. To her horror, however, she felt her head nod as instructed. *No! Stop it!*

Ericsson grinned. "Very good, Lieutenant McGivers." His fingers toyed with the Starfleet medallion around her neck. "Now then, Marla, I want you to listen to me very carefully. We're going to remove your gag, but you are not going to scream or call for help. Do you understand me?"

Marla nodded again, like a puppet on a string. *Don't!* she thought in dismay, unable to stop herself from obeying Ericsson's commands, no matter how hard she tried. It was like a bad dream she had no hope of waking from. *This can't be happening!*

"Do it," Ericsson told his wife, who undid the gag and removed the rubber sole from Marla's mouth. Austin kept a tight grip on the prisoner's arms, just in case Marla had not entirely succumbed to the eel's effects.

He needn't have bothered. Marla tried desperately to scream, but her treacherous throat refused to cooperate. Her frantic cries echoed inside her skull, but nothing emerged from her paralyzed lips.

"So far, so good," Ericsson observed. He shared a triumphant look with his two conspirators before returning his attention to their captive. "Are you still listening to me, Marla?"

"Yes," she heard herself say. She couldn't believe it was her own voice.

"Very good," Ericsson said, as though praising a well-behaved child. "Now stay right where you are until I say you can go." He nodded at Austin. "Release her."

Marla felt her arms drop limply to her side. She wanted to lash out at Ericsson and the others, kick and punch and bite until they were all broken and bleeding on the floor. Barring that, she wanted to run from this place as fast as humanly possible, all the way to Khan and anyone else who might be able to help her. *Get moving!* she shouted silently at her recalcitrant legs. *Run away—now!*

Instead, she just stood there, waiting helplessly for further instructions. *Like one of those androids on Exo III,* she thought bleakly.

Ericsson chortled at her unwilling obedience. "This just gets better and better." He put down the tongs and reached for the polished obsidian knife tucked into her belt. He stepped closer to her, until his face was only a couple of centimeters away from hers. Marla was unable to look away from his cold blue eyes.

"Listen to me, Marla," he said. Any trace of amusement evaporated from his voice and expression, as his tone became deadly serious. "I want you to find your husband. Do not tell him or anyone else what has happened here. You must act as though everything is normal and nothing is wrong with you. Can you do that, Marla?"

"Yes," she answered, against her will.

Ericsson thrust the blade into her hand and wrapped her fingers around its hilt. "Take your knife," he told her. "Use it to kill your husband. Get him alone first, then cut his throat, stab him in the heart, and keep on stabbing him until he is dead."

The part of Marla's mind that still belonged to her

reacted in utter horror. *Kill Khan?* The very thought scared her more than dying. She tried to hurl the knife away, but it remained securely within her grip. *I can't . . . I'd never . . . !*

"Repeat after me," Ericsson insisted. "Khan must die."

"Khan must die," Marla said hollowly.

"Precisely." Ericsson stepped back and gestured toward the door. "Go now," he commanded. "Your husband is waiting for you."

21

Marla walked through Fatalis, caught in a waking nightmare. Although she was free at last from her captors, Ericsson's words still echoed irresistibly in her mind.

Khan must die.

Assorted colonists, including Zuleika, greeted her in the tunnels and Marla responded calmly to each, unable to warn her friends and comrades of the danger to Khan. Meaningless pleasantries spilled from her lips as, moment by moment, she drew steadily nearer to the quarters she shared with their leader. The obsidian blade rested securely against her hip.

The trip seemed to last forever—and was over far too soon. Fear and anguish gripped her heart as she spotted Joaquin standing guard outside the arched doorway to Khan's private apartments. The zealous bodyguard took no chances; when he wasn't watching over Khan per-

sonally, one of Suzette Ling's handpicked security officers stood guard in his place.

"You're late," he grumbled as Marla approached.
Over the years, their mutual dislike had evolved into, at
best, a grudging tolerance for each other. They still
weren't friends, but Joaquin no longer distrusted her as
he once had . . . unfortunately. At the moment, Marla
would have given anything for the Israeli giant to eye
her with suspicion once more, perhaps even take her
into custody.

Please, Joaquin, she pleaded inwardly. *See what's happening to me. Don't let me near Khan!*

"I was busy," she told him. "One of the children was
having trouble with his homework." Guilt stabbed at
her soul as she heard herself lie effortlessly to her husband's guardian.

"Joachim?" his father asked.

"Of course not," Marla assured him. "Another child."

Joaquin grunted, having exhausted his interest in the
conversation. He stepped aside to let Marla pass, much
to her dismay. *No!* she thought hysterically. *You can't let
me get to Khan. You have to stop me!*

"He's waiting," the bodyguard said.

Screaming inside, Marla passed through the doorway.

The chambers beyond consisted of two interconnected
grottoes, both larger than the Ericssons' single cavern,
along with a natural sinkhole to serve as a private latrine.
The furnishings were rudimentary—a chair, a desk, a
handmade wooden bed bearing a mattress stuffed with
moss—yet Marla had done her best over the years to add

a few personal touches to their spartan accommodations. Dried flowers, procured before the desert swallowed up the savanna above, adorned limestone shelves and awnings. Her data disks and recharger occupied a carved marble bedstand. A miniature sculpture of a medieval knight and his lady, salvaged from the ruins of New Chandigarh, occupied a niche above the bed. Khan's old flag, now badly singed around the edges, served as a bedspread. A disintegrating grass carpet covered the floor.

She found Khan seated at his desk, updating his journal. The desk was actually an inoperative antigrav lift propped up by matching stalagmites. Khan's back was turned to the door, presenting an all-too-ready target. His gunbelt was draped carelessly over the back of the chair. Marla's hand drifted inexorably toward the knife at her own belt. She drew the blade and stepped toward her husband.

Khan must die.

He turned at her approach, however, and she hastily hid the knife behind her back.

"Ah, there you are!" he said warmly. His dark eyes lit up at her return, seeing only his wife, not the assassin who had taken possession of her body. "I feared you had been detained indefinitely."

Even with the eel nesting in her brain, Marla could not help noting, as she always did, how these long years of exile had taken their toll on him. His once-black hair was now liberally streaked with gray, while the constant strain of leadership had etched deep lines into his regal countenance. Like Ceti Alpha V, he was growing old before his time.

But even diminished, he still had five times the strength and determination of any normal man. *He can't die*, Marla agonized, *not like this! He's too magnificent, too larger than life.* An ocean of tears hid behind her clear brown eyes. *I love him too much.*

"It was nothing," she lied, hating herself but hating Ericsson more. "A conference with a parent." She prayed for Khan to notice the knife hidden suspiciously behind her back, but knew that she enjoyed his absolute trust. With her alone, he did not feel a need to be on guard, just as Ericsson and his fellow conspirators had counted on.

"I am pleased to hear it," Khan said. He sighed wearily, massaging his brow with his free hand. "This year's rice crop, alas, appears to be failing. I fear I shall have to cut rations once more." A scowl deepened the lines on his face. "The people will not be pleased."

"I'm sorry," she murmured, although the rice crop was the last thing on her mind. Her fevered brain fought a losing battle against the command consuming her being.

Khan must die.

"But I should not burden you with my own troubles," Khan said expansively, making an obvious effort to lighten the mood. He slammed his journal shut and placed his bone pen back in its inkwell. "Entertain me," he exhorted Marla, leaning back against his chair. "Tell me again about that singular production of *Hamlet* you attended upon the *Enterprise*. I find this Kodos individual intriguing. . . ."

"Certainly," Marla agreed, appalled at how easy Khan was making her mission of murder. She walked over to the chair and laid a hand on his shoulder. "Close your eyes."

Don't! she begged him in vain. *Stop me, please, before I hurt you!*

"As you command," he said indulgently. Shutting his eyes, he tilted his head backward, leaving his throat fatally exposed. "You have my full attention."

Marla sobbed inside as she drew forth her knife. Khan's jugular called out to the blade. She could already imagine its sharpened edge slicing through her husband's flesh as cleanly as a phaser beam. . . .

Khan must die.

She kneaded Khan's shoulder with one hand while raising the knife with the other. *This is it,* she realized abjectly. *I'm really going to do this. I'm going to kill the man I love.*

"NO!"

To her surprise, the word exploded from her lips. Marla yanked her arm away from Khan and staggered backward across the floor. Her entire body trembled.

Her outburst jolted Khan, who leaped from his chair. "Marla?" He stared at her, confusion written on his face. His dark eyes widened at the sight of the bared knife. "What is it? What's wrong?"

He stepped toward her.

"Stay back!" she warned him, slicing wildly at the empty air between them. It was taking all her strength not to lunge at him with the knife. "K-Keep away from me!"

Khan must die!

Marla knew she couldn't resist the ceaseless command much longer. She could feel herself weakening, despite her last-minute burst of defiance. The pressure at the back of her skull increased, as though the insidious larva was tightening its grip on her cerebral cortex. A single tear dripped from the corner of her eye. *My life doesn't matter,* she thought. *I'm dead already.*

"Marla!" Khan called to her, his face contorted with anxiety. "Please, beloved, let me help you!"

She knew what she had to do. It was the only way to save the man she had devoted her life to.

Good-bye, Khan. I love you.

Marla plunged the blade into her own heart.

Khan watched in shock and disbelief as Marla stabbed herself before his eyes. Blood gushed from her chest as she crumpled to the floor of the grotto.

"Marla! My wife!"

He sprang to her side, kneeling beside her as her life's blood spread beneath them, soaking the grass carpet. Gently he removed the knife from her heart and swiftly exerted pressure on the wound, desperate to save her.

Attracted by the commotion, Joaquin barged into the grotto, only to be struck dumb by the stunning tableau before him. Khan ignored the bodyguard's arrival, intent only on Marla's bleeding form. *The doctor,* he thought. *I must summon the doctor!*

But he knew it was already too late. He had seen too much of death and violence not to recognize a mortal wound when he saw one, especially on a planet lacking adequate medical facilities.

Marla was dying before his eyes.

Marla.

"Why?" he moaned in agony. He lifted her partly from the floor, cradling her body in his arms. She felt surprisingly light, as though the better part of her was already missing. "What madness possessed you?"

Her eyes flickered open, and a trickle of bright arterial blood leaked from the corner of her mouth. "Ericsson . . ." she whispered. "He . . . an eel . . ."

Joaquin growled nearby.

Her trembling hand found his. Large brown eyes gazed up at him for the last time. "No regrets," she murmured, trying to smile.

Gentle fingers went limp within his grasp.

Empty eyes stared blankly into oblivion.

She was gone.

Howling in torment, Khan clutched Marla's lifeless body to his chest. Blood pooled beneath him as he rocked back and forth upon the floor of their home. A sudden insanity tore at what remained of his reason as he realized that he had lost his wife—his Eve—forever.

"O' fairest of creation!" he ranted furiously, feeling the grief of Adam after the Fall. "How art thou lost, how on a sudden lost . . . Defaced, deflowered, and now to Death devote?" He bent to kiss Marla's tender lips, tasting her spilled blood before lifting his own lips at last from hers. "O' a kiss . . . Long as my exile, sweet as my revenge!"

A burning desire for retribution reminded him of Joaquin's presence. He glared up at the other man. "You heard her," he snarled. "Find Ericsson and his lackeys, everyone who has ever associated with him, and bring them to me now." Something moved beneath Marla's hair, and Khan watched, aghast, as a blood-slick eel larva escaped his wife's body. He lashed out angrily and crushed the creature beneath his fist, wishing it were Ericsson's skull he was smashing instead. "I will make them pay dearly for this atrocity! They will all pay, every last one of them!"

"Yes, Your Excellency!" Joaquin affirmed. He sounded grateful to have a duty to perform, especially one that took him away from this dreadful scene. "They will not escape!"

Harulf Ericsson paced around the edge of the compost pit, impatient to hear word of Khan's death. His kaffiyeh was tied over the bottom half of his face, while his visor was tilted upward so that it rested upon his forehead, above his eyes. The fetid chamber was far too dimly lit to make the visor's tinted lenses usable in this environment.

"How much longer must we stay here?" his wife asked him, clutching little Astrid to her waist. Like Ericsson himself, Karyn and their daughter were clad in full desert attire, as were the other rebels hiding out in the pit chamber. Ericsson counted fully fifteen adult colonists, along with assorted small children and infants. All of them knew that their very futures depended on the success of tonight's operation.

"Until Savine returns with confirmation of Khan's death," he answered, speaking loudly enough to address the entire assemblage. Handmade spears and axes waited in the sweaty palms of every adult. A "borrowed" resequencer rested in a canvas bag at Ericsson's feet. "Then we'll move against Joaquin and Ling and whatever pathetic resistance they manage to muster." He snorted derisively through his beard. "With Khan safely dead, there will be few willing to fight in his memory."

Khan was more feared than loved, Ericsson told himself confidently. He doubted if more than a handful of the old guard would oppose tonight's coup. And who were the loyalists supposed to rally around anyway? *Khan's widow? The woman has an eel in her brain!*

"This place stinks!" Astrid protested, wrinkling her nose. Impatience flashed in her striking blue eyes. "I want to go home!"

Ericsson knelt to console his daughter. Someday, when he was long gone, he fully expected Astrid to rule over Fatalis. Lord knew, she was certainly strong-willed enough!

"I know, *datter*," he told her. "Just a little while more. Then, maybe, we can move into a larger cavern where you might be able to have a room of your own. You'd like that, wouldn't you?"

"I suppose," the child conceded grudgingly. "This place still stinks, though."

She's not wrong there, Ericsson thought, rising to his feet. If anything the pit smelled even more revolting than it had when he and Panjabi had met there earlier. *Just wait until we add Khan's body to the heap,* he anticipated, *not to mention Joaquin, Marla, and the rest. . . .*

His eyes scanned the faces of his fellow conspirators: Austin, Panjabi, and Amy Katzel, among others. It had taken him years to build this clandestine alliance, but his hour had finally come round at last. Soon Khan would be no more and the people would turn to the leader they should have chosen long ago, the very day they first set foot on Ceti Alpha V.

"Be patient, my friends," he told his loyal allies. "Our long wait is almost over." He raised a gloved fist in triumph. "The tyrant's reign is done."

Racing footsteps sounded in the lonely corridor outside. A moment later, Juliette Savine dashed into the chamber. Ericsson had posted the widowed Frenchwoman, whose husband had been lost to the larva of a Ceti eel, in the hallway outside Khan's quarters, to keep an eye on what transpired there. Her ashen face immediately sent a chill through Ericsson's heart, even before she said a word.

"It's all gone wrong!" she gasped, breathless from sprinting all the way here. "Khan is still alive; they say his wife killed herself before his eyes." She leaned against a glazed flowstone wall, catching her breath. Horrified cries and curses arose from the other conspirators. "Joaquin is hunting for us now! They could be here any minute!"

Ericsson could not believe what he was hearing. Marla had committed suicide? How was that even possible? *This is insane!* he thought virulently. *She was under my control!*

Austin and the adults stared at each other, panic-stricken. The children, picking up on their parents' distress, began to cry loudly. Ericsson winced at the bawling, afraid that the noise would attract Joaquin and his storm troopers. *We have to get out of here*, he realized.

"Now what are we going to do?" Amy Katzel wailed.

She had broken with her brother to support Ericsson's rebellion. Now she clearly looked like she was regretting that decision.

"We flee Fatalis," Ericsson said plainly. He had planned for this eventuality, even though he had never expected it to happen; that's why they were all hiding out in their desert gear. "There's no other choice. Khan will kill us all if he catches us."

Unable to dispute their leader's prediction, Austin and the rest gathered up their children and belongings. Ericsson himself lifted the bag containing the stolen resequencer, along with provisions carefully hoarded over the last six months. Karyn, her face pale, took Astrid by the hand and removed a torch from a crack in the wall. "Follow me," he ordered.

He knew their escape route already: an uncharted tunnel that one of his followers had stumbled onto a year ago. The circuitous passage led eventually to the surface, many kilometers away from the heart of Fatalis. There a desolate future awaited them, assuming they managed to elude Khan's minions. Surviving on the surface would not be easy, but Ericsson knew that their odds of staying alive in Fatalis were even slimmer. After what they had attempted, they could expect no mercy.

Hurriedly, the conspirators disappeared into the shadowy depths beyond the compost pit. Acid churned in Ericsson's stomach as the gross injustice of it all galled his soul. Tonight was supposed to have been his moment of glory; instead he found himself scurrying away like a frightened rat. He felt as though he had gone from king to exile in one fell swoop.

Ericsson glanced backward, at the subterranean sanctuary he was now forced to abandon. *This isn't over, Khan,* he vowed. *Our war is just beginning. Someday I'll return in triumph to Fatalis—and it will be you who begs for your life!*

Joaquin's departure left Khan alone with Marla's body. Rising slowly, he lifted her from the blood-soaked carpet and laid her gently on the humble bed they had shared for more than half a decade. Her auburn hair spread out over her pillow.

Khan realized he could not consign such beauty to the compost pit, despite the colony's need for fresh fertilizer. For Marla, he would make an exception. *I shall carve you a tomb,* he swore, *worthy of an empress.*

A glint of silver caught the lamplight, drawing Khan's gaze to the Starfleet medallion hanging around Marla's neck. On an impulse, he took hold of the sculpted emblem and yanked it toward him, the slender chain snapping easily. He raised it toward his face, staring grimly at the medallion as it rested in his palm. The polished keepsake was free of tarnish even after all these years; Marla had seen to that. Its graceful design mimicked the golden insignia that had once adorned Marla's uniform—and Kirk's.

Kirk.

Khan's eyes narrowed in thought and a malignant scowl settled onto his features. Ericsson and his allies would be brought to justice. That much was certain. But, deep in his heart, he knew who was truly responsible for Marla's death.

James T. Kirk.

It was *Kirk* who banished Marla to this accursed world, rife with deadly cataclysms and bloodthirsty life-forms. It was *Kirk* who had never once bothered to check on the colony he had condemned to never-ending torment. It was *Kirk* who had foiled Khan's plan to conquer the starways, forcing him to accept exile on this planetary death trap instead.

It was *Kirk* who had left them all to die.

If not for Kirk, I would be ruling over a thriving interstellar empire by now, with Marla reigning beside me as my imperial consort.

Instead, she had met a miserable end in a gloomy hole deep beneath the surface of a dying world.

And it was all because of Kirk.

Wrapping the broken chain around his fist, Khan let the silver emblem dangle before his eyes. "I swear upon this token," he whispered to his beloved. "James T. Kirk will pay for your death—and for every other tragedy that has afflicted our people over all these doleful years. One way or another, no matter how many years may pass, I will find Kirk again—and, by all I hold sacred, you will be avenged!"

22

ONE PLANETARY YEAR LATER

Bit by bit, Marla emerged from the marble. Khan chipped away at the huge slab of stone, slowly liberating Marla's face and form from the stubborn marble. His hammer and chisel tapped repeatedly against the slab, which rested atop his late wife's heavy stone sarcophagus. Marble flakes littered the floor of the crypt. The crude oil lamps lighting the grotto were running low on fuel, an indication of how late into the night Khan had been working. Most of Fatalis had retired to bed hours ago.

But Khan slept only fitfully these days. Most nights he found he prefered working upon Marla's tomb to tossing fruitlessly in his empty bed, haunted by his memories—and his unfulfilled vow to avenge Marla's

311

death. "Work is the scythe of time," Napoleon had said, and Khan's nights passed very slowly now that his beloved wife was gone.

Exhausted, he paused in his labors. Powdered stone clung to his sweaty skin and garments. Purple shadows lurked in the hollows beneath his red-rimmed eyes. He wiped the perspiration from his brow, then stepped back from the sarcophagus to inspect the sculpture, which remained a work in progress. *The nose is not quite right,* he appraised, *nor is the mouth. Her expression should be more profound, more soulful . . . more reflective of her tender spirit.* Lacking any photos or paintings of his wife, he sculpted Marla's tomb from memory. *This will not do,* he resolved. *I must keep striving until the likeness is absolutely perfect. Marla deserves nothing less.*

The marble for the memorial came from a quarry far to the north. Khan had personally transported the slab from the mountains to Fatalis, albeit with the able assistance of Joaquin, who blamed himself, in part, for what had befallen Marla. It was among the tragic ironies of her loss that Marla's sacrifice had finally earned her, in death, the bodyguard's unqualified respect.

The image of Marla driving the knife into her chest flashed through his mind once more, stabbing into his own heart just as it always did. Driven by the ghastly memory, he took up his hammer and chisel once more. *This accursed world will never forget that you once graced its surface,* he promised Marla, *even if I have to work my fingers to the bone!*

He placed the edge of the chisel against the sculpture's lower lip, preparing to make a subtle but all-important adjustment to the marble portrait. His blood-shot eyes narrowed in concentration and he raised the hammer above the carefully positioned chisel. One quick tap would do the trick. . . .

Before he could deliver the blow, however, the sound of footsteps violated the sepulchral hush of the grotto. Khan turned angrily to see Zuleika Walker standing in the doorway. The Amazonian superwoman, clad in threadbare rags that scarcely covered her magnificent figure, regarded him nervously from several paces away. "Lord Khan?"

Khan did not wait to hear more. "You dare disturb me *here!*" he raged. "I have issued explicit instructions that I am to be left alone at such times, unless"—a vengeful gleam appeared in his eyes—"you have come to tell me that Ericsson and his band of traitors have been captured at last?"

Zuleika shook her head. "No, my lord. The renegades remain at large."

Disappointment stoked Khan's anger to a fever pitch. He hurled his tools at the floor in fury, causing Zuleika to flinch in alarm. *Of course they are still at large!* he thought vehemently. For perhaps the one-millionth time, Khan regretted letting Ericsson and the others slip through his grasp the night Marla died. *I should have seen to their capture myself, despite the enormity of my grief.*

Thought of that grief brought him back to Zuleika's unwelcome intrusion. "Then what brings you here?" he demanded.

"Concern for you, Lord Khan." Steeling her nerve, she stepped further into the tomb, her bare feet disturbing the stone shavings strewn upon the ground. Her braided hair was draped over her shoulders. "This is not healthy, my lord," she insisted, gesturing at the forlorn crypt. "You are here most every night, working until dawn and beyond." Pained eyes entreated him. "You don't sleep, you don't rest . . . Marla would not have wanted this."

"Do not presume to tell me my wife's desires," Khan upbraided Zuleika, bristling at the mention of Marla's name. "Nor to criticize the expression of my grief."

"I lost my love, too," she reminded him. "But life goes on, even here on this wretched dirtball of a planet." She stepped closer to Khan, until her supple form was only centimeters away from him. "You have to take care of yourself—for all of our sakes. The entire colony is depending on you." She swallowed hard. "*I'm* depending on you."

Memory of Keith Talbot's death in that sandstorm years ago took the edge off Khan's anger at being interrupted. Zuleika had indeed suffered as well. "I appreciate your concern," he told her sincerely, "but there are times when I must be alone with my memories if I am to stay sane."

"Are you quite certain of that, my lord?" Zuleika purred, pressing her taut body against his side. Her hand caressed his chest and he could feel the warmth radiating from her. "There's no reason you have to sleep alone tonight, or ever again. I am always here for you."

Khan was tempted. It had been many months since he had known the comfort of a woman's touch. Desire stirred him and he clutched her to him. His lips found her throat and Zuleika moaned in delight. A whiff of odorous perfume tantalized his senses. Then her questing fingers brushed against the silver medallion on his chest.

Marla's medallion.

His wife's martyred visage suddenly filled his mind, and he relived again that nightmarish moment when she plunged the obsidian dagger into her heart.

"No!" He thrust Zuleika away from him. She staggered backward, caught off guard by his abrupt change of heart.

"Khan?" she gasped. Powdery white handprints adorned her flesh. "What's the matter?"

"Go," he instructed her hoarsely. Averting his eyes from her inviting curves, he pointed forcefully at the exit. "Go . . . and never speak of such things again!"

His tone brooked no discussion. A stricken expression on her face, she scooted out of the grotto. Khan listened to her retreating footsteps disappear down the corridor outside.

When the last echoes of her departure faded away, he approached Marla's sarcophagus in contrition. A gloved hand gently stroked the marble planes of her face.

"Forgive me, dear one," he whispered. Marla had given her life for him. How could any woman hope to claim his affections after that? There could be no one else in his life, not while Marla's death remained unavenged.

Wearily, he retrieved his tools and went back to work.

23

FOUR PLANETARY YEARS LATER

Khan moved his queen into place. "Checkmate."

"Not again!" Joachim exclaimed, leaning forward to examine the board. His intense blue eyes widened as, with laudable speed, the boy discovered the trap Khan had laid for his king. "You always win!"

"Of course," Khan chuckled, "but not so swiftly as I once did." His snow-white hair hung to his shoulders, the color contrasting sharply with his thick black eyebrows. A king of shreds and patches, he wore a padded brown vest that bared much of his broad chest. "You are learning, my young friend."

Joachim sat opposite Khan on a rough limestone bench in Fatalis's cavernous meeting hall. Curtains of calcified flowstone draped the walls while the central firepit warmed the vast chamber. A makeshift chess-board rested on the bench between Khan and the boy, the pieces made up of miscellaneous nuts and bolts. Not quite as elegant as the polished onyx and turquoise set Khan had owned back on Earth, but sufficient to play with. He had come to enjoy his daily game with Joaquin's brilliant young son; the bouts provided a welcome relief from the endless ordeal of life upon Ceti Alpha V.

Vaster than empires, and more slow, the years dragged by. Khan had long since ceased trying to calculate how many Earth-years had passed during their stay here, and even Ceti Alpha V's longer years were becoming more difficult to reckon now that the seasons had blurred into a never-ending storm of heat, wind, and dust. Only the rapid aging of the children, and the gradual extinction of the native life-forms, marked the passage of time.

Although Joachim was still no more than ten years old, he looked at least fifteen, thanks to the accelerated maturity that was among the gifts bestowed by his superlative genetic heritage. He had grown into a slender, flaxen-haired youth, not quite as stocky as his father, but able-bodied and intelligent beyond his years. Khan often thought of Joachim as the son he'd never had.

Bittersweet memories, never far beneath the surface, arose once more as Khan reached out and lifted his queen from the board. Even after all this time, he still felt the loss of his one true queen—as well as an unquenched craving for revenge, against both Ericsson and Kirk. He fingered the tarnished Starfleet medallion resting against his chest. Recycled electrical wire, looped around his neck, held the emblem in place above his heart.

The medallion was a constant reminder of his unfulfilled oath to bring Marla's killers to justice—a sacred obligation that haunted him day and night. He had spent many a midnight hour these last five years lying awake upon his lonely bed, longing for the day he would finally avenge his martyred wife.

But this is not that day, Khan knew. Returning his queen to the board, he forced his attention back to the present. "I have another book for you to read," he informed Joachim, picking up a dog-eared volume from where it rested on the floor. "*Moby-Dick*, by Herman Melville."

"Another book?" Joachim regarded the tome with a mixture of curiosity and apprehension. Like any growing boy, he preferred exploring the caves and tunnels surrounding Fatalis to reading about a planet he had never seen. Khan wondered what Joachim, raised below a desert wasteland, would make of Melville's epic sea tale.

"A good book," he admonished the boy, "is the precious lifeblood of a master spirit, embalmed and treasured up on purpose to a life before life."

To his credit, Joachim identified the quotation at once. "Milton?"

"Excellent," Khan said, pleased that the treasures of his personal library had not been wasted on the youth. He began moving the chess pieces back to their starting positions. "Perhaps another game?"

Before they could begin, however, Joaquin rushed into the chamber. Joachim's eyes lit up at his father's arrival, but Khan could tell from the bodyguard's hasty entrance that something was amiss.

"Your Excellency!" Joaquin exclaimed. His alarmed tone belied his stoic expression. "The Exiles have struck again!"

Khan sprang to his feet, a familiar anger flaring inside his heart. His gloved hand went instinctively to the pistol at his belt. Ericsson and his desert raiders had been harrying Fatalis for years, striking out at the colony's vulnerable caravans and solar stills, then disappearing back into the rugged badlands that sheltered them.

"Where?" he demanded.

"Azar Gorge," Joaquin said gruffly. A moment later, two security officers entered the cavern, dragging between them an injured colonist, who bore the unmistakable marks of a grueling trek across the desert sands. His face was cracked and blackened, his eyes nearly swollen shut. Blood stained his badly shredded burnoose. His bare feet looked like gnarled claws. The man's features were so badly distorted that it took Khan a moment to recognize Vijay Nikore, one of three guards assigned to the gorge, the colony's primary source of fresh water.

Khan was shocked to hear that the precious hot springs had come under attack. "How could this happen?" he asked harshly, resisting a temptation to strike the haggard survivor, who had already suffered enough. "What of the guards?"

"Forgive us, Lord Khan!" Nikore pleaded through broken teeth. His tongue, swollen from dehydration, made speech difficult, but Khan managed to make out the man's garbled words. "They came upon us in force, without warning! Spears rained down on us from atop the gorge, killing Rivera and wounding Thomsen. Then they came charging down the ravine like berserkers. Men, women, even children! All armed to the teeth!" The traumatized guard shuddered at the memory. "I was the only survivor. . . ."

I should have posted more guards, Khan thought. *But how could I?* With these most recent fatalities, the adult population of Fatalis had been reduced to no more than twenty-three men and women. *Our security forces are spread too thin already.*

The only consolation was that the Exiles must be desperate indeed to risk everything in an all-out assault on the gorge. According to his best estimates, Ericsson's tribe now comprised roughly ten adults, plus an unknown number of offspring. It pained Khan to realize that the raid on the gorge would help keep the mutinous throng alive a while longer.

"How much water did they steal?" he asked.

"No, Lord Khan, you misunderstand!" Nikore blurted. He flinched in anticipation of his leader's wrath. "The rebels have taken possession of the gorge. They drove me out into the desert, then barricaded the entrances with boulders." His charred face grew more agitated. "I believe they hold it still!"

"What!" Khan reacted volcanically to the news, his unleashed fury startling Joachim, who backed away nervously. But Khan barely noticed the youth's discomfort, transfixed as he was by Nikore's disturbing report.

The Azar Gorge had long been key to the colony's survival, and all the more so as several other desert oases and watering holes had gradually dried up over the years. Without the precious water that bubbled up from the gorge's hot springs, Fatalis would be forced to rely on the meager supplies of morning dew harvested from the various solar stills installed upon the surface. Worse yet, they might be compelled to venture far into the barren wasteland in search of another rare spring— which might or might not exist!

"No," Khan declared. Ericsson had gone too far. "This shall not stand." Khan raised his gloved right fist, clenching it before him. "I have tolerated these incursions for too long. The time has come to dispose of Ericsson and his subversive rabble once and for all."

"We are with you, Your Excellency!" Joaquin said, sounding just as eager to take the battle to their foes. The other officers seconded his support, and even young Joachim looked ready to wage war in Khan's name. Vijay Nikore struggled to stand upon his deformed feet.

A superior breed, Khan thought proudly, *exemplary in strength and spirit!* He was touched by these people's loyalty, even as he wondered mournfully how many of them he would lose in the conflict to come. *Our numbers diminish with every year. The eels prey on our young. I can scarce afford to lose a single soul. . . .*

The Exiles had given him no choice, however. The

capture of the gorge demanded a swift and deadly response.

"Let us go to the armory," he announced. A battle strategy was already forming in his mind, one that he hoped might catch Ericsson unawares. "There are preparations to be made."

24

Three hundred years before, on his now-distant home-world, Khan had found himself locked in mortal combat with his fellow superhumans. Now, on Ceti Alpha V, history seemed to be repeating itself in what Khan fervently prayed would be the final battle of the Eugenics Wars.

Lying prone upon the sand, Khan peered over the crest of a towering sand dune at the enemy's stronghold. The cold of the desert night penetrated his robes, sinking into his bones. Overhead, roiling clouds blotted out the starlight, so that the only illumination came from the torches and campfires of the sleeping gorge. The wind howled in Khan's ears; with luck, it would drown out their preparations for tonight's sneak attack.

For perhaps the first time, Khan thought, *I am grateful that Ceti Alpha V has no moon.* The inky darkness would be a valuable ally, preventing the Exiles from realizing they were under assault until it was too late. *'Tis now the very witching time of night, when hell itself breathes out contagion to this world. . . .*

A handcrafted spyglass, its lenses painstakingly carved from clear volcanic glass, brought the entrance to the gorge within ready view. Nikore had not exaggerated the situation, Khan saw; the northern route into the ravine had been piled high with colossal boulders, of size and number enough to halt even the strongest superman. A robed sentinel, armed with a wooden bow and arrows of bone, patrolled a rocky platform built atop the barricade. Tarps and netting stretched over the top of the canyon, discouraging any attacks from above. Khan had to admit that the Azar Gorge looked ready to withstand any siege.

Khan lowered the spyglass. "It is as we expected," he informed his troops, who were gathered on the slopes of the dune below him, safely out of view of the Exiles. Joaquin, Ling, Daniel, Zuleika, Hawkins, and some thirteen more adult men and women waited to do battle against the faithless bandits who followed Ericsson. Only four adults, all wounded or disabled to varying degrees, remained back in Fatalis to care for the children—and to preserve the colony should tonight's campaign end in disaster. Nineteen full-grown superhumans, Khan had judged, should be enough to overcome how ever many Exiles opposed them.

Over his protests, Joachim had been left behind with the other youngsters. *Bad enough,* Khan thought, *that I am putting both of the youth's parents in jeopardy; I will not risk the future of Fatalis as well.*

Every warrior was armed with a variety of weapons. Khan himself had a Colt automatic pistol, a silver kirpan, a double-edged bronze sword, and five bronze chakrams threaded upon his left arm. All save the pistol were traditional Sikh weapons that he had mastered centuries ago on Earth.

Forging metal under the primitive conditions at Fatalis had not been easy, but five years and superhuman intelligence could accomplish wonders.

"We will proceed as planned," he announced. Through his visor, his eyes carefully gauged the distance between the top of the dune to the bottom of the barricade. He handed the spyglass over to Joaquin and reached for a carefully wrapped bundle, about the size of a medical tricorder. "Await my signal."

"Please, Your Excellency," Joaquin protested once more. "It is too dangerous. Let someone else perform this task!"

Khan shook his head. Five years ago, the night Marla died, he had delegated responsibility for apprehending Ericsson and his co-conspirators to others, and half a decade of bloody conflict had ensued. He would not make that mistake again. "No, my friend. My mind is set. This is something I must do myself."

The worried bodyguard conceded defeat. "Be careful, Your Excellency."

"It is Ericsson who should beware," Khan said grimly, "and all his treacherous renegades." Clutching the swaddled package closely against his chest, he crept over the crest of the dune and stealthily descended toward the gorge, counting on the blackness of the night and the ever-swirling dust clouds to hide his approach from the sentinel atop the barricade. He darted between wind-sculpted outcroppings of rock until he arrived at the base of the massive wall of boulders blocking the entrance to the gorge. Loose scree shifted alarmingly beneath his boots as he pressed his body into a crack between the bottommost boulders. Torchlight from the watch platform above filtered down through the hazy atmosphere. He could hear the footsteps of the sentry pacing roughly ten meters above.

Excellent, Khan thought. So far, he appeared to be undetected. His keen eyes scrutinized the imposing rockpile. Trained as an engineer centuries ago in Delhi, he quickly detected a potential weak spot in the deployment of the boulders. *That will do*, he decided.

Khan gingerly unwrapped the bundle beneath his arm, revealing a metallic food canister equipped with a lengthy fuse. He smiled behind his kaffiyeh as he contemplated the crude, but hopefully effective, bomb.

I trust Kirk would appreciate my ingenuity, he thought with bitter humor. Like the captain on Cestus III, Khan had taken pains to manufacture gunpowder from native materials: sulfur from deposits found along the banks of the late River Kaur; potassium nitrate from preserved bat guano and, later, human waste; coal extracted from Azar Gorge itself. Khan had been storing the raw materials in the armory for years, awaiting just such a challenge as this.

He wedged the bomb between two pivotal boulders. A spark from his flint ignited the fuse and he dashed for cover. In his haste, however, his heel dislodged a small heap of gravel, which rattled noisily onto the ground.

Khan froze, and glanced upward in alarm. To his dismay, he saw the robed sentinel staring straight down at him. The anonymous Exile reached for an arrow, but Khan's reflexes were faster still; in an instant, he plucked a chakram from his arm and hurled it with his right hand. The bronze ring spun through the air until its razor-sharp edge sliced into the guard's throat. The bow dropped from the sentry's grasp as he staggered backward, clutching his throat. A fierce gust of wind carried away his (her?) dying gurgle.

Had anyone noticed him dispatch the guard? Khan had no time to find out. Racing madly across the desert floor, he hurled himself behind a weathered outcropping only seconds before the bomb detonated.

A fiery flash, and thunderous blast, exploded at the base of the barricade, and the entire rockpile came tumbling down amid a rumble of crashing boulders. Smoke and dust rose in choking quantities. Khan heard the screams of injured Exiles.

He did not wait for the dust to settle. "Now!" he bellowed, running out from behind his temporary shelter. He drew his gun with one hand and his sword with the other, no longer afraid to let the enemy hear his voice. "Follow me—in the name of Khan!"

An answering roar, as from the brazen throat of war, arose from behind the dune. A second later, Khan heard the army of Fatalis stampeding down the sandy slope behind him. "For Khan!" they cried in unison. "FOR KHAAAAN!"

They charged the breach, leaping over the shattered remains of the barricade into a scene of utter chaos and disarray. Joaquin and Ling hurled gunpowder grenades into the enemy encampment. Exile bodies went flying as campfires and hot springs blew apart around them. Startled outlaws ran about frantically, snatching up weapons or children or both.

Sheltered by the canyon walls, few of the Exiles wore desert garb. Smoke and flames added to the confusion, along with the searing spray of detonated springs and geysers.

"Where is Ericsson?" Khan demanded over the din. A cloaked figure sprang up before, brandishing an axe, and Khan cut him down with his sword without a second's thought. "Ericsson is mine!" he called out to friend and foe alike. Khan had no intention of being cheated of his revenge, not even by Joaquin or the others.

The traitor has overreached himself, Khan thought triumphantly, savoring the success of their assault so far. As long as the Norseman and his raiders had stayed on the move, staging lightning raids, then disappearing back into the wastes, Khan had never had the troops or resources to track them down. But when Ericsson walled himself up inside the canyon, he had finally given Khan the opportunity to launch a major offensive against the renegades. Now he had them boxed in, trapped in a dead end of their own making. *I hope you enjoyed the water you found here, Harulf Ericsson. For now you will drink deeply of my vengeance!*

Khan tossed his visor aside, the better to see the nocturnal melee. Dark eyes searched the bloody scene around him, hunting for his foe. His eager sword cut down Exiles right and left, as the battle for the gorge swiftly evolved into a profusion of hand-to-hand contests being fought all throughout the crowded ravine. Amid the flames and screams, Khan caught fragmentary glimpses of heated combat.

Daniel Katzel squared off against his rebel sister upon an elevated ridge along the eastern wall of the canyon. Their tragic conflict struck Khan as emblematic of the internecine warfare that had turned brother against sister, superhuman against superhuman, for the last five years.

"How could you do it?" Daniel accused her. "Plot against Khan? Betray your oath?"

"Get real!" Amy shot back. "This isn't *Captain Proton!* Khan was leading us to destruction—and he wasn't going to step down without a fight!"

The twins were equal in strength and skill, but Daniel had the advantage in weaponry. Amy's obsidian-tipped spear of bone stood little chance against her brother's heavy bronze mace; Khan watched out of the corner of his eye, as the sister's spear shattered before the mace.

A follow-up blow knocked Amy from the ledge. She crashed to the floor of the canyon, where she sprawled motionlessly. Khan could not tell if she was dead or unconscious, nor did he much care. Amy Katzel had made her choice when she allied herself with Marla's murderers. Her fate was her own doing.

An angry shout called his attention elsewhere.

* * *

"There you are, Saraj!" Gideon Hawkins cried out. The loyal doctor had cornered Panjabi in a natural cul-de-sac formed by the craggy cliff face. Hawkins flaunted a tri-laser scalpel while his former partner sported only a single sputtering torch. "I can't believe you double-crossed our colony—and me!"

Khan watched with interest; he had long suspected the one-eared ex–cricket player of supplying Ericsson with the eel that had killed Marla. He would enjoy seeing Panjabi gutted.

"Come and get me, quack," Panjabi taunted Hawkins. A patch of loose scrub covered the canyon floor between them. The doctor charged forward, just as Khan guessed what was in store.

"Wait!" he called out, but it was too late. The moment his feet hit the scrub, the ground collapsed beneath Hawkins, plunging him into a hidden pit. His panicked shrieks drew Khan to the scene. Tossing other combatants aside, Khan ran to the edge of the pit and looked down, his eyes widening in horror.

The bottom of the trap was filled with Ceti eels, dozens of them. The scaly mollusks swarmed over the fallen doctor like piranhas, tearing him apart with their vicious pincers. Blood sprayed freely as the eels squealed in excitement.

Some deaths are too foul even for war, Khan thought in disgust. Raising his gun, he used a precious bullet to put the unfortunate physician out of his misery, just as so many of Hawkins' patients had been put down. Khan turned his outraged gaze on Panjabi. "Eels again, Saraj?"

he snarled. "I should have taken your head instead of your ear!"

He bounded over the pit, landing only centimeters away from Panjabi. The murderous renegade swung his firebrand, but Khan sliced the torch in half with one swipe of his sword. Shoving his gun back into his belt, he grabbed on to Panjabi and threw him headlong into the pit. New screams escaped the death trap, joining the frenzied squeals of the bloodthirsty eels.

Khan strode away. He was not about to waste a bullet on an Exile.

Several meters away, Zuleika caught Karyn Ericsson and her daughter trying to escape the gorge, along with Juliette Savine and some of the other Exile children.

"Forget it, girls," the Amazonian supermodel announced, blocking the pass out of the canyon. She had discarded her headcloth and visor, revealing braided dreadlocks, but threatened the fleeing Exiles with a pair of matching bronze *sais*. "You're not going anywhere."

"Please, Zuleika," Karyn begged from the forefront of the deserters, defending Astrid and the other youngsters with a crude spear. "We don't have to fight. Just let us by—for the children's sake!"

"So you can raise another generation of terrorists and thieves?" Zuleika asked mockingly. She jabbed the air between them with the sharpened points of her *sais*. "No way!"

Seeing no other choice, Karyn lunged at Zuleika with her spear. Zuleika deftly evaded the thrust by spinning to one side. Laughing, she came back at Karyn, her *sais* flashing in the torchlight.

It was a short battle. Zuleika was an ex-assassin, trained in armed and unarmed combat. Karyn Ericsson, although hardened by over a decade on Ceti Alpha V, was a former professor of linguistics.

The outcome was never in doubt.

Catching hold of Karyn's spear with one *sai*, Zuleika disarmed the other woman with one expert move. Her right leg slammed in Karyn's stomach, knocking Ericsson's wife onto the ground. Zuleika stood astride Karyn's sprawled form, staring down at her in contempt.

"Surrender," she growled, "and I won't have to kill you in front of your daughter." Zuleika raised her eyes to shoot a warning glance at Savine, who cowered a few meters away, clutching her ten-year-old son. "Khan's not much interested in taking prisoners, but he might be willing to make an exception where the kids are concerned."

A rock came whizzing through the air, striking Zuleika in the temple. Stunned, she raised a hand to her head and was surprised to see blood dripping from her fingertips. She tottered unsteadily upon her feet. Blurry eyes spotted little Astrid Ericsson standing a few meters away, a leather sling in her hand. "You . . . ?" Zuleika whispered in disbelief.

"Leave my mother alone!" the girl shouted. Fury blazed in her pale blue eyes. She let fly another rock.

The second missile struck Zuleika squarely between the eyes. The dazed Amazon toppled over, hitting the

ground with a crash. Astrid sprang forward, drawing the
tusk of a long-dead sabertooth from the folds of her small
burnoose. . . .

Moments later, Karyn and Savine hustled Astrid and
the other children out of the gorge into the darkened
desert beyond. Astrid clutched the bloodstained tusk
like a favorite toy.

Khan was drawing his sword from the belly of a fallen
Exile when he heard footsteps closing on him from
behind. He spun around to see Paul Austin swinging a
battle-axe at his head. The crazed American was naked
from the waist up, exposing a lean torso liberally
embellished with tattoos. "Die!" he yelled as the blade
of the axe came slashing through the air. "*Sic semper
tyrannis!*"

The speed of the attack tested even Khan's superhuman reflexes. He was still reaching for his gun,
unsure whether he could draw the Colt in time, when
the butt of a rifle suddenly struck Austin in the side of
the head, staggering him. "Do not fear, Your Excellency!" Joaquin shouted from the other end of the rifle.

Your timely assistance is much appreciated, my friend,
Khan thought. *I can always count on you to watch my back.*

The massive axe slipped from Austin's fingers.
Joaquin raised his rifle again, as though to deliver a
killing blow, but Khan had other plans. "Wait!" he fore-
stalled the eager bodyguard. "Hold the cur instead!"

Shouldering his rifle, Joaquin obediently grabbed on
to Austin, twisting the other man's arms behind his
back. The tattooed Exile struggled to free himself, but

could not escape Joaquin's unbreakable hold. Austin's efforts left him panting, a consequence, perhaps, of too much smoking over the course of his unworthy life.

Khan stepped forward to confront the prisoner.

"Where is your master, renegade?" he demanded, his face only centimeters from Austin's. "Where is Ericsson?"

Austin spit in Khan's face. "Go to hell!"

"Why this is hell," Khan snarled mordantly, "nor am I out of it." He pressed the point of his sword against Austin's throat, determined to wring the truth from the man, one way or another. "Where?" he repeated. The tip of the blade broke the skin, drawing a single drop of blood. "Where is Ericsson?"

"Here I am, Khan!" a sardonic voice called out. Khan looked away from Austin, his blood racing at the sound. *At last!* he thought savagely.

Harulf Ericsson stood at the far end of the gorge, at the foot of the southern barricade. Steam rose from a bubbling hot spring directly behind Ericsson, giving him the look of a demon making a far-too-theatrical entrance. No kaffiyeh concealed his hateful countenance.

To his horror, Khan saw that the rebel leader was not alone. Suzette Ling was caught in Ericsson's grasp, with one arm around her waist and a Colt pistol aimed at her head. Blood streamed from a bullet wound in her left shoulder.

An anguished grunt escaped Joaquin as he saw his wife in the enemy's hands.

"I am sorry, Joaquin, Lord Khan!" Ling blurted. Shock and pain showed on her ashen face. "I wasn't expecting the gun!"

"Quiet!" Ericsson barked at his hostage. Khan guessed that the revolver had been captured from one of the guards murdered when the Exiles seized the gorge. "Throw down your weapons," the Norseman shouted at Khan and Joaquin.

Khan wavered. Ordinarily, he would not hesitate to sacrifice a soldier or two in pursuit of victory, but Joaquin was his oldest and most faithful supporter. Khan still felt the pain of Marla's death. How could he ask Joaquin to endure the same torment?

He cast a sideways glance at Joaquin, who was maintaining his hold on Austin, seemingly frozen in place. Although Joaquin's expression remained as stony as ever, Khan glimpsed the agony in his friend's eyes.

Khan threw down his sword and gun.

"The chakrams, too," Ericsson ordered. "And tell your musclebound stooge to let go of Austin."

But Joaquin made his own decision. Forced to choose between Khan and the mother of his son, the huge bodyguard chose the leader to whom he had devoted his life. Bellowing like an enraged bull, Joaquin flung Paul Austin aside and charged at Ericsson. His big hands grabbed for the rifle strapped to his shoulder.

What happened next took only heartbeats:

"*Milde Makter!*" Ericsson exclaimed in surprise. His gun fired, taking off the top of Suzette Ling's skull. The security chief's body crumpled to the ground like cannon fodder even as Ericsson rapidly turned the gun on Joaquin as well. Multiple shots slammed into the bodyguard's chest, but Joaquin kept on coming, driven by momentum and pure animal determination.

Khan took advantage of the distraction to draw another chakram from his arm. The gleaming bronze ring flew from his hand, heading straight for Ericsson, who let out a horrified wail as the spinning chakram sliced off his gun hand at the wrist.

A flicker of movement to his right alerted Khan that Austin was scrambling for the discarded Colt. Annoyed at having to deal with an underling while the greater foe awaited, Khan reached out and administered a vicious nerve pinch to a pressure point at the base of the American's neck, which just happened to be adorned with the tattooed image of a black widow spider.

Austin dropped unconscious to the floor of the canyon.

Khan immediately turned his attention back to Ericsson. For a second, it looked as though Joaquin was going to reach the traitorous Norseman first, but not even the mighty Israeli could ignore Ericsson's bullets for long. His strength gave out less than a meter away from his target, and he collapsed to earth, landing in a heap not far from the body of his murdered wife.

Joachim had just become an orphan.

Khan felt a pang of grief for both loyal followers, but now was not the time for mourning. *Vengeance comes first,* Khan thought, as he advanced on Ericsson. *Vengeance long delayed.*

Clutching the spurting stump where his left hand had once been, the rebel leader backed into the rocky barricade behind him. Fear showed through a shaggy beard that was now more gray than gold. Khan was surprised at how much older the man looked.

"Well," Ericsson said with a toothy grin. "Here we are at last." He grimaced in pain, his sunbaked features growing whiter by the second. His voice, although grown hoarser with age, was just as insolent as it had been when he challenged Khan long ago, on the day they first set foot on Ceti Alpha V. "I don't suppose there's any point in pleading for mercy?"

Khan did not deign to answer so ridiculous a query. Ericsson's severed hand, still gripping the stolen revolver, lay upon the gravel between Khan and his quarry. He kicked it out of his path as he drew nearer to Ericsson. The spray from the nearby hot spring stung his face.

A cruel smile came to Khan's lips. He took hold of Ericsson with both hands and lifted him physically off the ground. Weak from blood loss, the Exile leader had no strength to resist.

"Marla once taught me an old Klingon saying—that revenge is a dish that is best served cold." Khan's smile faded as the memory of his wife's tragic end returned with full force. "In your case, however, I am inclined to make an exception!"

Before Ericsson could say another word, Khan hurled Marla's killer into the seething hot spring. The Norseman's screams echoed off the walls of the canyon as the boiling water scalded the flesh from his bones.

Khan savored every moment of Ericsson's demise.

25

The battle itself died shortly thereafter. With their leader gone, the remaining Exiles—mostly striplings no older than Joachim—surrendered to Khan and his forces. Weapons were confiscated, the wounded given varying degrees of treatment, and the dead laid out for disposal.

As the sun rose over Azar Gorge, casting a sickly yellow radiance over the blood-soaked canyon, Khan was left to contemplate the awful price of victory. The gorge had been reclaimed, yes, and his enemies routed, but at what cost?

Joaquin, Ling, Zuleika, and many others, all lost to death. In the end, his own forces had suffered a half-dozen fatalities, while the overwhelmed Exiles had lost seven adults and almost an equal number of youngsters. *There is not even a doctor to attend to the injured,* Khan real-

341

ized morosely, *not since Gideon Hawkins met his end in the eel pit.*

Ceti Alpha V was now without a physician.

Khan wandered numbly through the battle-scarred gorge. The stink of death and gunpowder assailed his nostrils. Even the canyon itself, he saw, had become a casualty of war. The rampant flames and explosion had destroyed whatever vegetation had once thrived in the gorge, the hardy cacti and other succulents. It would be many years before anything grew here again, if anything ever did.

A terrible weariness descended upon Khan. With Ericsson dead at last, he felt as though he had lost his reason to live. What remained to him now, except to preside over the slow extinction of the planet?

"Your Excellency!" A loyalist, whose name Khan vaguely remembered was Yolanda Aponte, hurried to catch up with him. Once a minor lieutenant, Aponte had received a battlefield promotion when Khan placed her in charge of the clean-up operation. "The prisoners await your justice."

The news brought no joy. He raised his gaze to consider the surviving Exiles, who had been chained together upon the floor of the ravine. Khan spotted Paul Austin among them, along with Amy Katzel, who was currently having her bandaged skull inspected by her brother Daniel. Armed warriors from Fatalis stood watch over the dispirited captives, despite their own assorted injuries.

"That is all of them?" he asked.

"All that are accounted for, Your Excellency." A frown

appeared on Aponte's soot-stained face. "Ericsson's wife and daughter are missing, I'm afraid. There are reports that they, along with a handful of others, escaped the canyon during the fighting."

Khan's spirits plunged ever deeper. *After all this bloodshed*, he lamented, *it seems the seeds of future conflict remain.* Although broken and leaderless, might not the Exiles someday rise to oppose him once more?

"We shall hear from them again," he prophesied. His voice held a bitter edge.

Aponte tried to lift his mood. "A few stray fugitives, Lord Khan. Nothing to be concerned about." She gestured toward the assembled prisoners. "In the meantime, there's those vermin to deal with. What is your command?"

What was to be done with the rebels? Deep in his heart, Khan had already decided their fates. The adults would be put to death, with the possible exception of Amy Katzel, whom he might pardon in payment for her brother's loyal service. Life at Fatalis was too precarious to risk adding a hostile underclass to the equation. The children, however, would be spared, to protect the genetic diversity of the entire colony.

They will have to be watched carefully, he cautioned himself, *perhaps for years to come. But they are still young enough to learn better of their parents' ways.*

"Leave me," he dismissed Aponte. He knew what had to be done, but found he had no stomach for the task at present. "I shall deal with the prisoners in my own time."

"As you say, Your Excellency," the woman replied, a

slightly puzzled look upon her face. Respecting his desire for privacy, she left him to his thoughts, which grew steadily darker as he looked beyond today's "victory" to the long years ahead. *Why go on?* he asked himself. *My wife and closest friend are dead, and my youthful dreams of empire have come down to this: ruling over a paucity of ragged castaways on a moribund planet.*

His hand fell to the pistol on his hip, reclaimed after he sent Ericsson to his eternal damnation. It would be easy, he realized, to end his torturous journey here in this desolate gorge, with a single bullet through his skull.

"I have lived long enough: my way of life
"Is fall'n into the sere, the yellow leaf;
"And that which should accompany old age,
"As honor, love, obedience, troops of friends,
"I must not look to have. . . ."

Khan lifted the gun. In his mind's eye, he saw Marla once more, as fair and enchanting as ever. *She is waiting for me,* he thought longingly. *Perhaps it is time to join her.*

But another face intruded upon his consciousness, staying his hand with a memory of flaxen hair and intense blue eyes.

The boy. Joachim.

Who will care for him once I am gone?

Khan's hand came away from the gun. "No," he whispered reluctantly. He must keep on living, if only for the sake of his people, who looked to him to keep them alive on a world infinitely harsher than the Earth they abandoned centuries ago. *I led them here, so I cannot abandon them now, even if it means ruling in Hell itself for many decades to come.*

He imagined Joaquin's spirit hovering nearby, standing guard over Khan in death just as he always had in life. "Do not fear for your son, old friend," Khan promised him. "I swear upon my life, I shall raise Joachim as though he were my very own."

The solemn oath reminded Khan of another vow he had once made years ago, and another, equally compelling, reason to stay alive. His hand went to his chest, feeling, beneath his blood-stained robes, the imprint of a silver medallion.

The face of James T. Kirk, captain of the *Enterprise*, appeared behind Khan's brooding eyes.

Kirk's hated visage stoked the embers of the all-consuming hatred burning in Khan's heart. *How could I have forgotten?* he chastised himself, ashamed to have even contemplated suicide while the true architect of his people's suffering traveled the cosmos with impunity.

I cannot die, he recalled, *until, someday, James T. Kirk has felt my wrath. . . .*

26

FIVE PLANETARY YEARS LATER

> *Which way I fly is hell; myself am hell;*
> *And in the lowest deep a lower deep,*
> *Still threat'ning to devour me, opens wide,*
> *To which the hell I suffer seems a heaven. . . .*

Khan's mood was dark as he led a procession of shrouded figures across the endless sands toward home. Today's expedition had been a discouraging one; the solar stills west of Fatalis had yielded less than seventy percent of the water supplies they had anticipated. There would be many thirsty days ahead.

The familiar wasteland stretched before him. The wind howled in his ears. Khan trudged wearily, feeling the weight of fifteen years of exile resting heavily on his aged shoulders. Swirling dust devils dogged his steps.

Just behind him, Joachim marched at his right hand, just as Joaquin had before him. In truth, if Khan was completely honest with himself, he sometimes forgot that the son was not the father, and that the present was not merely the doleful past prolonged unto eternity.

Most of those who followed him now were second-generation superhumans, their parents having long since succumbed to disease, accident, or the unceasing depredations of the eels. Of his original comrades from the twentieth century, only a handful remained. Khan suspected that only the simmering hatred in his own heart had kept him alive so long.

A gnarled stone outcropping loomed out of the murk before him, signifying that they were drawing near to the battered steel cargo bays that guarded the entrance to Fatalis. Khan's mind leaped ahead to the evening to come, as he pondered how he would spend the empty hours once the caravan returned to the caves.

Write in his journal? Play chess with Joachim? Neither sounded particularly inviting in his present mood. Perhaps he would simply seek out Marla's tomb and spend the time in quiet seclusion with his wife.

A bizarre flicker of light caught his eye, stopping him in his tracks. *I don't believe it! Can it be?* he thought in astonishment as his exceptional vision recognized the unearthly sparkle of a transporter beam. Peering through his visor, he watched transfixed as two space-suited figures materialized in the desert, only a short hike away from the refurbished cargo carriers.

Finally! he exulted, realizing that his superhuman patience had finally been rewarded. A smile lifted his lips for the first time in many years. He had no idea who had chanced upon their desolate abode, nor did he care. All that mattered was that the strangers must have beamed down from an orbiting starship, and where there was a starship, there was the possibility of escape.

Here at last, after so many years, is my chance for freedom . . .

And revenge!

PART FOUR

A.D. 2287

27

"The Pit" proved to be just that, a gigantic sinkhole whose smooth flowstone walls stretched at least three meters above Kirk's head. Human bones littered the bottom of the Pit, suggesting that he and Spock were not the first prisoners to be confined here. Squatting on the floor, his back against the cold calcite wall, Kirk hoped they weren't in for quite so long a stay.

Armed Exiles, young and feral in appearance, patrolled the top of the Pit, discouraging any attempt at rock climbing. *Not much danger of that*, Kirk thought. *Even if we managed to get out of here and past the guards, how far could we get without our environmental suits?*

Lacking any better option, at least for the time being, Kirk and Spock had compared notes on what they had read in, respectively, Khan's journal and Marla's data disks. The latter account seemed to jibe with Khan's versions of events, at least up to the point where Marla sacrificed herself to save Khan's life. *Just like Clark Terrell phasered himself to save me*, Kirk realized, *back on Regula.* He had been proud to read that, in the end, Marla had possessed the tenacity to overcome the coercive influence of the eel in her brain. *Was that a testament to her Starfleet training*, he wondered, *or to the extent of her unconditional love for Khan?*

"An intriguing, if tragic, narrative," Spock concluded. He maintained a meditative pose upon the floor of the Pit, conserving his mental and physical faculties as much as possible. "It is a pity that our investigation has encountered such an unexpected interruption. I would have prefered to have perused Lieutenant McGivers' data disks at greater length."

This trip is certainly proving more eventful than expected, Kirk conceded wryly. *Wonder how long Sulu will wait for us to check in before contacting Starfleet?* In any event, it would be some time before a search party could arrive to rescue them. *We're on our own, just like Khan was.*

Suddenly, he heard footsteps approaching the Pit from above. Spock arched an eyebrow and exchanged a silent look with Kirk. The two men rose quickly to their feet, the better to face whatever transpired next. *So much for discussing history*, Kirk thought. *At the moment, to paraphrase Spock, the needs of the present outweigh the demands of the past.*

Seconds later, he heard McCoy's familiar drawl echo through the caverns overhead. "All right, all right, I'm coming," the doctor groused. "There's no need to poke me with those damn pig-stickers."

A rope ladder, woven from flaxen human hair, tumbled down from the top of the pit. Prodded by the unfriendly guards, McCoy slowly clambered down the ladder to join his friends at the bottom of the pit. Kirk couldn't help thinking of the story of Rapunzel, even though the irascible physician made an unlikely Prince Charming.

"Good of you to drop in, Bones," Kirk said, glad to see that McCoy appeared unharmed. "What's the status of your patient?"

"The mother or the baby?" McCoy replied. He wiped bloody hands on his black bodysuit; apparently the Exiles couldn't spare water for washing up. "Both should be fine, although I've certainly performed deliveries in more sterile settings." He shook his head, obviously disturbed by the primitive conditions he'd witnessed. "It says something about these kids' enhanced immune systems that they don't lose more tribe members to infection. Good God, Jim, the mother herself was no more than fifteen, though she looked a bit older."

Kirk recalled that Khan had mentioned the children's accelerated maturation. He found it hard to accept that this whole new tribe of Exiles had grown up since he stranded Khan and the others here years ago.

"That's enough, Doctor," an icy voice interrupted from above. Kirk looked up to see Astrid Ericsson standing at the edge of the pit. The sabertooth tusk around her neck gleamed in the torchlight. "You can converse with your associates later, if you're still able."

Kirk didn't like the sound of that. *I have to convince her that we mean her people no harm.*

Eschewing the ladder, the youthful superwoman leaped into the Pit on her own, effortlessly landing on the uneven stone floor. Three more Exiles joined her, just in case the captives were tempted to try overpowering Astrid. Blades drawn, they glared at the unarmed Starfleet officers while a fifth young superhuman descended the ladder, a transparent aluminum container tucked under his arm.

A layer of rocky soil covered the bottom of the tank, which Kirk assumed to be Khan's missing terrarium. He had no doubt what lurked beneath the rust-colored dirt and gravel.

The Ceti eels.

Astrid smiled coldly, acknowledging the arrival of the terrarium. She fixed a menacing gaze on Kirk. "I trust you've had time to reconsider your situation." She gestured pointedly toward the eel tank, now resting in the arms of her subordinate. "Are you ready to reveal Khan's whereabouts, or shall I be forced to resort to more drastic measures?"

"I've already told you the truth," Kirk insisted. "Khan is dead." He threw up his hands. "Why would we lie to you? Khan was as much our enemy as yours."

"Then why not leave him to rot on Ceti Alpha V?" Astrid challenged him. Anger flared in her piercing blue eyes. "How else could Khan escape this world without the aid of your starship?" She laughed scornfully. "You expect me to believe the word of the Abandoner?"

"There are many starships," Spock pointed out calmly, as though he was conducting a seminar at Starfleet Academy. "Your enmity toward Khan is clouding your logic."

Astrid bristled angrily. "Shut your mouth, alien!" She nodded to two of the guards, who instantly took hold of Spock and McCoy from behind, trapping their arms to their sides. "I am tired of being lied to," she announced ominously.

Turning away from Kirk, she lifted the lid from the terrarium and impatiently tossed it aside. A pair of matching metal tongs appeared in her hands.

Astrid probed the eel tank with one set of tongs, provoking an immediate response from the creature hiding beneath the soil. Bony pincers grabbed onto the metal implement. An angry squeal assaulted Kirk's ears. Astrid pulled on the tongs, exposing a scaly, gray-blue life-form that could only be the infamous Ceti eel.

The monster looked just as ugly as Kirk recalled, and several times larger than the immature version that had crawled out of Chekov's ear back on Regula. He recoiled instinctively from the sight of the creature. A few steps away, McCoy gulped loudly.

"Fascinating," Spock observed. Kirk recalled that Spock had never seen an actual specimen of the eel before.

Frankly, the captain thought, *I could have done without this particular lesson in exobiology.*

Using the tongs, Astrid expertly shifted her grip on the so-called eel, seizing it behind its head so that it couldn't escape. The enraged mollusk thrashed and hissed furiously, rolling its slitted yellow eyes, but the determined superwoman held it firmly in place.

Next, she used the second pair of tongs to dig between the dorsal ridges of the eel's rigid carapace, extracting a single black larva. The procedure looked surprisingly delicate, as though Astrid were performing surgery, not preparing to torture an innocent prisoner.

"You don't have to do this!" Kirk called out to the Exile leader, trying one more time to get through to her. "We're telling you the truth. We're not your enemy!" He stepped toward her urgently, only to be driven back at spearpoint by the third guard. "Forget about Khan! Let us do what we can to help your people!"

"Abandon our crusade against the Tyrant?" Astrid reacted vehemently to the very suggestion. "Never!" Releasing the adult eel, she placed the lid back on the terrarium and turned toward the captives with the deadly larva still trapped within her tongs. Azure eyes swung from Spock to McCoy and back again, considering her options. "I am uncertain whether the larva will accept a host with green blood," she admitted. "Perhaps the doctor instead?"

Kirk could not contain his anger and frustration. "For God's sake, this man just helped one of your own people deliver a baby! He may even have saved two lives!"

A flicker of regret showed on Astrid's features. "A lucky happenstance for us," she conceded, "but hardly proof of your good intentions. The doctor's efforts may have simply been a selfish attempt to win our trust, in order to betray us later." Her gaze drifted to the blood-stains on McCoy's hands and clothes. "Still, I suppose there is no harm in starting with the alien."

His name is Spock, Kirk thought, unsure how to save both his friends, but painfully aware that he was running out of time. *This is just what Chekov and Terrell went through!*

I can't let it happen again.

Astrid approached Spock, who didn't flinch at all, even though Kirk couldn't imagine any fate more repellent to a Vulcan than having his brain and reason subverted by a destructive parasite. Could Spock's powerful mind resist the insidious effects of the eel?

Kirk knew he couldn't risk it.

"Wait!" he shouted. "You win!"

Astrid paused, keeping the squirming larva caught between her tongs. She eyed Kirk suspiciously.

"Earth is in trouble," he lied, making his story up as he went. "An alien race—the Corbomites—have attacked the United Federation of Planets, menacing the entire quadrant. They're a superior species: faster, stronger, smarter than us. We didn't stand a chance on our own. We needed Khan—and his genetically engineered intelligence. He was our only hope!"

Kirk heard McCoy choke. Astrid seemed to be buying the story, though, which had the virtue of playing to all of her preconceptions about the importance of Khan and the helpless inferiority of ordinary humans.

When in doubt, he thought, *bluff.*

"We rescued Khan and his people a year ago, offering him a full pardon in exchange for his help against the Corbomites. An enemy warship chased us away from here, before we could complete the evacuation, however. Khan was forced to leave several personal effects behind, including the remains of his late wife." Kirk let a note of genuine remorse enter his voice. "Now that the

Corbomites have been driven out of this sector of space, thanks to Khan, he has returned to transport his wife's body back to Earth." Kirk feigned annoyance. "Sadistic bastard that he is, he insisted that I personally handle the task of retrieving Lieutenant McGivers' remains, just to rub the fact of her death in my face."

McCoy snorted indignantly. "Isn't that just like the arrogant son of a gun!"

"Indeed," Spock confirmed, playing along. "Khan is nothing if not unforgiving, especially where the captain is concerned."

True enough, Kirk thought, *aside from the present tense.*

Astrid nodded, a look of satisfaction upon her face. "Of course," she crowed. "I knew Khan was behind this all." She dropped the larva back into the tank, which was sealed up and taken away at her command. "Where is Khan now?" she demanded of Kirk.

"Up there," he said, glancing at the rocky ceiling many meters above. "In orbit around the planet." Pushing his luck, he gave her a conspiratorial wink. "But I know just how to lure him down to the surface."

The punishing environment outside the refurbished cargo bays had not improved during their stint underground. Driving winds kicked up a furious duststorm that reduced visibility to near zero. "This would be easier," Kirk shouted at Astrid, straining to be heard over the howling wind, "if you'd just allow us to use our communicators."

The Exile leader had not permitted Kirk and his associates to put their environmental suits back on for this return trip to the planet's surface. Only primitive robes, headcloths, and visors protected the three men's faces from the never-ending sandstorm.

"No," Astrid shouted back, her striking features hidden behind her own desert garb. Although three of her lieutenants had donned the captured environmental suits for the occasion, she had preferred to stick to her accustomed attire. Kirk's phaser rested in her hand, while the other two phasers now resided in the grip of her bodyguards. "We will employ the emergency signal only, as planned."

"All right," Kirk agreed. *So much for giving Sulu a chance to beam us right up,* he thought. *Guess we'll have to do this the hard way.*

"Switch your phasers to full power," he instructed Astrid and the two bodyguards, "and point them toward the sky. You want the beams to converge, say, six meters above our heads."

He had convinced the Exiles that firing the phasers into the air constituted a universal Starfleet distress signal, one that would immediately draw Khan down to investigate. Kirk could only hope that Sulu would detect the fireworks from orbit and know what to do.

Astrid hesitated. "How do you know that Khan himself will respond to the signal?" she asked, doubt in her voice. Aside from herself and the three wolves in Starfleet clothing, the rest of the Exiles were hidden behind the granite bluffs surrounding Khan's former domicile, waiting to ambush the hated tyrant the minute he showed his face on Ceti Alpha V.

"Trust me," Kirk said, "I know the man much better

than you do." He gave his best impression of utter confidence and certainty. "He'll be here."

Offered a once-in-a-lifetime opportunity to lure Khan into her clutches, Astrid took the bait. "Let's do it," she ordered her guards as she raised her stolen phaser toward the oppressive yellow sky. "Now!"

Beams of crimson energy cut through the gritty haze from three separate locations, intersecting high above the party's heads. Kirk squinted behind his crude visor at the incandescent display, which flared above the desolate terrain like a reactor overload.

Come on, Sulu! he urged the absent helmsman. *Don't let me down!*

28

Hikaru Sulu stared at the sensor display with increasing anxiety. It had been hours since Captain Kirk and the landing party had last checked in; he had to assume that something had gone very wrong on the planet below.

But what?

"*Yakima* to landing party," he tried once more. "*Yakima* to landing party. Please respond."

Silence greeted his hails. He glanced in frustration at the transporter controls. Without a communicator signal, there was no way he could lock onto any of the missing men.

Sulu wished that he were at the helm of the *Enterprise*. On a full-fledged starship, it would be possible to send search parties down to look for Kirk and the others. A state-of-the-art sensor array could scan the entire planet for even the faintest signs of life. Stuck on the *Yakima*, however, Sulu's options were much more limited.

Now what do I do? he worried. The nearest starbase was days away at warp speed. By the time he got back with reinforcements, the captain, Spock, and McCoy could easily die of exposure on the hostile planet. *If they're not already dead,* he thought grimly.

An electronic beep from the sensors caused his pulse to race. His eager eyes scanned the display panel, which alerted him to a sustained energy discharge on the planet's surface, not far from the coordinates of Khan's primitive shelter. Sulu hurriedly recalibrated the sensors, determining that the mysterious energy surge appeared to be phaser fire.

That's good enough for me, he decided. Manning the helm, he took the *Yakima* out of orbit and headed the cruiser straight into the planet's turbulent atmosphere. He had no idea what the landing party was firing at down below, but at least he had an idea where they were now.

"Hang on, Captain. I'm on my way."

The ride through Ceti Alpha V's stormy skies was a bumpy one, testing Sulu's piloting skills to the extreme. Cyclonic winds buffeted the compact spacecraft. Dense particulate matter obscured the viewscreen, forcing Sulu to navigate by instrumentation alone. Thunder boomed all around him, while titanic bolts of lightning crackled against the ship's deflectors like disruptor fire. Sulu couldn't help remembering the *Galileo Seven*'s crash landing on Tarsus II. He hoped that history wasn't about to repeat itself.

The atmosphere thinned marginally as the cruiser neared the planet's surface. Sulu scanned the area around the phaser blasts with the onboard sensors and was surprised to detect the presence of multiple humanoid life-forms. *Looks like the captain ran into company,* he thought, both puzzled and concerned. *I thought this planet was supposed to be uninhabited.*

Unfortunately, there was no way to distinguish the landing party from the other humanoids, not under these conditions. The fierce sandstorms interfered severely with the sensors, making more precise readings impossible. Sulu realized that there was only one way to recover Kirk and the others safely.

"Sorry about this, Captain," he muttered as he set the phaser controls for maximum dispersal. He brought the *Yakima* in toward the center of the clump of individuals, aiming the phasers directly ahead.

A crimson flash lighted up the viewscreen as Sulu unleashed a low-level phaser barrage capable of knocking out every man, woman, and child in the immediate vicinity.

Then he looked for a good place to land.

Kirk's head was still ringing from the phaser blast when he confronted Astrid Ericsson in the *Yakima*'s pressurized passenger compartment. The clean air and comfortable temperature came as a welcome relief after his stay on Ceti Alpha V.

Astrid had been brought aboard the *Yakima* at phaserpoint, while her followers had been left on the planet below, sans their stolen phasers and environmental suits. Unarmed and outnumbered, the Exile leader found herself in orbit with Kirk and the others.

"Why should I believe you now?" she accused him, seated upon one of the cabin's padded seats. Kirk had to imagine that she found the cruiser's sleek interior disorienting compared with what she was used to. "After so much trickery?"

"Because," Kirk pointed out patiently, "I no longer have any reason to deceive you." He tilted his head toward Spock and McCoy who were standing nearby with their phasers ready. "In case you haven't noticed, I'm holding all the cards now."

Astrid seethed visibly, but was unable to refute his reasoning. "So what do you want with me?"

"To convince you that a better life is waiting for your people once you accept that Khan really is gone for good." Kirk felt an overpowering desire to get through to the young woman, before more lives were wasted on the hellish planet she called home. "Listen to me. Use your enhanced intelligence to overcome your obsession with Khan and look at the larger picture, for your people's sake. You must realize that Ceti Alpha V is dying. There's no future for you there, regardless of whether Khan is alive or not. What's more important to you: revenge or survival?"

For several long minutes, Astrid said nothing in reply. Kirk chose to take this as an encouraging sign. *Khan threw away his life and the lives of his followers in pursuit of vengeance,* he thought. *I can't let Astrid make the same mistake.*

"What precisely are you offering?" she asked finally.

Yes! Kirk thought, feeling a surge of hope. "You're all descended from refugees who fled Earth three hundred years ago. That makes you our responsibility. I'm sure I can convince Starfleet to relocate you to a more hospitable planet, where you can make a fresh start."

"What sort of planet?" Astrid asked. Her suspicious tone indicated that she was not yet convinced.

Kirk knew just the place. "There's a planet called Sycorax, which is already home to a colony of genetically engineered superhumans." Kirk had first visited Sycorax, and the so-called Paragon Colony, roughly fifteen years ago, only four years after his first encounter with Khan. "Sycorax has a thriving superhuman community, which I'm certain would be happy to add your enhanced DNA to their gene pool."

He didn't mention that Sycorax remained quarantined from the rest of the Federation, due to the UFP's age-old ban on human genetic engineering. The point was that the Exiles would be unwelcome anywhere else. *Plus,* he thought, *it can't hurt to keep Khan's descendants under quarantine as well.*

The ironic part, of course, was that his proposition was not entirely different from the one he had offered to Khan nineteen years ago: a new planet on which to begin again. *But this time,* Kirk vowed, *I'm putting them in the care of an established, successful colony. And I'm personally going to make sure that the Paragon Colony—and Starfleet—gives Astrid and the others all the assistance and supervision they require.*

The Exiles were not going to be forgotten again.

"You and your people deserve a better, a more superior life," he continued, "than fighting a battle that should have ended centuries ago. The Eugenics Wars are over, finally. It's time to put the tragedies of the past behind us and move on to the future."

And, perhaps, in this way, I can lay my own ghosts to rest as well, Kirk realized. *Part of me will always regret what happened on Ceti Alpha V, but, by helping the Exiles start over again on a new world, I can do what I can to put things right.*

The light of a bold new dream dawned in Astrid Ericsson's pale blue eyes. "Perhaps," she said. "You are no longer the Abandoner."

EPILOGUE

Kirk closed Khan's journal, having reached the final entry. He knew too well what happened next. *Khan must have sealed up Marla's crypt right before he used Terrell and Chekov to capture the* Reliant, *he realized. In fact, he probably used the two men's phasers to remelt the eighteen-year-old thermoconcrete.*

It occurred to Kirk that he was surely the last person Khan ever expected to find the entombed journal and data disks. *Chances are, Khan went to his end convinced that he had killed me in that final explosion. . . .*

He glanced out the starboard porthole at the very site of Khan's apocalyptic demise.

The Genesis Planet was no more, as was the nebula that birthed it. Kirk saw only the gaseous remains of the planet where his son had died—and Spock had been reborn. Khan and his followers had died in this same haunted sector of space as well, reduced to atoms by the primordial forces unleashed by the Genesis Device.

This is hallowed ground, he thought. Not literally, of course, but in every way that mattered. *Which makes it the perfect place for this last solemn duty.*

Technically, this region of space remained off-limits to civilian vessels, owing to the controversial nature of the Genesis Project, but Kirk had seen classified reports indicating that any residual contamination from the Genesis Device had long since dispersed. According to the experts, there was no danger in approaching this space. *And besides*, he acknowledged wryly, *it's hardly the first time I've skirted regulations for the sake of a former crew member.*

McCoy emerged from a compartment at the rear of the *Yakima*. The doctor's face bore a serious expression. "Jim, we're ready," he informed his friend.

Kirk rose from his seat. He placed Khan's journal on the seat beside his, next to Marla's data disks. The historian's electronic files awaited his further inspection. At the moment, however, another task demanded his presence.

He joined Spock and McCoy in the *Yakima*'s small transporter chamber. Like him, the two men had donned their best Starfleet uniforms for the occasion. Experience had taught the three officers to take their uniforms with them wherever they went, in the not-unlikely event that they were abruptly called into service or asked to attend some diplomatic function. It struck Kirk as highly appropriate to be wearing a captain's insignia again, since it was his decisions as a captain, nineteen years ago, that had led him to this moment.

On the transporter pad before him, a burnished steel capsule held the ashes of Marla McGivers Singh. After much deliberation, Kirk had decided to remove Marla's remains from her lonely tomb on Ceti Alpha V. He thought he knew what she would want done with her ashes.

"We are gathered here to pay our last respects to our former crewmate," he announced soberly. Spock and McCoy stood at attention, while the ship's intercom carried his remarks to Sulu, who remained stationed at the helm. "Some may fault Lieutenant Marla McGivers' service to Starfleet, but we cannot question her bravery and resourcefulness. She had the courage to follow her heart wherever it led, and the record shows that she accepted the consequences with grace and determination. As Marla McGivers Singh, she faced harrowing trials without complaint, and ultimately gave her life for the man she loved. Khan writes that, in the end, she had no regrets, and I, for one, do not doubt that this was the case."

Kirk was surprised to feel a pang of sympathy for Khan as well. Although he could not forgive Khan's bloody-handed exploits, reading the man's journal had given him some insight into the hellish circumstances that had fueled Khan's descent into madness. No one deserved to go through what the displaced dictator had endured on Ceti Alpha V, not even Khan Noonien Singh.

"For myself," Kirk concluded, "I regret that I did not take the time to know Marla better in the brief time she served aboard the old *Enterprise*, and, most of all, I regret that I never had the opportunity to know the strong, resilient woman she became."

Kirk nodded at Spock, who crossed the compartment to man the transporter controls. The three men watched in silence as the metal capsule dissolved into a cascade of shimmering energy that sparkled briefly before fading into nothingness. Spock beamed the energized atoms into the empty space where Khan had died, reuniting Marla with her beloved husband at last.

"Amen," McCoy murmured.

Kirk shared the doctor's sentiment. *Godspeed, Marla,* he thought. He hoped that somewhere, far beyond the Mutara Sector, Lieutenant Marla McGivers—and Khan Noonien Singh—had finally found peace.